My Highland Lord

Highland Lords Series

TARAH SCOTT

Broken Arm Publishing

BROKEN
ARM
PUBLISHING

My Highland Lord, Highland Lords Series
Copyright © 2012 by Tarah Scott.
All rights reserved.

ISBN: 1484179560
ISBN 13: 978-1484179567

Author's Website: www.TarahScott.com
Facebook: Facebook.com/TarahScottsRomanceNovels
Twitter:@TarahScott
Blog: TarahScott.TarahScott.com
Cover Design by Melissa Alvarez at BookCovers.Us
Cover Art: DepositPhotos @ Frencesco Cura

First Trade Paperback Printing by Broken Arm Publishing: August 2013

10 9 8 7 6 5 4 3 2 1

Acknowledgements

My deepest thanks to Nikki at *Close Encounters with the Night Kind* for being my first official beta reader. You rock, girl!

My undying gratitude goes to Evan Trevane, my good friend and critique partner, who read this book with an eagle eye. My hero wears a kilt, and you made sure no one mistook it for a skirt.

Thank you to Kimberly Comeau, who brainstormed with me, then edited this book into perfection!

No book is complete without a spectacular cover. Thanks to Melissa Alvarez at *Book Covers Galore* for another beautiful cover.

Reviews

Welcome to the Majesty that can only be Tarah Scott. Be prepared to be swept up in the intrigue and wonder of her newest addition to the *Highland Lords Series*. This books was completely engrossing and enraptured you from start to finish, and what an ending indeed!! A must read for all Historical Romance lovers. This book is sure to capture your heart and leave you in breathless anticipation for the next edition!! *Close Encounters with the Night Kind*

My Highland Lord is a hilarious and intriguing adventure in which all kinds of mysteries and romance surround our heroine. I give My Highland Lord five Stars out of five because it was supremely interesting and captivating. *The Romance Reviews Top Pick*

Fast paced and passion filled. If you enjoy conspiracies, romance, witty banter, danger and passion, then pick up this title. You will not regret reading this wonderful story! I can hardly wait to see what this author has to offer next. Sizzling hot with its plot and characters. Oh, did I mention sexy Highlanders. Well done!! A must read for Scottish and historical romance readers. *My Book Addiction and More*

The dialogue in this book was impeccable and made me love the love story between Phoebe and Kiernan all the more. This book was quick-paced and full of action, romance, and suspense. It is well written and beautifully timed and organized. It definitely embodied everything there is to love about historical romance novels. And on top of that it took root in real events, making it more realistic and interesting. This is a must read for any lover of historical romance or historical fiction in general. *Book Cracker Caroline*

Scott's command of character and plot keeps this epic saga from becoming too drawn out or convoluted. Part of the entertainment comes from cases of mistaken identity, and partly from the love/hate relationship between Phoebe and her highwayman. Sweeping scenery and colorful locals truly draw you into this freshly spun tale of culture clash and espionage. All the while, the mystery surrounding the estate of the Marquess, where Phoebe is held captive, keeps the reader desperate to discover the truth. A thoroughly enticing tale, "My Highland Lord" encases all of your favorite period romances and turns them on their head, offering something special and rare to the romantic at heart. *Silver Wood Sketches*

Chapter One

London, September 1837

"Please, Frederick," John Stafford rasped. He lifted his trembling hand from the bed's coverlet. Light from the candle on the nightstand flickered with the small disturbance. "Bring me that chest." John pointed at the desk in the corner of the bedchamber before his hand dropped back down beside him. He dragged in a heavy breath.

Frederick's mouth thinned in concern. "John, you must—"

"The chest," John cut in with a small measure of his old vigor.

His friend sighed, turned, and crossed the room. He lifted the small chest from its two-decade-long resting place. When last the chest had been moved, John was Sheriff of Bow Street and supervisor of the Home Office spies. The chest's contents proved the innocence of one of the conspirators in the most daring assassination attempts of their time.

Frederick returned to the bed, set the chest on the nightstand, and gave John a questioning look.

"Remove the documents," John said.

John closed his eyes in anticipation of the familiar creak of hinges as Frederick opened the chest. How many times had he raised that lid only to slam it shut again without touching the contents? The rustling of papers ceased and Frederick gave a low cry of surprise.

John opened his eyes. "Yes," he said as Frederick laid the stack of envelopes on the bed. "That is, indeed, Lord Mallory of the House of Lords." John pushed aside envelopes until he uncovered the one he wanted. He tapped it and whispered, "Read this aloud."

Frederick removed the sheets of paper from their envelope, sat beside John on the edge of the mattress, and began.

April 26, 1820

In early February of this year word reached me, John Stafford, chief clerk at Bow Street, and head of the Bow Street officers, that Arthur Thistlewood, leader of the radical Spencean Philanthropists Society, planned on February 15 to assassinate the king's ministers. Thistlewood had been reported as saying he could raise fifteen thousand armed men in half an hour, so we feared riots would break out, which might allow him to carry out his assassinations.

I sent one of my officers George Ruthven to infiltrate the Spenceans, then recruited from within their ranks, John Williamson, John Shegoe, James Hanley, Thomas Dywer, and George Edwards. Edwards was such an adept spy that he became Thistlewood's aide-de-camp. Little did I know the terrible part Edwards would play in this operation.

When I had investigated Arthur Thistlewood and the Spenceans in 1816 at Spa Fields, Home Secretary Lord Sidmouth sent me spies, and he was apprised of the men I now used — in fact, George Edwards reported not only to me, but to Lord Sidmouth. So I was surprised when Lord Mallory dispatched another spy from the Solicitor General's office, Mason Wallington, Viscount Albery.

Oddly, Thistlewood unexpectedly abandoned the idea of the assassinations planned for February 15. We feared he would make an unexpected move to murder the Privy Council, so we quickly set a trap. Thistlewood snapped up the bait like a starving lion. He believed that Lord Harrowby was to entertain the Cabinet in his home at Grosvenor Square Wednesday, February 23, 1820, and, as we anticipated, decided to assassinate the entire Cabinet while they dined. The Spenceans chose the Horse and Groom, a public house on Cato Street that overlooks the stable, as their meeting place, so we dubbed the operation 'The Cato Street Conspiracy.'

God help me, at the time, I felt no compunctions about entrapping Thistlewood and his men. Thistlewood was mad — he believed God had answered his prayers in finding a way to destroy the Cabinet — and his followers were, at best, murderers. The reform they claimed to be fighting for was nothing more than an excuse to seize power. However, given what I learned in the years since The Cato Street Conspiracy, I have questioned a thousand times our methods in bringing these men to justice.

On the day of the intended assassinations, I positioned Bow Street officers near the Horse and Groom. I had readied my own pistol when, at the last moment, a message from the Home Office deterred my participation in the arrests. How many times I have wondered at this bit of 'providence.' It was all too convenient that I was absent during the arrests that day.

I directed Richard Birnie, a Bow Street magistrate, to take charge, and left him with my officers to watch for the conspirators. Thistlewood's men soon arrived and, at seven-thirty that night, Birnie ordered the arrests.

A fight ensued and Thistlewood escaped. Several of the top conspirators were apprehended, but our spy Mason Wallington mysteriously disappeared. While making the arrests, Richard Smithers was run through by Thistlewood, and I was frantic at the possibility we had lost another good man. We arrested Thistlewood the next day, and eleven other conspirators were apprehended within days. Then, to my shock, Barry Doddard, a young officer from a neighboring magistrate, named Mason Wallington as the twelfth and only major conspirator to elude capture.

Upon hearing Doddard's accusations, I immediately wrote Lord Mallory informing him of the mistake. Mallory replied that Wallington had long been suspected of dissident actions and was believed to be in league with Thistlewood. I simply couldn't believe this. Wallington had a reputation as a devoted Englishman and spurned the tactics employed by the Spenceans.

I informed Mallory of this, but he countered that Wallington had openly criticized the government and had even quoted Thistlewood's philosophies concerning the lower classes and the rights of women. I couldn't accept this, but Lord Sidmouth intervened, ordering me to desist. Wallington was a wanted criminal and if he was found, Sidmouth ordered me to turn Wallington over to him.

I considered paying a visit to Thistlewood in Coldbath Fields Prison, but realized my visit would be reported to Sidmouth. Besides, Thistlewood was reported to have said that he had hoped it was me he killed instead of Smithers. I had no recourse but to obey Lord Sidmouth's orders. At the age of thirty-six, Mason Wallington became a fugitive.

Frederick lowered the document and John pointed to the envelope farthest from him. "Now that one."

Frederick picked up the second envelope and removed the letter. He cleared his throat and began again.

July, 1824

Four years have passed since Mason Wallington was branded a traitor. Despite Sidmouth's orders that I forget the matter, my conscience demands I act. Whether guilt or innocence is the result of my findings, I shall, as always, record all matters true and faithfully. I begin with Wallington's superior, Lord Niles Mallory.

Frederick looked at John, the short letter finished.

"Wallington has a daughter," John said. "She has been a victim of the lie too—" A heavy cough cut him off.

3

"John!" Frederick leapt to his feet and filled the glass on the nightstand with water from the pitcher.

Frederick slipped an arm beneath his back and lifted him forward until his mouth met the lip of the glass. John took several small sips. He breathed deeply, nodded he was finished, and Frederick settled him back onto the pillow.

Frederick set the glass on the nightstand. "Rest. We will finish later."

John grasped his friend's hand. "The girl has a right to the truth. I cannot go to my peace knowing I leave her in turmoil." John closed his eyes, remembering the day she had come to him. He couldn't escape her questions or the pain in her eyes when he turned her away without answers. He looked at Frederick. "See that she gets the letters." His voice weakened. "Swear." He tightened his grip on Frederick's hand in one final squeeze. "Swear."

"I swear," Frederick promised, and John lay back on his pillow and slept.

Chapter Two

Edinburgh, Scotland

The criminal was alive and well. Yet, the one man who could have exposed him was dead. Phoebe stared at the clipping of the obituary notice printed in the *Times* five days ago. The knowledge of his death settled around her as black as the darkness surrounding her carriage. The lantern flickered with the sway of the carriage as she slid her gaze over the paragraph that extolled Bow Street Sheriff John Stafford's criminal expertise, and past the mention of his involvement in The Cato Street Conspiracy. A man's life reduced to two paragraphs. For the hundredth time since she'd first read the obituary, she settled her gaze on the final line.

September 1837, John Stafford died in his London home.

Phoebe refolded the clipping, set it on her lap, and pulled another document from her reticule. She ran her fingers along the age-yellowed edges of the only letter her father had written to her mother, the letter she had shown John Stafford when she'd visited him in his home five years ago. She unfolded the foolscap and, with a deep breath, began reading. Her lips moved in tandem with the words she'd long ago memorized.

May 20, 1820
My Dearest Amelia,

    Please forgive this letter so long overdue. I am well and I have found safe haven — at least for the moment. You have, no doubt, heard the news that I am wanted for high treason, and now you know that my suspicions were correct. Amelia, you cannot know how my accusers make even the most abhorrent criminal look like one of God's angels. I sorely underestimated the depth of their deceit. Fool that I am, I did not anticipate being branded a traitor in their stead.

I know your heart is heavy, my love, but no more so than mine. It is shocking to learn that one's leaders are willing to sacrifice their countrymen for money and power. Ironically, had I known then what I now know, I would be guilty of their accusations. Do not shudder. I know I speak treason, but you cannot comprehend the fine line between reason and desperation when all choices have been eliminated.

Would it shock you to hear that I relish the day I shall destroy my accusers? They have taken all I hold dear: you, our darling Phoebe and, lastly, my freedom. While I cannot like Arthur Thistlewood — his motives are not pure as he would have us believe — in one thing he was right: those few rich and powerful men who rule supreme in our society have stolen our rights.

I have a plan, which, of course, I cannot elaborate upon here, but I must uncover the truth. Otherwise…well, otherwise, I am no better than Thistlewood — or those men who brought him to justice.

I do not know when I will have another opportunity to write. Give Phoebe my love, and do not despair. I have not.
Your loving husband,
Mason

It wasn't until her mother's death ten years ago that Phoebe learned her father sent this letter. The letter, hidden amongst her mother's personal correspondence, had been folded with a newspaper clipping dated February 24, 1820, the day after the Spencean Society's planned assassination of the Cabinet. The newspaper clipping, a statement made by Lord Sidmouth to the *London Gazette* concerning the charge of high treason against Thistlewood and his murder of Bow Street runner Richard Smithers, also mentioned the bounty on Thistlewood's head. The paragraphs were framed by a note written in her father's hand on the sides.

Sidmouth could not have yet known that Thistlewood killed Smithers. Here is proof positive the noose had been put around Thistlewood's neck before he even planned the assassinations.

"Why?" Phoebe whispered. Why had her father been falsely accused and why had he cared that the government ensured Thistlewood's capture? Thistlewood was a known murderer, a man—A sharp sideways jostle yanked Phoebe back to the present. "What in—" Another jolt cut short the exclamation.

She yanked back the curtain and peered into the darkness. No lights dotted the countryside as they should have, and moonlight revealed open fields beyond the road.

She quickly refolded the letter and clipping, stuffed them into her reticule, then opened the door an inch and called, "Where are we, Calders? I don't recognize this road."

"Taking a shortcut, Miss," came the muffled reply.

"Wha—" The coach listed, and she slammed the door with the force of the movement, tumbling back against the cushion. "By heavens."

Phoebe seized the handle again. The door was yanked from her grasp and flung open. A man filled the doorway. She jerked back as a rush of air guttered the lantern flame. Her heart jumped when she lost sight of the intruder for an instant, then the light flared to life again. The man gripped the side of the open doorway of the slowing carriage, one leg braced on the floor. She took in eyes bluer than any she'd ever seen, an angled face, and a fit body leaning forward on one powerful leg—a leg clad in finely cut trousers. Thievery paid well these days!

She cut her gaze to his and he grinned. Phoebe pooled her strength. Understanding flickered in his eyes the instant before she kicked his shoulder with a slippered foot. With a loud grunt, he toppled from the coach. She lunged forward, caught hold of the flapping door, and hung her head out the doorway, scanning the road behind for the brigand. The coach was slowing even more, and her heart leapt higher in her throat when he jumped to his feet and starting toward them.

"Calders," she yelled, "lay whip to the horses. Quickly!"

The coach halted so suddenly, she tumbled through the door, and landed on her side. A dull pain throbbed deep in her shoulder. She pushed onto an elbow and fingered the tender place on her arm. No blood. Thank God she'd worn a cloak.

The carriage creaked and Phoebe looked up to see the murky form of her coachman as he dropped to the ground. She scrambled to her feet and turned in the direction of the highwayman. He wasn't hastening to them as expected, but strolled forward while dusting off his trousers. She turned on unsteady feet to face Calders and her eyes came into sharp focus upon the face of a stranger.

She recoiled, then narrowed her eyes on him. "Where's Calders. What have you done with him? If you harmed him—"

"Never fear, madam, he is unharmed."

Phoebe whirled at the sound of the velvet, deep voice belonging to the highwayman.

"I promise," he said, "Calders was simply delayed."

A sudden pounding of hooves riveted her attention onto the distant shadowy forms of four approaching horsemen.

"There!" one of the newcomers shouted. "There she is."

She looked back at the highwayman in time to see him step toward her. He seized her arm. She tried to yank free, but he dragged her toward the carriage.

"Mather," he said in a low voice, "get this coach underway. Now."

Phoebe dug her heels into the ground and was abruptly hauled over his shoulder. She cried out, but he didn't slow his pace.

"Release me, you fool!" she shouted. His shoulder dug into her stomach with each long, hurried stride he took. Phoebe kicked, despite the pain.

"Be still" he ordered, and clamped his arm down on her legs.

She thrashed harder. A shot rang out. She jerked her head up, but found herself tossed onto the cushions of the carriage.

The highwayman jumped into the carriage after her. "Damnation." He slammed the door shut. "They mean to put a ball through me."

He pounded on the coach roof and they lurched into motion. Phoebe clutched at the door handle, but pitched forward despite the effort. Her captor shoved her back against the cushions, holding her firm as he pulled back the curtain and peered out the window.

"Bloody hell." He looked at her. "Fine time for shenanigans."

She frowned. "Perhaps you should keep a tighter hand on your band."

"They are not my band, madam." His gaze was still fixed out the window. "They are, however, a persistent band and will reach us momentarily." He twisted to look in the direction they were headed, then pounded on the carriage roof and shouted, "Mather, make for that abandoned farm up ahead."

The carriage veered and Phoebe bounced left and right despite his hold on her. Stories of runaway carriages conjured pictures of broken necks and twisted bodies, and she envisioned herself pitching forward head first into the opposite seat. The arm pinning her to the cushions suddenly encircled her waist. Another jolt of the carriage, and her unwanted companion yanked her tight against his chest.

Her senses flooded with the aroma of wool and musky sandalwood. They listed when the carriage swayed perilously to one side. Phoebe seized his lapel and buried her face deeper in his chest. If there was a God in heaven, she would land on the brigand when the carriage rolled and he would break his neck while saving hers.

The carriage halted. He threw back the door and jumped to the ground, dragging her with him. The farmhouse stood a few feet away. Phoebe scanned the distance. The riders approached at a gallop and would soon reach the barn that sat sixty feet from the house. The highwayman grabbed her hand and started around the side of the ramshackle farmhouse. She started to yank free, but hesitated. Two bands of extortionists? Why—and which was the more dangerous?

They rounded the building, then he pushed her against the wall, and demanded, "Which of your other admirers am I dealing with?"

Other admirers? Phoebe flushed. *Adam.*

She had refused Adam's offer of marriage three times this year alone, but hadn't considered that her childhood friend would kidnap her in an effort to coerce her into accepting his proposal. But if this man was Adam's friend, where was he — and who were the other thugs? God only knew, but at least Adam's friends didn't pose any real danger — other than the possibility of her ending up in Gretna Green.

Her kidnapper drew a pistol from the back of his waistband. Phoebe pressed closer to the rough stone of the farmhouse. He stepped forward two paces past her, extended a steady hand, and leveled the weapon on the oncoming riders. A shot rang out and shouts damned him to the darker parts of hell.

He ducked back behind the farmhouse. "Never thought I'd need more than one shot." He stuffed the pistol back into his waistband. "How many did you count, Mather?"

"Three, sir."

"Only three? Not terrible odds."

"If you say so, sir."

"Do you hear that?" the highwayman whispered.

Before Phoebe could reply, he hurried along the building to the rear. She took two quick steps to the corner at the front of the house and peered around the edge toward the road. The brigands were nowhere in sight.

"Bloody hell," her captor cursed, and Phoebe turned. "They left their mounts on the other side of the barn." He hurried back to her. "Mather, your second pistol, if you please."

The older man handed over the Murdock Scottish flintlock pistol he gripped.

"You haven't got a spare pistol you can give me?" she asked. The highwayman's head snapped in her direction. "I need protection," she said.

"I am your protection." He grasped her arm and hurried her along the farmhouse.

"Who will protect me against you?" she demanded.

Phoebe was sure she heard a chuckle as he continued around the back of the building. He halted and pointed at Mather, then jerked his head toward the far end of the building. Mather hurried to the edge and, a moment later, held up one finger, clearly indicating another of their attackers was closing in on the side he surveyed.

The highwayman motioned Mather toward the trees, then leaned toward her, his breath startling her as his mouth touched her ear. He whispered, "We'll make a dash for those trees. Hold tight to my hand."

He grasped her hand and sprinted forward. Phoebe yanked up her skirts as they raced across the short expanse. He glanced back in the instant before they entered the cover of trees, then muttered something and dragged her to the ground. His body rolled onto hers like the weight of a fallen carriage, and she gasped for air. A shot rang out and she

9

flinched. Mather shouted, then her companion sprang to his feet, pulling her up beside him. Phoebe dragged in a heavy breath, barely managing to keep pace as he hurried deeper into the trees. A man appeared up ahead. Relief eased the knot in her stomach upon recognizing Mather. The highwayman stopped once they reached his side.

A long moment of silence passed before her captor said, "I want to see if they've given up. Double back around to the north, Mather. You know where to meet should we become separated."

"Perhaps, sir, I should deal with the men?"

"I will be quicker in dispatching them."

"As you wish, sir," Mather replied. "But bear in mind, should anything happen to you, it is I who will face your father."

"Never fear," a chuckle tinged the highwayman's voice, "I won't leave you to so deplorable a fate. I have no intention of allowing these common brigands to get the best of me."

"Would that be common in comparison to a not-so-common brigand as yourself, sir?" Phoebe asked.

"You don't take kindly to being abducted by one brigand, while being pursued by another?"

"A comedian," she commented dryly.

"A comedian is a much safer wager than those fellows," he said, then slinked off in the direction they had come.

Phoebe followed Mather in the opposite direction. She waited until she was sure they were alone, then groaned and swayed.

"Miss!" He caught her before she collapsed.

She leaned heavily on him. "I-forgive me."

"Are you all right, Miss?"

Phoebe nodded. "You understand the strain of two abduction attempts in one night?"

"Well…" he began.

"I'm unaccustomed to skulking about in the forest." She shivered for good measure.

"Indeed," he agreed, and allowed her to lean on him as they started forward.

Phoebe sighed. "Perhaps…" she let her voice drop off.

"What is it, Miss?" He guided her around a large branch.

"If I were back in the safety of my carriage…"

"We'll soon have you back," he replied.

"Can't we go directly there? Your master will make short work of those men. We could—"

"Oh no, we must be sure those rogues are dispatched before we return."

"Which rogues do you refer to?" she demanded.

"Beg your pardon, Miss?"

His voice, she realized, carried a note that was just a bit too solicitous. She yanked free of his grasp. "Very funny, my man."

"Are you sure you're all right, Miss?" he asked with no change of demeanor.

"No, I am not all right. Would you be all right if you had been abducted against your will?"

"No," he answered thoughtfully, "I suppose not."

Phoebe distinguished the edge of the forest up ahead.

"We'll wait here." Mather grasped her arm and urged her down to the ground.

She resisted. "I don't want to sit on the ground. It is wet."

"Better wet than dead." He shoved her with enough force that she plopped onto the ground.

"You are no gentleman," she muttered.

They waited for what she estimated to be twenty minutes when Mather said, "You're looking fit, sir."

She twisted to see Mather's master approaching. Even in the darkness she discerned his limp.

"Well enough, Mather," he rejoined.

Phoebe rose as he neared.

"Shall we?" Grasping her arm, he started toward the road.

"That's a bit of a limp you've got there," she said as they broke from the trees. "Have a little trouble when you did away with those scoundrels?"

He looked sharply at her. "I did not do away with anyone, madam."

"You did away with the one you shot."

"I didn't kill him or the others. Though, they will have blazing headaches tomorrow."

"Payment for injuries inflicted?" Mather asked, keeping his gaze straight ahead.

"It was," he said with emphasis. "But only because the one fellow was reluctant to lay down his weapon."

Mather gave a single nod. "As you say, sir."

Phoebe glanced about for the carriage. The dilapidated farmhouse lay to the left a short distance, but the carriage wasn't where they'd left it in front of the building. She scanned to the right and spied the coach sticking out from the trees a little farther down the road.

"Why didn't they take the carriage?"

"Lack of funds, I would imagine," the highwayman replied.

"What does that mean?"

"It means, their employer didn't pay them enough to make it worth the possibility of getting their heads shot off."

"I did not hear your pistol discharge—and you said you didn't kill them," she said.

11

"I didn't kill them," he said irritably. "Still, they resisted. Once I relieved the one gentleman of this, however," he produced a pistol from his waistband at it his back, "they were much more docile."

Phoebe grasped his wrist. He halted.

"A Circa Percussion Dueling pistol," she remarked. "Deluxe nickel plated engraved barrel, trigger and butt plate." She dropped his hand and it fell limp at his side. Phoebe regarded him. "Rather fine weapon for a highwayman. But then, it would seem highwaymen live fine lives these days." She looked meaningfully at his clothes.

He lifted a brow. "As I have yet to rob you, madam, I don't see that you are justified in branding me a highwayman."

Phoebe extended her arms, holding tight to her cloak. The breeze filtered through the cloak and around the silk gown she wore. Locks of golden hair that had come loose from their pins fluttered before her vision. "I have nothing of value."

He grinned and a flash of white teeth shone. "But, my dear, you have a great deal to offer."

Phoebe blinked, then narrowed her eyes. "Tell Adam the answer is still no."

"Ahhh," he intoned. "Progress. Does Lord Stoneleigh know of the illustrious Adam?"

"Lord Stoneleigh? What has he to do with Adam?" A chill shot through her. These men weren't friends of Adam. "What does Lord Stoneleigh want with me?" she demanded.

The highwayman made a tsking sound. "Regan was right. You are in a fit."

"What are you talking about?"

He didn't respond, but stuffed the pistol into his waistband, then glanced at the sky. "We should be off."

"Aye," Mather replied and began again in the direction of the carriage.

The highwayman bowed slightly and gestured for her to precede him. Phoebe stepped back a pace. He didn't move until she retreated a second step, then he moved in tandem with her third step. His gaze didn't waver from hers but, on the fifth step, he halted.

"You can't go far."

"Far enough."

He leapt forward. Phoebe dodged his grab. Turning on the ball of her foot as he propelled past her, she kicked his rump. He stumbled, landing face down on the ground. Phoebe dashed for the trees. Mather's shout broke the quiet. She had just entered the trees when iron fingers seized her arm. He swung her around and into his arms.

The highwayman caught her with a grunt. "Perhaps you ought to have foregone the honey cakes at Drucilla's soirée."

Phoebe kicked his shin.

He yanked her roughly to him. "You will do no better in these woods than you would have at the hands of those footpads. Don't forget, they could awake anytime. Where would you be, then?"

He wrapped an arm around her waist and lifted her from the ground. She allowed her body to sag and her weight yanked him downward.

"Bloody wench." He hauled her over his shoulder.

For a horrible instant it seemed the momentum would land her on her head. She threw her arms around his waist as his arm clamped down on her legs. "By heavens, sir, I have been conked on the head once tonight as a consequence of you. I would prefer not to make it twice."

He muttered something under his breath and started toward the carriage.

Phoebe noted his limp had become more pronounced. "Does that injury hurt?"

He remained silent. When they stepped from the forest, the carriage sat within a few feet of the trees with Mather at the open door. For the second time that night, the brigand threw her onto the cushions of the coach.

"Mather," he said, stepping in behind her, "take us from this accursed place."

Mather closed the door. Phoebe edged toward the opposite door.

"Pray, do not force me to chase you again." He settled himself against the cushion opposite her. "Have you anything to say for yourself?"

The coach started forward and Phoebe was jostled to one side. "It is you who owe me the explanation." She righted herself. "*You* kidnapped me."

"I am no more a kidnapper than a highwayman."

She arched a brow.

"I am taking you to Regan."

Her mind raced. What did the earl want with her? Did this have something to do with Heddy? Heddy was furious with him for dallying with Lady Phillips, and decided to teach him a lesson by not meeting him this evening as planned. But Lord Stoneleigh hadn't seemed the least bit concerned about Heddy when he'd flirted with Phoebe earlier that evening. In any case, the earl certainly didn't make a habit of kidnapping ladies. As for the man sitting across from her...

"Sir, whatever your game, this has gone far enough. One does not kidnap a lady."

"Miss Ballingham, really—"

"Miss Ballingham—you think I'm Heddy?" Relief flooded through her. "This is nothing more than a case of mistaken identity."

"Indeed?"

13

"You have mistaken me for Hester Ballingham. Understandable, given that I am in her carriage."

"A fine barouche-landau."

Phoebe gave him a recriminating look. "I understand it is a rare vehicle, but I am not her."

"I see," he replied. "So aside from sharing an expensive carriage, you also share the same unusual hair color?"

"Only somewhat," Phoebe said. "Heddy is fair haired, but not so golden."

"Your hair is, indeed, golden," he said in a soft voice. Before Phoebe could reply, he added, "Where is Miss Ballingham this evening? Why isn't she in her own carriage?"

"Heddy is ill." Or she would be once Phoebe got her hands on her. Heddy knew the barouche would be recognized, so had sent the expensive carriage for Phoebe, while she used a nondescript chaise she kept for assignations with gentleman she wished to keep secret from her current protector—in this case, Lord Stoneleigh.

The highwayman leaned forward and placed a hand on hers. "You needn't worry. I didn't lie when I said I would deliver you straight to Regan."

Phoebe snatched her hand away from beneath his. "I do not wish to go to Lord Stoneleigh."

He sat back. "You will, no doubt, be just as pleased to see him as you were Lord Beasley earlier this evening."

Phoebe narrowed her eyes. "You were spying on me."

"I was at the ball."

"Then you saw Lord Stoneleigh dance with me."

"I didn't see Regan at the party."

"He was there," Phoebe insisted.

The corner of the brigand's mouth twitched. "You carried on shamelessly with Lord Beasley."

"What? I danced with him twice. That is hardly shameless."

"Indeed, it is," he said. "But you were also dancing much too close."

She groaned inwardly. Lord Stoneleigh's cupid clearly knew of Hester's reputation for shameless flirtations and feminine tantrums, and—

"Wait," Phoebe exclaimed. "If you saw me at the ball, how could you possibly mistake me for Hester?"

"It wasn't until I saw you in the coach that I knew you were the woman I saw dancing with Beasley."

"By heavens, why didn't you speak with me then, make sure who I was before embarking on such a numskull plot?" she demanded.

"I fully intended to seek an introduction to you, sweetheart, but when I received word that Miss Ballingham had left in her coach I was forced to leave." He smiled. "Imagine my disappointment when I discovered you were Regan's paramour."

"Disappointment?"

He regarded her. "I wonder what Regan would do if I kept you to myself instead of giving you back."

She stared. "Give me back? I'm not yours to give — or his to have!"

The highwayman sighed. "I suppose he would fret if we didn't meet him as promised. He explained his offence, by the way. Really? Is it fair to punish him for a slight indiscretion — or were his trinkets not expensive enough to sooth your wounded pride?"

"I hardly call disappearing into Lord Rupert's gardens with Lord Phillip's young widow a slight indiscretion." The words were out of her mouth before she realized her mistake.

"So I thought," he said.

"I am not Hester," she shot back.

"The trip to Brahan Seer is only two days — "

"Two days?" Phoebe exploded.

"Two days there and two days back. Then there are the days you and Regan will reconcile."

Four days — or more? Panic coursed through her. Her uncle would be frantic, not to mention, she couldn't begin to comprehend the affect this affair might have on her career as an English spy. Her employment with the Crown was tenuous, despite the fact she had proven her worth when information she gathered two years ago exposed Lord Capell of Parliament as the man responsible for the disappearance of a dozen young girls. He'd been supplying brothels with the girls, many of whom had been murdered by the brothel owners.

Phoebe saw her hard work going up in smoke. Her mentor, Lord Alistair Redgrave, might overlook the fact she'd been spirited away in the dead of night by a man, but her superior, Lord Briarden, wouldn't appreciate the attention such a scandal would bring to one of his agents. This is what she got for allowing her maid to leave when she'd claimed illness. Phoebe should have gone home with the girl.

"I can't be away for four days," Phoebe insisted.

"My apologies for interfering with your other assignations," the highwayman said.

"There will be hell to pay when my absence is discovered," she snapped.

"Regan will sooth your pride."

"I am speaking of my family, you fool. My uncle will have your hide."

"I wager Regan will appease him as well," he replied.

She stared. "You truly are mad."

"You don't wish to snare an earl?" he asked.

"I do not."

"Perhaps you have your sights set higher?"

She didn't break from his stare. "Has it occurred to you that if I am telling the truth, you will be the unfortunate who is forced to marry me?"

"So you are ambitious," he murmured. "But at least you're honest."

"Take yourself out of my carriage," she ordered.

"We're in the middle of nowhere. Where would I go?"

Phoebe gave him a sweet smile. "Go to the devil."

"And my coachman?"

"You will need him more than I."

"You would drive these chestnuts yourself?"

"Why not?"

"Interesting," he said.

She scowled. "That I can drive a pair of horses?"

"No. That you haven't yet resorted to fainting."

Phoebe prayed the man sitting across from her believed she was sleeping. He had left off further conversation when she relaxed into the corner and allowed her mouth to go slack. She cracked open one eye and observed him. Eyes closed, he too, appeared to be resting. She didn't believe that for an instant. The carriage slowed and the highwayman opened his eyes. Phoebe sighed as if the slight disturbance had intruded upon her sleep and she slumped more heavily into the corner.

A moment of silence followed before the door opposite her opened, then clicked shut. The carriage swayed slightly and she knew he had climbed up top. The vehicle settled and she opened her eyes and scooted closer to the door. They swayed left as the road curved. She gripped the handle and carefully opened the door. The latch released with a tiny click.

Phoebe held her breath, but no cry of discovery came from above. The carriage hugged the shoulder of the road so that she could nearly touch the tree branches. She lifted her skirts, poised to jump, but hesitated at sight of the fast moving ground.

She had fallen from the carriage earlier and was none the worse for wear. Hadn't they been moving slower then? She glanced at the dark forest. If she injured herself, how far would she have to walk to civilization? That challenge, she realized, paled in comparison to her uncle's reaction if he discovered she'd been closeted away with a man for days. Phoebe jumped.

She hit the ground quicker than anticipated. The impact knocked the wind from her. She wheezed for air as a sharp pain shot through her head. The retreating carriage blurred in her vision, seeming to vanish into the yawning mouth of a black cave. She scrambled to her feet and plunged into the fuzzy darkness of the trees.

A sound emanated behind her, but the pounding inside her head muffled it beyond recognition. Phoebe closed her eyes and tried willing the pain into submission. She opened them just in time to miss a low hanging branch. The quick swerve brought her to her knees.

Chapter Three

*F*lickering light penetrated Phoebe's consciousness. Orange and red flames swam before her vision and she blinked into focus the fire that burned in the hearth beyond the foot of the bed where she lay. She moved her gaze to the left and saw a door leading to... Phoebe concentrated in an effort to place her surroundings, but the world outside that door—the world beyond this moment—remained a mystery. She looked to the wall on her left, saw an armoire, then the deep alcove farther left. She started at sight of the tall form standing at the alcove's end, staring out the window.

The highwayman.

He shifted. She clamped shut her eyes. The pad of boots on the carpet drew near and continued around the bed to her right. A faint rustle of clothes followed, then silence. She waited a moment before slitting open one eye. The highwayman reclined in a chair beside the bed. His legs, stretched out before him, spanned the remaining length of the bed. His head rested against the chair back and his eyes were closed. He reached up and rubbed the bridge of his nose with thumb and forefinger as if to ward off a headache. His hand fell away from his face and Phoebe closed her eyes. Had he seen her? She abruptly felt the dislocation of air near her face, the sense of his nearness, though she had heard no sound of movement.

"What possessed you to take such a foolhardy risk?" he whispered.

A wisp of air brushed her eyelashes. *His sigh.*

A soft scratching sounded at the door and a dull pain rumbled through her head.

The door clicked open and a voice said, "You must rest, sir."

Mather.

"If the lady wakens with you hovering over her as you are, you're likely to give her a start."

"Unlikely," the highwayman replied in hushed tones. Phoebe knew by the location of his voice, he had straightened away from her. "Any woman who would jump from a moving carriage isn't easily frightened. I'll be glad when Connor has another look at her. Until now, she hasn't moved a muscle."

"He promised to be here bright and early," Mather said.

"Yes," the highwayman replied in a dry tone. "I wonder if his dedication is due to concern or curiosity." He chuckled. "The good doctor gave me an odd look when I told him Heddy had *fallen* from the carriage. Damn, but I hope he doesn't take it in his head to contact my father."

"Old Connor knows which side his bread is buttered on," Mather said with such loyalty, Phoebe wanted to roll her eyes.

"My father is the one who butters Connor's bread," the highwayman said.

"Speaking of," Mather began.

"Please," he cut in, "no more lectures on how my father will whip you should you allow me to stray from the path of righteousness."

"As you wish, sir. If I must, I can face him with the news that you collapsed from fatigue."

"I doubt he'll pay that news much heed."

Phoebe could contain herself no longer. She opened her eyes and said, "Such a paragon of a father would surely have your despicable hide for this foolish stunt."

Both men looked at her.

She stared back at them. "I heartily wish to meet your father and inform him what a beast of a son he sired."

"I see that crack to your head did nothing to diminish your wit," the highwayman said.

Phoebe gingerly touched the gash on her forehead. "My head pounds dreadfully. What happened?"

"You jumped from the carriage."

She shot him a reproachful look. "I know that. What I do not recall is how I came to be here. How did you find me?"

He raised both brows. "I believe I mentioned you might have done better to leave off eating those honey cakes."

Phoebe frowned.

"When you jumped," he explained, "the carriage rocked."

She narrowed her eyes, but ended up squinting due to the sudden sharp throb in her head. The pain subsided, and she said, "If the carriage rocked, it was your large girth tramping about up top that caused it to do so."

The highwayman angled his head. "As you say, madam. We shall call it luck, then."

"Whose?" she muttered. "Certainly not mine."

"I beg to differ. If I hadn't discovered you, you might be among the dead instead of the living."

"Rubbish," she retorted, then added in a quieter tone when the pounding in her head again thrummed, "Where are we?"

"Glaistig Uain."

"What is that and where is it?"

"The Green Lady Inn, not far from where you jumped from the carriage."

"Oh," she replied, then, "I require some privacy."

"Whatever you need, Miss Ballingham, just ask."

Phoebe flushed.

He regarded her more closely. "Is something wrong?"

"Nothing that a moment of privacy won't cure."

"Mather or I can attend to anything you need," he insisted.

"Of all the bloody inconvenience," she burst out. "The day I can't manage a chamber pot myself is the day I meet my maker."

A distinct stillness cloaked the room. "Considering the circumstances," he said in a tight voice, "I find that jest in bad taste."

"Never mind." Phoebe sat upright and swung her legs over the side of the bed.

"Miss Ballingham," he strode around the bed, "you are to remain in bed."

"I can't remain in bed when the chamber pot is in the corner."

She shoved to her feet as he neared. The room spun. Her stomach lurched and she felt herself falling forward. Strong arms grasped her shoulders and pulled her against a solid body. Phoebe recognized the smell of sandalwood and clutched at the lapels of the highwayman's open jacket. She squeezed her eyes more tightly shut against the nauseating sense of spinning.

"B-by heavens." Her voice, she noted with distress, was not as clear as it had been when she lay in bed. "I am a bit dizzy."

Phoebe felt herself lifted in his arms. She tightened her grasp on his coat against a sense of falling she knew was ridiculous, but she couldn't keep from burying her face in his chest in an effort to anchor herself.

"Easy," he soothed.

"Stupid," she managed in a mumble.

He didn't answer, and she was eternally grateful when he didn't move. She became aware of the warmth that seeped through his shirt and into her cheek, then the sure, strong beat of his heart. She released a slow breath and he must have sensed that her orientation had returned for he settled her back onto the bed.

Despite the heat of the room, he pulled the blankets up to her chin then began a methodical tucking in of the blankets around her. When he bent over her and switched to the other side, she found herself staring at his angled profile. A hint of whiskers shadowed his jaw, giving him a dangerous look that had been absent when he'd appeared in her carriage. His raven dark hair brushed the collar of his shirt. She had the urge to see if the tresses were as soft as they appeared.

He paused and turned his face to her. Phoebe pressed back into the pillow before realizing the action. He lifted a brow and she flushed. Damn the devil, he was pleasant to look upon and knew it—knew she'd been thinking just that. Something flicked in his eyes—understanding—and she cursed him again. He went back to securing the blanket in a business-like fashion until she felt as if she were being mummified.

She squirmed.

"*Lay still,*" he commanded.

The warmth of the blankets bordered on stifling. She wriggled, then realized the garment she wore wasn't her gown. "What am I wearing?"

The flash of gray flannel she'd seen before swooning came to mind. Her cheeks warmed again. Someone had removed her gown, then dressed her in the nightgown she now wore. Phoebe glanced from the highwayman to Mather, then fastened her gaze back onto the highwayman. There was no question which of the two men would have undertaken the task of undressing her. The culprit straightened, apparently finished with making her a veritable prisoner beneath the blankets.

"Perhaps you should take yourself off for a rest." Phoebe said, gritting her teeth as much against the throbbing in her head as to control her rising temper.

He gave her a quizzical look.

"Sir." Mather stepped forward.

"Mather," the brigand said without looking at him, "I'll stay." He glanced over his shoulder at the window where soft light had begun to filter into the room. "Mrs. Grayson may already be about. If she isn't, please wake her and inform her Miss Ballingham requires tea and some of those cakes I know she prepared yesterday."

"I thought you said I was too fat and shouldn't eat more cakes," Phoebe said.

"I said nothing of the kind."

"You most certainly did," she replied. "You said the carriage nearly tipped over when I jumped from it."

He bent, placed a hand on each side of her and leaned in close to her face. "I didn't say the carriage nearly tipped over. I do say, however, let both those incidents be a lesson."

"Lesson?"

21

"Yes. Not to repeat such addlepated actions in the future. Mather," he straightened, "see to Mrs. Grayson."

"Aye, sir." Mather left.

Phoebe, covered to the chin, wriggled beneath the blankets. "It's intolerably hot under here." She squirmed more. "And I can't do without that chamber pot much longer."

"Had you continued sleeping, you could have done without it."

"What do you think woke me?"

The corner of his mouth twitched. "I'll help you with the pot, Heddy."

"You will not."

"But I will." He fetched the pot and returned to the bed.

She eyed the pot, then him. "I can manage."

"As you did a moment ago?"

"Mrs. Grayson, then."

His demeanor turned thoughtful. "Mrs. Grayson is a stout woman. Still...perhaps another maid might assist her."

"Slip the pot under the blanket."

"If you miscalculate—"

The door opened and an older woman entered, tray in hand, followed by Mather.

"Just as you said," Mather said. "She was already bustling about the kitchen."

Mrs. Grayson set the tray on the nightstand. At sight of the tea and cakes on the tray Phoebe's stomach growled.

"Of course I was," the housekeeper said with an indignant sniff. "It is nearly five in the morning."

"Good morning, Bridgett," the highwayman said.

"Morning," the woman replied as she slipped an arm beneath Phoebe's back and gently lifted her away from the pillows.

The covers fell forward. Phoebe grabbed for them, but Mrs. Grayson had propped the pillows against the headboard and was easing Phoebe back against them before she could grasp the blanket. The housekeeper urged her arms out of the way, then twitched the blanket up over her breasts.

"There, now, dearie." Mrs. Grayson plucked a folded napkin from the tray and gave it a smart shake before placing it on Phoebe's lap. "Are you hungry?"

"That's not all," Phoebe said.

Mrs. Grayson gave her an inquiring look, but the brigand said, "Miss Ballingham requires assistance." He lifted the chamber pot for all to see.

Use of the chamber pot, along with hot tea and cakes, revived Phoebe. She set her cup of tea on the tray and glanced at the armoire where Mrs. Grayson said her cloak hung. Any hope of discovering if her reticule was there with the cloak was dashed by the presence of her highwayman. Phoebe studied the scoundrel. He rested, once again, eyes closed, head reclining on the high back of the chair.

"I didn't think to ask your name," she murmured.

"Kiernan MacGregor, at your service." The sound of his voice startled her. He opened his eyes and sat up. "How's your head?"

"Better."

"That was a foolish move, Heddy."

Phoebe opened her mouth, but the intensity in his gaze stopped the retort. She took a deep breath. "I did it because I wish to avoid the scandal of being away for days with a strange man."

Surprise melted into a cool look. "A man you know will do, though?"

Her response was forestalled by a knock at the door.

"Come in," Kiernan instructed.

The door opened and Mather stepped inside. "Dr. Connor here to see the lady, sir." Mather stepped aside and a small, gray haired man entered the room.

Kiernan came to his feet. He strode forward, hand extended. Dr. Connor grasped one side of the gold-rimmed glasses he wore and set them farther back on the bridge of his nose. He switched the black bag he carried from his right hand to the left and grasped Kiernan's hand in a warm greeting.

"Good to see you, Connor," Kiernan said.

"How are you, lad?" the doctor asked. "Mather, here, tells me you're not taking care of yourself as ye ought."

Kiernan laughed. A deep rich laugh, Phoebe grudgingly noticed, that filled the room and settled deep inside the heart of the listener.

"Mather, long ago, appointed himself my mother," he said, giving him a stern look.

Mather bowed and backed out of the room, closing the door behind him.

Dr. Connor frowned. "You look as if you could use a rest."

"Soon, Connor, soon. But first," Kiernan motioned to Phoebe, "you have a more pressing patient."

The doctor approached. He sat down on the bed beside her and, setting the black bag on the floor, eyed Phoebe. "A nasty fall, my dear." He placed a hand on her forehead, tipping her head back slightly. "Let me have a look." He leaned in closer and studied the gash on her forehead, then said with a glance at Kiernan, "Have you a candle?"

Kiernan looked around the room, then strode to the small secretary in the alcove. He picked up the candle sitting there, and hurried to the fire and lit it.

"Put it on the nightstand," the doctor said as Kiernan approached.

Kiernan placed the candle beside Phoebe's tea cup on the tray and Dr. Connor placed a thumb on her right eyelid and gently pulled the lid up as he tilted her head toward the candle light. He studied the eye for a moment, did the same with the left eye, then released her.

"How is your sight?" he asked.

"Fine now," she replied. "When I first awoke, it was blurry."

He nodded, then reached into his black bag and pulled out a stethoscope. Phoebe grasped the end of the stethoscope and examined it much as he had her head.

She looked at him. "A binaural stethoscope. Where did you find one?"

His face lit with surprise. "You're familiar with this instrument?"

"Indeed I am." She fingered one of the tubes. "The article in the *London Gazette* was most informative."

"You read that article? That came into print in eighteen twenty-nine."

Phoebe thought for a moment. "August twelfth, I believe." She looked from the incredulous doctor to Kiernan, who regarded her with a tilt of his head. "A woman can read as well as a man," she said.

"Aye," Dr. Connor agreed, pulling her attention back to him. "That she can. That-she-can."

"How did you come by it?" she asked. "I didn't think they were in use."

"You're correct. But I have a friend who knows the inventor."

Phoebe's gaze followed when he looked at Kiernan.

"You know Nicholas Comins?" she demanded of Kiernan.

"Not I, Miss Ballingham, my father."

"Now, if you don't mind," Dr. Connor pried the stethoscope from her hands, "I will finish."

The poking and prodding came to an end twenty minutes later with Dr. Connor's instructions that Phoebe was not to move from her bed, and that her head was to remain elevated. "You took a nasty blow," he admonished. "You're lucky it didn't crack your skull wide open."

"Is that any indication of how hard the head is?" Kiernan asked.

Dr. Connor chuckled. "It has more to do with luck. But it wasn't very wise." He looked pointedly at Phoebe.

"You would have done the same had this—this—"

"This what?" Kiernan inquired.

"*This man,*" she retorted. "If he had kidnapped you, you would have done the same."

"Kidnapped?" Dr. Connor's attention riveted onto Kiernan.

Kiernan shrugged. "The fall addled her brains."

"Kiernan," the doctor began.

"You remember Lord Stoneleigh?" Kiernan cut in.

"Aye."

"Miss Ballingham is his special guest."

Comprehension lit the doctor's eyes and Phoebe knew Lord Stoneleigh's reputation as a womanizer had preceded him even here, in the wilds of Scotland.

The doctor snapped his bag closed and rose. "Remember," he said in a stern voice, "you're not to get out of that bed today. I'll see you tomorrow." He started for the door.

"Doctor," Phoebe cried.

He turned. "Yes, Miss Ballingham?"

"You aren't going to leave me here?"

"You can't be moved, young lady," he replied in a kindly, but firm voice. He looked at Kiernan. "Inform Lord Stoneleigh she isn't to be moved until I give permission."

"I'll see to it, Connor. Thank you for coming."

Phoebe watched, mouth agape, as Kiernan escorted him to the door. Dr. Connor exited, and Mather entered.

"I am returning to Edinburgh the moment I recover," Phoebe burst out.

"Don't excite yourself," Kiernan said.

"Cease this foolishness," she snapped.

"I'm not the one who jumped from a moving carriage," he replied.

"I am not Heddy, I tell you."

"Who might you be, then? Cleopatra?"

Phoebe stiffened. *I will seek recompense for this, Heddy*, she telepathed. "For a man who thinks so little of the lady, you are going to a great deal of trouble to keep her in your company."

A smile twitched one corner of his mouth. "A man has a right to change his opinion."

Phoebe cut her gaze to Mather. "Sir, do you write?"

"Aye, Miss."

"Fine. Be so good as to fetch paper and pen."

"Miss?"

"Oh, for heaven's sake." She shook her head in exasperation. Her vision blurred and she pressed the fingers of her right hand to her temple.

"Heddy?" Kiernan demanded.

"You are to write a letter for me," she ordered Mather.

Mather looked at his master.

"Do you intend to inform your other…er, friends that you are no longer at their disposal?" Kiernan asked.

"Never mind, Mather," Phoebe said. "I will not require your help after all."

Kiernan made a tsking sound. "You're going to keep the poor fellows hanging?"

"All I need from you, Mather," she went on, "is an address."

25

"An address?"

"Yes. One I am sure you have."

"I know very few addresses," Mather hedged.

"I'm in need of only one address. I must—no, it is my duty—" she pinned him with a hard look "—your duty, as well, to inform this person's father of his dishonorable actions."

Mather paled and satisfaction surged through her.

Kiernan took the two steps to her bed and squatted down face level with her. "Miss Ballingham, I have been far more honorable than I would have preferred. I assure you, my father would agree."

Phoebe blinked, aware of a frustrated heat rising to her cheeks. Her head began to pound. "Please leave," she rubbed her temples. "I require privacy."

"Mather," Kiernan said, rising, "fetch the chamber pot."

Phoebe put one foot in front of her, careful to take each descending stair slowly. Though loath to admit it, Dr. Connor was correct. She would be unable to ride for another day. Tomorrow would be four days since she disappeared. Her uncle must be frantic, and the fact she hadn't been contacted or rescued by one of Lord Redgrave's spies had her worried. Where was this Green Lady Inn that she was out of his network? Phoebe paused on the final step. No dizziness. She released a breath, thankful she hadn't given in to the sense of unease she experienced while staring down from the top stair at what seemed to be an abyss.

She tugged the bodice of her dress. "A might small it be for ye, lass," Phoebe mimicked Mrs. Grayson's tone when the housekeeper had produced the dress. "A might small, indeed," she muttered.

How was it possible to have ripped her skirt from hem to hip when she jumped from the carriage? Mrs. Grayson had given the gown to the village's seamstress for repair so, until she got the gown back, Phoebe was stuck with the tight dress. She tugged harder on the bodice. Blasted thing was made for a twelve year old girl.

Phoebe fidgeted with her shawl, but her efforts to flatten it over her breasts were useless. Tied over itself, the shawl only emphasized the fact her breasts nearly spilled over the narrow lace. She finally gave up and loosened the tie, throwing the corner over her shoulder so that the edge hung over the bodice. She started down the narrow hallway at a sedate pace. Halfway down the corridor, Mrs. Grayson's voice filtered to her from a room up ahead.

"Dora swears we will no' have snow for at least two months," the housekeeper said.

Masculine laughter followed.

Kiernan MacGregor.

Phoebe slowed.

"Dora hasn't always proven reliable," he said. "I shall hazard the ride north."

A chair squeaked and Phoebe realized one of the two was rising. She turned on her heel with the intention of hurrying back down the hallway, but the corridor spun in a dark swirl around her. She groped at the wall.

"*Heddy.*" Kiernan's voice closed in on her.

Phoebe found herself swept off her feet, her face crushed against the velvet lapel of his wool morning coat.

"What are you doing out of bed?" he demanded, bringing his face so close to hers, Phoebe swore she could taste the saddle soap he had washed with that morning.

"I see by your coat you have already been riding this morning," she complained.

"I am allowed that privilege," he replied tersely. "You are not."

"Dr. Connor said I might leave that cursed bed," she retorted.

"I—" Kiernan began, but was cut off by Mrs. Grayson.

"Good Lord, what's happened?" She touched a hand to Phoebe's forehead. "You're a might flushed, dearie."

"No doubt due to being surprised," Phoebe grumbled. "Put me down, sir."

"That I will. Step aside, Bridget." He hugged her so tightly a rush of air was forced from her lungs.

"By heavens," she wheezed.

"Now, Kiernan," Mrs. Grayson began as he started down the hallway.

"I don't wish to spend any more time in bed," Phoebe protested.

"Kiernan!"

Mrs. Grayson's shout stopped him. He faced her. "Bridget—"

"Dinna' Bridget me," she ordered. "Bring her into the kitchen. She can sit with me at the table. It'll do her good to be up and about. She is less likely to do herself harm under your watchful eye."

He hesitated. Mrs. Grayson gave Phoebe a knowing look.

He must have discerned its meaning, for he started down the hallway toward the kitchen as he muttered the single word, "Women."

Chapter Four

Kiernan leaned back in his chair and studied Heddy. There was a flush in her cheeks and her eyes were clear. Being out of bed agreed with her. And he couldn't deny the ridiculous dress she wore agreed with him.

"More tea?" Mrs. Grayson asked.

Heddy shook her head and the housekeeper looked inquiringly at him.

"I've had quite enough tea for one day, thank you, Bridget."

"Perhaps, then," Heddy said, "you should be off attending to business."

Kiernan rubbed his chin. "I have no business as interesting as you."

Her lips thinned. "I am not Heddy."

"You keep saying that. Yet, not once, have you offered an alternate identity."

"I'm sure I told you that I'm Phoebe Wallington, Lord Albery's niece."

"No," he said. "I don't think you did. I haven't had the pleasure of Lord Albery's acquaintance." She raised a cool brow. "He spends little time in Scotland." She faced Mrs. Grayson. "After three days, it must be clear I'm not who he thinks I am." Heddy shot him a sidelong glance. "Even if I were, he had no right to kidnap me."

"Kidnap?" He tsked. "Come now, Heddy, we have discussed this. If not for me, God knows what those brigands would have done—" The barking of dogs outside interrupted him. Kiernan rose and went to the window where he lifted the curtain and surveyed the street.

Mrs. Grayson stepped up beside him. "Oh dear."

"What is it?" Heddy asked.

"Strangers," he replied.

Kiernan studied the man who walked in the forefront of the newcomers. The carved walking stick he leaned on showed wear and the haunted look in his eyes confirmed he'd been too long on the road.

Mrs. Grayson clucked her tongue. "Look at the women, as thin as rails. I made bread yesterday." She turned from the window.

"Wait." Kiernan caught her arm. "I don't care for the looks of the leader."

"They're hungry," she protested. "Ye can't expect the homeless to look like proper lords and ladies."

"Bridget," he released her, "forego the bread for just a moment."

Kiernan exited through the kitchen door and headed toward the small crowd gathered around the strangers. A cold nose nuzzled each hand and he glanced down at two hounds that nudged for attention. He gave each an affectionate pat, then brushed them aside as he stopped before the newcomer's leader.

"M'lord," the man said.

Kiernan nodded an acknowledgment and surveyed the group before returning his attention to the man. "Where are you from?"

"Hay territory, m'lord."

"Hay? Are things still so bad in the north you couldn't find work between there and here?"

The man looked surprised. "'Tis powerful bad, m'lord. We found what work we could, but..."

"There are only seven of you?"

"Aye." The man pointed to the man and woman at the rear of the company. "That is George and Sharon." He went on to name the remaining three men and the other woman, ending with himself, "Alan Hay."

"No children?" Kiernan asked.

Alan pointed to the second woman. "Rebecca's bairn died two days into the journey." He nodded toward Sharon. "She had a wee one, but not enough milk for the babe. We buried the children in fields."

"Good God," a female voice behind Kiernan said.

He whirled. Heddy stood a few paces away. "What are you doing here?"

Her attention remained on the newcomers and a look of surprised recognition flitted across her face.

"We only ask a bit of food," Alan broke in.

Kiernan faced him. "Food will be provided."

"Thank you. Thank you very much."

"What is your destination?"

Alan frowned. "Wherever we can find work."

"The Glaistig Uain can offer no work for one man, much less four. You'll do well to move farther south. For tonight, you may sleep in the stable." Kiernan motioned to the stables across the lane.

Alan's mouth thinned. "Kind of you to let us sleep with the animals, m'lord."

"Aye," he replied, then, "Baths can be arranged, if you like."

Alan nodded. "The women will be glad for that."

"I imagine so," Kiernan agreed. "Particularly if the men avail themselves of the luxury, as well." He gave a final nod and took two steps to Heddy. Her gaze remained fixed on Alan. "What is it, Heddy?"

"You see that?" She nodded at the thick, wavy stick Alan carried.

"The walking stick?"

"A swordstick. Silver mounted buckhorn handle, if I'm not mistaken. Certainly disguises the sword hidden within quite well, doesn't it? And those." Kiernan followed her line of sight to the combination weapon stuffed into Alan Hay's belt. "The short hanger, a hunting sword. Ideal for mounting a flintlock. Queen Anne cannon barrel type. And that one." She nodded at the weapon in George's belt. "At least forty years old, but still deadly. Four barrels, two on each side."

The group turned, led by one of the villagers, and started for the stables.

With a final glance at Alan Hay, Kiernan returned his attention to Heddy. "They have traveled far. Weapons would be a necessity."

"True," she agreed. "But those look well used."

"It's likely they survived the journey by hunting."

"But what do they hunt?" Heddy murmured.

His gaze caught on the shawl that had fallen afoul of her bodice. "You'll catch your death." He grasped the shawl's edges.

Her attention broke from the strangers and she looked at him. Kiernan tugged the shawl across her breasts. He would have to find a way to thank Mrs. Grayson for giving Heddy this particular dress. Heddy glanced down at the shawl, then raised her face to his, her mouth turned down in a dry expression. Kiernan laughed and dropped his hands to his sides. He glanced again at the retreating Hays—his attention flicking over the walking stick—before grasping Heddy's arm and leading her toward the inn.

"How is it you're acquainted with weapons?" he asked.

"My uncle is an amateur collector. I have been subjected to long lectures on weapons and their uses."

"You spoke of your uncle before." Something Regan hadn't mentioned about her. One of the hounds bounded up to his side and woofed. Kiernan gave the dog a playful cuff on the nose.

"My father died when I was seven," Heddy answered. "My mother when I was fourteen."

"I'm sorry," he said.

"It was long ago."

"What of your remaining family?" he asked.

"They are...a mixed cup."

The dog bounded off in pursuit of the other hound that had shot across the lane toward the stables. "How so?" Kiernan looked down at her.

One corner of her mouth twitched in the first indication of amusement he'd observed, but she answered with gravity, "My father's brother is a good man. His wife, however, isn't so amiable."

"Why?"

Heddy laughed, the sound devoid of warmth. "The most common reason: money."

"MacGregor!"

Kiernan turned at the call. Davis Hamilton rode toward them. He brought his horse to a halt beside them. "'Tis good to see you, MacGregor."

"It's good to see you. What brings you south?"

Davis reached down the neck of his shirt and pulled out a letter. "Clachair sends his thanks." He handed Kiernan the letter.

Kiernan took the document and slipped it into the front pocket of his jacket. "We have visitors from Hay territory. They tell me things are still bad up north. I hope you are faring better."

Davis nodded. "Times aren't easy, but we're managing."

"How long can you stay?"

"I'm returning home immediately. I've been gone too long."

"A shame. How are the children?"

Davis shrugged. "They are adjusting to losing their mother."

"And you?" Kiernan asked.

Davis' expression clouded. "I canna' get used to her being gone." He cast an embarrassed glance at Heddy, then said, "I'll be going." Without further conversation, he pulled on his horse's reins and returned in the direction he had come.

Kiernan turned back to Heddy. "Shall we." He gestured toward the kitchen door.

She turned with him and they began walking. "Your friend doesn't look nearly as bad off as the others. The Hays look half starved." She lifted her skirts for the single step that led into the kitchen. "Are they from the same place?"

Kiernan opened the door. "Hay country is farther north than Davis' home."

"Is that where you plan to visit when you go north?"

31

Kiernan shifted his gaze onto her. "Are you thinking you would like to accompany me north, instead of staying at Brahan Seer? Perhaps you'll miss me just a little?"

He didn't miss the annoyance that flickered in her eyes, but she said, "I have never visited the northern Highlands. I've heard they are beautiful."

"You would like it there," he said, and, oddly, thought it was true.

They entered the kitchen and Kiernan escorted Heddy to the chair she'd occupied earlier. "Bridget." He looked at the housekeeper who stood at the counter cutting bread. "Ah, I see you are already preparing food for our guests."

"The famine," Heddy remarked, pulling his attention back to her. "It has lasted nearly two years now." She frowned. "Did the two hundred thousand pounds Dr. MacLeod raised to assist with the famine not help?"

"They say the Duchess gave aid to three thousand people on her estate," Mrs. Grayson interjected in a mocking voice.

"Three thousand?" Kiernan repeated. "Kind of her, considering she's likely displaced that many this year alone—despite her advanced age."

Mrs. Grayson snorted. "More like ten times that many."

"Ah, Bridget, perhaps not quite so many?"

"It might as well have been," she answered in a lofty tone, "for all the damage she caused."

"True," he agreed.

"Duchess?" Heddy asked.

"The Duchess of Sutherland," he said.

"She displaced these people? Then the famine isn't the cause of their plight?"

"The famine is the final nail in the coffin. The real cause is the clearances."

"Clearances?" Heddy repeated. "I've heard the word bantered about, mostly as propaganda voiced by elders not in favor of progress. I understood the changes in Scotland were for the better."

"For the noblemen," he replied. "For the tenants who have been farming the land for generations, the switch to cattle ranching has meant eviction, homelessness, and starvation. The duchess has been clearing her land for years and, though she alone can't be blamed—the Morenish and Breadalbane evictions are just as terrible—she has displaced nearly fifteen thousand Highlanders."

"By heavens," Heddy said. "I can see why the three thousand she aided is paltry in comparison. Why is she doing this?"

Kiernan gave a wry smile. "The most common reason." Heddy gave him a questioning look, and he said, "Money."

Phoebe waited until the occupants of the Green Lady Inn had retired for the night before stealing to Kiernan MacGregor's room, a taper in hand. A clock inside the room struck a muffled gong. She waited until ten more gongs sounded and the room fell silent before tapping lightly on his door. As hoped, silence followed. If her instincts were correct, Kiernan was checking on Alan Hay. Earlier, when the strangers arrived, there had been no mistaking Kiernan's curt remarks. He clearly didn't trust Alan Hay.

She knocked again. When no answer came, she turned the knob and eased open the door. Silence. Phoebe stepped inside and clicked the door shut behind her. She lifted the candle and scanned the room. An empty bed sat against the far wall and a chair and small desk were located in the far right hand corner. Her gaze caught on the single letter lying on the desk. Was that the letter from Clachair that Davis had given him?

When Davis handed Kiernan the letter and said it was from Clachair, she recalled four years ago, reading a notice in the paper about a five thousand pound government bounty on a man with the unusual name. The likelihood of the wanted man being the man who'd written the letter was slim, but this was just the sort of information she was obliged to investigation. Phoebe hurried to the desk and picked up the envelope.

A thrill raced through her. Was this how her father felt when he investigated Arthur Thistlewood? For the first time since she had agreed to spy for Great Britain, Phoebe felt the kinship with her father she had always sought. They hadn't shared their lives, but they shared patriotic passion. The exhilaration was replaced by unexpected regret. If this Clachair was the man wanted by the government, that meant Kiernan MacGregor was himself a criminal. By heavens, she hadn't liked any of the criminals she'd come in contact with—hadn't considered the possibility she could like any of them. But then, Kiernan MacGregor wasn't like Lord Capell, who sold women, or Lord Wallace, who would sell his Parliament vote to the highest bidder. Phoebe suddenly wished she knew nothing of the letter. But she did. She withdrew the single piece of paper from the envelope and read.

> *Dear Kiernan,*
>> *All is well here. I received the writing paper you sent. As always, your generosity comes at the most opportune time. I have distributed the paper amongst my students. They shall make good use of it. Thank you for thinking of us. I look forward to seeing you when next you come north.*
> *Clachair*

There was nothing the least bit suspicious about the letter, and Kiernan had left it in plain sight. Tension eased within her as she slipped the letter back into the envelope, then placed it back on the desk. How many times would she suspect a man of criminal activities and find out she was wrong? Not many she feared.

The small but distinct creak of the windowsill to the left of her bed alerted Phoebe that someone had entered her room. Only a few minutes earlier, the clock had softly gonged once. So, the intruder had had chosen climbing the trellis leading to the portico, instead of risking the lighted hallways. Choices a practiced thief would make.

Through slitted eyes, Phoebe watched him move stealthily from the window to the armoire. He inched open the door and rifled through her cloak and gown. She had removed her reticule and stuffed it beneath the mattress, her father's letter intact. Had Kiernan read the letter, he would have realized his error in mistaking her for Hester. If only she could show him the letter. But the one piece of evidence that could free her was the one thing she couldn't hazard revealing for fear of incriminating her father.

The intruder cursed softly. Phoebe tensed. He abruptly turned as though to exit the way he had come, but paused and gazed at her. Moonbeams shone through the window in front of him, but he remained in the shadows. She resisted the urge to squeeze her eyes shut. He couldn't possibly discern the fact her eyes were cracked open. He lingered, and Phoebe realized he struggled with some inner decision. Could it be the same indecision she had sensed in Alan Hay that afternoon? Was this Alan Hay, or had he sent one of his men to do the robbing?

He hurried back to the window and climbed back onto the roof. Phoebe waited until the count of three before throwing back the covers that hid her fully clothed body. She sat up. No dizziness or pain. Just as Dr. Connor had predicted, today was a turning point in her recovery. She hurried to the window. Peeking outside, she spied the man on the edge of the roof. He turned and fitted a boot into a trellis rung and quickly disappeared from view. Phoebe thrust her hand forward, intending to shove the curtains aside, only to have her fingers catch in the intricate weave of the Nottingham lace.

"By heavens," she muttered.

She disentangled her fingers and yanked aside the curtain. She grasped her skirts, but hesitated. Climbing through the window was no difficult task, but climbing from the roof to the ground might prove too much despite her improvement. She scanned the lane between the inn and the stables, but the intruder didn't appear as expected.

Phoebe hurried to the door and, a moment later, reached the hallway's end and crept down the stairs. At the bottom, she paused and listened to the silence for a moment, then headed for the kitchen door. Once outside, she sidled alongside the building to the corner. The lane between the inn and the stables stood empty. She hurried to the stables, around the building, and located a stall door. Phoebe eased open the bolt on the upper half of the Dutch door. When no sound came from within the stall, she opened the door and reached inside for the bolt that locked the lower half. The bolt held firm. She pressed harder, with no better luck.

Phoebe grasped her skirts and hoisted herself up and over the door into the hay-littered stall, then eased the door shut. She inched forward until her outstretched hand contacted the far wall and felt her way to the stall door leading into the main part of the stable. The metal of the bolt was cool beneath her fingers and she held her breath while easing it free. A tiny creak of hinges sounded behind her. Phoebe jerked her head around in time to see the upper door she had entered through opening. Her heart thudded. The door opened more and a large figure became visible in the doorway.

"Heddy," came a harsh whisper.

Despite recognizing Kiernan MacGregor's voice, Phoebe knew an instant of confusion.

"*Come here*," he commanded.

Before she could respond, a door creaked and muffled voices broke the silence within the stables. Kiernan muttered something incoherent and she startled when he hoisted himself over the door and started toward her.

Upon reaching her, he grasped her arm and yanked her to him as he whispered, "What in blazes are you doing here?"

"I could ask you the same," she retorted.

"No, you could not."

She started to reply, but the voices grew louder.

"Rest assured we will discuss this later," he said.

"Nothing," a low voice was saying. "I told ye they were too poor."

"Did you search the fine gentleman's room?" another said.

"Are you daft?"

Phoebe recognized Alan Hay's voice.

"Hush," the other said.

"Never mind," Alan shot back. "No one inside the inn can hear us."

"You didna' find anything in the woman's room?" the other voice asked in such a miserable tone Phoebe felt sorry for the speaker.

Kiernan's hold on her arm turned painful.

"He was in your room?" Kiernan demanded in a harsh whisper.

Phoebe pressed a finger to his lips to quiet him. His free hand closed over her hand, but he stilled when Hay's companion said, "What are we to do next? We canna' go on much farther without provisions."

"We've come this far," Alan replied. "We'll make do the rest of the way."

"But we have come only half way," the other replied, "and 'tis the easy half. The north is rough land."

35

Kiernan's lips tensed beneath Phoebe's fingers.

"There will be plenty once we get there," Alan said. "Just wait. We'll make that bitch pay for what she and her kind have done to us — to us and every other Highlander."

"I still say she's got too much power," another grumbled. "It won't be so easy."

Alan laughed, low and cruel. "Even someone as powerful as the Duchess of Sutherland isn't invincible. She's seventy-two. She won't be hard to kill."

Phoebe jerked. The duchess.

Kiernan pulled her hand to his chest. "Be still," he hissed.

"Still…" the other man said.

"Are you a coward?" Alan demanded.

"I'm no coward," he replied, "but I'm no fool either."

"If you don't have the stomach for it, get out now," Alan said.

"I didn't say I wanted out," the accused said sullenly.

A sound like that of a slap on the back was followed by, "It's been difficult, George. You lost the wee one and Shannon hasn't been the same since."

"I should have left her with her father in MacEwen territory," George answered.

"We agreed," Alan said, "no one suspects us with the women along."

Phoebe drew a quick breath. Kiernan must have understood her horror, for his free hand shot around her waist and he gave her a squeeze. She felt the hard shape of the pistol stuffed into his belt and wished mightily for an opportunity to aim it at the men who sacrificed women and children for their own ends.

"What's done is done," Alan said. "It served its purpose."

Phoebe started at sight of another figure appearing in the doorway through which Kiernan had entered.

He backed her into the corner. "Stay here," he ordered.

The man in the doorway disappeared as Kiernan hurried back to the door that opened into the stables. He pulled the pistol from his waistband and, in unison with the groan of the main stable doors abruptly opening, yanked open the stall door.

"Lay down your weapons in the name of the Marquess of Ashlund!" a man yelled.

Kiernan lunged into the stables and out of her view.

Phoebe rushed forward as Alan Hay's voice boomed above the female screams, "Lads! Dinna let them — "

A shot rang out.

She skidded to a halt in the doorway. Mather stood between the robbers and the main stable door, gun raised heavenward, smoke rising

36

from the barrel. Six men in a semi-circle around the robbers pointed weapons at them.

The women screamed again and Phoebe's snapped her gaze upward. The women cowered away from the edge of the loft. Two of Hay's men dropped to their knees, their drawn weapons falling to the ground beside them. The man standing beside Alan Hay whirled toward Kiernan. Kiernan halted as the man thrust a hand inside his coat.

Phoebe's heart leapt. Kiernan leveled his pistol. A heartbeat passed and she thought in that horrible instant that Kiernan had somehow frozen. The man pointed his revolver. She opened her mouth to shout a warning, but Kiernan fired. The man twisted to the side and blood stained the shirt at his shoulder even before he crumpled to the ground. Alan Hay dropped to his knees beside his comrades and Kiernan motioned the women from the loft. They backed away from the edge, but when one of his men moved toward the ladder, the first woman started down.

"Take them to the salon," Kiernan instructed his men.

Once the women descended, they pleaded innocence for their men. Phoebe glanced left at the pitchfork leaning against the wall and decided it might do for herding them out the door. She froze at seeing the barrel of a revolver suddenly protrude from the stall to her right. Muscular fingers gripped the weapon, and an arm followed, the weapon aimed at her.

She met the eyes of the gun's owner. His face, devoid of emotion, chilled her. She grabbed for the pitchfork. He leapt forward, knocked the handle from her grasp, and jammed the barrel of the revolver against her neck.

"Nay, lassie," he said in such a reasonable tone, he might have been cautioning her against paying too much for a scarf at the market.

He snaked an arm around her waist and tugged her close while backing away from the stall and from his comrades. The women were at last being led toward the main door, but Charlotte looked over her shoulder and her eyes widened. Kiernan glanced over his shoulder.

His attention centered on Phoebe's assailant as he turned and took a step in their direction. "You don't have to do this, lad."

"Dinna' come any closer," the man warned.

Kiernan halted. A hushed tension hummed through the room.

"Where are you taking them?" The man's chin brushed the back of Phoebe's head when he motioned toward the women.

"What do you hope to accomplish?" Kiernan said. "You won't get ten feet."

"I will get ten feet and more." The man pulled Phoebe closer. "Me and my friends."

"Ye tell him, Robbie," one man yelled before he was silenced by a pistol leveled at his head.

"I can't let you take her." Kiernan took a step left and forward.

"You want her dead?" the man demanded.

Kiernan angled his head slightly. "I don't think you want to kill her."

"I've done many things I didn't want to do," Robbie replied.

"That's right, m'lord," said Alan Hay. "We've done many a thing we didn't like. Don't think we won't do so again."

"Aye," Kiernan agreed, taking another step forward and to his left, "but I don't think one of them was murder."

The man's hold on Phoebe tightened and she wondered if Kieran had miscalculated in assuming the man's conscience was free of murder. Kiernan took another step forward, and Phoebe's assailant shifted to the right.

"You aren't like the duchess," Kiernan said. "She is the one capable of hurting innocents, not you." When the man made no reply, Kiernan went on. "It's a hard line to walk, seeking justice against one so powerful."

"Watch him, Robbie," Alan called. "You have them right where we want them. Don't be taken in by his soft manner."

"We haven't a prayer in heaven," the man said as if he hadn't heard Alan.

"Aye," Kiernan agreed. "You haven't a prayer of committing murder. But justice is another matter."

Robbie laughed bitterly. Alan opened his mouth to say more, but Mather shoved the barrel of his pistol against the man's temple. Robbie retreated a step. Alan looked at him, and Phoebe read the message conveyed in his eyes: take no prisoners. She shifted her gaze to Kiernan and sent him her own message: be ready. Surprise flickered across his face and his eyes narrowed in a command to remain still, but she jammed her elbow into the ribs of her captor and shoved the gun barrel pressed against her neck heavenward.

No shot rang out as she broke free. Kiernan leapt forward. He caught her, pushed her aside, and lunged for Robbie. Kiernan rammed his fist into Robbie's jaw. Robbie staggered back, arms flung out to his sides like a rag doll. Kiernan drove his left fist into the man's abdomen. He doubled over and the gun jettisoned forward. Kiernan swung again and hit beneath Robbie's jaw.

Phoebe leapt to her feet. "Stop him!" she yelled.

No one moved and she realized they had no intention of interfering. Kiernan grabbed Robbie by the collar and dragged him to his knees. Phoebe stumbled forward, latching onto Kiernan's arm as it reared back for another blow. The force of his strength dragged her forward and she dangled at his side before his muscle relaxed enough that her feet touched the straw laden floor. He looked at her as if trying to recognize her.

"You'll kill him," she whispered.

"Yes," he answered just as quietly.

"But the pistol wasn't loaded."

Doubt crossed Kiernan's features.

"He intended no harm," she said.

Kiernan's fingers slowly unclenched as he lowered his arm and looked at Robbie. Utter silence reigned in the stable until Kiernan turned to Phoebe and said, "A simple request, Heddy. Stay in the stall."

"I didn't leave it." She released his arm.

His lips pursed and he gave a grim shake of his head. "You're splitting hairs." His gaze abruptly shifted onto the men, "Mather," he called. "Tie them up." Then he swung her into his arms.

Phoebe cried out and threw her arms around his neck. Kiernan strode through the stall door and lifted her over the Dutch door through which they had entered and set her down. He vaulted over the door, then grasped her arm and pulled her toward the kitchen door of the inn. Once inside, he paused to open a drawer and rifled through it until he produced a wad of twine.

Phoebe's pulse jumped. "What are you doing?"

Kiernan again swept her off her feet and stalked from the kitchen.

"Put me down," she ordered, but he didn't slow his march down the hallway. Phoebe thrashed, but his hold tightened so that she felt as if bands of steel crushed her against stone—stone that smelled of sandalwood and man, and radiated a warmth that brought a rush of heat to her stomach. "Sir," she managed, but only the powerful thump of his heart answered as he took the stairs two at a time.

At her room, he threw open the door, crossed to the bed, and tossed her onto the mattress. She bounced and tried to gain her balance, but Kiernan grabbed her hands. He hesitated, and relief shot through her at the thought he had come to his senses. But he released one hand and snatched a napkin from the nightstand, then wrapped it around her wrists in one quick motion.

"You can't be serious!" she cried, but his gaze remained fixed on winding the twine around her napkin-protected wrists.

Phoebe jerked her hands, but Kiernan yanked the knot closed too quickly.

"That hurts," she cried.

He made another knot and yanked harder.

"How dare you!" She struggled against the ties.

Kiernan responded by winding the two ends of the twine around the bedpost and finishing off with another knot. Phoebe stared, dumbfounded as he stared back, blue eyes startlingly dark, and chest lifting and falling with each heavy breath he took. His gaze dropped to her breasts, inches from his face.

She flushed. "You can't," she began, but he shoved away from her and strode to the door.

"In a few minutes, Mather will be outside your door," he said without looking back, then slammed the door as he left.

Chapter Five

Phoebe shifted against the bed pillows and glanced at the mantle clock. Ten minutes before six. Her gaze fell to the low burning embers in the hearth. Morning was upon them and the commotion of the earlier hours had long since died. Yet, as Kiernan MacGregor promised, Mather stood outside her door. Mather had shown the good sense to untie her before positioning himself as guard. Her first thought had been that Kiernan regretted his rash outburst of temper, but Mather's, "You ought not to have ignored his commands, Miss," did away with any notion that his master had enough sense to comprehend his sin.

A perfunctory knock sounded on the door, then it opened and the object of her anger filled the doorway. Phoebe straightened.

"My one burning question, Heddy," he said, closing the door as he stepped inside—she noted Mather no longer stood outside the door—"is why you were following Alan Hay?"

"That offense didn't warrant you tying me up as if I was the criminal," she retorted.

Kiernan snorted. "I would have done far worse if you were a criminal." He strode to the chair to the right of her bed and sat down. "Answer the question."

"If I answer incorrectly, will you tie me up again?"

"I might."

Phoebe forced herself to relax against the pillows and raised a brow. "A simple case of ennui."

He blinked, and Phoebe feared she had earned another trussing up, then his expression grew speculative. The look abruptly disappeared and he settled into a corner of his chair.

He draped an arm over the chair's back and drawled, "Ennui, you say?"

Despite his lazy expression, Phoebe was startled by the decided lack of interest in his voice. "Yes," she replied.

He gave a single nod. "Your quest for adventure nearly got you killed, my dear."

"It was an exciting adventure," she rejoined in a bright voice. "Wouldn't you agree?"

"Indeed."

"Indeed," she emphasized.

"I am pleased," Kiernan said.

Phoebe frowned. "What are you talking about?"

"This fine bit of coquettish flirting."

She stiffened. He was right, which made the analysis all the worse. "This isn't an evening ball," she snapped.

"And I am not an earl."

"You could be a merchant—or a farmer—for all I care." Phoebe narrowed her eyes. "Who are you? You keep company with Lord Stoneleigh, which means you're not lowborn, and the villagers here look to you for leadership. You are no merchant—or a farmer, for that matter."

He laughed. "If I was a merchant, would my money be enough for you, or is a title required?"

She forced her temper back. "Sir, I understand you believe I am Hester—"

He coughed as if to clear his throat.

Phoebe crossed her arms beneath her breasts. "I understand you believe I am Hester and that you're doing your friend a service."

"Heddy." He leaned forward and reached for the hand she had stuffed beneath her arm.

Phoebe stiffened, but he pried the hand free and lifted it to his lips. His mouth against her hand caused her pulse to jump and warmth spread up her cheeks. His eyes registered curiosity, but he released her hand and reclined in his chair.

"Forgive me for laughing," he said.

"I can forgive the mistaken identity—as inconvenient as it is—but tying me up goes beyond the pale."

"I'm pleased to have your forgiveness, regardless of the reason."

"When this escapade is finished, you will find yourself at a disadvantage."

"Heddy," he said with resignation, "I find myself at a disadvantage now."

She gave him a dry look. "I doubt that. When do you plan on sending word to the authorities of the murder plot against the duchess—or have you already done so?"

"No need to concern yourself with that."

42

"But — my God, you don't intend to report them. You will stand idly by while a murder is planned and executed?"

"What is one murder in exchange for fifteen thousand?" he replied. "Or do fifteen thousand Highlanders hold less value to you than a single noblewoman?" He paused. "Perhaps, the gratitude of the duchess' male relatives interests you more?"

Phoebe shot to her feet. "Even Heddy wouldn't lower herself to such debased actions."

"Lower herself?" Kiernan laughed, although the sound held none of his characteristic humor. "Heddy, I have seen — "

"By heavens," she burst out. "I am not Heddy."

"No?" he murmured. When she gave a frustrated growl, he rose. "Well then — " He yanked her against him.

His mouth crashed down on hers and she froze. One arm slipped around her waist while the other cupped her neck. She gasped, but he hugged her closer. His tongue invaded her mouth, the taste of him, shocking *and* intoxicating. His arm tightened, but the kiss, the thrust of his tongue, softened to a feathery touch. He shuddered, and her heart leapt into a furious rhythm.

His mouth moved slowly against her lips. She became aware of the hard bulge pressing against her abdomen and clutched at his shoulders. Heat streaked from the unexpected throb in her breasts to her stomach, then lower. He abruptly tore his mouth from hers and buried his face in her neck. Phoebe swayed. His low laugh washed warm across her ear and she shivered.

"You temptress," he breathed. "I understand what Regan sees in you."

"Just because I borrowed Heddy's coach doesn't mean I am her," she said through a gulp of air.

Kiernan straightened away from her and stared down at her, eyes intense. "I wonder if Regan would believe me if I swore I didn't know you're his lover." His gaze slid down her body, and she couldn't find the will to turn away as his eyes lifted again to her face. "You make testing the theory tempting. In fact — "

His fingers tightened on her arms and she realized he intended to *test the theory* that instant.

Her head swam. A mental picture rose of Kiernan's large hands on her naked breasts, his mouth — Phoebe managed the presence of mind to tug free of his grasp. "I-I care nothing for what Lord Stoneleigh believes."

Kiernan tweaked a lock of her hair. "I think you do, sweetheart."

She feared her knees would buckle. By heavens, she had to get away from the man. Despite the shakiness in her legs, Phoebe crossed to the window and stared out at the road leading to the trees in the distance. "What have you done with the prisoners?"

43

"Prisoners?" The lazy drawl had returned to his voice.

Phoebe turned. "You freed them, didn't you?" But he had said as much a moment ago. He'd been in a rage when Robbie threatened to shoot her, then he had let them go. Why? "You have made yourself a conspirator to an assassination attempt," she said.

"I had hoped Regan would meet us here," he said, "but I can't wait any longer. I must press north. Connor will be here to see you early this morning. If he says you can ride, we'll travel together."

How was she going to escape him and get word to Alistair of the plan to assassinate the duchess? Phoebe closed her eyes and rubbed her temples.

"Are you ill, Heddy?"

"There's a good chance I will be."

"Shall I fetch the chamber pot?"

"Only if you wish me to brain you with it." She looked at him. "Don't you understand what this means?"

"That you are ill, or that you wish to do me bodily harm?"

"Lord Stoneleigh isn't coming — because I am not Hester."

"If that is true, when I return, you and I will get better acquainted."

Her pulse quickened. "It is imperative I return home."

"And I must continue north," he replied.

Why force her to go with him? At this point, his attempt to play cupid was dashed. Had he come to doubt she was Heddy? Surely he wasn't serious about getting better acquainted? He'd said he'd planned to secure an introduction at Drucilla's soirée.

"What is so pressing that you must return to Edinburgh, Heddy?"

She shook her head. "Not Edinburgh, England."

"England, then?"

"What awaits you in the north?" she said. "You don't strike me as a man displaced from his home."

"My home is nowhere near the duchess."

"I see." Phoebe nodded. "Kidnapping women, stalking robbers in the night, dabbling in murder conspiracies, it is you who suffers a nasty case of ennui."

"But you have solved that problem, my dear," he replied.

"Lord Stoneleigh won't appreciate you kidnapping me," she shot back in desperation. By now her uncle must know she was missing. If he was on following her as he had been she'd eloped with Brandon, Kiernan MacGregor was likely to receive a bullet through his heart.

"So my money isn't enough, then?" Kiernan said.

Phoebe narrowed her eyes. Perhaps he deserved the bullet.

Baron Ty Arlington closed the door to his mother's bedchambers as he entered. She sat on the settee overlooking the small garden in their Carlisle home, and looked up. The smile on her face faltered.

He strode to her, his fury barely held in check. "Where is Phoebe, mother?"

"W-what? How should I know?"

"She's been missing four days. Don't toy with me. I'll wring your beautiful neck, then make sure your precious Clive hangs for your murder."

Her eyes widened. "Ty, I don't know what you mean by Clive—"

"I am well aware you've been spreading your legs for him these last three months," Ty snarled. "Unlike your husband, I am no fool. What did you do with my cousin?"

"We—I—did it for you," she sobbed

Blood roared through his ears. "Did what?"

"You know she won't marry you," his mother rushed on. "We must gain control of her inheritance. If she is dead—"

Ty seized his mother's arm and dragged her to within an inch of his face. "If she dies before I marry her, we won't get a damned thing. There's a stipulation in her mother's will that if Phoebe dies before marrying, her money goes to a distant cousin."

His mother gasped.

"That's right," he said. "Lady Wallington didn't trust us."

"Us? But we never hurt her."

"Only because she had the good grace to die of a fever first." He gave his mother a violent shake that jarred dark curls loose from their pins. "What did you do?"

"Phoebe isn't dead," she got out between sobs, then began to cry harder.

Rage flashed in a blinding light through his brain before her words penetrated. Ty shoved her back onto the couch and she fumbled in her pocket for a handkerchief. He pulled the handkerchief from his pocket and shoved it in front of her face. She hesitated.

"Take it," he ordered.

She took the handkerchief and dabbed at her eyes. "You can be so cruel," she said through a dramatic hiccup.

"Like mother like son."

Her head snapped up and her eyes locked onto his.

"Where is she?" he demanded.

"I don't know. Clive said there were two men with her who protected her from him and his men."

"His men? Bloody hell, do you realize I could hang if he tells a single soul what I have planned?"

"Clive would never tell anyone."

"He's a damned coachman. Once he tires of fucking you, he'll find a wealthier woman who's just as bored as you are."

"*Ty.*"

Ty sat down beside her. "Listen carefully, you are to leave Phoebe to me."

"Clive can help."

"No one can help. Now calm yourself. If your husband sees you, he'll demand to know why you've been crying."

"He would take it for a touch of melancholia."

Ty gave a disgusted snort. "Twelve years of marriage and he doesn't know you at all."

"He sees what he wants to see."

There was a rap on the door, then it opened and a young maid entered, a tray of tea in hand. She stopped. "Forgive me, my lady." She gave a small curtsy. "I didn't realize you had company."

"Never mind," Ty said. "Bring the tray."

The girl cast a nervous glance at Lady Albery, but did as instructed. She set the tray on the sideboard. Ty rose and approached as she poured the second cup.

She paused and looked up at him. "M-m'lord?" she asked in a whisper.

Ty placed a hand over her fingers, steadying her as she finished filling the cup. "No need to be afraid," he said softly.

"Y-yes, m'lord," the maid stammered, then set the pot down and made a hasty exit.

"Really, Ty," his mother said once they were alone again, "must you have every maid that passes through these doors?"

Ty carried the two cups of tea to the table in front of the settee, and sat down beside her. "Don't meddle in any of my affairs—especially Phoebe. Do you understand?"

"Surely you can find a better prospect than her?"

"Few heiresses are willing to wed a mere baron," he replied. "And even if I were to find an heiress, few can boast fifteen thousand pounds a year."

And even fewer had no one left in the world to protect them.

Two towers came into view atop the mountainside to the west. Cool morning air rippled across Phoebe's cloak, tickling her arms. She cast a furtive glance at Kiernan MacGregor. He rode to her left with Mather to her right. Kiernan sat straight in the saddle, his body moving in a fluid motion with the horse, which gave testament to the countless hours he must have spent riding.

A tremor rippled through her. The memory of his kiss rose to the surface as it had a hundred times in the three hours since they'd left the inn. Kiernan wasn't the first man she'd kissed, but he was the first highwayman she'd kissed and—her stomach twisted—the first man she'd suspected of being a traitor. That, however, didn't stop her heart from fluttering with the memory.

For the thousandth time, she cursed her curiosity. Had she stayed in bed last night instead of following Alan Hay, she would halfway back to Edinburgh, where she could warn Alistair of the plan to assassinate the duchess. She would also be far away from Kiernan MacGregor. Though had she not followed Alan Hay, she wouldn't know about his plan. Either way, her fate had been sealed the moment Kiernan MacGregor appeared in her coach doorway…or perhaps it was his fate that had been sealed. Her attention snagged on the way his trousers hugged his muscled thigh. Phoebe snapped her attention forward.

"Is something wrong, Heddy?"

She shifted her gaze to him.

He was regarding her. "I didn't think to bring a chamber pot with me."

She scowled. "I have no use for a chamber pot here."

Mischief lit his eyes. "Not even to brain me with?"

The brute was enjoying himself far too much. She turned her gaze to the castle, now in full view as they crested the hill.

"Do you like it?" he asked.

Phoebe noted the dozen armed men arrayed along the battlements. "This is the nineteenth century, why so many guards?"

Kiernan motioned with his head to the forest that surrounded them. "This is untamed country, far beyond the reach of traditional law. The nineteenth century won't ride to our rescue any quicker than the Queen's men will."

She pointed past Mather to the sparkling lake that stretched out in the valley to the east. "What lake is that?"

"Loch Katrine."

"It's beautiful," she said.

They lapsed into silence. As they rode through the castle gate, three ruddy-faced children shot across the courtyard. Three women walking toward the castle slowed, their attention on Phoebe. She gave a cordial nod and they continued on. No one looked thin or underfed. What shielded these people from the catastrophe that had devastated Alan Hay and his people?

They halted and Mather dismounted. Kiernan slid from the saddle and tossed his reins to Mather. "If you would, Mather," he said, and came around her horse.

Mather cast her a nervous glance that reminded Phoebe of when she'd told him she wanted help in writing a letter to Kiernan's father.

Surely the rogue's father couldn't be at the castle? Kiernan halted beside her and she looked down at him.

"When will I meet your father?"

He grinned. "He isn't here."

Of course not. The kidnapper wasn't about to be so easily caught. "Where is he?"

"In the south."

Kiernan clasped her waist and lifted her from the horse. He set her down so close that she caught the familiar scent of sandalwood.

His gaze dropped. "That's a fine dress you're wearing, Heddy."

Phoebe looked down to find her breasts nearly spilling over her bodice. She scowled and pulled her cloak more closely about her. "I would have preferred my own dress."

"I think that one suits you just fine."

She was sure he did think that. In fact, she had a suspicion he was responsible for the fact that the seamstress hadn't been able to finish her gown before they left.

He released her and turned to a man who had stopped behind him. "Johnson, how are you?"

"Well enough." Johnson nodded. "Daniel wants to see ye."

"Where is he?"

"The library. Harris is training the new steward and had business with Daniel."

"Excellent." Kiernan turned back to Phoebe. "Shall we?" He offered an arm.

Phoebe rolled her eyes and started toward the castle without taking the proffered arm. "How long do you plan on keeping me prisoner?" she asked.

Kiernan fell into step alongside her. "Are you so anxious to be rid of me?"

"Beware your choice of words, sir."

He laughed. "I sent word to Regan. I expect he'll be here soon."

"Don't you find it odd he hasn't yet arrived? Has it occurred to you I might be telling the truth?"

"It's my guess that my original message didn't reach him." Kiernan gave her a serious look. "He is likely frantic with worry. You are, after all, missing."

Phoebe looked sharply at him.

They had reached a side door of the castle and Kiernan opened it. "After you," he said, waving her through.

She stepped inside and found herself in a large eating hall. Phoebe stood, transfixed by the variety of weapons mounted along the length of the wall on the far side of the room.

"An arsenal," she breathed.

"Not quite," Kiernan said. "Just a few relics we've collected over the years."

Phoebe recalled her father's mention of Arthur Thistlewood's claim that he could amass fifteen thousand armed men within half an hour. The weapons that covered the wall in front of her were a far cry from fifteen thousand, but if Kiernan MacGregor flouted this small arsenal to the world, how many more weapons had he hidden in the bowels of this castle? Who was Kiernan MacGregor, and why hadn't she heard of so powerful a man? But he'd given her the answer; Brahan Seer was far beyond the reach of *traditional law*.

"Come along." Kiernan cupped her elbow and led her toward the kitchen.

They stepped through the doorway into the busy room and a woman Phoebe guessed to be in her seventies looked up from a table in the middle of the room where she sat shelling peas.

"So, ye decided to grace us with your presence?" she said in voice clear for a woman of her advanced years.

"Aye, m'lady." Kiernan swept a low bow. "I have returned to the nest."

"Who's that with you?"

He winked at Phoebe. "A friend of Regan's."

"Does she have a name or is she like the others?"

Phoebe shot him a questioning look—though she well knew what the others must have been like. Lord Stoneleigh was a well-known rake.

Kiernan shrugged and said, "No, Winnie, she is nothing like the others."

"Well," Winnie said, "what is it?"

"What is what?" he asked.

The old woman gave him an exasperated look and Phoebe had the distinct impression her own frustrating experience with this man wasn't unique.

"Her name," Winnie said. "What is it?"

"My apologies," he said. "Hester Ballingham, may I present Winnie MacGregor."

Phoebe angled her head. "A pleasure to meet you, ma'am. Allow me to make a proper introduction. My name is Phoebe Wallington."

Winnie studied her for a moment, then looked questioningly at Kiernan.

"I told you she wasn't like the others." Before Phoebe could respond, he said to Winnie, "Heddy will be staying with us until Regan arrives."

"Sally," Winnie called, and a woman kneading bread at the counter turned and wiped her hands as she approached.

"We have a guest," Winnie said when the woman stopped beside her. "See to the guest room on the second floor."

The woman looked at Phoebe. "Would you like a bath, my lady?"

"I would, indeed," Phoebe said, "and Phoebe will do. I am no lady." She cast him a Kiernan a glance, but he stared at the peas Winnie was shelling, his expression akin to that of a man who had struck gold.

Chapter Six

Phoebe startled awake to the sound of footsteps running past her bedchamber door. She threw back the covers and jumped to her feet, reaching the door in three paces. She yanked it open in time to see two women, arms laden with blankets, disappear down the corridor. Phoebe dressed and hurried to the great hall. The room was filled with women racing in with more blankets and tossing them onto an already full table. She dodged a young girl who dashed up the stairs, then headed toward a woman who was pulling blankets from the table and piling them into the arms of another woman.

"What's happened?" Phoebe demanded.

"A fire in the village," the woman replied tersely.

"My God," Phoebe exclaimed as the woman with the blankets whirled and headed for the postern door. "Is anyone injured?"

"Two men and a child, but Winnie is tending them."

"The blankets," Phoebe said, "they are for the fire?"

"Aye."

"I'll help."

"Take these blankets to the village." The woman grabbed several blankets and shoved them into Phoebe's arms as three other women scooped up armfuls. "Go with them." She waved Phoebe toward the women who were already hurrying toward the door.

The instant she stepped outside, Phoebe gasped at sight of the red glow in the sky. Thick, dark billows of smoke trailed a haze across the moon. She kept pace with the women across the courtyard. Even before they reached the gate, the smell of smoke assaulted her nostrils and the shouts of men filled her ears. The women hurried through the gate and down the hill at a near run. Phoebe's heart pounded harder at sight of the bucket brigade that led from the well in the middle of the square to the two burning cottages sixty feet away.

She followed closely behind the women as they neared the bottom of the hill. Another pail of water was thrown on the burning cottage to the left and she shuddered at the hiss of the water over the flames. She stayed with the other women as they pushed past the old women and children who watched in stunned silence. Men dunked blankets in a tub of water beside the well, then raced along the muddy trail created by the dripping blankets to a cottage adjacent to the burning cottage.

A child shrieked, and Phoebe's heart jumped into her throat as a flame leapt in a furious gust from the cottage on the left to its neighbor. Small patches of red glowed in the thatched roof of the endangered cottage. She hurried forward and dropped her blankets onto the others piled beside the tub. A man pulling water from the well hauled up another bucket. Sweat glistened on his forehead as he handed the bucket off to his companion. The man throwing water directly onto the first cottage hurled another bucket of water onto the inferno. Nothing more than a drop on hell's flames, she thought. The man turned in her direction.

Kiernan MacGregor.

He yelled something to the man next to him — Mather — then snatched the bucket Mather held and threw the water high onto the roof of the cottage with the highest blaze. Searing smoke blasted across him. Phoebe stepped forward, but was forced back by a man who shoved past her to grab a blanket. He gave it a quick dousing, then raced to the cottage. The man pulling buckets of water from the well dumped more water into the tub. He shot her a questioning look and Phoebe dropped to her knees in the mud beside the tub. She grabbed the top blanket and dunked it elbow deep in the water, then barely lifted it to have it snatched from her by another man. She doused blanket after blanket, and handed them to men until her arms ached. At last, the pile of blankets had been exhausted.

For the first time since she'd begun the task, Phoebe looked up and saw the fire had diminished significantly. She looked back at the ground. No more blankets. They needed more. She jumped to her feet and dodged through the maze of people, only stopping when she found an open door several lanes down. She hurried inside. A woman, ransacking a large chest at the foot of the bed, looked up in surprise.

"What have you got?" Phoebe demanded.

"Take that." The woman pointed to two heavy blankets on the bed.

Phoebe scooped them up, then dashed for the door. When she dropped the blankets at the well, the man who had just dunked a blanket in the tub of water thrust it into her arms. She ran to the cottage and dumped the wet tartan into the arms of the nearest man.

She turned and started back into the village, but slipped. Sharp pain lanced through one knee. She gritted her teeth against the tears that sprang to her eyes and started to push to her feet. A strong hand gripped her arm and yanked her upright. She looked at the man as he released her, then he seized the bucket his companion shoved into his view.

Phoebe backed away and, once clear of the bucket-line men, halted and rubbed her knee. She felt something slick on her wet dress and sniffed her fingers. *Animal oil.* She looked at the blaze. Smoke still rose in dark clouds from the flames. Heavy clouds, like those thick with the sort of oil meant for a lantern. A woman sped past, nearly colliding with her. Phoebe whirled and hurried back through the village.

An hour later, she stepped from the cottage of a young girl who had given her two linen sheets. The girl had seen her passing by with the single blanket she had found and insisted she take the sheets, but the men had finally reduced the fire to a smolder, and Phoebe felt certain it wouldn't be necessary to burn such lovely hand-made sheets. Phoebe headed for the square, but slowed at sight of a figure sprinting between cottages.

She hesitated, exhaustion warring with the impression that the man was purposely keeping in the shadows to avoid detection. She recalled the oil she'd slipped in. Her knee still ached. Phoebe glanced down the deserted lane. All the villagers had gathered at the fire, so who would be skulking through the deserted lanes? She tucked the blanket and sheets under her arm and crept along the front of the cottage until she could peer around the edge. The moon shone dimly through thin clouds, lighting the empty lane. A tiny splash drew her attention farther down the narrow road.

Phoebe crept forward between the cottages. She caught sight of trees and realized this row of cottages butted up against the forest. She stopped and cautiously looked around the cottage to her right. The figure hurried away from her toward the trees. She slipped around the cottage after him. He made an abrupt right turn as if heading back toward the lane. Phoebe halted. Maybe he simply took a short cut. She started at the unexpected bark of a dog, then whirled at a rustling in the trees.

"Kiernan."

Kiernan drew back after tossing up another bucket of water onto the smoldering ash to find Munro MacGregor looking anxiously at him. "If you have come to tell me Brahan Seer is ablaze, you can go to the devil," Kiernan said.

Munro shook his head. "No. It's the Englishwoman."

"Heddy?" Kiernan thrust the bucket into Mather's hands and stepped clear of the bucket line.

"Aye," Munro said. "Rebecca says her dog, Surry, chased her."

"What's she doing in the village? Where's Rebecca?" he demanded before Munro could answer.

Munro pointed to Rebecca, who stood in the forefront of the crowd of onlookers.

Kiernan strode to her. "What's this about the Englishwoman?"

"We were coming from the north end of the village," Rebecca replied, "when Surry barked and ran between the cottages. I chased him and spotted her running into the woods."

"Damnation," Kiernan cursed. "You're sure it was her?"

"Aye," Rebecca replied. "Ye can't miss that hair."

"No, you can't. Mather," Kiernan yelled, then said to Rebecca. "Show me where you saw her."

Mather appeared at Kiernan's side. "You called, sir?"

"Yes. Mather, seems our work is not yet finished.

Moments later, Kiernan spotted a boot print where Heddy had jumped a puddle, then frowned, upon noting another much larger boot print in the mud inches from hers. A dog's growl jerked his attention to the trees. He lunged forward in tandem with a woman's muffled cry. An instant later, he and Mather crashed through the trees as Heddy shouted, "Take a large bite of him, lad!"

The dog snarled and a man's curse followed. The dog gave a sudden high-pitched yelp. Kiernan squinted in a frantic effort to pierce the darker shadows of the trees.

"Bastard!" Heddy shouted in a breathless voice.

"Heddy!" Kiernan yelled.

Boots pounded away from them, headed deeper into the forest.

"MacGregor!"

Kiernan veered left, toward her shout and spotted her slim figure amongst the trees. She shifted as though to run. "Heddy!" he shouted. "Stay put!"

She whirled toward him.

A moment later, Kiernan arrived at her side. He grabbed her shoulders. "What in God's name is going on?"

"A man," she said in a rush, pointing deeper into the forest, "he went that way."

"Mather," Kiernan said, and Mather rushed forward in pursuit of the man as Kiernan began dragging Heddy from the forest.

"Sir!" she exclaimed. "You're hurting me."

"Nothing compared to what I plan to do." Once they stepped from the trees, Kiernan yanked her around to face him. "What the hell were you doing in the forest?"

She frowned. "The forest—you think I was trying to escape? By heavens, if I wanted to escape, I wouldn't waste time helping with the fire and I certainly would not go on foot."

"Then what were you doing?" Kiernan demanded. "Who was the man?"

"I don't know. I saw someone behaving oddly and went to investigate. I believe I startled him."

"Startled him? What do you mean? Did he harm you?"

"I am well, sir," she said. "There's no need for hysterics."

There was a rustling and Kiernan looked up as Mather emerged from the forest, Surry, Rebecca's Border Collie, in his arms. The dog thumped his tail against Mather's arm.

"What's wrong, is he hurt?" Heddy demanded.

"Looks as though he's hurt his leg." Mather stopped beside them. "Nothing serious."

Heddy stroked. "Well, done, lad." She looked at Mather. "You're sure he will recover?"

"I caught up with him limping through the forest." Mather smiled fondly at the dog. "He wasn't about to give up the chase."

"And the man?" Kiernan demanded.

"Horace and Thomas heard the cries and came running. I instructed them to continue looking, but I fear we lost them."

"Them?"

Mather nodded. "I believe there were two."

Kiernan swung his gaze onto Heddy. "You said there was only one."

"I encountered only one."

"Only one? When this mess is sorted out, you will pay the piper. That is me, madam, in case you think otherwise."

Her mouth dropped open in genuine surprise. "I have done nothing wrong."

"Just as you did nothing wrong the night you followed Alan Hay?"

"I don't owe you an explanation for my actions," she retorted.

"No matter how foolhardy the actions?"

"I would think men skulking about on the night of an arson would be of greater interest to you than what I was doing in the forest," she replied.

Kiernan stilled. "Arson?"

"Are you saying you didn't notice anything strange about the fire?"

"I notice many things, Heddy, many things, indeed."

"You changed your dress." Kiernan squinted against the morning sunlight at Heddy, who walked alongside him on the path to the village.

She glanced down at the bodice that covered her full breasts. "Yes. Winnie noticed my dilemma."

Her dilemma was turning into a distraction he was having a devil of a time ignoring. He returned his gaze to the path, using the stick he'd picked up on the trail like a cane. "I shall miss your, er, shawl."

"You may have it, sir, if it means that much to you."

He would have that, and more. After a moment, he said, "We found no trace of your attackers."

"Not attackers, sir. I encountered only one man, and he did not attack me."

Kiernan looked at her. "No?"

"As I told you last night, it seemed more that I surprised him."

"Heddy, there isn't a man in this village who would accost a woman — or attack her — because he was *surprised*."

Phoebe nodded. "I know. If he was at all familiar, my description would have jogged your memory, I'm sure. Who do you think they were?"

"What of the man you thought hired the men who tried to kidnap you the night—"

"The night you kidnapped me?" she cut in.

Kiernan canted his head. "The night I kidnapped you. Adam, I believe was his name?"

"Adam couldn't possibly know I am here," she said. "Not to mention, he wouldn't associate with violent men."

"He tried to kidnap you."

"Many men have attempted to woo a lady by abducting her to Gretna Green." Before Kiernan could reply, she added, "I assure you, sir, Adam would never set a fire to a home *for any reason.*"

"You believe the men who fled are connected with the fire?" Kiernan demanded. "You said nothing of this last night."

"There's always the chance the fire was an accident, but there is no mistaking the animal oil I slipped in. Did you find the oil as I said?"

"I did." Just as he found papers on his father's desk in the library in disarray, which wasn't how he'd left them earlier that night.

They reached the bottom of the hill and a passing villager nodded to Kiernan. "Hugh." He returned the nod and continued toward the burned homes.

They entered the square and Heddy halted. "Good God."

"Terrible sight, isn't it?" Kiernan stared at what remained of the two cottages.

The first cottage had burned nearly to the ground, while the back wall of the second cottage and stone chimney was all that remained of that building. He strode to the cottage on the left and stepped through what used to be the doorway, then dug the stick into the ashes and began shifting through them.

"Be careful, sir," Heddy called. "Coals are sure to still burn in spots."

"Yes."

Nothing but ash turned up in his search and he went to the second cottage. The doorframe stood waist high, and he stepped carefully over the threshold. He shuffled throughout the cottage, stopping to turn a board over with his boot or prod at the ash with his stick.

After several moments, Heddy said, "Does anything of interest remain?"

Kiernan turned and met her gaze. "What of interest could remain? Perhaps the coverlet that Evvana's great-great grandmother made? Or the new pair of boots Logan's brother sent him for his birthday?"

"Any of those things would be of interest." Her eyes softened. "The girl was not badly hurt in the fire."

"So Winnie says," he said, and began picking his way to the far corner.

"How many tenants live on your land?" Heddy asked.

"It isn't my land."

"How many tenants on your father's land, then?"

Kiernan's stick hit something solid. He pushed aside more ash until the remains of a glass lamp became visible. "Heddy, come have a look at this."

She started forward.

Her skirts swished and Kiernan jerked his head around. "No. I forgot your skirts. It's too dangerous to walk through the cinders."

He stuck the stick through the handle of the lamp and lifted it carefully.

She stepped back as he carried it over the threshold. He squatted and set the lamp on the ground at her feet.

Heddy followed suit and studied it for a moment. "The glass is still intact. Had the lamp been the cause of the fire, it would have fallen over. Why didn't it break?"

Kiernan tipped the lamp slightly to one side. "Good question."

"Are you, by chance, involved in a feud?"

He looked up to find her studying him. "We're not at war," he replied.

"I only thought…"

"Thought what?"

"If you are helping tenants evicted by the duchess…"

Kiernan came to his feet, pulling her up with him. "Be careful, Miss Ballingham. Such accusations are dangerous. The duchess wouldn't take kindly to being accused of arson."

"I didn't accuse her."

"Who then?"

Heddy shook her head. "I'm not accusing anyone. It's just that such associations—"

"What associations?"

"Associations such as Alan Hay."

"Do not meddle in things you know nothing of. That's just as dangerous as throwing allegations at someone as powerful as the Duchess of Sutherland."

"For whom?"

"The person making them." Kiernan looked around, searching the men milling throughout the square. "Nelson," he called. "Come here, if you please." When Nelson reached them, Kiernan said, "Be so kind as to see Miss Ballingham back to Brahan Seer." He turned to her. "I'm going north. I won't be back for at least two days. This is goodbye, Heddy."

"Goodbye?"

"I expect Regan will fetch you before I return."

Her lips pursed.

Ah, so she didn't regret seeing him go at all. "You're not still angry with him?" he asked.

She sighed. "I can make the short walk to the castle myself. No need for your man to accompany me."

"I wager you can, but I prefer you not wander about alone."

Her brows lifted in polite inquiry.

"You remember my mention of the piper?" he asked.

Her regard remained detached. "Once you're gone, what is to stop me from leaving?"

"Good sense, I would hope. If you should decide to leave, I suggest you don't stop. I am known as a relentless hunter." With that, he strode away.

Phoebe had consulted the maps in the MacGregor library immediately after Kiernan left that morning and, as Alan Hay had said, the duchess' land was far to the north. Earlier, on her way to the kitchen, she had calculated their journey. They wouldn't reach her anytime soon, especially on foot. But by the time Phoebe reached London and Lord Briarden dispatched someone to warn the duchess, it could be too late. Her best choice was to slip away from Brahan Seer and ride as fast as she could for London. Kiernan had been gone several hours now, long enough for her to have a head start that would ensure he didn't catch her. From the corner of her eye, Phoebe caught sight of a tall figure that filled the kitchen doorway.

She shot to her feet, toppling her chair. "Lord Stoneleigh."

"Phoebe," he said.

At his one word, the bustle in the kitchen ceased. Phoebe didn't have to glance at Winnie to confirm her intense gaze. Phoebe groaned inwardly as the earl made his way past the women who stared at him with unabashed curiosity.

He reached for Phoebe's hand. "Why so formal, my dear, we're old friends, aren't we?" His brown eyes held hers as he pressed a kiss to the tips of her fingers. Releasing her, he looked at Winnie. "Winnie, you grow lovelier each time I see you."

"Off with you, you scoundrel." She waved him away and turned her attention to the batter she'd been stirring.

Phoebe wasn't taken in by the old housekeeper's casual manner, but faced the earl when he said to her, "I take it you've had a bit of an adventure?"

"That is one way of putting it, my lord."

He grinned. "That bad?"

"It has been…interesting."

"Kiernan does have a way of livening things up."

The activity in the kitchen resumed at a slow pace.

Phoebe inclined her head and murmured, "Again, my lord, aptly put."

He burst out laughing and she groaned inwardly when the women stopped work altogether.

"Forgive me," the earl said. "This is my doing. I received Kiernan's note the day after the ball. I assumed he would realize his mistake, and gave it no further thought."

"Don't blame yourself. He was the one, after all, who…detained me. How did you discover the truth?" she asked, but added before he could reply, "My uncle, has he raised a fuss?"

"Not to my knowledge. It was the letter from Kiernan asking why I hadn't come to Brahan Seer that told me of my error. It wasn't until the ride here that I began to sort things out. Please, my dear—" his lip twitched"—I—" His body shook with silent laughter, and Phoebe scowled.

"I know," he said. "Abominable of me." He wiped an eye with a forefinger. "But the look you must have had on your face when you found yourself in the clutches of the Marquess of Ashlund." Phoebe gasped, and his sputters of laughter abruptly ended. "What is it—Lord?" His eyes widened with even more hilarity. "Don't tell me you didn't know?"

"I did not."

She recalled the shout she'd heard when the men had burst in upon Alan Hay and his men. *"Lay down your weapons in the name of the Marquess of Ashlund!"* She groaned and reached for the chair, then remembered it lay on the floor.

"By heavens, when it becomes known the Marquess of Ashlund held me against my will—"

"Against your will?" Winnie interjected. "You can leave any time you like."

"He brought me here against my wishes," Phoebe replied coldly. "The fact that he thought I was Heddy won't signify in the eyes of polite society—my God, what a mess."

Winnie pinned Phoebe with an impatient stare. "Does anyone in England have to know what happened?"

"Good question," Lord Stoneleigh said. "Since your family hasn't sounded the alarm, we may yet avoid a scandal."

"I'm at a loss to understand why my uncle hasn't created a fuss."

59

"I can't say," the earl replied. "But I heard nothing, so perhaps no one in England knows."

"Everyone here knows." She waved her hand, indicating her surroundings.

"You needn't worry about anyone at Brahan Seer," Winnie said. "We don't associate with English gentry."

"There are those at the inn," Phoebe said.

"The Glaistig Uain?" he asked. When she nodded, he said, "Is it possible to say you were visiting someone?"

"I don't know. I can't understand why my uncle hasn't searched for me."

"I wish Kiernan hadn't left," he said. "Oh, Phoebe," he added with genuine feeling, "this is my fault. Had I not complained to Kiernan…"

"You couldn't know that His Lordship would concoct such a ridiculous scheme. He should clear up the mess, but that is impossible."

"True," Lord Stoneleigh agreed. "Even if he were here, he's the last person you want to be associated with, at this point."

"Sir," Phoebe said, "you have no idea."

Lord Briarden had long ago instructed her to be a lady of society. What would he think once he knew that by obeying his orders, she'd gotten herself mistaken for Lord Stoneleigh's mistress, then whisked off to the Scottish Highlands?

"You're sure you want to leave today?" Lord Stoneleigh asked as they walked along the village lane on their way to the stables.

Phoebe nodded. "I know we'll only make the Green Lady Inn, but I am anxious to reach London as soon as possible. If there is any chance I can head off a scandal, I must try."

"Of course," he said. "And once we reach the inn, I'll procure a maid to travel with us the rest of the way. It wouldn't do to escape one scandal only to be foisted by our innocent trip home."

"Thank you, my lord. I am deeply grateful."

They rounded the corner and the burnt cottages came into view.

"Good God." He stopped.

"It's beyond comprehension, isn't it?" she asked.

They started forward again. "What started the fire?" He lifted his hand to shield his eyes against the afternoon sun.

"I don't know. I'm sure His Lordship will insist upon a full investigation.

"Aye," came a deep voice from behind them, "that he will."

Phoebe turned to see a man, Kiernan's height, with the same striking build, striding toward them.

"Your Grace." Lord Stoneleigh affected a bow.

"Regan," he replied.

Phoebe's mouth dropped open as His Grace, the Duke of Ashlund, shifted his attention onto her. "You're his father," she breathed.

"If by 'his father' you mean, the father of Kiernan MacGregor, aye, lass, I am."

Phoebe reddened. "Forgive me, Your Grace." She lowered into a deep curtsy. "I-it is just that I—" She rose. "Forgive me, Your Grace, I have had a trying day."

"So I see." He turned to survey the cottages. "I was under the impression my son had some idea what happened."

"He sent word informing you of the fire?" she asked.

"Aye." The duke strode to the cottage Lord Stoneleigh stood nearest. "This would have been Evvana and Logan's cottage. Where are they staying?"

"Winnie made space for them in the castle. The couple who live in the other cottage is away."

"In Graham country, visiting her family," the duke said.

He went to the other cottage and stepped across the threshold with the same care Kiernan had demonstrated. His gaze moved along the ruins. "There is nothing to salvage here. Work on a new cottage will begin immediately." He turned. "But that will be tomorrow. The day is nearly done. Shall I escort you back to Brahan Seer?"

Phoebe cast a glance at Lord Stoneleigh, then said to the duke, "We were leaving, Your Grace. I must return to England right away."

"Surely you can spare an hour?"

"As you can see, it's growing late. We had hoped to reach the Green Lady Inn before dark."

"I spoke with Winnie, lass."

A shock reverberated through Phoebe. Winnie had informed the duke of his son's indiscretion.

"Marcus," interrupted a passing villager. "'Tis been a season since we've seen you."

"Aye," he replied. "Too long. The twins keep Elise busy. She sends her regards."

"Those rascals, eh?" The man beamed. "Are they giving you trouble?"

"Not nearly so much as my eldest son, I suspect."

Phoebe choked back a groan.

"What has the rogue done?" the man inquired with a grin.

"That," the duke said, "is what the lass, here, is about to explain. Would you excuse us, Wallace?"

"Aye, Marcus. We will see you later?"

The duke clasped his arm. "You will," he said, and looked at her. "Shall we?"

Phoebe nodded and she and Lord Stoneleigh fell into step alongside him.

"Would you mind beginning with your name?" the duke asked.

"Phoebe Wallington."

She startled when his head snapped in her direction. "Wallington?" he repeated.

"Yes, my uncle is Charles Wallington, Viscount Albery. Do you know him?"

He shook his head. "Nay. I knew a Wallington, a man in Inverness. I'm pleased you're not related to him."

Her heart suddenly pounded. "May I ask why, Your Grace?"

"The man was a cold-blooded killer." Before she could digest his answer, he said, "Why is Viscount Albery's niece visiting Brahan Seer?" She dropped her gaze, and he added, "Is it so bad that you fear telling me, Miss Wallington?"

"Your Grace, I ask that you leave the matter between me and your son."

He looked at Lord Stoneleigh as they started up the hill. "Have you anything to say, Regan?"

"As the lady, says, Your Grace, this is between her and Lord Ashlund."

"I can always ask Winnie."

Phoebe inhaled sharply.

"You don't strike me as the sort of young woman who traipses about the country with men."

"I assure you, I am not."

"Good. So, when we arrive at Brahan Seer, I expect you both to go directly to my library. I will ask Winnie to join us."

"Your Grace," Phoebe said, "I beg you, leave the matter."

"He's my son. I cannot."

Phoebe steadied her breathing. "No need to ask Winnie to join us. She knows very little of the matter."

"A heartening thought," he replied as they crested the hill.

Chapter Seven

*F*our days travel had tired Kiernan. He entered Brahan Seer's great hall desiring nothing more than a good meal and several scotches. He made his way through the crowd gathered for the evening meal. The last three men who stood between him and the table stepped aside and Kiernan halted upon seeing his father seated at the head of the table. He noticed Heddy sitting on his father's left and frowned.

"Evening, Kiernan," the duke said.

"Father," he replied, and started forward.

His father raised a brow just as a hand clasped Kiernan's shoulder from behind.

"Well, now," came the voice of Regan Langley.

Kiernan faced his friend. An odd light played in Regan's eyes and Kiernan looked back at his father. "What's wrong?"

The duke only stared at him.

"Damnation, Father, what is it? Is something amiss with the twins—Elise?"

"Nay. She and the children are well."

"Heddy," Kiernan turned to her, "I expected you and Regan to be gone. Are you ill? For God's sake, someone tell me what's wrong."

"What's wrong is that you are addressing the lady by the wrong name," his father said.

Kiernan's frown deepened. "What?"

"Her name—Phoebe Wallington."

Kiernan yanked his attention back to her. The low drone of voices in the hall, the clatter of pans in the kitchen, all faded into the background of a silence that hung between the four of them.

"Good God," he whispered.

"Not quite my reaction," his father said. "But considering the lady's presence, it will do."

"Father," Kiernan began, but halted at the warning look on his face and turned again to Phoebe. "Heddy—"

"Phoebe," the duke cut in sharply.

Kiernan nodded. "Phoebe—Miss Wallington, I had no idea."

"Nay?" his father demanded. "Miss Wallington informed me she revealed her identity the night you abducted her. You are saying it's not true?"

"It's true."

"Then do not compound your wrongs by lying."

"I'm sorry."

"'Tis not me you should apologize to." His father cocked his head in Phoebe's direction.

Kiernan turned to her. "Miss Wallington, I am sorry."

"That's all?" the duke demanded.

"I will, of course, make it right. I'll have an announcement immediately sent—"

"No," she interrupted. "As I told your father, things aren't as bad as they appear."

"What?" Kiernan stared.

"Lord Stoneleigh assures me my uncle hasn't acknowledged my disappearance. I have already sent word that I am well and visiting friends in the north."

"The devil you say?" Kiernan looked at Regan, who gave a nod of confirmation, then turned back to Phoebe. "You said he would move heaven and hell for you."

Her lips tightened. "Sir, I would not look a gift horse in the mouth. I'm offering you a way out."

"Offering me a way out? Madam, honor dictates there is no way out."

"My freedom for your honor?"

"I would think it would be your honor, as well." He shook his head in frustration. "I'm sorry. Get whatever notion you have of avoiding a scandal out of your head. You have no choice."

Her eyes blazed and she faced his father. "Your Grace, I remain firm in my resolution. I will not marry your son. This is Scotland, and women here have the right to refuse any offer, no matter how fantastic it may be."

"But you aren't Scottish," he replied.

"We are in Scotland, therefore, Scottish law prevails."

"But your uncle is English, and he will demand you marry."

"Think of the life you sentence me to," she begged. "You force me into a marriage that neither of us wants."

Doubt flickered in his father's eyes and Kiernan burst out, "Heddy, bloody hell!"

The din of the room quieted.

"Kiernan," the duke admonished in a low voice.

Kiernan gave the men nearest him a glare that sent them about their business, then he stepped closer to Phoebe. He placed a hand on the back of her chair and said in a low voice, "Forgive me, Phoebe, but you mistake my surprise for reluctance."

She rolled her eyes. "Don't act as though you are a willing groom."

He scowled. "You know I want you."

She gasped. Regan cleared his throat, and his father sighed.

"Don't pretend you have no idea what I'm talking about," Kiernan muttered.

"Miss Wallington," his father cut in, "you said my son didn't force his attentions on you."

"Of course, I didn't," Kiernan retorted. But he'd come damned close, truth be told.

"You said he was a perfect gentleman."

"I knew, er, thought she was Regan's." He looked at Regan and shrugged. "That didn't stop me from—"

"*Sir.*" Phoebe shot to her feet and shoved at her chair with the back of her leg, but it didn't slide and she nearly fell back into the seat. Kiernan and his father reached for her. She slapped at them, then her eyes widened on the duke.

"Your Grace," she whispered, then added under her breath, "By heavens."

"Phoebe," Kiernan said, then, "love."

"Oh no, you don't." This time she managed to shove the chair aside. "I am not some schoolgirl who will swoon with your charm." She started to turn, but whipped back around and poked her finger in Kiernan's chest, causing him to jerk back with every jab of her forefinger. "I am not your *love*. I wasn't your love before, and I—ohhh—" her blazing eyes turned on his father "—and I am not your—your—anything." She stalked to the far side of the room and disappeared up the narrow staircase.

"Interesting," his father remarked.

"Interesting?" Kiernan scowled. "Has everyone gone mad?"

The duke regarded him. "You are a fine one to talk. Abducting a woman?"

Kiernan sat in Phoebe's chair. "I had no idea who she was."

His father's mouth twisted down reprovingly.

"Yes, yes," Kiernan said impatiently, "she told me her name, but did she tell you the circumstances?"

"I believe she explained things quite thoroughly," Regan said.

"Did she explain she was in Heddy's coach?"

Regan and his father nodded.

"Did she tell you she was flirting with Lord Beasley?"

His father reached for the mug of ale sitting before him. "I would be careful about mentioning that, lad."

Kiernan stared at him.

"A future wife doesn't care for being reminded of past flirtations."

Phoebe took a sip of her morning tea just as the Duke of Ashlund stepped from the staircase into the great hall. She took another slow sip in the seconds before he reached her side, then set the cup aside and rose from her seat.

"Your Grace." She dipped into an elegant curtsy.

He grasped her hand, lifting her to her feet. "Lass, you needn't be so formal, you will soon call me father." He smiled. "You may begin now, if you wish."

"You're too kind," she said, then, "Might we speak privately?"

"Of course." He looked toward the kitchen. "Marinda," he called to a girl passing by the door, "have tea sent up to my library."

Phoebe followed him up the stairs and down the long hallway to his library. He opened the door and motioned her in. She entered and seated herself in the chair opposite his desk as he stepped behind his desk and lowered himself into his chair.

Phoebe took a deep breath. "Your Grace, there is something about me you must know. When I was seventeen, I eloped with a man to Gretna Green."

"Seventeen is young to marry," he said.

"My uncle thought so, too, and came after us. I will be blunt. He did not arrive in time."

"In time?"

Phoebe's cheeks warmed. "You must know what I mean."

"I assume your reputation was tarnished?" he asked.

She gave a nod. "With good reason. So you see, your son can't possibly marry a woman like me."

"A woman like you?" There was no mistaking the amusement in his voice, but before she could reply, he added, "No need to worry, Miss Wallington, no one will dare impugn your reputation once you and Kiernan are married."

"Your Grace, a marquess simply does not marry a tarnished woman."

He laughed. "I think a marquess marries anyone he chooses."

"I am certain your son won't be so blasé about the situation."

"Miss Wallington, as Kiernan said last night, you have no choice."

"But society—"

"Society will likely make the Marquess and Marchioness of Ashlund their darlings," he said.

"You—you can't be serious," she breathed.

"Society thrives on just such a story as yours," he replied.

Panic swept through her. Did he really consider himself that far above society's reach? Was there nothing that would sway him, nothing he cared about? She understood all too well society's barbs. She enjoyed parties and received many invitations, but no man of rank would think of offering for her and—she abruptly recalled the Duke's reaction yesterday when he thought she was related to the Wallington he knew. By heavens, the answer was right in front of her. Why hadn't she thought of it before? The duke might think his position put him above society's rules, but even a man of his rank couldn't flout society's view on a woman whose father was wanted for high treason.

Phoebe's stomach twisted as she said, "Your Grace, there is something much more serious than a green girl's mistakes."

His brows rose in polite inquiry.

"When I was a child, my father involved himself with the wrong sorts of men: dissidents, malcontents, murderers. In a word: traitors." She suddenly realized the irony of the fact that the lie that had enslaved her all her life was about to buy her freedom. "These traitors, along with my father, planned to assassinate a group of nobleman. All but my father were hanged. He escaped and hasn't been heard from since. Your Grace, he is wanted for high treason."

"High treason," the duke repeated. "That is serious business."

Hope surged through her. "Indeed it is."

"A very interesting tale," he said.

"Tale? It's the truth. The incident is known as the Cato Street Conspiracy."

His forehead wrinkled thoughtfully. "I seem to recall...the Spenceans, correct?"

"Why, yes. I'm surprised you know of it."

He smiled, the light in his eyes indulgent. "My generation does read the papers."

Phoebe flushed. "Forgive me. Of course, I-I didn't mean to imply otherwise—oh, surely you see, your son can't marry me?"

"Why not?" said Kiernan MacGregor from the doorway.

Phoebe cursed and, an instant later, when he stood at her side, she demanded, "What are you doing here?"

He lifted a brow just as his father had a moment ago and she experienced an urge to box his ears.

"I live here, my dear."

He took her hand in his. She tried to yank free of his grasp, but his hold tightened and he bent over her hand, brushing his lips across her knuckles.

Kiernan's gaze captured hers. "Good morning, Phoebe," he murmured.

His thumb brushed the spot he had kissed, then he released her. She snatched her hand back so quickly, her elbow banged the cushioned back of the chair.

"Are you all right?" He glanced meaningfully at her elbow.

"Fine, no thanks to you," she muttered.

"Your future wife was just telling me of her father's involvement with Arthur Thistlewood," the duke said. "You wouldn't remember, you were a boy then, but Thistlewood was found guilty of high treason and hanged in May of 1820."

A tremor rocked Phoebe's stomach. The duke remembered the incident even to the details of Thistlewood's execution?

"What did your father have to do with him?" Kiernan asked.

"He was accused of taking part in Thistlewood's plan to assassinate the Cabinet," she answered.

"I see. So you know a bit more about assassinations than I first thought."

She didn't miss the flicker of surprise on the duke's face, but had no time to consider it when she noticed—what, recognition?—in Kiernan's eyes.

"Why didn't you say something?" he asked.

"If you recall, my lord, you thought I was Heddy."

He cleared his throat in an obvious attempt to keep from laughing. "Indeed. Was your father also hanged?"

"Good God, no," Phoebe blurted before catching herself.

"What happened to him?"

"He was never caught."

"You told me your father died when you were seven."

She gave him a deprecating look. He would have the memory of an elephant. "What should I have said, my lord?"

"Was he guilty of the accusations?" Kiernan asked.

"I-I beg your pardon?"

"Was he guilty?" Kiernan asked again.

By heavens, she hadn't expected this question—hadn't expected any questions. "I have accepted that he wasn't the man my mother thought he was." The truth. But she'd had enough of this. Phoebe looked at the duke. "Your Grace, yesterday you asked if I understood the gravity of my situation. I ask you the same. When you thought I was related to the Wallington you knew, you weren't pleased. My father is no better than the man you knew."

"What are you talking about?" Kiernan said.

"Never mind," the duke said, then regarded Phoebe. "The Wallington I knew was a deranged killer. Is that the case with your father?"

"No, Your Grace, but—"

"Excuse me, laird," a woman entered the room. "The tea you asked for."

"On the sideboard," he instructed.

She hurried to the sideboard and set the tray down, then began filling the cups.

"I'll take care of the tea," Kiernan said.

The girl cast a blushing glance in his direction, then hurried out the door. Kiernan crossed to the sideboard as Phoebe leaned toward the duke's desk. "As I was saying, Your Grace—"

"How do you take your tea, Phoebe?" Kiernan asked.

She glanced at him, exasperated at the interruption. "Cream, two sugars." Focusing again on the duke, she said, "Dukes do not marry their sons to the daughters of traitors."

"Even if the duke himself descends from a traitor?" he asked.

"I beg your pardon?"

Kiernan returned with the tea and set it on the desk in front of her. He leaned against the desk, one leg brushing hers as he stretched them out before him. Warmth rippled through her and she froze at the realization that he was purposely enticing her.

"We come from just that sort of stock," he said.

"What?"

"About two hundred years ago, our ancestor Ryan MacGregor was a hunted traitor. Didn't stop him from marrying into the Ashlund line."

Kiernan's eyes flashed the same devilishness she glimpsed the night he had burst into her carriage, and her stomach did a flip. What was wrong with her?

"You'll fit in just fine," he said.

She gave a questioning look to the duke.

"He's right."

Good Lord, had she stumbled into a family of traitors? Did this explain Kiernan turning a blind eye to Alan Hay's assassination plot? Maybe it was in the blood. This cast a new light on the idea of the *family business*.

"Has it occurred to either of you I don't want to marry?" she demanded.

"Why not?" Kiernan asked.

Phoebe hesitated, but knew she had no choice. "My twenty-fifth birthday is a few months away. I come into a sizeable inheritance. The money will allow me to do as I please."

"So that is what you meant by *my honor for your freedom*," Kiernan murmured.

"You do understand? Well, perhaps not. My uncle is a wonderful man, but his wife isn't so wonderful, and her son—well, he's a nuisance."

"What's he done?" Kiernan demanded, and Phoebe realized he thought Ty was trying to get into her bed.

Damn him, she had no desire to explain Ty's love of gambling or her fear that Ty's mother would find a way to access Phoebe's inheritance.

Phoebe planned to take possession of her money, then ensure that Lady Albery and Ty didn't ruin her uncle. But first she had to escape this mess.

"You misunderstand," she told Kiernan, "Ty—they simply aren't my family."

Kiernan squatted beside her, bringing his face level with hers. "I will be your family now."

"I have a life," she went on in a rush, "things I wish to do, things that don't include being at the beck and call of a husband."

"As to whether or not those things include being at the beck and call of a husband," the duke said, "I cannot say, but they do now include *having* a husband."

Phoebe stiffened. "Even you, Your Grace, cannot force me into marriage."

"It is done. The notice has been sent to the papers and a letter to your uncle."

She reeled. A message already sent. How—when? How long to reach London with a message? Two days, if the messenger changed horses along the way? When had the messenger left?

"You sent the message last night," she said in a whisper to the duke. "When you allowed me to send a message to my uncle." Her pulse quickened. "Sweet God in heaven, what have you done?"

An acute silence fell upon the room, broken a moment later by Kiernan's, "Phoebe, love."

She looked dumbly at him.

"It wasn't my father's doing."

She stared. "You?"

He smiled slightly.

"Not your damned honor?"

The smile never wavered.

She couldn't believe it. *A traitor with honor.*

Phoebe looked at the duke. "I wish to return home."

"We have time," Kiernan said. "If we leave tomorrow—"

"I wish to leave now," she insisted, her gaze still fixed on his father.

"All right," Kiernan said. "It's best if the announcement appears in the papers before we arrive in London, so we will go to Ashlund first."

"I bloody well plan to cancel that announcement," Phoebe said. "And I have no intention of going anywhere with you."

"You can't go without me. In fact, we will ride with a large company of men in case your other *admirer* decides to waylay you again."

"What's this?" the duke demanded.

"Did my future wife neglect to tell you of the men who tried to abduct her the same night I did?"

The duke's attention sharpened on Phoebe.

70

"It was fortunate that I got there when I did," Kiernan said. "If not for me, God knows what would have happened."

"You're being melodramatic," she said.

"Miss Wallington," the duke said in a stern voice that forced her attention to him. "Who is the other kidnapper?"

The same man I encountered in the woods the night of the fire, she wondered? But said, "I haven't the vaguest idea."

Five minutes later, Phoebe begged Kiernan to give her time to think, and closed the library door on him and his father. She hurried to her room to collect the three articles she had hidden there earlier that morning. First, the *sgian dubh*, which she'd taken from the great hall. Lifting her apron, she stuffed the sheathed dagger into the pocket of her skirt. Next, she retrieved the small derringer she had found in the duke's library and pocketed the weapon with the dagger. Lastly, she picked up her reticule, which contained the ruby ring her mother had given her before she died, along with her father's letter. She stuffed the bag into her pocket and stood.

Blood pounded in her ears in tandem with the rhythm of her thudding heart. She smoothed her skirts, until certain the bulge wasn't noticeable, then hastened from her room and down the stairs to the front entrance. Phoebe forced her pulse to slow and her mind to quiet as she pushed open the door and stepped into the busy courtyard. She resisted the urge to glance at the upper level of the castle. If luck smiled, father and son would be in conference long enough for her to reach the village. If all went well, Kiernan wouldn't seek her out until she was long gone. Leaving on her own was a huge risk, but she couldn't see any other choice. It was simply out of the question for her to arrive in London engaged to a man who she had already reported as a possible traitor to England. The letter she'd sent to Alistair was among those the duke thought was to her uncle, and would reach London with Kiernan's announcement for the papers.

Keeping her gait casual, she started toward the gate. Halfway across the compound, a high-pitched shriek caused her to jerk her head in the direction of the scream. Two children raced across the courtyard. Phoebe shoved her hands into her pockets and slowed her pace. The open gate was only a few feet away. Easy, she told herself. A man stepped from the battlements as she crossed the gate's threshold. He glanced at her, but she kept her gaze straight ahead as if not having seen him. She felt his gaze linger on her and her heart sank. But he didn't call out, and a third of the way down the hill she couldn't refrain from quickening her pace.

Upon reaching the village, she spotted two women she'd met the night of the fire. They smiled. By heavens, they intended to stop her. Phoebe gave a cool nod and one woman flashed her a disgusted look. Phoebe winced inwardly, but kept walking. The minutes it took to reach the stables ticked by with the sluggishness of a nightmare. She reached the stables and slipped inside. A quick inspection of the horses revealed two stallions, a mare, and two geldings. She backtracked three stalls to the first gelding, a nice looking chestnut.

Phoebe ran a hand along the strong back of the animal. "Your brethren in the keep's stables are finer than you," she cooed, "but pay them no mind. We have the element of surprise and will outrun them."

With a precision born of practice, she had the gelding saddled in ten minutes. Phoebe took a deep breath. "Ironic. Of all the villains I have had to escape, it is a duke insisting I marry his son that makes me quiver in my shoes."

Leading the horse toward the rear door, she halted at the squeak of a wagon wheel halting at the front of the stable.

"There, there," a raspy voice called.

The creak of wood indicated the wagon's driver was dismounting. She would have to make a run for it after all. Phoebe urged the horse the final paces to the rear door. She shoved the door open and, yanking her skirts past the point of propriety, vaulted into the saddle. She dug her heels into the stallion's belly just as light streamed into the stable from the other end.

"What the—" Phoebe heard behind her as the beast lurched forward into the morning light.

The ride through the lane was finished in seconds. She shot past the last cottage, and the young boy who stood on its step staring after her.

Phoebe didn't slow the gelding when the forest thinned, but kept him at a cantor as she glanced up at the early afternoon sun. Four hours had passed since she'd fled Brahan Seer and only one hour since she'd spotted three riders half a mile behind her. Her stomach churned. Despite the fact that she'd circled north before heading south, they had picked up her trail. Phoebe urged her horse up the hill she had been riding alongside the past fifteen minutes. His neck muscles strained with the effort.

"That's it, laddie," she said. "Let's have a look."

They topped the summit and she brought the horse to a halt beneath the cover of trees. She surveyed the sparsely treed terrain directly below, moving her gaze northward where the forest thickened. Her gaze snagged on shadowy movement within the trees and her pulse jumped. She couldn't discern the men's faces, but there could be no doubt who led the men: Kiernan MacGregor. Phoebe yanked the reins and whirled the horse around and back down the hill.

"Easy," Phoebe instructed the gelding as he tried to veer west and deeper into the forest.

She estimated the border to be about two hours south. Darkness had fallen and, though she would have preferred the cover of thicker foliage, she feared getting lost without the aid of the moon and stars which, thankfully, shined bright that night. The horse neighed loudly.

"Quiet." She pulled back on the reins.

He neighed again, this time, succeeding in veering off course. Phoebe distinguished the soft rush of water and realized the horse's intent. She relaxed her grip on the reins and the gelding quickly broke through the foliage and into a small clearing. Phoebe spotted a stream ten feet away, glistening in the moonlight. The horse trotted to the water's edge. She dismounted as he bent his neck and drank. She lowered herself to her knees and did the same. A rustle of leaves beyond the brook caused her to pause.

For a moment, the faint sound remained lost in the babble of the brook, then slowly distinguished itself as the light tread of a horse. Had Kiernan MacGregor separated from his men? Or maybe this was one of his men. Phoebe pulled her skirt calf-high and jumped noiselessly across the brook. She crept to the nearest tree and listened. The rider's approach was still faint. She glanced at her horse. He grazed contentedly beside the brook.

Phoebe stole deeper into the forest following the discerning the horse's step. She stopped behind the trunk of a sprawling chestnut tree. The moon sliced through the branches in thick stabs of light and she was rewarded with the sight of a rider picking his way through the trees. This short, stocky man was not Kiernan MacGregor. Two men on horseback materialized from the shadows of a large oak beyond the rider.

Phoebe started, then her heart skipped a beat. None of the men wore kilts, but instead, wore the loose fitting trousers and badly cut woolen coats worn by the lower class English.

"Ain't but three o' 'em," the man she had followed said in rough English accents.

"You sure?" another demanded with authority.

"I can count," the first retorted.

A twig snapped in the darkness beyond the men.

"Bob," called the one Phoebe believed to be the leader.

"Aye, Zachariah." A large man astride a massive horse entered the circle of men.

"Where's Cary and John?" Zachariah demanded.

Bob jerked his head in the direction he'd come as two more men became visible behind him.

Zachariah looked back at the first man. "You and Frank hide in the trees near Borthwick Bridge. When they cross, fire a shot so that we know they're there, then block their rear." Zachariah looked at the other men. "You four get down below the bridge. If they try to jump, give them a taste of your pistol. But whatever you do, aim for the sky. Kill the wrong man and we end up with nothing."

Phoebe's blood went cold. The 'wrong man' Zachariah referred to could be none other than Kiernan MacGregor, the Marquess of Ashlund, son of a wealthy duke. He would bring a fine ransom.

"What about our employer?"

"What about him?" Zachariah said.

Yes, Phoebe wondered, what about him?

"Don't strike me as the type to like being double-crossed."

"He doesn't run this band," Zachariah growled. "I do."

"What if he comes looking for us?" another asked.

"It won't matter, we'll be long gone. You men want to keep working this drudge of a country?"

Grunts of agreement went around.

"Get going, then," Zachariah commanded.

The men turned their horses east and Phoebe knew they were headed for the valley she had left half an hour ago. She waited until they disappeared, then hurried back to her horse. She mounted, then urged him back through the holly bushes and down the mountainside toward the valley. Fifteen minutes later, the terrain leveled out and she snapped the reins against the gelding's rear. He shot forward.

"Heddy," Phoebe muttered as she hunkered down, "I'll choke every last breath from you when I return home. As for you, Ashlund, I'll shoot you myself if these brigands don't do it for me."

Chapter Eight

The wide valley became visible beyond the thinning trees and Phoebe brought her horse to a standstill on the hill's edge. The moon illuminated a grass-covered basin strewn with rocks and ground-hugging brush. Further scrutiny was halted by the discovery of riders entering the long valley at a gallop from the north. She squinted at the tall figure in the lead. A cloak lashed behind him in the wind. Kiernan MacGregor. She looked south where the valley narrowed and spotted the bridge where Zachariah and his men waited. She pulled the derringer from her pocket and kicked her horse's ribs. He neighed and lunged ahead. Phoebe leaned into him as he sped down the hill. The chill of the autumn night penetrated the sleeves of her dress. She tucked her head down and bent closer to the horse's neck.

Moments later, the ground leveled and they shot from the trees. Directly ahead, Kiernan and his men were midway into the valley. Shouts went up from his party. Kiernan whipped his horse around on an intercept course. The two men with him followed. In less than a minute, they were within shouting distance.

"You're riding into a trap!" Phoebe yelled. "There are brigands waiting for you at the bridge."

Kiernan glanced over his shoulder in the direction of the bridge, then faced her.

"Two men are acting as lookout," Phoebe brought her horse up short as Kiernan and his men did the same beside her. "They mean to block your retreat," she panted. "Four men are below the bridge and another waits on the other side."

"What?" Kiernan demanded. Then, before she could respond, "Damnation, woman, are you trying to catch your death?"

Tarah Scott

He whipped off his plaid cloak and edged his horse closer. Her gelding shied, but before she could pull back on the reins, Kiernan grabbed the beast's bridle and stilled him.

"MacGregor!" one of his men cried as he threw the cloak around her shoulders.

Kiernan whirled his horse in unison with shouts that abruptly emanated from the opposite side of the valley. Phoebe jerked her attention toward the shouts and saw two riders emerge from trees near the bridge.

"They spotted us," she said. "There are six of them."

"How do you know that?" Kiernan demanded. "Never mind. When this is finished I'll beat it out of you." He looked at his men. "Take care of them." He motioned toward the approaching brigands and the men started toward them. He brought his gaze back to bear on Phoebe. "Get to the other side of the valley and stay inside the trees." He snapped the reins across his steed's rump. The horse leapt into action.

"Ashlund!" she shouted. "They intend to kidnap and ransom you."

"Do as I say or I'll beat you *here and now*," he called over his shoulder.

A shot rang out. Phoebe cut her gaze to the approaching brigands who aimed a pistol at the MacGregor men. Her pounding heart skipped a beat. The ball had missed its mark and the would-be kidnappers still raced toward the MacGregor men.

She looked at the derringer. Why hadn't the duke had anything better in his library? Shooting the derringer at a target more than fifteen feet away was like spitting. She clasped the cloak about her throat, then spurred her horse back the way she'd come. Another gunshot pierced the night air. She glanced back and saw Kiernan holding his weapon level, and a riderless horse charging toward him.

The fallen man's comrade whirled and raced back toward the bridge. Phoebe urged her horse into the forest, then reined south toward the river. Beyond the trees, she glimpsed the man who had fled. He reached the bridge and raced across. Indistinguishable shouts reached her when Kiernan and his men disappeared down the riverbank left of the bridge.

Minutes later, Phoebe reached the bank. She pulled her horse up short and dismounted. She discarded Kiernan's cloak, then slid down the riverbank to river's edge. The bridge lay a hundred feet away. Waist high bushes grew in sporadic patches along the bank. The slow moving water whispered in a gentle flow downstream. She gave a final glance around the deserted riverbank, then scurried between the bushes toward the bridge. Thirty feet from the bridge, something rustled in the foliage within its shadows, and Phoebe halted behind a bush. Her heart jumped into her throat when a figure emerged from the shadows and started up the bank.

She aimed the derringer, then hesitated. He was too far away to hit with any accuracy, and his back was to her. Her stomach took a sickening turn. She'd never shot a man, and she wasn't about to start by shooting

76

him in the back. Crouching, she headed for the next bush. Another shot discharged. The man spun toward her before she reached cover and she stopped. Their gazes locked, then he stepped toward her and she fired. He jerked to his right and fell. Her heart jumped into her throat. Thank God, the bullet hit his shoulder, as planned. She'd feared the gun would pull even harder to the left than anticipated, and she would miss him altogether.

Phoebe rose on shaky legs, but forced herself to hurry forward. Another brigand appeared from beneath the bridge and she halted. His glance flicked from his fallen comrade to her — then the derringer she still gripped. He leveled the double barrel revolver he held. Phoebe dove behind the bush an instant before he fired. She looked up, expecting to see his pistol aimed at her again, but he wasn't there. A strong hand clamped onto her arm and yanked her upright.

Her captor began dragging her up the bank and Phoebe fumbled for the *sgian dubh* in her pocket. The dagger bounced off her thigh with the long strides he forced her to take. She caught sight of two revolvers stuffed into his waistband, then gave a tiny cry upon recognizing the MacGregor plaide of his kilt. Phoebe looked up and searched his face, but didn't recognize him.

"Who—" She tripped as they crested the bank. He grabbed her around the waist and yanked her off the ground. "Barbarian," she yelped, and elbowed him in the ribs.

He grunted. At the sound of more gunfire, Phoebe glanced back, but saw nothing as he hauled her up the bank. They entered the trees and she twisted to face her captor.

"You would do better to help Lord Ashlund," she said. "Those ruffians will shoot his companions and take him."

"You have a fine opinion of MacGregor men," he replied in a placid voice that didn't hide the sarcasm.

Phoebe jammed her derringer into his side. "Release me and go help the others."

"You used your one shot on that fellow."

"Useless piece of iron." She tossed the weapon aside.

Her horse came into view a few feet ahead, alongside a stallion. Her captor set her on her feet, but kept hold of her arm, while directing her toward the horses.

"They need your help." she burst out.

"I can't take you near the fighting, and I canna' leave you alone. MacGregor will have my head."

"Lord Ashlund will understand."

"Not him. His father."

They reached the horses. Phoebe spied a branch the size of her arm near the stallion's feet.

"What will his father say when you return with me and his son's ransom demand follows?" she demanded.

More gunfire echoed through the trees and he cast a glance in the direction of the sound. He shook his head. "I must do as the MacGregor ordered." He reached for her horse's reins.

Heart pounding, Phoebe bent and grabbed the branch. *Sorry about this, lad.* Her stomach tensed as she shot to her feet, swinging the branch against the back of his head. He fell to the ground with a groan. She dropped the branch and grabbed a revolver from his waistband. He groaned again.

"You'll live." Her stomach relaxed a fraction and she headed for the river.

Upon reaching the forest's edge, Phoebe once again crept down the riverbank and ducked behind the first bush she reached. She surveyed the quiet riverbank. Was Lord Ashlund on this side of the river or had he crossed over? The moonlight dimmed behind filmy clouds. She scurried from bush to bush toward the water. Nearer the river, the bushes thinned, then stopped altogether. She bent low and darted from the cover of the last bush. Gunfire broke the silence and she dropped to the ground fifteen feet from the water's edge. Her knee smashed against a small rock. She winced, biting back a cry of pain.

"Give it up, Your Lordship," Zachariah's call drifted across the river. "You're outnumbered. We won't hurt you, I swear."

Silence met his demand.

"You can't escape. I have men guarding your retreat."

Still no answer.

"Come, now. You're only going to get you and your men killed."

A soft splash in the water jerked Phoebe's attention sideways.

"If you come out now, I promise to release everyone except you," Zachariah shouted.

A figure rose from the river near her. He turned slightly and the silhouette of the revolver he held above the water became visible. She realized the giant was the man Zachariah had called Bob. Phoebe rose to her knees and aimed her revolver as Bob stepped up onto shore and started toward the bridge.

"Not another step, Bob," she said in a whisper, "or I'll blast a hole in you."

He halted. Her thudding heart skipped a beat.

"Do we have an agreement?" Zachariah called.

"Drop the weapon," Phoebe ordered.

Bob remained motionless.

She drew back on the hammer. The chamber clicked over with an audible grate. "Throw down the weapon," she ordered again.

He looked over his shoulder. His gaze latched first onto the weapon, then slid up to her shadowed face. He whirled and she fired. He staggered back with the force of the ball that hit his belly.

He looked down at the spreading stain, then at her. "Ye shot me."

Her stomach turned. *Two men in one night.* And this one, she guessed, wouldn't live.

He fell to his knees, hitting the ground with a choked groan. "Done in by a woman." He raised his weapon.

Phoebe froze. The man she had killed was about to kill her. Another shot fired. She jumped as Bob fell face forward onto the ground. Something rustled behind her and she twisted, losing her balance and hitting the ground on her backside. A figure emerged from behind a bush and she barely stifled a scream upon recognizing the MacGregor man she'd left unconscious.

He hurried forward. She stared dumbly at him as he halted beside her and dropped to his knees. She allowed him to disengage the revolver from her grasp and help her kneel. Revolver at ready, he grasped her arm.

"Can you crawl?" he asked.

She nodded and started on all fours alongside him toward the bridge.

"Now," came Zachariah's voice again, "you see what happens? You're forcing me to kill your men. Who did we kill, Your Lordship?"

Phoebe yelled, "Bob didn't kill anyone, Zachariah. He is dead."

An instant of silence passed.

"What?" Zachariah demanded.

"Come along." Her companion urged her toward the bridge.

"That's right, Zachariah," she shouted. "Bob is dead."

"Who is that?" he shouted back.

There was a scuffle, muffled voices, then the sound of footsteps running through the trees—running *away*, Phoebe noted.

"Come back, you cowards," Zachariah called.

A moment later, Phoebe and her companion reached the bridge, and he called out softly, "MacGregor."

A man's voice answered a few feet away, beyond the bushes. "Donald?"

"Aye," he replied.

A man showed himself and waved them forward. Donald got to his feet, pulling Phoebe with him. He hurried her past him and she pushed through several bushes, snagging her skirt on brambles. Donald yanked the skirt free and pushed her forward. They broke through the bushes where three men stood, and she stopped short at seeing Kiernan sitting on the ground, back against a large rock as he loaded a revolver.

"Phoebe Wallington," he said without looking up, "when this affair is finished, I do swear to beat you."

There was a gritty edge to his voice Phoebe didn't like. "Indeed, my lord? I was thinking I would shoot you." Her gaze caught on the tartan wrapped around the uppermost part of his left thigh. "Good God, what have you done?"

She hurried forward and dropped to her knees at his side. A splinter of pain shot up her leg. She winced, but ignored the discomfort and touched the tartan around his leg. She pursed her lips upon recognizing the moist stickiness of blood and pressed down on the wound.

"Phoebe," he said in a raspy voice.

She shot him a quelling look. "You were the one person who was not supposed to get shot."

"Save your reprimands for the wedding night," Kiernan said with a grunt.

"Don't be a fool." She pressed gingerly on his leg.

"Madam," he growled, "if you would kindly cease your ministrations until we are finished with—" Phoebe pressed harder. "By God," he cursed.

"Hush, or you'll have no business to attend to at all." She looked at his men. "How is that, of the four of you, he is the one shot?"

"It was the sniper." One of the men pointed at the bridge.

She gave a disgusted snort, then eyed Kiernan critically. "Hurts like the devil, I imagine."

He scowled. "A mere flesh wound. See to that fool threatening us," he ordered, and two of his men slinked off into the darkness as he returned his attention to sifting the powder into the muzzle of his weapon.

"From the looks of that fabric, you've lost a fair amount of blood." Phoebe touched his damp forehead. "You're flushed." She rose and turned from the men, slipped off a cotton petticoat, then turned back and thrust the petticoat into Donald's grasp. "Tear this into one long bandage."

"I suppose you'll insist on a new petticoat," Kiernan said as the sound of fabric ripping filled the quiet air. A large portion of the powder he had been trying to force into the barrel of his revolver missed its intended mark and ended up in a heap on his lap. "Damnation," he cursed.

Phoebe snatched the weapon from him.

"What the devil—give me that, woman."

She dodged his swipe for the weapon. "Why wasn't I able to get my hands on this belt pistol when I needed it?"

"What's that you say?" Kiernan made another grab for the pistol.

"Be patient," she ordered. Phoebe pointed the barrel upward and pulled back the hammer to the half cock position. Another rip of her petticoat rent the air. "Give me the powder." Instead of waiting for him to comply, she grabbed the horn from his hand. She measured powder into the chamber. "Keep pressure on that wound," she told Kiernan. "I don't like the way it's bleeding. Where is Mather? He would have kept you out of trouble."

Kiernan shifted the tartan back onto the wound and pressed gently. "I gave him leave to visit family before I saw you this morning—and he didn't succeed in keeping me out of trouble the night I met you. Who taught you to load a pistol?" He retrieved a ball from the pouch lying beside him and offered it to her.

"I told you, my uncle is an amateur collector."

Phoebe took the ball and placed it on the face of the cylinder. Using the loading lever, she depressed the ball into the cylinder, watching as a small ring of lead was shaved off the ball in the process.

"Excellent." She reached for more powder and began loading another chamber.

A moment later a shot rang out from across the river.

"I pray that was a MacGregor weapon." Phoebe pressed the last ball into the chamber and gave the weapon a final examination. Satisfied, she handed it back to Kiernan, then turned to Donald. "Finished ripping that petticoat, I see."

"Aye." He handed the mass of fabric to her.

Phoebe set the bandage on Kiernan's lap, then reached beneath her apron and retrieved the *sgian dubh* from her pocket.

"What the devil?" he muttered.

"Where is the closest doctor?" she asked as she unwound the tartan from his leg.

"Edinburgh is three hours away," Donald answered.

Phoebe tossed aside the tartan. "Nothing closer?" She grabbed Kiernan's breeches at the right thigh, and positioned the dagger over the cloth.

"Phoebe," he said, "I don't care for the way you are holding that knife."

She stuck the point of the dagger into his pants.

"Phoebe!" He twitched.

She gave an exasperated sigh. "Lie still, and I won't cut you." She slit the fabric to his knee, then scooted down and finished cutting the pant leg. "Has anyone got any liquor?"

Both men shook their heads.

"Use the powder," Kiernan said.

"That'll do." She set the dagger on the ground and grabbed the horn. Kiernan had shut his eyes. "What of English soil, Donald?" She sprinkled the powder on the wound.

"What?" he asked.

"A doctor," she said. "Where is the nearest doctor in England?"

"There is a respectable village an hour away," he answered.

"Come here," Phoebe ordered.

Donald knelt beside her.

"Hold his leg up as I wrap the bandage."

81

He did as instructed and she reached beneath Kiernan's leg and handed the bandage from one hand to the other, keeping the fabric taut with each pass.

"Phoebe," Kiernan said, his voice sleepy, "be gentle, lass."

She paused, concerned that she had applied too much pressure to the wound.

"I'm wounded, not dead," he said.

Phoebe frowned, then noticed the bulge in his pants a couple of inches from her hand. "By heavens, shall I have Donald finish the job?"

"No," Kiernan's voice held a trace of amusement. "I shouldn't enjoy it half as much."

She continued wrapping his leg. "Zachariah has an employer who it seems has an interest in you."

"What are you talking about?"

"I overheard them in the forest," she said.

"We will speak about the fact you were in the forest at length when I am in better condition to deal with you," he said.

"We are speaking now." She tugged the bandage tight.

"Don't be obtuse, Phoebe."

She ignored him. "Reference was made to an employer who wouldn't like being double-crossed. Who is after you, my lord?"

Kiernan shrugged. "Not everyone understands how delightful I am."

"So it seems." She ran her hand along the makeshift bandage, satisfied it was the best she could do, then looked at Donald. "He has lost a substantial amount of blood."

"Aye," he agreed.

"Don't talk about me as if I'm not here," Kiernan complained in a whisper.

"If we don't hurry, you are likely not to be with us much longer."

"I would think that would solve your problem, Miss Wallington," he replied.

"Had I known you would be fool enough to get yourself shot, I wouldn't have bothered to come back and warn you."

Kiernan grasped her hand, his grip still quite strong, she noticed with relief. "Why did you turn back?"

Phoebe shook him off. "You owe me for this, Ashlund. I deduced that it would be easier getting you to repay this debt my way, than trying to fight you—and your father."

He took a slow breath. "It doesn't signify. Neither my father nor your uncle would allow that, even if I agreed. Which—" he broke off, glancing at his two men, who had reappeared "—I do not."

Phoebe looked at Donald. "Where are our horses?"

"I last saw them when you hit me," he said.

82

"Had you done as I told you and helped Lord Ashlund, I wouldn't have had to brain you. If luck is with us, they're still there. Please retrieve them."

If luck were with her, she would reach London before the announcement reached the papers — and before Kiernan MacGregor had a chance to recuperate. God willing, he did recuperate.

A little over an hour later, they reached the inn. Donald was off his mount and at Kiernan's horse as Phoebe stepped to the ground. Kiernan had managed to stay in the saddle, but his eyes were closed and he had grown pale. Aaron had dismounted and reached Kiernan as Donald helped him from the saddle. Each man grasped one of his arms and slung it over a shoulder, then started toward the inn. Phoebe hurried ahead of them as the remaining two MacGregor men pulled the injured brigand from his horse. The man she had shot looked worse than Kiernan, but she prayed he would live. As suspected, Bob hadn't lived. If they were fortunate, this man would name his employer.

Phoebe held the door of the inn as Donald and Aaron crossed the threshold with Kiernan between them. She frowned when Kiernan's head lolled to one side. Blood had soaked the white cotton of his makeshift bandage, as well as the pant leg that flapped about his calf. A wave of panic swept through her. She had never dealt with a wound that bled so much. Perhaps she had bandaged it improperly. She hurried past them into the wide foyer. A long hallway lay straight ahead and to her right was the drawing room. She entered and a young, brown haired serving girl and the two guests seated at a corner table looked up.

"We need three rooms," Phoebe said, "and send for a doctor immediately."

The girl hurried past her, eyes widening when Donald and Aaron entered with Kiernan.

"Put Lord Ashlund in that chair." Phoebe pointed to a chair positioned in front of the fireplace.

The men complied and she bent and felt Kiernan's forehead. He had developed a fever. She straightened when a tall man entered the room.

"You are the proprietor, sir?" she inquired.

"I am," he replied. "What's all this?"

Phoebe followed the man's gaze to Donald and Aaron. Their kilts, she realized, held his attention and not the bleeding man.

"This is Lord Ashlund." She motioned toward Kiernan. "We were set upon by highwayman, and His Lordship was shot."

"Lord Ashlund?" came a nasally feminine voice from behind the man.

The proprietor stepped aside, allowing a short, plump woman to enter. She gasped as her gaze fell upon Kiernan. "The man's indecent."

She jerked her attention to Phoebe. "How dare you bring a half dressed man here? This here's a respectable establishment."

"Don't be a fool," Phoebe snapped. "He's wounded, and he's the Marquess of Ashlund."

"A Scot," the woman said with derision, then added with a sweep of her gaze across Phoebe, "And you're no more a fine lady than Mildred down the lane."

Phoebe faced the proprietor. "I would advise you, sir, to take quick action. His father is the Duke of Ashlund."

"Another Scot," the woman repeated with outrage.

"You do not wish *this* duke's son to die on your carpet," Phoebe said without taking her eyes off the proprietor.

"Sally," he called. The serving girl rushed into the room. "Ready the room at the end of the hall."

"Now, Roger," the plump woman began.

"Be quiet," he hissed.

"Send for a doctor immediately," Phoebe said.

"Send Jack for the doctor," he said, and Sally dashed through the doorway.

"There is another man in your stables who must be attended to as well," Phoebe said, then turned. "Donald, see His Lordship to his room."

Donald and Aaron lifted Kiernan by his armpits.

"I, too, will need a room," Phoebe added.

"We ain't got no more rooms," the proprietor's wife snapped.

"Roger." Kiernan's low voice quieted the room. Donald and Aaron halted as he said, "The lady is my future wife. You will see to her comfort?"

"Aye, my lord, I will," the proprietor said with a quick bow. "My wife isn't always aware of the rooms we have available. Rest assured your lady will be looked after."

Kiernan closed his eyes and Phoebe prayed no more would be heard from him that night.

Phoebe watched Dr. Wilcox place a bottle of laudanum on Kiernan's nightstand before he turned to her.

"He lost a great deal of blood," the doctor said.

Phoebe agreed. It showed in the paleness of his skin. The doctor had made short work of extracting the ball from his leg. Now, an hour later, he rested, and they waited.

"The fever concerns me," the doctor went on. "If it breaks, he'll do well. He's a healthy lad, the chances are in his favor. You did a fine job on the bandage. Chances are it saved his life. Administer the laudanum if he wakes. As it is, he should sleep through the night."

"His lordship will see to the bill in the morning," Phoebe said. "You will see to the other man, as well?"

"I will."

He rose and she escorted him to the door. "Thank you for coming."

The doctor nodded. "I'll look in on him in the morning."

She opened the door and said again, "Thank you," then closed the door behind him. "So," she faced Kiernan, "the tables are turned. It is I who must attend to you."

Phoebe crossed to the bed and placed a hand on his forehead. He was still hot to the touch. In sleep, Kiernan MacGregor's features softened, but the masculine angles remained. His mouth...his mouth she remembered with more clarity than she cared to admit. She had yet to forget the damn kiss, and that was the one thing she should forget.

Her mother's ruby ring, her father's age-yellowed letter, and Dr. Connor's binaural stethoscope danced around Phoebe's head. She jumped, desperate to snatch each one as they dipped closer, but every time she caught one, they melted in her fingers. From the corner of her eye, she caught sight of the only sentence in her father's letter that was legible: *I give my blessing to this marriage.*

She didn't remember that line in his letter. How had her father known about Kiernan MacGregor? The stethoscope made a sudden dive, then snapped back, causing the end to crack like a whip and hit her head. She cried out in pain and the letter followed, lashing across her face. She swatted viciously, ripping the corner. She wadded the fragment of paper and flung it after its whole.

The three objects turned in unison, forming a line as if for a coordinated attack, then lunged for her—Phoebe awoke with a start. At sight of Kiernan MacGregor asleep in bed, she leapt to her feet. She looked wildly about for her three foes, but saw nothing flying about in the soft glow of the fire-lit room.

She touched her head where the stethoscope had hit her, but found no soreness. A dream. Phoebe collapsed back into the chair, the beating of her heart so loud she wondered how her patient could sleep through the noise. Even with the phantoms gone, fear gripped her. She considered lighting a lamp, but suddenly remembered her plans for the evening. She touched Kiernan's forehead with the back of her hand. Sweat dotted his brow, but he was cooler to the touch than he had been when they arrived. He would recover. She released a slow breath, then stood and pulled the bedcovers up to his chin.

"When next we meet, I shall be home." Phoebe crossed to the door and opened it. Stepping into the dark hallway, she closed the door with a soft click. "Blasted innkeeper," she muttered, then realized it was probably the innkeeper's wife who was too cheap to light the hallway.

85

She started forward. Her toe jammed against something hard. A man grunted. She stumbled when her next step landed on hard flesh. She tried to sidestep again, but lost her balance completely and toppled on top of the man, knocking the breath from her lungs.

"My lady!" he cried, and Phoebe recognized Donald's voice.

She gasped for air as he shoved her away and leapt to his feet, pulling her up.

"I didn't know you would be leaving the laird this evening," he said. "Are you hurt?"

She glared at him. "Why are you sleeping in the hallway? Did that odious innkeeper deny you a room?"

"Nay. I, uh, well, that is, I can't leave the laird unguarded."

Phoebe narrowed her eyes. "You mean you can't leave me unguarded."

"I didna' say that," he answered too quickly.

"What gave you the notion you need to guard me?"

"I can't leave you unguarded in a foreign country."

"You're telling me this is for my own good?" she demanded.

"Aye. I would be drawn and quartered if anything happened to you."

That, Phoebe knew, was true. "You weren't instructed to see that I don't escape?" She left off the word *again.*

Donald didn't answer.

"How did that devil of a man have the strength to give any orders?"

Donald straightened with obvious pride. "He's a strong one. He said it didn't matter if none of us got a wink of sleep, we are to watch over you until his father arrives."

By heavens, Phoebe cursed inwardly. *They sent word to the duke.*

"I "have no intention of sleeping in His Lordship's room the remainder of the night," she said. Someone must attend to him. I give that task over to you. I shall fend for myself. You needn't worry. I'll lock my door from inside."

Five minutes later, ear pressed against her bedchamber door, Phoebe heard a shuffle outside her room. Damn the man. Donald had recruited help with guard duty. This time, she had no choice: it was to be the rooftop.

Chapter Nine

At the muffled thud of approaching horses, Ty reached for the revolver he'd set on his log backrest and rose from the side of the long dead fire. He had expected one rider this morning, no more. His horse tugged uneasily on the reins Ty had secured to a nearby branch, and he flicked the animal a glance just before spotting the riders through the trees. He recognized Bernard, the man he'd hired to locate Ashlund and Phoebe, and with him, was Clive Randal. So, despite his warning, his mother had involved her lover. Clive's gaze met his and didn't waver. Apparently Ty's warning to Clive had gone unheeded, as well.

Ty should have known the coachman would coerce his mother into interfering again. He saw this situation as a chance to help Lady Albery spend the money he believed she would have access to once Ty took possession of Phoebe's inheritance. Dammit, he should have killed Clive after he'd questioned him the night he tried to kill Phoebe. Once Clive described the two men who were with her, Ty recognized the description of Kiernan MacGregor—and Clive had outlived his usefulness.

"Arlington," Bernard said, halting in front of Ty. Loosely gripping the reins, Bernard raised his hands in mock surrender and nodded toward the revolver Ty aimed at them. "You wouldn't shoot your own men, would you?"

He would. Ty lowered the weapon.

Clive dismounted as Bernard swung his leg over his horse's rump and stepped to the ground. Clive reached inside his coat.

"Clive." Ty stepped toward him, but Clive already had his pistol pointed at Bernard as he emerged from between their horses. "Clive!" Ty shouted.

Bernard's eyes widened in the same instant Clive fired. The horses squealed and lunged to the side as Bernard staggered back, arms flung wide. He made a gurgling noise, then twisted, falling face down onto the ground.

"You bloody fool," Ty snarled. "I needed him."

"The man was a risk." Clive stuffed the pistol back into his waistband. "He led me to you without question."

Ty slipped a booted foot under Bernard's belly and turned him over. Blood stained his dirty, white shirt in a large circle over his heart. Ty looked at Clive. "You could at least have waited until I got the information I needed."

"He learned that Ashlund was at the inn a week ago with your cousin."

A week ago? Damn it, was he too late? "Are they married?"

Clive shook his head. "No, and there's something odd about the situation."

Ty tensed. "What?"

"She's going by the name Heddy Ballingham."

"Ballingham? Why is she using that bitch's name?"

Clive's brow rose. "You know her?"

"A baron's daughter. She married young, to an elderly man who left her with a small stipend. She is currently associated with Lord Stoneleigh. Are you sure it's Phoebe with Ashlund and not Hester?"

Clive shrugged. "Bernard seemed convinced."

"Did he find out where were they headed?"

"Ashlund's castle north of Glasgow."

"God damn it, Clive. Bernard had men working for him. Now I'll never know if they discovered anything more."

"His men never returned."

"What are you talking about?"

"Bernard sent his men to find Ashlund, but they were a day overdue in returning. My guess is they tried to rob the marquess and either they killed him and ran, or he killed them."

"They simply might not have discovered anything yet," Ty countered.

The coachman gave him a deprecating look. "You don't know the criminal sort, my lord." *My lord* held his usual condescension.

Ty nodded. "Not as well as you."

"That's right. Trust me when I say they made plans of their own."

Ty hated to admit it, but he was probably right. "What are you doing here?"

"Your mother sent me with this." Clive reached into his pocket.

"Easy," Ty warned.

Clive's mouth twisted into an arrogant grin as he pulled an envelope from his pocket, then handed it to Ty.

Ty took the envelope. "How is it you found Bernard?" he asked as he broke the seal. "I didn't inform my mother I'd hired him."

"I immediately pegged him as someone who didn't belong at the Green Lady Inn. When I told him I had a message for an English friend I was sure he knew, his description of you told me I was right."

"Many people come and go at the Green Lady Inn. You could have been wrong." Ty withdrew the two sheets of paper from the envelope, unfolded them, and read.

Humphrey,

You must read the enclosed letter immediately. It will explain all. I managed to intercept the letter, so Charles is yet ignorant of this news.

Ty paused to unfold the other letter. He sucked in a breath at sight of the letterhead. *Marcus McGregor Duke of Ashlund.*

To Charles Wallington, Viscount Albery
Sir,

> *I write in regards to the marriage of my son, Kiernan MacGregor, Marquess of Ashlund, to your niece, Phoebe Wallington. This announcement will come as a surprise, but be advised there are circumstances surrounding this engagement we must discuss privately. The formal announcement has been dispatched to the post and will appear in print, at the earliest, the day you receive this letter, at the latest, the next.*

> *I will be in London within the week and shall call upon you immediately.*

Signed,
Marcus McGregor, Duke of Ashlund

"Bloody hell." Ty cursed, and finished reading his mother's note.

> *You must tell me immediately how to proceed. The announcement did not appear in today's paper, but it will surely be all over London by tomorrow. Do make haste.*

Lady A

Phoebe had made no noises about marrying the marquess. To Ty's knowledge, she didn't even know him. Ashlund must have compromised her somehow and his father was forcing the marriage, though why he would do that, Ty couldn't understand. The Duke of Ashlund was rich as the devil and very powerful. He didn't have to do a damn thing he didn't want to do.

Ty refolded the letters and put them in the envelope. "Tell my mother I'll speak with her when I return."

"You have plans for the girl?"

Ty looked up. "Stay out of this, Clive."

He shrugged. "I'm just saying that sons die, even the sons of rich men."

"The duke is not one to dally with," Ty said.

Clive gave a deferential nod. "I only thought perhaps you might not realize how easy it is for a man to die while walking down the street after a night at his club."

Ty knew. He also knew that Clive might decide to prove how right he was before Ty had a chance to take care of Ashlund himself.

Phoebe brought her horse to a stop at the inn where a group of bedraggled travelers faced a man in the doorway. She threw the cloak from her shoulders and dismounted.

"Please, Sir," one of the travelers said with a light Scottish brogue, "all we ask is a wee bit of food for the women and children, and that you let them sleep in the stables." The traveler towered over the innkeeper, but kept his gaze lowered as he pointed to the three women and four children. "We men will sleep in the forest."

Phoebe glanced at the sky. The sun would set within the hour and already a raw chill hung in the air. The men faced a bitter night if exposed to the elements. As did she.

"Sir—"

The innkeeper cut off the traveler with a derisive snort. "Off with you, you Scottish bastards," he snarled.

"Why doesn't he like us?" the smallest girl said in a half-whisper. She clung to another child, a boy not much older than herself.

The innkeeper jerked a startled look in the children's direction. They stared back, eyes wide in gaunt faces. Embarrassment shadowed the innkeeper's face and Phoebe thought he would relent.

"You ought not to speak that way in front of the bairns," the traveler said in a soft voice that didn't quite hide his effort to maintain control.

The innkeeper's face mottled with anger. "Watch your tongue," he snapped. "We don't want the likes of you here. Now get out before I have you jailed for trespassing."

The traveler's jaw tightened and he flushed a deeper red.

By heavens, the fool of an innkeeper will start a row that will end in half the village being burned.

"I'll pay for their lodgings," she interjected.

The group turned toward her.

Phoebe met the traveler's gaze. "How many rooms do you require, sir?"

"We—I—" He dropped his gaze. "My lady, we can't—"

"Money isn't the issue," the innkeeper interjected.

Phoebe pinned him with a cold stare. "What is the issue, sir?"

His jaw clenched. "I have the right to turn away anyone I please."

She started forward and the travelers parted as she passed through their midst. She halted before the innkeeper. "A fine thing to be able to turn away paying customers."

He gave another snort, this one even more scornful. "They ain't paying customers."

"Four rooms," she said. "Three for these people and one for myself. Supper for everyone, as well as breakfast, and dinner for tomorrow's travel."

The innkeeper's expression melted into a confident sneer. "That's a lot of money."

Phoebe reached into her dress pocket and pulled out her reticule. She loosened the drawstring and retrieved her mother's ruby ring. Her heart wrenched as she held it out. A murmur rippled through the travelers.

"This will more than cover the cost," she said.

The innkeeper's eyes widened and Phoebe knew she had him.

His gaze lifted to meet hers. "How can I be sure you didn't steal the ring?" He ran his gaze down the length of her. "You don't look the sort to own something so fine. I don't need—"

"Don't be a fool," she cut in. "If I had stolen the ring, I wouldn't be trading it for simple lodging. The ruby is genuine, and the gold of the highest quality. I will require a bath as well and—" the innkeeper opened his mouth and she went on in a more forceful tone "—and your other guests will be given the same privilege should they choose."

The innkeeper glanced at the travelers. "If there's any trouble—"

"If there is any trouble, I shall call the constable myself." She brought her gaze to bear on the traveler's spokesman. "I expect that won't be necessary."

"My lady," he began, but she turned again to the innkeeper.

"Please see to my horse." With that, she brushed past him and into the inn.

Shyerton Hall in London. Despite the fact the townhouse hadn't felt like home since her mother died, anticipation swept through Phoebe when the cab turned onto the dead end lane and the house came into view at the end of the road. She surveyed the neighborhood as they rolled along the lane. Autumn leaves littered the cobblestone street and rustled with the wisps of air created by the cab. The hour was early yet, nine-thirty or so, and no signs of life were evident in the homes they passed. Phoebe breathed a sigh of thanks for the small favor. She had dreaded any neighbors witnessing her arrival. The bath at the inn had refreshed her, but that had been two days and many dusty roads ago.

Water enough for drinking had been offered on the ride from Yorkshire, but no more. Phoebe had dipped a corner of her dress in the quarter cup she was given at the last stop the previous night and, without the aid of a mirror, had cleaned her face. The looks she'd gotten from drivers at the London depot told her she'd been unsuccessful in elevating herself above the status of street prostitute. Her hair hung in limp tresses around her shoulders. If the dusty taste in her mouth was any indication, even her tongue needed a good cleaning. All would be well, however, if her good fortune included her aunt and uncle's absence when she arrived.

What of the travelers' good fortune, she wondered? The man who had begged shelter from the innkeeper had introduced himself the following morning as David MacEwen. His gently offered thanks had wrenched her heart, but it was the children's faces that haunted her. The meal they'd eaten at the inn and the night in a warm bed had restored some of the glow to their cheeks, but no hope illuminated their eyes. Suffering through the ride in the public carriage from Yorkshire to London had been worth the price of giving her horse to David. If they sold the beast, they would get enough for passage to a larger city where the men could find work. She laughed. It wasn't her the travelers had to thank for the horse, but the Duke of Ashlund.

The cab jostled as the driver turned off the street and onto the gravel drive that circled Shyerton Hall. A moment later, they came to a halt at the townhouse steps. Phoebe opened the door, knowing the driver wouldn't bother to assist her, and stepped to the ground.

"Wait a moment," she instructed, and hurried up the steps.

"This is your home, is it?" the driver said in a doubtful voice.

"Be good enough to wait," she called over her shoulder.

"I'll wait," he said.

Phoebe tried the knob. Locked. If not for the driver, she would enter through the rear servant's entrance. She glanced at him. His eyes were narrowed in suspicion. Phoebe faced the door and knocked several times with the ball of the knocker.

The door opened with a jerk and the butler stood in the doorway. "What—"

Recognition flooded his angular face and his mouth fell open.

Phoebe smiled reassuringly and stepped into the foyer, forcing him back. "Is there any money to be had in the house, Gaylon?" she asked.

"Money?" he repeated.

"Yes, money." She pointed to the driver, who watched them intently. Gaylon glanced past her, and she added, "I find myself short of cash. If you don't have any, I'll fetch some from my room."

"No, Miss. I'll deal with the gentleman."

"He was most kind," Phoebe said.

Gaylon nodded understanding, then stepped past her out the door. Phoebe hurried toward the stairs to the right. Gaylon would keep silent about her present state of dress. If she could avoid the other servants, she might yet circumvent any gossip. Her foot touched the third step when a woman behind her shrieked. Phoebe jumped, then cursed, and slowly turned to face Molly, the downstairs maid. Linens lay strewn about her feet.

With a sigh, Phoebe stepped back down onto the hallway carpet. "It's all right, Molly."

A quick, heavy tread of feet echoed down the corridor that led to the kitchen and Phoebe groaned. An instant later, the housekeeper appeared in the foyer. Phoebe started at sight of the large butcher knife Mrs. Harkin held even as the housekeeper's eyes widened and she halted.

"Hello, Mrs. Harkin," Phoebe said.

"Lord," Mrs. Harkin said, circling Phoebe, eyeing her, "you look terrible."

"Mrs. Harkin," Phoebe said mildly.

"Huh?" Mrs. Harkin's head jerked up and she met Phoebe's gaze.

Phoebe nodded toward the knife. "Do you mind?"

The housekeeper gave her a blank look, then glanced at the raised knife. "Oh." She laughed. "I was cutting ham." She lowered the knife. "Where have you been, Miss? There's been something of a stir this past two weeks, what with you missing and all."

"A stir?" Phoebe asked in a light voice.

"Oh, yes, Miss," Molly broke in. "Calders returned home hoping to find you here."

"I thought he was in Scotland," Phoebe said with a laugh.

"Said he'd been poisoned," the maid said. "Said, when he woke up, you were gone."

"Poisoned?"

Mrs. Harkin snorted. "He wasn't poisoned. Got a hold of bad brandy, is all. If he hadn't been drinking to begin with, he wouldn't have lost you."

"He didn't lose me," Phoebe replied. The beginnings of a headache pressed against her skull.

"Who was it made off with you?" Molly asked, wide eyed.

"No one made off—"

"Miss!"

Phoebe whirled at the sound of Calder's voice. He stared at her as if she were a ghost. By heavens, all the thought she had given to keeping quiet her abduction, and not once had she considered Calders.

"Calders—"

"I nearly got you killed," he said with such anguish that Phoebe stood dumbstruck. "Your uncle will never forgive me."

93

"It wasn't your fault," she said. "As you can see, I am well." She prayed no one would notice she looked more worn than she should.

"Calders," Gaylon's low voice drew everyone's attention to him. He stood behind the group. "I believe you have work in the stables."

Calders nodded, shoulders slumped, and turned.

"Calders," Phoebe called.

He halted, but didn't face her.

"Calders," she repeated firmly, and he turned.

"It wasn't your fault," she said. "If it hadn't been the brandy, it would have been something else. I'm thankful you weren't a casualty. The jest was in very bad taste."

"Jest?"

"Exactly."

His brow furrowed, then his eyes narrowed shrewdly. He started to say something, but Phoebe raised a brow. His expression melted into his usual placid look.

"As you say, Miss."

"One more thing, Calders."

"Yes, Miss."

"What did my uncle say when you told him I was, er, lost?"

"He hasn't said anything," Calders replied.

"Lord and Lady Albery left for their estate in Carlisle before Calders returned," Gaylon interjected.

Hope surged through Phoebe. "You didn't tell them I was missing?"

"I did, indeed. I sent them a message."

"And?" Phoebe prodded impatiently.

"Lady Albery wrote back that they were dealing with the situation."

Dealing with the situation? What did that mean? Had the duke's letter reached her uncle? Or had Uncle been wise enough not to make a ruckus about her disappearance until he could find out what happened?

"Has there been any further communication?" Phoebe asked.

"No," Gaylon said.

She turned. "Calders, why didn't you stay in Scotland?"

"Your cousin sent me home."

"Ty? What has he to do with this?"

"We assumed he was assisting in the search for you," Gaylon said.

"Quite right," Phoebe quickly put in. She smiled at Calders. "You did the right thing."

"I don't think so, Miss." He hung his head again. "I should have been watching you closer."

"What were you to do? Follow me about in the ballroom?"

He gave her a sharp look. "If need be."

She laughed despite herself. "A fine sight, indeed. No, I think we can do without the drama. Don't forget, I am unharmed."

94

He surprised her by running an assessing eye over her. "If you'll excuse me for saying so, Miss, you don't look as well as you usually do."

"No, I suppose not. But all in all, none the worse for wear."

"You shouldn't have any wear on you at all," he grumbled.

Phoebe would have commented, but he turned and headed down the hall. "Well," she bestowed a smile upon the remaining staff, "I shall begin with a bath. Will you have one prepared for me in my room, Mrs. Harkin?"

"Molly," the housekeeper shot the girl a stern look, "there's water on the fire. Take it up and begin another pot—but for goodness sake, pick up these linens first."

The girl quickly gathered the linens, then scampered off to do her mistress' bidding.

"Thank you, Mrs. Harkin." Phoebe turned to leave, then stopped. "Gaylon, are any messages for me?"

"A package came for you," he replied. "It's in your bedchambers."

"From whom?"

"There was no return address on the envelope."

Phoebe nodded. "It would seem all has been quiet."

"There was that message from the Duke of Ashlund," Mrs. Harkin commented.

Phoebe jerked her head in the housekeeper's direction. "Message?"

"The letter was for your uncle, Miss," Gaylon said.

"Where is this message?"

"The messenger insisted on delivering it personally. I gave him your uncle's direction in Carlisle."

Phoebe swallowed. "When did this message arrive?"

"Yesterday morning."

"I see," Phoebe mumbled. "Nothing else, then?"

"No, Miss. Hardly seems anything else was needed."

Phoebe's stomach flipped. He was right. Not a blessed thing more was needed.

Phoebe dropped her shoulders and allowed her dress to slide onto the carpet beside the tub in her bedchamber. She stared at this last piece of Highland garb she had worn. Could she shed the memories of that place and time as easily as she had the dress? She thought of David MacEwen and his people and knew she would never forget the innkeeper's derision, or the confusion on the children's faces. Just as she would never forget Kiernan MacGregor; the flash of his smile when he appeared in her coach doorway, the smell of sandalwood, and the steel of his arms around her.

By now, Alistair would have shared with Lord Briarden the information concerning the assassination attempt against the duchess, which she sent when the duke allowed her to send a letter to her uncle.

What might Alistair have already uncovered in his investigation into the marquess' affairs? Phoebe was suddenly very tired, more tired than she could remember being since her mother's death. She picked up the dress and tossed it onto the chair left of the fireplace. A fire crackled in the hearth as she stepped into the tub and sank chin deep into the blessed water. The door opened and Molly entered.

The maid crossed the room to the chair and gathered up the dress. "Do you need anything else, Miss?"

"That will do for now," Phoebe answered.

"You'll want this." Molly placed a package on the table beside the tub.

"The package Gaylon mentioned?"

"Yes, Miss."

"Thank you, Molly," Phoebe said.

A moment later, the door clicked softly shut. Phoebe thought about opening the package, then closed her eyes.

The chime of the grandmother clock brought Phoebe bolt upright in the tub. She blinked the room into focus before realizing she was in her own chambers in Shyerton Hall. She shivered. The water had grown cold. She glanced at the grandmother clock in the corner. Eleven o'clock. An hour had passed. She rose from the tub. Goosebumps raced across her arms when the chilled flesh collided with the warm air of the room.

Phoebe grabbed the towel from the table beside the tub, knocking the package Molly had left there to the floor. She picked it up and her gaze caught on the London postmark before she tossed it onto the bed. She began drying herself. As Gaylon had said, no return address. Phoebe grabbed the robe Molly had laid out and picked up the package as she stuffed an arm into one of the sleeves. She tore open the package and slid the other arm into the remaining sleeve, then pulled out several documents folded around four letter-sized envelopes. When she unfolded the documents she startled upon seeing the date at the top of the first page.

April 26, 1820

April 1820 was two months after her father disappeared and the month he sent the letter to her mother. Phoebe lowered herself onto the mattress as she began reading.

> *In early February of this year word reached me, John Stafford, chief clerk at Bow Street, and head of the Bow Street officers, that Arthur Thistlewood, leader of the radical Spencean Philanthropists Society, planned on February 15 to assassinate the king's ministers…*
>
> *…So I was surprised when Lord Mallory dispatched another spy from the Solicitor General's office, Mason Wallington, Viscount Albery.*

Phoebe halted. John Stafford had known her father was a spy for the Crown? She remembered vividly the one and only meeting with Stafford five years ago. She had shown him her father's letter, insisted she wouldn't leave until he read it. He had acquiesced, but his agitation after he'd read the letter made her think he couldn't even speak the name of a traitor, much less abide the company of his daughter. Stafford, for all his civility, had been austere, advising her to accept things for what they were. But all the while he'd known…

A moment later she finished the letter, ending with;

> *At the age of thirty-six, Mason Wallington became a fugitive. When no trace of him was found, he was thought to have perished.*

Phoebe drew in a shaky breath, set the letter aside and began the next one.

July, 1824
> *Four years have passed since Mason Wallington was branded a traitor. Despite Sidmouth's orders that I forget the matter, my conscience demands I act. Whether guilt or innocence is the result of my findings, I shall, as always, record all matters true and faithfully. I begin with Wallington's superior, Lord Niles Mallory.*

Phoebe reread the name: Niles Mallory. At last, she knew the identity of her father's direct superior.

August 1824
> *Lord Mallory, member of the House of Lords. Resident of London. Married, one child. Wife died in 1819.*
> *Two months, and my investigations yield no derogatory reports about Lord Mallory. Surprising, considering the devils that surround him in the House of Lords.*

January 25th 1825
> *While I have yet to discover the significance of the meeting I observed tonight, I cannot deny the excitement I feel. Tonight, Mallory left his home at about eleven o'clock and visited Lord Harrington, a man whom I had not observed in Mallory's company before now. Mallory stayed but a few minutes, then set out, despite the late hour, straightaway to a residence in a neighborhood in the docks.*
> *Though I have no previous knowledge of the place, I was quite familiar with the man who lived there: Peter Jenkins, a former law enforcement officer who made a name for himself as a thief, liar, and suspected rapist. He was eventually discharged for taking bribes.*

The meeting between him and Mallory lasted three quarters of an hour. From there, Mallory went directly home.

January 30th 1825

A quick investigation proved that Jenkins hadn't changed. When in the employ of the London magistrate, Jenkins consorted with criminals who were involved with everything from blackmail to black market French brandy. Dealing with a man like Jenkins called for drastic measures. I would chance no discovery before my investigations bear fruit therefore; for the first time in my career, I stepped outside the law.

Disguised, I hired two felons from the docks, and accosted Jenkins in a side street not far from his home. My cohorts and I had only just thrown Jenkins against the wall when he began to blubber that he would repay the loan. All he needed was a little more time. I realized he had mistaken me for the owner of one of his gambling debts, and demanded to know when I might expect payment. Jenkins blathered on about how he had landed a big 'fish,' and would that next day receive an advance that would more than cover his current payment.

The man is a coward at heart and it was easy to force from him the name of Mallory as his client. I insisted on knowing what Lord Mallory would want with a river rat like him. I nearly gave myself away when he revealed that Mallory had hired him to discover if any trace of Wallington could be found.

Phoebe's breath caught. Lord Mallory was searching for her father. Her heart pounded as she read on.

On the surface, it seemed a simple enough matter. Despite Jenkins' unscrupulous nature, he was a superb investigator, which made Mallory's choice understandable. Oh, how I wanted to believe Mallory planned to right matters. Yet, that special sense, the sense which every investigator must have to survive, screamed with that his motives were not altruistic.

When I questioned Jenkins as to why Mallory hadn't gone to a legitimate Bow Street runner, Jenkins said Mallory didn't want a particular member of the House of Lords to learn of his inquiries. Jenkins denied knowing who the man was and I realized he must be telling the truth. Why would Lord Mallory reveal this information? However, I recalled that Lord Mallory had once gone from Lord Harrington's home to see Jenkins, and I wondered if Lord Harrington wasn't the man from whom Lord Mallory was hiding his investigation.

Phoebe paused and searched her memory, but found no recollection of a Lord Harrington. She put the question to the back of her mind and read on.

March 1825

    Two months, and Mallory has visited Harrington on several occasions. Not once, however, have I observed Mallory visit Jenkins again. In the meantime, I began investigating Harrington. Thus far, the information is much like that of so many in the House of Lords, mainly, the taking of bribes for judgments in the favor of the party offering the bribe.

September 1825

    When two months passed and all remained quiet with Mallory, I decided to focus on Jenkins. Another month passed and Jenkins didn't appear, so I took a look inside his home. It appeared he hadn't been there for some time; therefore, for the next three months I split my time between Jenkins, Harrington, and Mallory. At the end of the third month, Jenkins returned home. On the night he returned, I arrived to his street with the intention of stationing myself in the alleyway across the street, but I observed another man watching Jenkins' establishment from that spot. I continued around the block to the rear of the alley and watched from there.

    At four a.m., Jenkins returned home and the waiting man closed in on him and stepped inside the doorway just as Jenkins shut the door. I hastened to the window I had previously used to gain entrance into his home. As before, the window was not locked. I —

A knock caused Phoebe to jerk her head up as the door opened and Molly stepped in.

"Miss Wallington," she said, "Lord Redgrave is here to see you. Gaylon informed His Lordship you weren't accepting callers, but he insisted you would see him." Molly gave a derisive snort. "It's almost as if he knew exactly when you returned."

Damn him, Phoebe silently cursed. *That is precisely the case.*

Molly reached for the towel Phoebe had discarded on the bed. "You've scarcely finished your bath, and not even a morsel of food for your stomach, and already folks are demanding to be entertained."

Phoebe folded the papers, then gathered the envelopes lying beside her. She picked up their envelope and slid the papers inside.

"Tell His Lordship I will be down directly," she said.

Molly scrutinized her. "You'll need help dressing. I'll tell Gaylon you'll be down, then come back and help you." She started for the door, but paused beside the bed and lifted a lock of Phoebe's hair. She tsked. "You've let your hair dry all helter-skelter. It'll need combing, then we'll put it up."

Phoebe raised a brow. "You have no compunctions about Lord Redgrave waiting to see me?"

The maid's face remained composed, but the flicker in her eyes gave her away. "You can't entertain a gentleman looking anything but a lady."

Chapter Ten

*H*alf an hour later, Phoebe opened the parlor door. She looked into Lord Alistair Redgrave's brown eyes as he rose from the settee at the window.

She closed the door behind her. "Lord Redgrave."

"Phoebe." He smiled and started toward her.

Phoebe warmed to this man who had been her father's friend, then her friend and mentor after her father disappeared. As a young girl, she had fancied herself in love with Alistair. It wasn't uncommon for women to marry men twenty years their senior, and Phoebe had fantasized about their life together. In some small way, she had—did—love him. The impulse to confess Stafford's letters surfaced. *Steady*, she told herself. Finish reading them before sharing secrets. That was a precept Alistair himself had taught her.

"Alistair."

He clasped her hands in his. "Phoebe." He kissed her cheek, then held her arms out to her side and surveyed her. "You look well."

"Do I?"

"Indeed." He released her. "It's been too long since I've seen you. How have you been?"

Phoebe scowled. "You know very well how I've been. You received my letter?"

"I did, so you need not worry. The duchess is safe. There have been no attempts on her life. Come, tell me everything that happened."

"Must I?"

"You have never before hesitated to give a report," he said.

The report had never been so...personal, she thought, but said, "It has been a long journey, my lord."

A speculative glint appeared in his eyes, but he said nothing more until they sat in the two chairs placed before the fire. "I am curious as to exactly what happened."

"Curious? I had hoped for concern."

A hint of amusement lit his eyes. "I admit to a moment of uncertainty."

Phoebe raised a brow. "How is that, sir? I have never known you to be uncertain of anything."

"It was the two days between your disappearance and my discovery of your whereabouts that befuddled me."

"My God," Phoebe cried. "I was still at the Green Lady Inn at that time. Why didn't you free me then? It would have been an easy piece of work."

He lifted a brow. "What happened, Phoebe? What prompted the marquess to kidnap you?"

"He mistook me for someone else."

"Miss Ballingham?"

"Yes. I borrowed her carriage."

"Indeed, and you also cavorted with her protector."

She gave him a reproving look. "I danced with Lord Stoneleigh, nothing more—and Lord Ashlund didn't see me with the earl. Had that been the case, we would have avoided the whole fiasco."

"So why did Lord Ashlund want to kidnap Miss Ballingham?" Alistair asked.

"Hester and Lord Stoneleigh suffered a falling out." Phoebe waved her hand in a disgusted motion. "Everything with her is a drama. She decided to teach him a lesson, and made an assignation with another gentleman. Hence, she leant me her carriage."

A corner of Alistair's mouth twitched. "I see. But that doesn't answer why Ashlund kidnapped you—or Miss Ballingham, as it were. He didn't have designs of his own on her? No," Alistair amended before Phoebe could reply. "He would have known her and wouldn't have made off with you." A mischievous twinkle lit his eyes. "Unless, that is, he discovered his better fortune."

Phoebe rolled her eyes. "He had the ridiculous idea of playing cupid."

"Well," Alistair said, "this fills things in nicely. You can imagine the drama that played out in my mind. I must scold you," he added. "You should have notified me the moment you arrived in London."

"I have been home for two hours, my lord, and already you are here. You couldn't have arrived any sooner had I sent word. I only hope it wasn't that odious Barrister who you had watching Shyerton Hall. He can't keep a secret."

Redgrave laughed. "No, I would not be so unkind."

"I think it is you who needs a scolding," she said. "Why didn't you demand my release or, at least steal me away in the night?"

"What?" Horror appeared on his face. "And be guilty of the marquess' crime? No, thank you." He shrugged one shoulder. "And, as I said, I was curious."

"Your curiosity may have cost me a great deal."

"Hmm," Alistair intoned. "The duke wasn't pleased with his son's antics?"

"He was not."

"He's insisting the marquess make things right?"

"And being quite pigheaded about it in the bargain," Phoebe added darkly.

"The duke can afford to be as pigheaded as he pleases. He is a powerful man."

"And he knows it," she muttered. "With your help, however, I can better deal with him."

"You have been in the company of one of Britain's most eligible men for two weeks."

Phoebe stiffened. "You don't think—"

"I think nothing in particular," Alistair interrupted. "But it isn't my tongue that will wag all over London."

"Tongues can't speak of something they don't know."

Lord Redgrave gave her a *fool yourself if you like* look.

"Calders will keep quiet," Phoebe insisted.

"And your servants?"

"They know nothing."

"The marquess won't pursue the matter?" Redgrave paused, then added, "Once he makes known his suit, word will be all over London in a day."

Phoebe thought of the letter probably already read and acted upon by her uncle. "He can't force me into marriage," she said with vehemence.

Redgrave angled his head in ascent. "Ultimately, you can refuse him, but your uncle will be pigheaded about the matter as well. Not to mention, you're likely to receive no other reputable offers. Though, fortune hunters will hound you. You will soon be a rich woman."

She snorted. "I care nothing for offers, reputable or not. I am well past marriageable age."

His lip twitched. "On the shelf, are we?"

"I haven't had an offer in years."

He lifted a brow.

"A reputable offer," she said. "Adam does not signify."

"Adam would disagree."

"I have more pressing matters," Phoebe replied.

"More important than a family?" His face softened. "Do you so fear another mistake that you will deny yourself happiness?"

Phoebe blinked. "What—you don't mean—"

"You were but seventeen. Surely you understand what an impressionable age that is?"

"I realize he was a fortune hunter," she replied. "A very patient fortune hunter."

"Patience is a fortune hunter's greatest asset," Redgrave replied. "You understand why your marriage to him had to be annulled?"

She regarded him. "This is the first time you asked me that question. Why now?"

"Perhaps my advanced years have given me a different perspective."

"You're not so old. What, forty-six this year?"

He scowled. "Forty-five, my girl."

She studied him, noticing the flecking of gray that highlighted his brown hair and, for the first time, she wondered why he had never married.

"I am no longer seventeen," she said. "Long past the girlish idea of true love."

Alistair didn't reply, and Phoebe realized he wondered the very thing everyone else did: whether he and her uncle had reached her and her new husband in time to prevent a true wedding night.

Alistair and her uncle had arrived in time to find her in her shift and Brandon, his trousers hanging open as if in hurried disarray. She remembered all too well the rare look of disappointment in her uncle's eyes.

She straightened. "Enough of this. Alistair, I expect your help in dealing with the marquess."

"Don't you mean the duke?"

"Both. I have no intention of marrying. It would interfere with my work. Lord Briarden wouldn't be pleased."

"On the contrary, he may be very pleased. You wouldn't be the only married woman employed by the British government, and it will give you a fine cover. Your reputation, I might add, has been sorely compromised as a result of this escapade."

"How can I possibly consider marriage to a man who might be connected with criminals?"

"You don't know that Lord Ashlund is connected to this Alan Hay. When you consider the facts, it doesn't make sense. You said Hay happened to come into the village. Why would the marquess conspire with a stranger to murder the duchess?"

"I don't know," Phoebe admitted. "But there's more."

Alistair sat patiently as she told him all that happened and ended with, "When I questioned Lord Ashlund about contacting the authorities to report the planned assassination against the duchess, he told me to keep my nose out of it. I saw nothing suspicious in the letter from Clachair, but given Lord Ashlund's attitude about the planned assassination attempt on the duchess, everything is suspect."

"The last you saw of Ashlund he was laid up at the inn?" Alistair asked.

"Yes."

Alistair nodded. "I have apprised Lord Briarden on the situation with the duchess. If anything comes to fruition, we'll have our answers, at least in regards to Lord Ashlund's involvement. As for Clachair, we have heard nothing of him in years. I'm doubtful the Clachair of Ashlund's letter is our man. We have suspected for some time that he may be dead."

"What are his crimes?" Phoebe asked.

"He is charged with trying to overthrow the government."

"Just like my father," she murmured.

"He is of your father's generation, in fact."

Phoebe scowled. "Was there something in the water in those days, my lord?"

He laughed. "It was a tumultuous time. Many changes for the positive were taking place and, as is always the case, there were those men who tried to use the uncertainty of the times to gain power."

"Men like Arthur Thistlewood."

"In fact, Thistlewood had some good ideas," Redgrave replied. "But he intended those ideas as a means to gain followers who he hoped would seat him in power. As we know—" A sharp rap cut him off and the door opened and Gaylon entered.

"Forgive me, madam, but you have more visitors."

Phoebe frowned. "I wasn't expecting anyone. Who is it?"

"Lady Carlton, Lady Mansford, and Miss Smith."

"What do they want? By heavens, I just returned home. Tell them I'm busy."

"As you say, Miss," Gaylon replied. "However, I suggest you see them."

Phoebe paused. "I have never known you to suggest a blessed thing, Gaylon. What has happened?"

"There is talk of a certain announcement in the paper, Miss."

"An announcement?" Feminine voices in the hallway caused Phoebe to glance sharply in that direction. "Gaylon, who is that I hear on the second floor of this house?"

"I believe that would be your visitors, Miss."

She snapped her gaze onto him. "What are they doing up here?"

Gaylon looked as if he were exerting a great deal of patience. He opened his mouth and Phoebe shot him a narrow-eyed look.

105

He cleared his throat and said, "I informed the ladies I would inquire as to whether or not you were entertaining. I left them in the drawing room. They must have followed me upstairs."

"Which room is it, girls, do you remember?" Leticia Mansford's voice was uncomfortably close.

"Get rid of them," Phoebe said in a low voice. "And make it quick."

"Here we are," Leticia said as she appeared in the doorway.

Phoebe caught sight of the golden brown satin of Leticia's dress as Gaylon took a step back against the door. The ridiculously puffy sleeves of her dress were a strange contrast to the tiny corset-constricted waist. The combination made Leticia look like a cartoon.

Alistair rose as Leticia said, "She's hiding, just as I said."

Her gaze slid onto Lord Redgrave and Phoebe caught a flicker of malicious satisfaction in her eyes. So, Lady Mansford believed she'd caught the future Marchioness of Ashlund in the middle of a private moment with a man other than the marquess. Phoebe wondered if a scandal would discourage Kiernan MacGregor.

"Phoebe, darling." Leticia glided past Gaylon and across the room. "It's so good to have you back." Upon reaching her side, Leticia placed a hand on her shoulder, then bent and kissed her cheek. "Look darlings," Leticia glanced over her shoulder at her companions, "isn't she radiant?" She faced Lord Redgrave. "My lord." She extended a gloved hand, which he graciously grasped and brought to his lips.

"Lady Mansford." He looked over her hand at Phoebe, amusement twinkling his eyes. He straightened and looked at the other two women, who stood near the door. When they didn't approach, he strode to them. "Lady Carlton," he said, as he neared them. He grasped her hand and kissed it as he had Leticia's. "Miss Smith." He turned to her and bent over her hand, as well. "It is good of you ladies to visit Miss Wallington on her first day back."

Phoebe's jaw tightened when Lady Mansford ensconced herself in the chair Alistair had vacated. He offered an arm to each of the other two ladies and escorted them to Phoebe's side. He released them and looked about the room.

"Ah," he said, and hurried to Phoebe's desk. He picked up the chair there, and carried it to the ladies. He placed the chair beside Leticia's chair. "Now." He again looked thoughtfully around the room.

"By heavens, Redgrave," Phoebe blurted, "seat them on the settee."

"Miss Wallington," he said, his voice brimming with reproof, "the settee is too far from the hearth. There is a definite chill in the air today, and the ladies have just arrived. I strongly advise the four of you stay as close to the fire as possible. Gaylon," Redgrave's expression brightened, "be so good as to find another chair for," he glanced back at Brenda Smith, who still stood, "Miss Smith."

106

"Of course, sir," Gaylon said, and disappeared into the hallway.

"What do you want?" Phoebe demanded of Leticia.

Leticia gave her companions a knowing look, then produced a newspaper clipping from her purse.

"You naughty girl," Leticia chided, waving the clipping. "Matty, Brenda, and I were quite peeved that you hadn't uttered a peep about the marquess' intentions. Isn't that right ladies?" They murmured agreement and she went on. "You must tell us all about him." Leticia leaned forward in her chair, expectantly.

There was no mistaking the gleam of excitement in her eyes, but Phoebe noted an underlying trace of malevolent jealousy. "There's nothing to tell," she said.

"Nothing to tell?" Leticia pouted. "You mean to keep us in suspense?"

"What I mean—" Phoebe stopped when Gaylon reappeared, carrying a wing backed chair. He set the chair next to hers, and Miss Smith sat down.

Phoebe glowered at Lord Redgrave who hovered over them like a mother hen. "Have you nowhere to seat yourself?" she demanded.

"I will do very well standing. Thank you, my dear."

"My dear, indeed," she muttered, then looked at Leticia. "There is nothing to say, because the announcement was a mistake."

Lady Mansford studied the announcement. "No," she pointed with a gloved finger at the text. "It says right here, His Grace, the Duke of Ashlund, is proud to announce the—"

"I don't care what it says," Phoebe snapped. "The announcement is incorrect."

The room fell quiet. Leticia refolded the clipping, creasing each fold with deliberate precision. She placed it inside her reticule, then looked Phoebe in the eye, and said, "He is no child. He must understand the need for discretion. Also, there are your sensitivities."

Phoebe frowned. "What—"

"A newly married man won't flaunt his dalliances to the world. Never fear," Leticia patted Phoebe's knee, "I'm certain his father will take him to task for forgetting he is about to be a married man."

Phoebe stared. "You think I am denying the engagement because he dallied with some—" Alistair coughed discreetly. She scowled. "This is rubbish."

"His father married that American woman some years ago," Leticia said. "I don't recall even a whisper of infidelity." She smiled. "Yes, I am correct. His father will take him to task. If Lord Ashlund is half as discreet as his father, you will be a lucky woman. I wager this will be settled in time for the two of you to attend the Halsey soiree."

Phoebe shot to her feet. "I assure you, Lord Ashlund has not been unfaithful. It would be impossible."

Leticia made a tsking sound. "I wish you all the happiness in the world, but don't delude yourself as to the nature of the male of our species."

"Nature of the male of our species?" Phoebe looked helplessly at Alistair.

"Perhaps we should leave Lord Ashlund's reputation to him?" he offered.

"Indeed," Phoebe agreed. "Considering he has dragged my repu—"

"Miss Wallington." Redgrave's voice was low, but firm.

Phoebe glanced from him to the two women who had remained mute throughout the meeting. "Ladies," she said, "I had not intended to entertain today. Good day."

With that, she quit the room.

Three days later, Phoebe closed the door to the drawing room and Alistair turned from the window overlooking the gardens.

"Where is Susan?" he asked. "Isn't she to accompany us to Lady Halsey's party?"

Phoebe hurried across the room.

"You look beautiful," he said, when she reached him.

She shook her head. "I have decided not to go."

"But you're dressed."

"Alistair, you are well aware that the only reason I received this invitation is because of my engagement to Ashlund. Lady Halsey has never before invited to me to one of her parties. I don't move in her circles."

"That has changed," he replied.

"I'm in no mood for a party."

"So you have said for the last three days. It's time you resign yourself to the notion."

"Resign myself to the notion of spying on the marquess, you mean," she said in a whisper.

"Your engagement will circumvent the gossip that is sure to ruin you. Cut off the beast at its head, sort to speak."

"That is not the head I would choose to cut off."

"I understand your consternation."

"*Consternation?*" She grimaced. "You have a talent for understating a situation, my lord."

"Better that than melodrama," he replied

"You haven't heard anything on Ashlund's whereabouts?" She would have liked to believe the marquess had changed his mind about marrying her, but that, she suspected, would be too good to be true. "I don't like the

108

fact that we haven't heard anything from him." Or her uncle, for that matter.

"Once I hear from my man, I'll fill you in on the marquess' movements. Alistair's expression gentled. "We have no proof that Ashlund has committed any crime. If he is an honorable man, you could do worse."

"By all accounts I have made the match of the decade," Phoebe said, "perhaps even the century." She was suddenly struck by a thought. "You don't believe he's guilty." Redgrave didn't immediately answer, and she said, "I've known you all my life, Alistair. You would never try to marry me off to a criminal." *Would you?*

"I am slow to come to judgment in such matters." He smiled. "You, of all people, can understand why."

"I do. Only, you weren't there, you didn't see what I saw." Kiernan MacGregor telling her to mind her own business…Kiernan MacGregor blind with rage when he attacked Robbie, and Kiernan MacGregor holding her until her dizzy spell passed…then him tucking her into bed.

"Is marriage so terrible?" Redgrave asked.

Phoebe stirred from the memories. "Marriage isn't in my plans."

He sighed. "Have you considered putting the past behind you, letting your father's memory rest?"

Stafford's letters came to mind. The memory of what she read in the remaining documents brought a chill just as it had the first time she read them. Was what Stafford said true? Had Alistair kept her in the dark all these years about the truth concerning her father?

"No," she replied. "I won't stop until I have my answers."

"As you wish. Cry off from the marquess—when the time is right, not before."

"Yes," she replied caustically. "I understand my duty."

"Do you?"

"I agreed to spy for England, now I can't renege because it's too hard."

"Or too personal."

She gave a deferential cant of her head.

"Whatever transpires with Ashlund, I advise you to forget the past," he said. "Keep the memory of your father with you always—though we both know his memory has interfered with your life. If not for this obsession, you would have married long ago."

"I beg your pardon?"

"You changed after Brandon."

Phoebe felt as if she'd been slapped. There was no denying his words, though she hadn't thought anyone knew. Redgrave must have read her mind, for he said, "Don't look so surprised. I am a master at keeping secrets. I may have taught you all you know, but I haven't taught you all I know."

Indeed? her mind fired back.

Would her father's oldest friend really keep quiet and allow him to keep the name of traitor? What would her father think if he knew she was being forced to marry a man who was in all likelihood a traitor?

Phoebe passed through the French doors of the overcrowded ballroom out onto the balcony. The hour was half past one in the morning. Early by London Society standards. The echo of the orchestra receded as she crossed to the low stone wall overlooking the gardens. Soft moonlight soothed her tired eyes after the bright lights of the room. Her ears roared with the buzz of the crowd occupying a room meant to accommodate two hundred, instead of the nearly three hundred that now milled about the space. The soirée would likely prove to be the crush of the season. Phoebe grimaced at the thought that the success of the party had something to do with the fact the future Marchioness of Ashlund was present.

She leaned against the stone wall. Darkness blurred sculptured bushes that outlined the grounds while bare-limbed trees in the arboretum beyond them reached heavenward. The cold of the stone penetrated her full gauze over-sleeve, and the stifling heat that had driven her outside began to dissipate. She took a cleansing breath, thankful she had foregone the torture of the corset Molly had tried to force onto her.

"Certainly God will avenge us that one," she said into the air.

"Avenge us what one?"

Phoebe turned to face Jane Halsey. "Lady Halsey." She inclined her head. "Forgive me for not speaking to you earlier. As always, you've outdone yourself."

Jane gave a low tinkle of laughter and glided across the terrace to Phoebe's side. "It was not I. This is my mother's home and her affair."

"True," Phoebe agreed, "but all of London knows it is you who makes it the gala of the year."

A flush of pleasure reddened her cheeks. "I do try." She leaned stiffly against the banister.

Lady Halsey, Phoebe noted with amusement, did wear a corset.

Jane gazed out over the garden. "Forgive me for being so blunt," Jane said, "but I was shocked to hear of your engagement."

No more than I, Phoebe mentally complained, but said, "Were you?"

"I understand your reticence. Did your uncle bother to consult you in the matter?"

Phoebe regarded her. "What exactly do you understand, Lady Halsey?" She should have beaten Leticia Mansford when she'd had the chance.

Jane straightened. "You needn't pretend with me. It is true, Lord Ashlund is rich, and he does possess a certain charm."

The memory of Kiernan MacGregor's *charm* ignited a warmth inside her stomach. "A certain charm, you say?"

110

"He is large," Jane gave a shiver that Phoebe sensed was not revulsion. "Imagine," Jane went on, "if he decided to beat you."

Phoebe recalled the night Kiernan had tied her to her bed and wanted to laugh. "I, er, hadn't noticed that inclination in him."

"You'll live in luxury," Jane went on, "but is it worth being forced to bear Scottish children?"

Phoebe's amusement vanished. She regarded Jane. "I was sure you were going to repeat Lady Mansford's ridiculous rumor that Ashlund had been unfaithful."

"That is to be expected."

Phoebe gave her head a slow shake. "In these past weeks, I have met far more fools in England than in Scotland."

Jane gasped.

"I wonder, Lady Halsey, if Lord Ashlund had offered for you—"

"I would never entertain such an offer," she interrupted with a lift of her chin.

"Indeed not," Phoebe agreed, "when you have such illustrious offers as Lord Phillips. How old is he, sixty-two?"

"It does not signify," Jane hissed. "His family ties are impeccable."

"What happened to that fellow, what's his name, ah, yes, Andrew Paxton? Young fellow, about thirty-three or thirty-four, if I recall."

"He wasn't suitable," Jane fired back.

"I should say not," Phoebe replied. "He is just the sort to demand his husbandly rights."

"When your Scottish bastard of a husband beats you, don't turn to me for help," Jane whispered in a voice shaking with anger.

Phoebe blinked in genuine surprise, then grinned. "You err in thinking he is a bastard. The Ashlund line is also impeccable. As for my coming to you for help should my husband entertain the numskull notion to beat me, that isn't possible, as I shall likely end up in Newgate for murder."

Phoebe felt the presence of someone behind her even as Lady Halsey stiffened. When Jane's eyes widened, Phoebe cursed silently, for she knew exactly who stood behind her.

Chapter Eleven

*K*iernan kept a straight face when Phoebe faced him, despite the expression on her face that said *I may yet end up in Newgate for murder.*

"Lord Ashlund," she said, "what kept you?"

Kiernan sauntered to her side. The flick of her attention to his leg, then the gleam in her eyes told him she noticed his slight limp. That was the price he paid for cutting his convalescence short. The ride to London hadn't helped and, if he'd had his way, he would have rested instead of attending this party. But his discomfort was worth the element of surprise. And Phoebe was definitely surprised.

"Will we dance tonight, my lord?" she asked sweetly.

But she'd taken back the edge—fast.

He lifted her hand and caught a whiff of the violet soap she used to bathe as he brushed his lips against her skin. "I insist upon the first dance." She shot him a look that said that first dance would be taxing on more than just his sore leg.

He released her, then addressed Lady Halsey. "Jane."

She curtsied, gripping her skirts with such ferocity it was obvious she meant to keep from offering him a hand. Kiernan grasped her hand and pulled her up. He fixed his gaze on hers and brought her fingers to his mouth.

Her face reddened and she snatched her hand back. "I-I have guests," she stammered.

"But of course." He stepped aside.

She hurried across the balcony toward the ballroom.

"Strange girl," he said as she cast a backwards glance at them before blending into the crowded ballroom. "One would think she didn't like me." He faced Phoebe.

Her narrowed eyes didn't quite hide her amusement. "How long were you eavesdropping?"

"Long enough," he replied. "You look especially lovely tonight. The bodice of that dress is particularly fetching."

She glanced at the tightly fitted beaded bodice of her olive green damask gown. "For a man, you have an unusual interest in women's dresses, my lord."

"I have an interest in how you look in them. I like your hair up."

"Lord Ashlund, if you think you can charm me with sweet words you are quite mistaken—and that devilish smile will not aid you either."

"Indeed?"

A blush crept up her cheeks.

"Lovely," he murmured.

Her mouth parted in surprise. Good.

"I suppose we would return to the party," Kiernan said. "My father is looking forward to seeing you. We'll have to greet Lady Halsey first. We weren't officially invited. I'm sure she'll understand that we couldn't bear to remain parted." He winked.

"Ashlund, I'll murder you with my own hands."

"Missed me that much, did you?" He grinned. "We'll take care of that later. Your uncle is anxious to see you as well."

She paled.

"Phoebe, love, it's not as bad as all that." He smiled gently. "Is it?"

"I can imagine what my uncle thinks," she cast a glance toward the ballroom, "considering the rubbish you must have told him."

"Actually, it was the rubbish my father told him that saved my head."

"My uncle wouldn't waste time with a scoundrel like you."

"That's exactly what your uncle said about you." Kiernan grinned. "Of course, that didn't stop him from wanting to cut my heart out."

"Would have served you right," she retorted.

"That's what my father said. Nonetheless, he convinced your uncle to give me a chance. Though, I did have to agree to certain…terms."

Her eyes widened, then narrowed with suspicion. "What terms?"

"That I take excellent care of you."

"Rubbish," she muttered.

"In fact, he was adamant on the point."

"How is a forced marriage taking excellent care of me?" she demanded.

"I am saving you from yourself, Phoebe. If you"—a woman halted near the open doors and Kiernan cupped Phoebe's elbow and urged her to the far corner of the balcony. "If you care anything for your reputation, you'll marry me," he said. "After what's happened—"

"If you are referring to the fact you held me cap—"

"I'm referring to the fact you will be seen as a loose woman."

113

She gave him a smug smile. "I have been seen as a loose woman for some time."

"Indeed?" He leaned his hip against the balcony wall.

"It may interest you to know I eloped when I was young. As far as the polite world is concerned, my innocence ended then. If it is a virgin you have your heart set on…"

Kiernan gave a soft snort. "Is that all you've got?"

Phoebe frowned. "What?"

"If you expect me to be put off with that nonsense, you've miscalculated."

A dangerous gleam glinted in her eyes. "My uncle filled you in on the details, didn't he? Or perhaps it was your father."

"My father?" He should have known she would try and slip out of the marriage by telling her father about her elopement. "It was your uncle, as a matter of fact."

"Including the details concerning the period between the time Brandon and I left the magistrate and the time he and Lord Redgrave arrived?" she asked.

Redgrave? Her uncle hadn't mentioned the earl. "He told me enough," Kiernan replied. "I can surmise the rest."

"Then you know you're getting no vestal virgin."

"I could hardly think that, considering the way you were throwing yourself at Lord Beasley that first night I saw you."

She gasped. "How dare you?"

"I wish you would make up your mind," he said. "You're insulted by the possibility I might consider you a virgin, yet angry when I point out the fact that you were flirting publicly with a man."

Phoebe opened her mouth, then her gaze shifted past him.

"Lord Ashlund," a female voice said.

Kiernan grasped Phoebe's hand, tucked it into the crook of his arm, and turned to face Lord and Lady Dawney.

He guided Phoebe forward and stopped a few feet from the pair. "Lady Dawney," he said.

Lady Dawney curtsied, then proffered her hand. Kiernan released Phoebe and bent over the older woman's hand, then straightened and looked at Lord Dawney.

"Horace."

"Lord Ashlund," the viscount replied with a stiff bow.

Kiernan stepped back. "You both know my fiancé, Miss Wallington?"

"Indeed." Lady Dawney's gaze fastened onto Phoebe. "The instant we spied you in this private spot, we knew you could be speaking with none other than Miss Wallington." Lady Dawney gave her husband a knowing look. "Remember, Horace, what it was like being so young and in love?"

Lord Dawney cleared his throat. "Indeed."

"Yes, indeed," Lady Dawney added unabashedly. She leaned forward and whispered in a confidential voice. "You needn't concern yourselves that we misunderstand the time you two spent together in Scotland."

Phoebe gave a tiny gasp and Kiernan repressed a groan.

Lady Dawney giggled. "We understand the magic of love on the young heart." She gazed up lovingly at her husband. "Lord Dawney and I were involved in just such a scandal before we married."

"Lydia," Lord Dawney admonished.

"Quite all right," Kiernan said. "May I ask what is the commérage?"

"It is said you whisked Miss Wallington off to your father's castle in Scotland." Lady Dawney's eyes turned dreamy. "Quite romantic."

Kiernan chuckled. "An interesting interpretation." He grasped Phoebe's hand.

Lady Dawney's gaze focused on the action.

"When Miss Wallington came to my father's home in Scotland, she wasn't alone." Kiernan lifted her hand to his lips. Phoebe tensed and her expression darkened, but she didn't resist. "That was my misfortune." Her look turned murderous. He gave her a small wink and placed her hand in the crook of his arm, then looked at Lady Dawney. "You know how these things get started, one grain of truth and a mountain of gossip."

"Indeed," Lady Dawney agreed. "Things do get out of hand."

"The truth," Kiernan said in a sorrowful voice, "is far less romantic." He looked down at Phoebe. "Though, I am fortunate that my father facilitated the marriage arrangements for me." Kiernan gave her a roguish wink. "Had he not done so, I would have been forced to take matters into my own hands."

"You have taken quite enough into your own hands," said his father from the doorway.

Phoebe started and Kiernan gave her hand a squeeze.

"Father, you know Lord and Lady Dawney."

"Horace." The duke nodded.

"Your Grace." Lord Dawney gave another of his stiff bows.

"Lady Dawney," the duke said.

"Your Grace," she said in a titter, and curtsied.

"Kiernan," he said, "you have had Phoebe to yourself long enough. Her uncle is anxious to see her."

"Kiernan looked down at Phoebe. "So I told her."

Phoebe didn't move when Kiernan grasped her elbow and started toward the ballroom.

He looked down at her. "What's wrong?"

"I…" She glanced at the duke. How was she to face him?

"Father," Kiernan said, "Phoebe and I need a moment."

115

Annoyance flickered in the duke's eyes and Phoebe feared he would deny the request, then he turned to Lord and Lady Dawney.

"Shall we?" He held out an arm for Lady Dawney.

"Oh, well," she fluttered, then slipped her plump hand into the crook of his arm. "You're too kind, Your Grace."

"Don't be long," he called as he led the pair back into the ballroom.

They disappeared into the ballroom and Phoebe whirled on Kiernan. "Lord Ashlund—"

"Shhh." With a sideways glance at the ballroom, he grasped her hand and guided her across the balcony and down the stairs to the gardens.

The light from the ballroom receded. She glanced back at the open door. "Lord Ashlund, perhaps we ought to stop here."

He ignored her and continued across the lawn.

"Where are we going?" she demanded.

They passed the bushes and, a moment later, entered the darker shadows of the arboretum.

"By heavens, slow down or I'm liable to—" The toe of her slipper hit a small branch and she stumbled.

Kiernan pulled her upright, then swung her around to face him. "How long are you going to be pigheaded?"

Phoebe felt her eyes widen, and she fell silent for an embarrassingly long moment before saying, "I don't know."

He released her. "Well, that's a start."

Anger lanced through her. "Don't blame me for balking at the idea of marrying a stranger. Or do you think I should count my blessings that the groom is a marquess?"

"Damnation, Phoebe, I never said that."

"Have you considered what this is like for me?" she demanded.

He hesitated. "I thought I had." He stared at her, though she couldn't discern his expression in the shadows. "How is it for you?"

Phoebe stilled, completely unprepared for this response. "Damn you," she muttered.

"What's that you say?"

"You would have to ask me straight out," she said.

"Phoebe," he began with obvious frustration.

"I have no wish to marry anyone," she blurted. "Yet I'm being forced to marry a complete stranger."

"Not a complete stranger," he said softly. "We know one another better than many who marry."

"I want freedom, sir, not marriage." By heavens, if Redgrave could hear her, he would paddle her, then dismiss her from Her Majesty's service.

"You act as if marriage is a prison," Kiernan said.

"Easy for you to talk. You won't have to change your life one iota."

"Your opinion of me is gratifying," he said in a dry tone. "What sort of freedom do you want?"

Another question she was unprepared to answer. Alistair's words came back to her. "If he is an honorable man, you could do worse." If her spying turned up no incriminating evidence against Kiernan, she would still be able to call off the wedding.

"The kind that doesn't put me at the beck and call of a husband," she muttered.

"I don't plan on making a slave of you," he said.

The gentleness in his voice startled her. "Yes—well, I didn't mean to imply you meant to chain me up."

"Oh?" he murmured. "That idea has some appeal."

"I beg your pardon?"

"Never mind. I'm a reasonable man. I promise not to ask too much of you."

"No heir, then?" she asked.

"I had hoped, of course."

"Since I didn't plan on marrying, I didn't plan on children."

"A logical conclusion," he agreed. "Now that you will marry, however…"

"There we have it," Phoebe said. "By the time I'm fat with your third child I will have no other choice but to follow your every command while you continue on as you always have."

"My dear," she heard the smile in his voice, "only a moment ago you were defending my fidelity."

"You weren't guilty of Lady Halsey's accusations."

"But I will commit future crimes."

"You aren't marrying me for love, Ashlund. Don't pretend you will be faithful to a wife for whom you feel no tenderness."

"I feel a great deal of tenderness for you, and to prove it, I will allow you all the freedom you desire."

"You won't question where I go at night?"

A long silence drew out between them before he replied in a neutral tone, "If you are asking, if I will stop you from going where you please, the answer is no, as long as you have no secret assignation."

"If I wish to travel?"

"What man would deny his wife the luxury of travel?"

"What of my finances?" she asked.

"Your inheritance is yours to do with as you please."

"I have no intention of changing how I dress, my friends, the parties I attend. I am often not home until sunrise."

"It will please me to watch the sunrise with you." He grasped her shoulders. "Do we have a bargain?" He pulled her close.

117

"I'll give it thought," she said, though her mind had gone blank at the pressure of his thighs against hers.

"Do my terms please you?"

"I-I can't say."

Kiernan chuckled. "I can please you in many ways."

"I'm sure you will do your best, sir." Her heart, she realized, was pounding.

"Are you?" he asked. "It's only fair you understand exactly what you're getting. Perhaps, then, the sunrise will hold less attraction."

Kiernan's arms slid around her as his mouth brushed hers. His teeth closed gently over her bottom lip. Phoebe froze, startled by the tender nips. He released her lip then ran his tongue along the edge of her mouth. She gripped his shoulders, intending to push him away, but when he prodded her mouth with his tongue, she forgot the impulse in favor of the surprise that parted her lips. He slid his tongue inside and suddenly she was aware of his heat and — heaven help her — the bulge that dug into her abdomen.

A low groan rumbled from his chest and an answering heat pooled between her legs. He angled her head back and deepened the kiss, pressing her closer, though she wouldn't have thought that possible. An unexpected ache throbbed in her nipples and she tightened her hold on his shoulders before realizing the action. His mouth slid from hers, down along her cheek and to her neck. Her flesh seemed to shiver where he touched her and the shiver traveled down her back and stomach to meet at the juncture between her legs.

Kiernan broke off his kiss and buried his face in her hair. "I've wanted to do that since the last time I kissed you."

Her legs felt like jelly.

"I understand what you want," he whispered. He ran his tongue along her ear. By heavens, her legs were going to buckle. "I'll court you as I should have in the beginning," he said.

"I won't marry before a year," she managed.

"A year?" He sucked gently on her earlobe.

"A year." Phoebe cursed the unsteadiness in her voice.

"A year's engagement is proper." He nibbled on her jaw. "In that time, I will pursue you, court you, and, lastly, seduce you." He hugged her tighter, pressed the hard length of himself closer. "Beware," he whispered, "this is but the courting. When the seduction begins, you will be unable to resist."

By heavens, had she just whimpered? "You're certain I will surrender?"

His hand cupped her neck, and he pressed his lips against the hollow of her neck. "Quite willingly," he said against her flesh.

"Why?" she breathed.

Kiernan leaned back. "Because our union will be no bondage, rather, I will please you." He exhaled a slow breath. "Where else will you find a man willing to give you all you want?"

What did she want?

He wrapped a hand around her waist and began a slow walk back toward the ballroom. "It was foolish of you to run off as you did from Brahan Seer," he said. "And then the inn." He made a tsking sound. "You can imagine my concern when I learned you were gone."

"For all the good it did me," she said under her breath. Were her legs ever going to feel strong again?

He laughed. "Don't expect me to believe you would have it any other way. By the way," he added, and reached into his breast pocket, "I believe this is yours."

He took her hand and pressed something into her palm. Phoebe discerned the cool metal of a ring and held it up in the moonlight.

"What—my God, it's not?"

"Yes, it's your mother's ring," he said.

"But how—"

"I can't take credit. It was Donald. He realized the importance of the piece and procured it for me. I am eternally grateful, of course."

"How did you know it was my mother's ring?" Phoebe asked.

"Your uncle recognized it. How else?"

How else, indeed? Phoebe groaned. She had all but forgotten about her uncle.

When Kiernan led Phoebe back into the ballroom, his father turned from the group he was talking with as if aware of their entrance. Over the heads of the couples dancing, their eyes met and Kiernan knew exactly what his father was thinking: *any more stolen moments alone in the garden with your future wife and I'll horsewhip you.*

The twitch of a smile pulled at Kiernan's mouth and his father's expression darkened. Kiernan shifted his gaze to Phoebe and understood his father's irritation. Her left sleeve had slipped too far down her shoulder, exposing the curve of her breast more shockingly than did the low bodice of the olive green gown. That would teach him to half undress a woman—his betrothed—in public.

Kiernan pulled her tight, pressing the lovely breast against his side.

Her head snapped up, eyes dark with indignation. "Sir, I am not some streetwalker to be mauled."

"I quite agree," he said. "Which is why you might want to adjust your sleeve."

She frowned and looked down. "By heavens."

Phoebe grasped the sleeve and jerked it up. His cock jerked in response to the shift of creamy flesh as she pulled the bodice back into place over her full breasts. Damnation, he'd only managed to control his lust so that he didn't draw stares when they entered the ballroom.

He looked up to see his father still staring. Kiernan sighed. "Shall we, my dear?" He guided her through the crowd surrounding the dancers toward his father.

They neared the duke on the far side of the ballroom and her eyes widened when he smiled at her.

Kiernan bent his head and whispered, "You jumped from a moving carriage, but my father terrifies you?"

"Your father is determined that I marry you," she said under her breath.

"Phoebe, *I* am determined that you marry me."

"You, I can ignore."

"You weren't able to ignore me in the garden."

"My lord," she exclaimed, then blushed at a woman who was staring.

"Good evening, Lady Benette." Kiernan canted his head in the woman's direction. Her gaze flew to his and he lifted a brow. She visibly swallowed, then whirled away from him. "Lovely woman," he commented. "I believe her daughter ran off with Lord Phillips when she was eighteen," Kiernan said in a loud whisper. He didn't miss the stiffening of Lady Benette's shoulders as he and Phoebe passed her. They neared his father and Phoebe slowed. "Courage, my dear," he whispered. "He isn't an ogre."

"No," she said under her breath, "that would be you."

Kiernan brought them to a halt before his father, and Phoebe dropped into a low bow. "Your Grace."

He grasped her hand and pulled her upright. "None of that. As I said before, you can call me Father. You're well?" he asked.

"Yes, Your-er, sir."

He gave her hand a gentle squeeze. "Lass, we welcome you into our family."

Surprise flickered in her eyes. "I see where your son gets his straightforward manner."

Kiernan's father shot him a look that said he'd better not be too straight forward, then said to Phoebe, "Honesty is the best, wouldn't you agree?"

"I do," she said.

He released her hand. "Your uncle is here, he and your aunt accompanied us. I understand you haven't seen him since your arrival in London."

"He came with you?" Her eyes narrowed. "So my new father and uncle are ganging up on me."

"I wouldn't say ganging up."

"No?"

"No. We had business to settle."

"Is that what you call me: business?"

"Phoebe," Kiernan began, but her gaze shifted past his father. Kiernan followed her line of sight and saw Regan talking with Lord Mallory. Lord Harrington joined their group.

"When did Lord Stoneleigh return to London?" Phoebe asked.

"I believe he arrived two days ago. If you recall, I was forced to convalesce," Kiernan said.

"You saved my son's life," his father said.

Phoebe smiled sweetly. "One good turn deserves another, wouldn't you agree?"

"Aye," he replied. "But allowing you to become a pariah isn't a good turn."

"Your Grace—" She stopped when Regan, Mallory, and Harrington arrived at Kiernan's father's side.

"I believe congratulations are in order," Regan addressed Kiernan, then faced Phoebe. "Miss Wallington." He gave a slight bow. "May I present Lord Mallory and Lord Harrington.

Lord Mallory bowed. "Miss Wallington."

"Madam." Lord Harrington inclined his head.

"My lords." She offered a graceful bow that was the epitome of gentility, but had her gaze lingered for a bare instant too long on Lord Mallory?

Lord Redgrave appeared at Phoebe's side and Kiernan was sure he heard her groan.

"Your Grace," she addressed his father, then looked at Kiernan, "Lord Ashlund, may I present Lord Alistair Redgrave. He is a long time family friend and my escort tonight."

"Your Grace," Alistair said to the duke, then looked at Kiernan, "Lord Ashlund, my congratulations on your upcoming marriage."

Kiernan nodded. "Thank you."

"So, when is the wedding?" Regan said.

Phoebe shot him a look filled with daggers, but his grin didn't falter.

"We're in the planning stage," Kiernan said.

"A year from now," Phoebe put in.

The duke cut his gaze onto her.

"As I said," Kiernan quickly added, "a proper wedding takes some time to plan."

"A year," Phoebe emphasized.

Her gaze moved past him and her eyes widened. Kiernan glanced over his shoulder to see her uncle headed toward them.

Kiernan grasped her hand and slipped it into the crook of his arm as he turned to face her uncle, and whispered, "Forgot all about him, didn't you?"

121

Her head snapped up and he read in her eyes that she would avenge herself on him for having brought his father and her uncle to corner her at the party. He was sure she would have said something had her uncle not reached them and pulled her into a hug.

Chapter Twelve

*P*hoebe wished she could forget about her uncle. It was immediately clear a night's rest hadn't softened him. They sat in his library, him behind his desk, her in the chair opposite him. She glanced at the portrait of her mother and father hanging on the wall behind him. Lord Albery had never replaced the picture with one of him and his wife. Tenderness rippled through her and she looked back at him.

"Uncle," she said, "Lord Ashlund has explained the circumstances. Surely you understand my position?"

"The marquess was wrong to have taken you against your will," he replied. "But he wouldn't have mistaken you for Miss Ballingham had you not been in her company."

"I wasn't in her company—"

"You're friends with her, aren't you?"

Phoebe sighed. "Yes."

"You were in her coach and," he paused to give her a reproving look, "you were cavorting with her lover."

"It's not as bad as all that, I assure you, Uncle."

"Phoebe, I have tried my best to guide you." Guilt replaced her earlier tenderness when his expression turned anxious. "But this sort of behavior... It is past time you married. Your aunt and I had never hoped to make such a fine connection for you. You will marry Ashlund."

"I have told him I will marry him," Phoebe replied, "but not before a year."

"A year, is it?"

"A year is an acceptable engagement."

"Given the circumstances, don't you think that is a bit overdone? Not to mention, women of your age don't usually wait any longer than necessary."

"Afraid the marquess will change his mind?"

"Not in the least. The special license he obtained proves his intentions."

"Special license?" Phoebe blurted. "He said nothing of this last night."

"My guess is, he knew better."

"I won't marry before a year," she said.

"If you think to wait until after your twenty-fifth birthday, collect your inheritance, then thumb your nose at the lot of us, you can think again."

"The money isn't the issue."

"Indeed, it is," he replied. "The arrangements have been made." He paused, then added, "You are aware that I am in charge of your finances?"

"Of course." She angled her head. "And a fine job you have done. I have no complaints."

"Enough of the flattery. I have more control over matters than you might like."

She stilled.

"There's a codicil to your mother's will that gives me control of your inheritance."

"What sort of control?"

"Your mother was concerned that fortune hunters…"

Phoebe kept her gaze steady. "Fortune hunters such as Brandon?"

"Yes."

"You have the authority to withhold my inheritance?"

He nodded again.

"So, it would have done Brandon no good to marry me. Did he know this?"

Her uncle didn't answer immediately, but finally said, "He did."

"Most interesting. Yet he married me anyway. How do you account for that?"

Silence drew out between them so long, Phoebe wondered if he would answer, but he did. "He told me that if I didn't pay him, he would ruin you."

Phoebe drew a sharp breath.

"Forgive me, Phoebe. I didn't tell you then, because I felt you had suffered enough at his hand."

"So," she said, "when you wouldn't pay, he made good on his threat."

"Not exactly."

Phoebe frowned.

"I did, indeed, pay."

"Oh, Uncle," she cried, "you didn't."

"Of course I did." Lord Albery's eyes softened. "I knew you were very much under his spell, and he had no compunctions about carrying out his threat."

Phoebe reached across the desk and took his hand in hers.

A small smile touched his mouth. "It was well worth the money, my dear."

"Why, then, did he marry me?" she asked.

Albery's hand tightened on hers. "He thought to play both ends. He believed that when he told you I had paid him off, you would hate me, and I would do anything to regain your good graces to the extent of sanctioning your marriage."

"Might I ask how much you paid?"

A bushy brow shot up. "You may not."

"That much?" She released his hand and sat back in her chair. "And I wager you paid with your money, not mine." Red tinged his cheeks and she knew she'd hit the mark. "I have caused you a great deal of grief, haven't I?" How much more would she cause if he knew she was a spy for the Crown?

"Enough of that," he said. "You're my brother's daughter. I could not..." His words trailed off.

Phoebe smiled. "I know."

"You understand, my dear, why it is I must withhold your inheritance?"

"You mean, the fact that you won't allow me to wait a year just so I can, as you say, *thumb my nose at the lot of you?*"

"Yes."

"I suppose I do. But I tell you, Uncle, I won't be rushed into marriage."

Lord Albery leaned forward onto his desk. "He does seem a decent sort, Phoebe. His father was in full accord that the boy make things right. You know how rare that is for a man in his position."

"Yes," she admitted. "I do. But that doesn't change the fact that I will be marrying a man I hardly know, and one who, despite his honor, doesn't care for me."

"Such alliances aren't based on love."

"True, but I hadn't thought I would be forced into the typical marital mayhem."

Memory surfaced of Kiernan's hard body pressed against hers and she couldn't help wonder what the *typical marital mayhem* would be like with him. His words from the night before came to mind, "*I will pursue you, court you, and, lastly, seduce you.*" Desire sent a tingle through her. Yes, the seduction would be everything he promised. The marriage, however, was another matter.

Phoebe released a breath and was surprised to realize her heart had picked up speed. "I promise to give the matter full consideration," she said in an even tone.

Lord Albery sighed. "The marquess has agreed that your inheritance will remain yours. However, if you don't marry him, I will see to it your inheritance does not fall to you until the age of thirty."

She was dumbstruck. "You can't be serious."

"Five more years, Phoebe."

"Why? My inheritance will see me safely through life. Surely you see that?"

"Phoebe," he implored, "the money will see you have a house, but not a home. Not children, not a man to care for you."

"He will care for me only as far as obligation demands. Once obligation is fulfilled, he will amuse himself elsewhere."

A speculative light came into Lord Albery's eyes. "Why argue, then? That will leave you free to do as you wish."

Oddly, the idea brought a stab of sadness, and she realized what she'd never let herself admit: her parents had been a love match and, in some distant future, she'd hoped for the same. To be tied to a man who had married her out of obligation was the worst prison she could imagine. No, she realized with a jolt. There was one worse fate: To be tied to a man she cared for who didn't care for her in return.

The clock struck one and Phoebe rose from her bed. She lit the taper on the nightstand, then went to her bedchamber door. As expected, the hallway was deserted, and she closed the door, then carefully turned the lock with a soft click. By now her uncle would have retired, and her aunt had left hours ago, intent upon attending several soirées.

Phoebe retrieved a small locked chest in a corner behind other boxes in her armoire and carried it to her bed. She pulled the key from the nightstand drawer and unlocked the box. Her hands shook as she lifted Stafford's letters from the chest. She laid the envelope containing the journal on her mattress beside her, feeling as if they weighed more than her strength could hold. She settled back against the pillows and unfolded the documents she wanted to reread.

> It came as no surprise to hear the terror in Jenkins' voice when the brute demanded to know why Mallory was dealing with the likes of him. Jenkins related the same tale he had to me of how Mallory wanted Jenkins to discover if Wallington still lived. The brute demanded to know why Mallory wanted information on Wallington. Jenkins denied knowing his client's motives. I heard a sound that was clearly a fist against a man's jaw, and Jenkins cried out. The man threatened worse if Jenkins didn't

come up with something more. Jenkins sniveled that it was all because of that 'Lord Redgrave.'

The brute asked the very question I burned to know: who was Redgrave and what had he to do with the affair? Jenkins explained that Redgrave had been a close friend to Wallington, and since Wallington's disappearance, Redgrave had made half a dozen trips to France.

"Nothing strange about that," the brute said.

"There is when you go through Scotland," Jenkins replied. "Mallory says Redgrave is trying to throw us off the track because he's in contact with Wallington."

"Where in Scotland does he go? the brute demanded.

"Tain.

"Tain?" the man repeated. "Then he's got to be going out of Dornoth Firth. Where does he go in France?"

"Paris."

The brute made a few more threats, but Jenkins, no matter the menace, had nothing to add. The brute at last left and I followed. We soon left the seedier part of town and even as we entered the more affluent section of London, I knew where he was going. I instructed the hackney driver to slow as the brute's hackney turned onto the alley I'd expected him to take and, as we made the same turn, I saw the brute entering through the rear entrance of Lord Harrington's mansion.

December 1826

My investigations turned up nothing to indicate Redgrave was involved in any illicit activities. In the six months I observed him, he made one trip to France. It wasn't until the fifth month, however, that I discovered that, like Wallington, Redgrave was employed as a British spy.

I began these investigations a year and a half ago, and only now does it occur to me that I should find out more about the one man who played the key role in Wallington's condemnation: the young constable, Barry Doddard.

March 1827

I quickly learned that Doddard was a notorious rake, gambler, extortionist, and was quite willing to take bribes — just the sort of fellow from whom we are sworn to protect the citizens of London. There is only one way to deal with a man like Doddard. I waited outside the Golden Mount, a favored hell of his, and followed him until he was alone. He took me for a brigand set on killing him for his money, but I showed him my pistol before he could produce his, and said I only had questions for him. He lit a cigar, leaned against the wall of the building we stood near, and gave me leave to ask any questions I liked.

The instant I mentioned Mallory and Wallington's names, however, he straightened and demanded that I stand aside. (I purposely kept Lord Harrington's name to myself. I have yet to understand Harrington's part in the Wallington affair, but it's obvious he is a big fish.) I threatened to expose Doddard's illegal actions to his superiors if he didn't answer my questions, to which he laughed and asked how I thought he had been able to maintain a position with the magistrate to begin with. My threat to pass on the information to the Bow Street Sheriff, John Stafford, had quite another affect, however.

He demanded to know how he could be certain I would keep quiet if he complied. "No guarantees," I told him, "other than, if you do not answer my questions, I will have a runner on you before you reach home."

By now, I deduced that Mallory must have paid him to denounce Wallington, and confronted Doddard with this accusation. "What did you expect?" he snarled. "Every war has its casualties."

I was stunned by this response and recalled my collaboration with Lord Sidmouth to entrap Thistlewood and his men. To my knowledge, only the Home Office and Cabinet knew of our operation — we were careful to keep all news of our plans from the public. Still, even if Sidmouth had informed Doddard of our plans, his manner implied knowledge of something beyond the fact we had purposely deceived known criminals...and my stomach turned with the sickening comprehension of what that something was.

"I see you didn't like Thistlewood's revolution any better than Lord Sidmouth did," I said.

The shock on Doddard's face told me I'd hit the mark — and the suspicions I'd long ago quelled were correct: Lord Sidmouth had made sure Thistlewood's revolution never took place.

I grabbed Doddard by the scruff. "What has Sidmouth to do with Wallington?"

Understanding lit Doddard's eyes. I had overplayed my hand. But he surprised me by saying, "Sidmouth isn't the only man with secrets."

Doddard yanked free of my grasp and sauntered away as if he hadn't a care in the world. And he didn't. The men who paid him to lie had maintained their power by enlisting the aid of men like me to stop the Thistlewoods of the world.

I stared as Doddard disappeared into the shadows. He hadn't told me why he had been paid to denounce Wallington, but he had told me that whoever paid him had a secret. I wager that Wallington was — is — a threat to that secret.

September 12, 1827

I have, again, taken to watching Mallory and Harrington.

Phoebe paused at recollection of the night before when Lord Stoneleigh had introduced her to Lords Mallory and Harrington at the Halsey soirée. This was one of the answers she'd been searching for all these years, yet it was strange finally putting names and faces to the men responsible for her father being falsely accused. Her chest tightened and she took a deep breath to ease the constriction. This was only the beginning. Knowing who was behind the lie was only the first step. No telling how long it might take to uncover their motives. Then came the task of proving their guilt—and her father's innocence. She returned her attention to the letter.

> The many hours of solitude give me too much time to think. I have replayed the events of the Cato Street Conspiracy. Of the half dozen spies I had inside the Spenceans, there was one man recruited by Lord Sidmouth, George Edwards. It was Edwards' reports that we most relied upon. He is the one who showed Thistlewood the notice we'd placed in the New Times announcing the Cabinet's fictional meeting at Lord Harrowby's, and Edwards even supplied the Spenceans with weapons. Wallington once made a comment about Edwards that I dismissed, then forgot. "The real instigator in the Cato Street plot is George Edwards." Recollection of Wallington's words sheds new light on the fact that Edwards was never caught and, though a warrant was issued for his arrest, no real efforts were made to capture him.
>
> I did my duty in capturing the would-be murderers. Now, however, I must discover exactly what fruits my handiwork wrought. Should I be surprised to have discovered that during Thistlewood's and his cohorts' trials the defense put forth the notion of Edwards as the instigator behind the assassination plot? They even argued that the conspiracy was 'nothing more than the artful invention of hired spies and secret agents.' Yet the prosecutor retaliated with evidence of a man who claimed that Thistlewood had approached him with the plot to assassinate the ministers days before we made it known they would meet at Harrowby's. Such evidence simply could not have existed...just as the defense couldn't have known the depths of Edwards' part in the conspiracy— unless someone told them.

Pride welled up in Phoebe as she ran her fingers over the last lines of this letter as she read them:

What had Doddard said? "Every war has its casualties." Wallington's single comment showed me he was in the forefront of that war. How could his enemies possibly ignore the threat?

January, 5 1828

Tonight I met with Lord Alistair Redgrave.

At promptly eight o'clock, Redgrave arrived at the private dining room I engaged for the evening. I wasted no time in revealing my identity and that I was investigating the charges against Wallington.

"So, you have discovered that Mallory hired Doddard," he said once I'd told him enough of my investigation." It isn't strange that Lord Mallory would enlist aid to ensure that Thistlewood and his men were arrested. You of all people know that Thistlewood escaped justice once before." He referred to Spa Field, of course, four years before the Cato Street Conspiracy, and Thistlewood's acquittal of high treason charges. "How can you be surprised that Mallory wishes to locate Wallington?" Redgrave went on. "Mallory suspects I am in contact with Wallington. It is, of course, untrue, but understandable that he would make the connection. I am among one of the few men Wallington might contact were he alive."

"You think he is dead?" I asked.

"Of course he's dead. Lord Mallory is correct, were Mason still alive, he would have contacted me."

"Indeed," I replied, "given the two of you are in the same business, you would be the most logical choice." This, I saw, surprised him.

"You are well suited to your profession," he remarked. "And I applaud your loyalty to a man you believe has been innocently condemned."

This was simply too much. "You're saying he is guilty?" I demanded.

"Tell me," Redgrave said, "if he is innocent, how might it be proved? Even the information you have indicates the only man who can exonerate him is Lord Mallory. Why hasn't he done so?"

Here I put myself in an even more precarious position and told him that I believed it had something to do with Lord Harrington, and told him of the brute's involvement. I was befuddled as to what Harrington's part could be, he hadn't been part of the Cabinet during the assassination attempts, but there was no doubt he was involved.

"What do you want from me?" was Redgrave's reply.

I stared, suddenly more unsure of my position than at any other time in this investigation. I had enjoyed a prosperous career. If he ended it for me now, I could retire in the country and live a simple life. Perhaps take on a position as a local constable.

"To give this man back his life," I said.

Redgrave released a sigh. "The criminals you deal with are nothing like Harrington. He has power and connections that are unimpeachable. Has it occurred to you that to stir the pot is to take away what little life Wallington has left?"

I could barely conceal my excitement. So Harrington was involved. "Are we to simply let his accusers get away with this crime?" I demanded.

"How do you propose to stop them?" Redgrave asked.

"Mallory had Doddard falsely accuse Wallington," I said. "Once we interrogate him — "

Redgrave's laugh cut me off. "Doddard wouldn't live long enough for you to interrogate," he said.

"Why did Lord Mallory have Doddard falsely accuse Wallington?" I shot back. "What is he hiding?"

Redgrave smiled. "Come now, surely you of all people know?"

"I know because I was there?" I retorted, but immediately relented. Lord Redgrave was not responsible for my mistakes. "Lord Mallory wasn't one of the men Thistlewood planned to murder," I said. "He was in no danger."

"Do you believe anyone in the government would have survived Thistlewood's revolution?"

That included Mallory, Harrington... and me. I didn't reply.

"We all make mistakes, Stafford. You're an honorable man, but I pray you understand this isn't your affair. Leave it be." He gave me a last look, then left.

This has brought my investigation to an end I wouldn't have thought possible. Perhaps Redgrave is right. I am accustomed to dealing with baser criminals, the dregs of society, those we have no trouble identifying as men deserving of our contempt, or those, like Thistlewood, who dare defy their overlords. Men like Harrington are beyond my reach. I can save us from men such as Thistlewood, but who might save us from the Harringtons of the world...or from men like me?

Phoebe let the hand that clutched the letter fall to her lap. She knew what she had to do.

Chapter Thirteen

*A*t just past noon the following afternoon, Phoebe looked up from her desk at the sound of a knock on her study door. The door opened.

"Excuse me, Miss," Gaylon said, his voice graver than usual. "You have a visitor."

Her heart skipped a beat. She had wondered how she would elude Kiernan MacGregor when she sneaked away to Scotland to follow Redgrave's trail, forgetting that she must avoid him between now and then, as well.

"Need I ask who it is, Gaylon?"

"I don't know if you do, Miss," he replied as if answering a perplexing question.

"Have I the honor of a visit from the man who insists I marry him?"

"Indeed, Miss, he does insist you marry him."

She eyed Gaylon. "I would rather avoid seeing him." The butler remained mute. "Might he barge into my study should you tell him I'm not at home?"

"He does seem determined, Miss."

"Is my uncle home?"

"I regret to say, he is not."

She sighed. "Please inform my—him—I shall be down directly."

Gaylon took his leave and, ten minutes later, Phoebe entered the drawing room only to stop dead in her tracks at sight of the man awaiting her.

Adam faced her. The two stared at one another for a moment before he spoke. "Allow me to offer my felicitations." Before Phoebe could say a word, he went on. "Kind of you to allow me to read about your engagement in the papers, Phoebe. While I was away, no less."

"Adam," she began.

"No, madam, you needn't explain. I understand fully."

"Do you?" With a sigh, she walked to the sofa near the window and sat down. "If that is so, why the agitation?"

He stiffened. "I understand you mean to put me in my place."

"You presume too much, Adam."

"Perhaps," he replied. "But is it too much to ask why you would turn down my proposal of marriage, only to return from Scotland no more than a month later betrothed to another?"

"Yes," she said, "it is too much to ask."

Adam blinked as if he'd been struck.

"Mr. Branbury, you knew perfectly well I wouldn't marry you. What has your proposal to do with the events that took place afterwards?"

"I don't intend to let this pass, Phoebe."

"What do you propose to do, have me abducted against my will?"

He gave her a look of such surprised horror that Phoebe knew she'd been right. He wasn't associated with the men who tried to abduct her the night Kiernan had done the same. Who was the other would-be kidnapper?

Adam came to stand before her. "I know who this Ashlund is. Rich as the devil himself. So that's it, is it?"

"I don't find this side of you very becoming, sir."

"There is no other explanation."

"Aside from being tiresome, Mr. Branbury, you border on insulting. The affair is none of your concern."

"I wouldn't have thought it of you," he said.

She regarded him. "What are you saying?"

"You know perfectly well what I am saying. All the while playing the innocent with me, you were—"

"Adam," Phoebe cut in, "I understand you feel slighted, though, God knows, you have no call, but I won't sit in my own house and be insulted."

A sharp rap sounded on the door. Gaylon opened the door and stepped inside. "Pardon the intrusion, Miss, but you have another visitor."

"Good Lord, who—" Phoebe halted, realizing that the newest arrival was in all likelihood Adam's rival. She stood. "Perhaps you should have the visitor shown into the parlor, Gaylon." Even as she spoke, Gaylon stepped aside and a finely dressed woman entered the room.

"Elise MacGregor," Gaylon announced, "the Duchess of Ashlund."

Phoebe gaped at the woman who looked nothing like the duchess she had expected. She knew the duke to be at least fifty, but the dark haired woman standing before her could be no more than thirty-six, maybe thirty-seven, and she radiated a youth that belied even that age. A faint twitch at the duchess' mouth told Phoebe her thoughts reflected on her face.

"Your Grace." Phoebe dipped into a deep curtsey, then rose. "Please, Your Grace," she looked toward Adam, "may I introduce Mr. Branbury."

Adam strode to the duchess and bent over her hand in a formal bow. "Your Grace." He released her and stepped back.

"Have I come at a bad time?" the duchess asked.

"No, Your Grace," Phoebe said, "not at all."

"I will ask two favors," the duchess said.

"Anything you wish."

"First, don't address me as 'Your Grace.' I tolerate that only at court and certain parties. You may call me Elise."

"But you—madam," Phoebe said, genuinely shocked, "I couldn't."

"You can. As for the second favor, may we sit down?"

"By heavens, yes." Phoebe motioned to the sofa. "Gaylon, please have tea sent in. Mr. Branbury," Phoebe gave him a curt nod, "I believe our visit is finished."

"I have come at an inconvenient time," Elise said.

"I assure you, Your-er, Elise, you have not." She turned to Adam. "Mr. Branbury, Gaylon will see you out."

Adam gave her a hesitant glance and Phoebe feared he might force a scene, but he nodded and followed Gaylon out of the room. Phoebe seated herself next to her guest.

"Please forgive me for coming unannounced," the duchess said. "To be honest, I didn't want to give you the opportunity to avoid me."

"I assure you, I would have done nothing of the kind."

Elise laughed. "Maybe not, but I wouldn't have blamed you, if you did." She added, "I am a surprise to you?"

"I hadn't expected you, ma'am."

The duchess laughed. "Of course you didn't." She leaned forward, a twinkle in her eye, and said in confidential tones, "I don't think my husband did either." She raised her eyes heavenward in a fashion that said she found the whole thing humorous. "And Kiernan was most surprised of all." Elise gave her an impish look. "Serves him right, wouldn't you agree?"

"I couldn't say, ma'am,"

"Phoebe," Elise paused. "May I call you Phoebe?"

"Of course."

"Phoebe, my husband has explained how you and Kiernan became acquainted. Kiernan deserves to be thrashed." She snorted. "Don't think his father didn't consider it. The only consolation was the rogue didn't try to weasel out of his responsibility."

A knock sounded on the door. Both women looked up as the door opened and a maid entered with a tea tray. She set the tray on the table in front of the sofa.

"That'll be fine," Phoebe said. "I'll pour."

The girl bobbed a curtsey, then backed out of the room.

Phoebe lifted the teapot and poured. "Sugar?" she asked.

134

"Lemon," Elise replied, "no sugar."

Phoebe complied, then handed the cup to her.

"Now," the duchess said, "what were we talking about? Oh, yes, Kiernan not weaseling out of his responsibility."

"Indeed," Phoebe replied, pouring cream into her cup of tea.

The duchess sipped the tea, then replaced her cup on the saucer. "And we have arrived at the heart of the reason for my visit." She smiled. "Aside from wanting to meet you, of course. I understand you aren't keen on marrying Kiernan."

"Madam—"

"Please, Phoebe, don't call me ma'am, or madam. I despise the formality. You're going to be part of the family, and it's bad luck for us to start off as if we intend to be anything but friends." Her eyes twinkled. "Perhaps even allies? Therefore, call me Elise. Yes," she went on, "when we're in public you must adhere to formalities, but here, in the privacy of your home, we don't need to act like strangers. Now, I'll be honest, I don't care for British formality. A woman can't go here, a woman can't do this. I can't tell you how often my husband and I have disagreed over that foolishness. However, what happened with you and Kiernan goes beyond these petty constraints."

Phoebe sighed. "Yes, though I'm loath to admit it, you're right."

"Good." The duchess took another sip of tea before saying, "You have decided to marry him, then?"

There was something in her manner that made it impossible to be anything but straightforward. "I'm beginning to wonder if I have any choice," Phoebe said.

"Phoebe!" The duchess laughed in a hearty manner that would have made British nobility scowl. "You're an honest woman. I like that. Still, it's not quite as bad as walking the plank. All men can be a trial, but Kiernan is a good man. To be frank, I had wondered what sort of woman would catch his eye."

"I did not exactly *catch his eye*, ma-Elise."

"Not in the usual sense, true, but he is enthusiastic about the marriage." She halted, her expression turning speculative. "You don't really know anything about him, do you?"

Phoebe lifted her teacup to her lips. "No, I don't." She took a sip of the tea.

"Well, the fun in your marriage will be getting to know him, but I'll tell you one thing, he doesn't form attachments easily. Oh, there is the occasional infatuation," Elise smiled broadly, "but nothing he doesn't get over within a month or two."

"I see." Phoebe leveled her teacup on her lap. "So you and the duke had begun to despair of him marrying?"

135

Elise laughed again. "I'm sorry to disappoint you, but his father hasn't thought much about it."

"But how is that? He is no young man."

The duchess' expression softened. "His father and I didn't marry until he was forty. I was nearly thirty myself."

"How long have you been married?"

"Nearly thirteen years."

"Forgive me for saying so, ma-er, Elise, but I can't believe that."

"So I've been told before," she replied. "Though, I don't mind hearing it again." She set her tea on the table. "You realize, Kiernan isn't my son?"

"I knew the duke remarried."

"Marcus married young, and Kiernan was born when he was twenty-one. Marrying you at thirty, Kiernan is ahead of Marcus' forty years. Don't you think? Still, this isn't what you had planned, is it?"

"In truth, no."

"Pardon me for asking, but do you plan on marrying here, or in Scotland?"

Phoebe started. "I-I hadn't thought of it."

"We have a wonderful home in Scotland. It is large—immense, actually—just the sort of place for a wedding. Before deciding, perhaps you would like to see it?"

"See it?"

"Yes."

Scotland. Could it possibly be this easy? Why not? It was only fair that Kiernan MacGregor help her out of the mess he'd gotten her into.

"That is most kind of you, Elise."

"Not at all," she replied. "It's the least I can do. And if you decide you want to have the wedding there, you can leave the arrangements to me."

The door opened and Lady Albery entered the room. Her gaze fell on the pair sitting on the sofa and she stopped.

"Phoebe," she said, "you didn't tell me we had a guest." Lady Albery crossed to the sofa and curtsied. "Your Grace," she murmured, and rose. "Please forgive my niece for not informing me of your arrival."

The duchess regarded her with an unconcerned air. "Don't trouble yourself, madam. I came to see your niece."

"But of course." Lady Albery sat in the chair nearest Phoebe. "You must have been most anxious to meet your future daughter-in-law."

"Tea, Aunt?" Phoebe inquired.

"Yes," she replied, "if you please," then turned back to the duchess. "I hope you find London to your liking."

"London is always to my liking," she replied.

"Aunt." Phoebe handed her the tea.

"Thank you, my dear."

"Your niece and I were just discussing her visit to our estate in Scotland," the duchess said. Phoebe caught the surprise on her aunt's face. "We may go at your convenience, Phoebe," Elise added.

"What is this?" Lady Albery asked. "You've only just returned to us, Phoebe, and already you're leaving?"

Phoebe paused in lifting the cup to her lips. What had her aunt cared one wit for her being at home?

"What about the wedding?" Lady Albery cried. "Surely, you can't consider a journey before your marriage. What will your husband think?"

Phoebe took the sip of tea, then set the cup on the table. "I have no husband yet, ma'am. Therefore, that isn't a consideration."

"I am sure you would do well to consult Lord Ashlund before making any plans," she insisted.

"I have informed Lord Ashlund that if I marry him, I will not be consulting him on anything. Why should I do so now?"

"*Phoebe*." Lady Albery set her cup onto her saucer with such force, the china rang. "I am sure your uncle wouldn't approve of such a philosophy."

"Forgive me, Aunt, but I suspect my uncle will be pleased if I simply make it to the altar." Phoebe turned to Elise. "Forgive us, madam. As you may have guessed, there is some doubt as to the outcome of this affair."

"Phoebe," her aunt scolded. "Really."

Phoebe ignored her and said to the duchess, "I warned the duke that I might not be the sort of wife he wants for his son, but he wouldn't listen. Having met me, you may feel the need to warn him. I would fully understand."

The twinkle returned to the duchess' eyes. "Far be it from me to contradict my husband."

Phoebe nodded politely. "You're the epitome of womanly virtue, ma'am."

A look of comical horror crossed Elise's face. "You probably shouldn't repeat that to my husband *or* Kiernan. Well, I believe I have overstayed my first visit."

Lady Albery came to her feet. "No, indeed, Your Grace. You're welcome to stay as long as you like."

Elise looked at Phoebe. "Decide when you would like to visit Ashlund. Though I've only just arrived, I will be glad to return." She smiled. "My decision to come to London was a bit hurried, therefore, my children didn't accompany me."

"I imagine you miss them."

"Very much." She rose and Phoebe followed suit as the duchess addressed Lady Albery. "Madam."

"Your Grace." Lady Albery curtsied.

Phoebe escorted the duchess to the door.

"If I might suggest, ma'am," Phoebe said as she opened the door "Don't wait for me to return to Scotland."

Elise stopped. "I assumed we would travel together."

"Don't stay in London on my account. Return home and your children," Phoebe said. "My uncle will see to my travel arrangements."

"Phoebe," Lady Albery said, "surely it is wise for you to travel with the duchess."

"It is neither wise, nor unwise," Phoebe said. "I shall come to Scotland, Elise." Lady Albery gasped, but Phoebe went on, "Only don't press me as to the time just yet. I promise it won't be long, within a fortnight, I think."

"I can wait," Elise said.

"I ask that you don't. If, by chance, I'm not ready within the allotted time, I don't wish to have kept you from your children."

The duchess smiled. "No matter your decision concerning where you will hold the wedding, you will stay for some time."

Phoebe nodded. "I think I will."

Elise lifted a brow. "You realize what will happen if you don't come to Scotland?"

"I imagine," Phoebe said, "there will be another abduction."

Phoebe picked up William Godwin's *A Tale of the Sixteenth Century* from the bookstore shelf and opened the book. After Elise left earlier that day, Lady Albery was all agog over her visit, and Phoebe had been forced to flee her aunt's company. The bookstore was her final stop on her list of errands, but she dreaded returning home where her aunt would likely ply her with more suggestions for her wedding. It was clear that Lady Albery disapproved of the wedding being held in Scotland.

"So," came a familiar male voice, "I understand we are to return to Scotland?"

Phoebe whirled, knocking a stack of books from the store shelf. "By heavens, sir," she exclaimed.

She started to reach for the scattered books, but halted, narrowly missing a collision with Kiernan's head as he bent to pick up the books. He gathered them in one arm. Phoebe took a step back when he straightened, and tilted her head back in order to keep eye contact. He set the books on the shelf.

Her stomach did a somersault. "Are you going to make a habit of scaring the life out of me?"

Curiosity flickered in his eyes. "I can't say," he replied. "Catching you unawares has its appeal." He smiled. "The blush on your cheeks is quite becoming." She froze when he trailed a finger along her cheek. "What man wouldn't be gratified to incite such a reaction in a beautiful woman?"

Warmth pooled between her legs. Could he sense this reaction as easily as her blush? He took her free hand and lifted it to his lips, eyes locked with hers as he pressed his lips to the back of her hand. When he released her, she realized her heart was pounding...and that he had, indeed, sensed her desire.

"Have you any purchases you wish to make?" he asked.

Phoebe broke from the trance. "Yes, these two novels."

He took the books she held and read out loud, "William Godwin, *A Tale of the Sixteenth Century*." He looked at the other volume. "*The Pickwick Papers* by Charles Dickens. I'm not acquainted with this fellow."

"He has only just published." Phoebe took the books. "I heard he is quite good."

"They will make fine reading during the trip to Ashlund." Kiernan cupped her elbow and directed her toward the front of the shop. When they reached the counter, he plucked the books from her grasp. "Tate," he addressed the man behind the counter, "please add these to my bill."

"Sir." She reached for the books, but Kiernan handed them to Tate, who began wrapping them in paper. "Ashlund, I don't need you to pay for my purchases."

"Of course you don't," he replied. "But it's my pleasure to do so." He smiled the same soft smile she had witnessed two nights ago at the Halsey soirée, and memory of his lips on hers caused her knees to weaken.

Tate offered the books to Kiernan, who seemed not to notice.

Phoebe reached for the books, but Kiernan captured her hand in his and took the books with his free hand. "Thank you, Tate." Kiernan tucked the books under his arm, then maneuvered her past other shoppers and out the door.

"Have you a carriage?" he asked.

"I took a cab. It's chilly, but the day is so lovely, I planned on walking at least partway home."

"A wonderful idea," he said. "I'll accompany you."

He grasped her hand and placed it in the crook of his arm. They started down the street, and the slight movement of his arm as they walked caused the muscle beneath her fingers to flex. She couldn't halt her gaze from snapping onto the hand covering hers. His long, tanned fingers enveloped her hand and she became aware of the warmth of his flesh.

"Have you decided upon a date for going to Ashlund?" he asked. "By carriage, it's four or five days. Really, you needn't bother your uncle for a coach. We can travel in mine."

This caught her attention. "I can't say when I'll go. It's likely, I will decide the day before I leave."

"I require no more than an hour's notice." He directed her to the right of the walkway when another couple approached.

"Don't rely on me for notice," she said.

He smiled genially. "I'll ask your uncle to inform me. I understand you'll be busy with the details of the journey."

"My lord," she said in frustration, "I don't plan on traveling with you."

"Don't worry about imposing on me, Phoebe. I'm looking forward to spending time with you. You'll forgive me if I ride horseback most of the way, but we'll stop for refreshment at your pleasure and, of course, we'll have the evenings."

Phoebe started. Was that a sultry note in his voice?

"Phoebe?"

She realized he was staring and could only think to say, "I don't plan on riding in your carriage—any carriage, for that matter—all the way to Scotland."

He grinned. "Of course, I should have guessed. It's obvious you wouldn't enjoy the confines of a carriage for long." He halted at the end of the lane and waited for a cab to pass before leading her across the street. "I have an Andalusian," he went on like an excited school boy. "You must ride him." Her astonishment must have shown on her face, for he added, "He's a gelding. You can handle him with ease. You will love him. He's a bay. The shading on his coat is magnificent and his presentation is spectacular."

"Where did you get such a horse?" she asked.

"My father's doing. A trader recommended the beast, and he had the horse imported from Spain. Do you know the breed?"

"I do, though I've never ridden one." And she couldn't deny a thrill at the prospect of riding such a fine animal.

Kiernan applied gentle pressure to her hand. "Now, you shall."

He hailed a passing Hansom cab. The driver pulled up and Phoebe found herself handed up into the seat with Kiernan sliding in beside her.

"I'm not finished with my shopping," she said.

His brow lifted in surprise, but she had the distinct impression he wasn't surprised. When he said, "It's growing late. You'll need rest before attending the Blakely soirée this evening," she knew she was right.

"I'm not going."

"Surely you don't want to miss the party?"

She regarded him. "How did you know where to find me?"

"Your aunt, of course."

"Of course."

"I'll call for you this evening at ten," he said. "Perhaps your aunt would care to join us. It's beneficial that we're seen in public together and she's a perfect chaperone."

"Beneficial for whom?" Phoebe asked.

"You did say a year's engagement," he replied. "And I said I would court you in that year."

He'd said "...*pursue you, court you and, lastly, seduce you*" to be exact, and she had yet to decide on a firm course of action to avoid his suit while she investigated the information in Stafford's journal.

"I have been straightforward with you," he said.

"Really?" she replied. "You never mentioned that you obtained a special license."

"I would be remiss not to be prepared."

"May I see it?"

A corner of his mouth twitched. "Had I known you wished to see it, I would have brought it with me."

"I would think you would keep it on your person at all times. You know," she raised her brows, "in the interest of being prepared."

"Quite right," he said with more enthusiasm than she cared for. "I'll put it in my pocket the moment I return home. Shall I procure a change of horses for my carriage tonight?"

"If you like. That way you can ride onto Scotland early."

"No," he said. "I'll await your pleasure."

"My pleasure, indeed."

"What's that you say?" he inquired in a polite tone that told her he had heard her.

"When we arrive to Scotland, will you take me about the countryside?" she asked.

He gave a genuine smile of pleasure. "Of course. Anywhere you like."

"I wish to ride north. I've never been farther into Scotland than Brahan Seer. The castle is in the very south of the Highlands, isn't it?"

"It is," he replied.

"I would like to visit Kildonan parish, or even farther north to Ldderachylis."

He showed no consternation at hearing that she wished to visit territory owned by the Duchess of Sutherland.

"Kildonan and Ldderachylis are some distance away," he replied amiably. "Perhaps we should save that trip for after our marriage." The cab came to a halt. Kiernan peered out the window. "We have arrived." He opened the door and helped her from the carriage. He raised her hand to his lips. "Until tonight, my dear."

"I make no promises."

He caressed her cheek. "I'll be here at ten."

He turned and his coat went taut over his broad shoulders as he grasped the door and vaulted back into the carriage. Phoebe didn't move, her legs once again weak as a kitten. He waved once, then leaned back and disappeared into the depths of the carriage. Phoebe released a breath and turned, but halted suddenly, whirling. She raised her hand to gain the rider's attention, then dropped it back to her side when the carriage turned the corner.

"My books." With a sigh, she started up the walkway to Shyerton hall.

Chapter Fourteen

At hearing her uncle's voice through the partially open door of the drawing room that evening, Phoebe halted in the hallway. "Lady Albery," he was saying. "would you see what is keeping Phoebe, please?"

"What keeps Phoebe," Phoebe muttered, "is the question of whether life in Newgate is worth shooting a certain marquess." She opened the door and saw Kiernan rise from the chair located beside the couch where the Duke and Duchess of Ashlund sat.

"Phoebe." He crossed the room. "I'm pleased to see you."

"Forgive me, Lord Ashlund. The time slipped by. Before I knew it, the clock had struck nine." The hour she received his note saying that the duke and duchess would accompany them to the soiree.

Kiernan kissed her hand, lingering a second longer than was appropriate before releasing her. "You look lovely tonight, my dear. My father and Elise are here."

"Yes," Phoebe replied. "I received your note *an hour ago.*"

He gave no outward sign of noticing her reprimand and led her forward, stopping before the duke and duchess.

"Your Graces." Phoebe curtsied.

The duke rose and took her hand in his. "Remember, lass, call me Father."

Elise stood and gave her a hug. "So good to see you again, Phoebe. I hope all is well with you."

"Very well," she replied. "But I have kept you waiting long enough. Shall we go?"

"Phoebe," Kiernan said, "before we go, I have something for you. My father and Elise accompanied me this evening for a very special reason." Kiernan reached into his pocket and produced a square velvet box.

Phoebe's heart jumped into her throat. "Lord Ashlund—"

"This was my mother's." He opened the box to reveal a single strand, diamond and emerald necklace, matching earrings, and a heavy banded emerald ring. He removed the ring and handed the box to his father.

Phoebe took a step back, but Kiernan caught her hand. Her hand felt ice cold against his warm fingers and her hand trembled as he slid the emerald onto her finger.

He looked at her and gave her hand a gentle squeeze. "She would have liked you."

"You should have waited," Phoebe whispered, and cast an anxious glance at the duke. "Nothing has been decided."

He gave a soft smile that said everything was, indeed, decided.

Kiernan released her and when he took the necklace from the box, Phoebe stood stock still while he walked around behind her. As she had the first night he'd kidnapped her, she wore her golden hair up. He settled the necklace around her neck. The cold stones seemed to seer her flesh, to scream *faker*.

While closing the clasp, he leaned forward and whispered, "One year, Phoebe. It would be wrong for me not to give you what is rightfully yours." He grasped her shoulders and turned her, then reached for the earrings. Kiernan clipped one on each ear, then took a step back and surveyed her.

"Perfect. Have you a cloak?"

"In the hallway."

"Then we are ready?" Kiernan surveyed the group.

"Oh, yes, indeed, sir," Lady Albery said, dabbing at the moisture in the corner of her eyes.

"My dear." Lord Albery retrieved a handkerchief from his breast pocket and gave it to her.

She took the handkerchief, again dabbed at her eyes, then pulled Phoebe into a hug. "Phoebe, my dear." Lady Albery straightened, then paused and touched the necklace. "Breathtaking. You are most fortunate." She blushed. "Do forgive me, everyone. I hadn't realized how this would affect me."

Phoebe frowned. "You knew of this?"

"Of course. Lord Ashlund informed us he would be presenting you with the family jewels tonight. I couldn't be more pleased."

Phoebe looked at her uncle. "And you, sir, are you pleased?"

He gave a nod. "I am."

Kiernan took her arm. "Shall we go?"

She looked at him. "It seems I am at your full command."

Or was that at his *beck and call*?

"You received my letter?" Ty's mother asked as they sat on the couch in her chambers' anteroom the following morning.

"I did."

"My God," she exclaimed, "can you imagine? The marquess kidnapped Phoebe."

No, he couldn't imagine.

"Have you seen her yet?" Lady Albery asked.

"I only just arrived and you waylaid me before I could find her."

"Ty, what are we to do? Albery has ordered her to marry him. To make matters worse, Ashlund gave her his mother's jewels last night. Emeralds and diamonds."

"Worth a fortune, no doubt," Ty commented.

"Yes," she replied. "You must take action immediately. She can't marry him."

Ty eyed his mother. "That's a new morning dress you're wearing. Madam Bellievau, if I'm not mistaken."

"Well, yes," she said in a fluster. "This is one of her creations. You always did have a good eye."

"That dress must have cost a king's ransom. What does Albery think of that expenditure?"

"He can't balk over this," she said in a rush. "I must dress well. After all, I am the wife of a viscount."

"So he has yet to see the bill."

"I didn't ask you here to talk about my wardrobe," she shot back.

"But you did. I tell you, madam, that when I come in possession of Phoebe's money, I no more intend to finance your whims than does your husband."

"So you haven't given up hope. Oh, Ty, I can't tell you how relieved I am."

"Mother," he began.

"Don't discipline me, Humphrey. I am quite capable of staying within a budget."

"On the contrary, you have never even seen a budget."

"Never mind that, you must make haste if you are to marry her before the marquess."

"I have no intention of marrying her just yet."

His mother's eyes widened in horror. "How are we to survive if you don't?"

"You will survive quite well," he said. "As for me, I have matters in hand."

A speculative gleam lit her eyes. "Clive mentioned that the marquess might meet with an accident."

"Clive will do well to mind his own business."

"Still, isn't it taking a chance to wait?" she went on as if not hearing him. "How long would you have to wait before — ?"

"No more expensive dresses, Mother, and more important, no more gambling. I don't want your husband learning of your indiscretions — which includes Clive." She opened her mouth, but he cut her off. "Defy me, and I'll leave you to drown in your debt." He rose, dropped a kiss on her cheek, then left.

Ty paused in the hallway, outside the door. So Clive was cultivating his own plans, despite Ty's warning to stay out of the affair.

Perfect.

Phoebe stared down at the card sent by Lord Redgrave saying how much he was looking forward to seeing her tomorrow. Her two-day reprieve had ended. Tomorrow evening, the Duke and Duchess of Ashlund were hosting an intimate dinner party of one hundred or so of their and her uncle's closest friends in order to officially announce her and Kiernan's engagement. Redgrave's note was a warning to be there.

Guilt tightened her stomach. The duke and duchess were making a sincere effort to draw her into their family. She liked them. Heaven help her, she liked Kiernan — more than liked, if she was honest. How would she face the duke and duchess if she became the instrument of their son's downfall? How would she face them even if she simply cried off from the wedding? One way or another, things weren't going to end well.

The pad of feet on the carpet snapped her attention in the direction of the door. She groaned. Not another visitor. The endless stream of well-wishers her aunt had allowed into the house had become a nuisance. Before she could think of an excuse to deny her aunt's latest visitor, the door opened and her cousin entered.

"Ty," she said with relief. "I didn't know you were back in London."

He crossed to the couch where she sat and lowered himself onto the cushion beside her. "You sound glad to see me."

She laughed. "I am, of course, but I'm just as glad you're not another gossip monger come to see for herself how it's possible that the daughter of a traitor snagged a marquess."

He draped an arm over the top of the couch. "As bad as all that?"

She grimaced. "Worse. How have you been? I haven't seen you in some time."

"The damn property Albery has in Coventry is giving me trouble," he replied. "I've had a devil of a time with the carpenter hired to reconstruct the walls in the blue bedroom."

Phoebe frowned. "I was there three years ago and didn't notice that house was in such disrepair."

He shook his head. "Wood rot. I only just discovered it myself."

He couldn't be any more surprised by the wood rot than she could by his caring about the house. Was her cousin finally accepting responsibility for the property that would one day likely be his?

"I understand congratulations are in order," he said, and she was even more startled by the *brotherly* expression on his face.

"Oh. Yes, thank you."

His brow lifted. "You don't seem ecstatic."

"As I said, the never ending visitors have grown tiresome."

"That'll end soon enough," he said.

"Not nearly soon enough."

"Surely that can't have you so disheartened? What's wrong? Has something happened with Ashlund? Is he getting cold feet?"

Embarrassment rushed through her at the realization that Ty must know what had transpired between her and Lord Ashlund. Of course, that made sense. Her uncle might not tell him, but his mother, her aunt, would.

"Not at all," Phoebe replied with light airs. "If anything, he's too ardent."

"If he's giving you trouble, I'll pay him a visit."

She snorted. "If he gave me any trouble, his father would deal with him." Damn the duke.

Ty scrutinized her. "You're not keen on his suit."

"You're aware that I am not interested in marriage."

He shrugged. "I knew you weren't interested in any of your recent suitors, but surely you knew marriage was inevitable?"

"I did not."

"Ahh," he intoned. "You believed you would be left to amuse yourself with your inheritance."

"Why not?" she replied irritably, then released a sigh. "Forgive me, Ty. You're being kind, and I'm not."

"Ashlund is filthy rich. How could he possibly need your paltry fifteen thousand pound yearly income?"

"He said I could keep the money," Phoebe replied.

"There you have it. Once your new husband has his heir, you'll be free to go on as you always planned." Ty rose. "I'll see you tomorrow night."

Frustration welled up in her, but she nodded.

"Chin up, Cousin," he said. "You love a good party. Especially of late." With that he was gone.

Phoebe stared at the door after he'd closed it, wondering what had inspired her cousin's familial interest in her, and what he meant by 'especially of late.'

Kiernan looked up from the article in the *Satirist*. The newspaper wasn't his regular read, but he'd found it with his morning mail, sent from someone signed *A Friend*. He could well imagine the friend was any number of London society women who delighted in vicious gossip. Even a so-called gentleman or two might be the culprit. Either way, by now, all of London society would have read or been told about the article.

Regan took a swallow of coffee, then set the cup on its saucer and picked a piece of bacon off the plate that sat alongside a platter of scrambled eggs. "Miss Wallington is going to be none too happy with this turn of events."

Kiernan set the newspaper on the table beside his breakfast plate. "News of our time together in Scotland was bound to reach London. She was foolish to think otherwise."

"True. But one wonders who filled in the intimate details."

"Yes." Kiernan looked at the paper and the headline, *London Heiress kidnapped by the Marquess of Ashlund.*

"Who do you think sold the story?" Regan asked.

"No one in my household," Kiernan said. "It must be someone in Phoebe's house."

"Her coachman, Calders?"

"Perhaps, but it's just as possible one of her other servants got their greedy hands on my father's letter to Lord Albery."

As if Kiernan had summoned the duke, he appeared in the doorway.

Regan rose. "Your Grace."

"Sit down, Regan," he said, his eyes on Kiernan, "What is it?" he asked as he seated himself at the head of the table.

Kiernan passed the newspaper to him and poured coffee for his father, then refilled his and Regan's cups.

A moment later, his father folded, then laid the paper on the table. "A year's engagement is unreasonable. Every move you and Miss Wallington make will be scrutinized."

"Phoebe has expressed an interest in returning to Scotland," Kiernan said with caution. "We won't be under the critical eye of London society."

"Ashlund will be little better, and," he added when Kiernan started to reply, "Brahan Seer is out of the question."

"You've become a mind reader, Father." Though he knew his father was right. It didn't matter that Brahan Seer was crawling with servants, soldiers, and villagers, all of British Society would believe that he had whisked Phoebe off to the castle in order to continue their *affair* as portrayed in the *Satirist*.

"I can't force her to the altar," Kiernan said.

The duke reached for the platter of eggs. "A shame you didn't consider that when you forced your way into her carriage."

"I know. It's too bad, really. When I saw her at the party that night, I fully intended to make her acquaintance. Had she not been in that coach, I would have pursued her."

"The way you pursued her the other night at the Halsey ball?" The duke spooned eggs onto his plate.

148

"Damnation, Father." Kiernan broke off at sight of his father's brown eyes lifting to meet his. "What would you have me do?" Kiernan asked.

"You may begin by not adding fuel to *that* fire." He motioned toward the paper and set the plate on the table.

"Then you might consider hiring a chaperone."

His father looked at him, nonplussed. "You're no rake."

"No. But I won't lie. Phoebe...excites me." Kiernan winced when his father's jaw tightened. "I won't make love to her until we're married," he said. His father's expression turned speculative, and Kiernan shook his head. "No. I haven't taken that liberty—and neither has she offered."

"She likely won't."

"I seem to recall that didn't stop you with Elise." The words were out of his mouth and even Regan stilled. "Father—"

"That was a different time and a different place," the duke cut in—to Kiernan's surprise, without rancor. "And as you know, not all my choices were the wisest."

"I'm sorry," Kiernan said. "I shouldn't have said that."

"Nay," he replied. "But I knew you someday would. You might ask yourself why that time was now."

Her Grace, the Duchess of Ashlund, insisted that Phoebe avail herself of her dressmaker and Phoebe agreed. She had to choose her battles between now and the time she parted company with the Ashlunds, and she had, after all, been ordered to agree to the marriage.

Phoebe stepped from the dressmaker's shop behind the duchess, who was resolute that she be present for the final fitting. She had supervised the design of white-work embroidery with sleeves of puffed and ruffled mancherons, and had chosen the delicate ruffles for the skirt. Elise MacGregor had exquisite taste.

The duchess pointedly ignored her guard Niall, who stood beside their carriage on the bustling London side street, and turned to Phoebe. "I'm relieved that is over with," she said.

Phoebe laughed. "I was afraid you would be offended if I said that."

"Not at all. I despise fittings—even when I love the dress. I imagine the gown will arrive at your uncle's home before you do."

"Oh," Phoebe said, and Elise laughed.

"I don't intend on keeping you out all afternoon. Mrs. Gilly will be quick about the final touches on the gown and will have it delivered immediately. Do you like sweets?"

"Why, yes," Phoebe replied.

"Good. There's a confectionary nearby. Well worth the walk. I visit every chance I get." The duchess didn't look as though she indulged in sweets and Phoebe said so. Elise patted her arm. "You and I are going to get along very well. Niall," she said, "Phoebe and I plan to walk to Madam Araquette's."

"Aye, Your Grace," he said, and motioned to the driver.

The driver snapped the reins and the carriage started forward as Elise and Phoebe began walking, with Niall following on foot.

"So, tell me the truth," Elise began, "what do you think of marrying Kiernan?"

Phoebe had wondered when she would ask this question. "I have agreed to a year's engagement. You might ask me six months from now or perhaps even nine months." Honesty was the best policy—as long as it was possible.

"If you find in the year you can't tolerate him, do you plan to call off the wedding?"

"I imagine few women would not be able to *tolerate* Lord Ashlund."

"He's a good man," Elise said. "But that alone isn't enough for marriage." She lapsed into silence for a moment. "You do seem to find him attractive." Phoebe cut her gaze onto her, and Elise said, "I have eyes."

Phoebe returned her attention to the sidewalk. "He is a…" A couple passed them and she felt her cheeks heat.

"A fine specimen of masculinity?" Elise finished.

Phoebe thought she heard Niall groan, and could only manage, "Indeed."

The carriage stopped behind two other carriages that had halted to let other vehicles pass at the intersection, but Niall kept pace with them. Amidst a hackney driver shouting at a carriage driver that had veered too close, Elise said, "It's all right to admit you like him."

"I-well, yes, Your Grace," Phoebe sputtered.

They reached the intersection. "Turn right," Elise instructed. They started down the block and she added, "I should warn you, the MacGregor men are relentless. The only way he will give up the chase is if you can prove you…dislike him."

Or if I denounce him as a traitor, Phoebe thought, but said, "I suppose if I don't dislike him, I may not want to call off the wedding."

"Exactly," Elise said. "And I don't blame you one bit for wanting to be sure he's worth having. Some of England's most respected husbands care nothing for pleasing their wives."

Phoebe looked at her. What was she saying?

"I suspect that isn't the case with Kiernan." The duchess looked Phoebe in the eye. "After all, the apple doesn't usually fall far from the tree."

Phoebe stared. Was the Duchess of Ashlund saying that the Duke of Ashlund was a good lover; therefore, his son would be as well?

Elise cast a glance behind her and Phoebe couldn't help following suit. Niall had fallen back a few paces. Elise leaned into her and whispered, "The damage has already been done to your reputation. If you have any doubts about the marriage, it's only right that you investigate his suitability."

"Investigate?" Phoebe repeated dumbly. "Suitability?"

"Try out the goods beforehand," Elise prodded.

Phoebe recalled Kiernan's words the night of the Halsey soiree, "*I will pursue you, court you, and, lastly, seduce you.*" By heavens, if she didn't know better, she would swear Kiernan had colluded with his stepmother.

"I see," Elise said.

Phoebe jarred back to the moment.

"Perhaps your investigation is already underway," she said. "Or...," her gaze turned speculative, "Kiernan has begun a campaign of his own."

Phoebe realized her cheeks were flaming. "Ma'am," she began, but Elise cut her off.

"Here we are." She entered the shop with Phoebe following on unsteady legs. "There isn't a thing here you won't love," Elise said. She stepped up to the counter where various pastries were displayed.

The petite, middle-aged woman behind the counter looked up. "Your Grace," she said with a slight French accent. "How lovely to see you."

"And you, Madam Araquette. How are you?"

Phoebe watched them, lost in the wonder of what sort of duchess suggested that her stepson's future wife *should try out the goods beforehand*. Were Scots that...loose?

"Why, Miss Wallington."

Phoebe turned at hearing Jane Halsey's voice. "Lady Halsey."

Lady Wilmington stood alongside her with a look in her eye that Phoebe didn't like. Jane, too, looked self-satisfied and Phoebe had the sneaking suspicion she was about to discover why.

"Lady Wilmington," Phoebe said with a deferential cant of her head.

"You look well," Lady Wilmington replied. "I suppose a Scottish marquess can do that for a woman."

"I am fond of His Lordship," Phoebe said.

"Fond?" Lady Wilmington exchanged a glance with Jane. "Is he fond of you?" Phoebe frowned, but before she could answer, Lady Wilmington added, "How long do you think his fondness will last now that all of London knows you made a fool of him by trapping him into marriage?"

"I beg your pardon?"

Lady Wilmington opened her reticule and produced a newspaper clipping and handed it to her. Phoebe's gaze snagged on the headline *London Heiress kidnapped by the Marquess of Ashlund*. She caught the word Green Lady Inn and her heart thumped so hard she couldn't hear anything save the rush of blood that pounded in tandem to the beat.

"What's this?"

Phoebe snapped from the horrible spell. Lady Wilmington and Lady Halsey's faces went white and they stared at Elise as she stepped up beside Phoebe.

"Your Grace," they murmured in near unison, and curtsied deep.

Elise took the clipping from Phoebe's hand. Her eyes flicked over the paper, then she looked at the two women. "Jane, you will inform your mother that His Grace and I will not be attending your party this week as planned. I will send a note explaining why. As for you, Katherine, if I'm not mistaken, His Grace was recently considering a business venture with your father—shipping, I believe. My husband will not be investing as your father had hoped, and His Grace will send a letter of explanation. In fact, I feel certain His Grace will visit your father. It's only right, wouldn't you agree?"

"Your Grace," she began, but Elise faced Phoebe.

"Come along, Phoebe."

Phoebe's attention caught on the clipping as it fluttered to the floor in their wake.

Phoebe waited until Gaylon had closed the door and left her alone with Alistair. The shock of seeing the article in the paper that afternoon had worn off, and now she was furious—for several reasons.

"I arrived home to find a note from Lord Briarden asking when my wedding date was," she said.

Surprise flickered in his eyes—barely.

"Don't toy with me, Redgrave," she said. "Does Her Majesty now expect British spies to marry their quarry?"

"Of course not."

"Then what is Briarden about?"

"Something's happened, but I have no idea what."

"None?"

He gave her a sharp look. "Now who's playing games, Phoebe?"

"All right. She pulled from a drawer the copy of the *Satirist* she had had Calders purchase for her, and handed it to Redgrave."

His face remained impassive as he read the article and Phoebe wondered how many times throughout their friendship he'd worn that same look while hiding something from her, something like the fact he knew her father was still alive.

His gaze shifted back to her. "You can't be surprised by this."

"Indeed, I can. There are too many intimate details in that story for this to be someone who happened to see Lord Ashlund and me in Scotland."

He lifted a brow. "You suspect me?"

"You have your reasons for wanting to see me married to the marquess."

"Once we are sure he's an honest man, yes, but even then I wouldn't stoop to these tactics."

She snorted. "You would."

"All right," he said. "I might. But I didn't."

"Briarden?" she asked.

Alistair shook his head. "He would *not* stoop to such tactics."

Phoebe wasn't so sure. Briarden had made it clear that she was employed by the Crown to gather information, and as the future wife of a suspect she was in a perfect position to carry out that duty. But how much better would her position be as wife...and lover?

"The only other person who knows enough is Calders, and he wouldn't do it," she said.

"No," Alistair said, "I don't believe he would. But he isn't the only possible suspect."

"My aunt and uncle, but they would never report to the papers." Or would her aunt?

"True," Alistair replied. "Remember, you stayed in that inn on the English border. From what you told me, the innkeeper's wife sounds like the type to sell such a story."

"But she would have to know there was a story to sell."

"What about someone in Ashlund's entourage?"

"If what I saw in Scotland is accurate, highly unlikely. Those men practically worship him and his father."

A rush of emotion barreled through her. There was one other candidate, and she suddenly wondered just how much he hated losing a battle.

Chapter Fifteen

The emeralds Phoebe wore around her neck seemed to seer into her flesh as she paused in the entry of the Ashlund mansion ballroom. Everyone's attention turned toward her, eyes on the jewels that proclaimed she was an Ashlund.

"Easy, girl," her uncle said. He patted her left arm.

His wife stood to his left, and Ty stood next to her.

The crowd to Phoebe's right parted and she drew a breath at sight of Kiernan MacGregor passing through their ranks, his gaze fixed on hers as though she was the only woman in the room…the only woman in the world. He wore a black dress coat, ivory silk waistcoat, white shirt, and black trousers—and white gloves. By heavens, he embodied the perfect gentleman. And he was stunning. When he reached her side and grasped her hand, she felt the tremble in her fingers as he lifted them to his lips. As always, his mouth was moist, warm, and deliberate in its work on her flesh. Heat crept up her cheeks and, from her belly, moved downward to where a now familiar ache tightened.

"You are the Devil," she murmured when he released her hand.

"Phoebe," her aunt remonstrated in a whisper.

The Devil danced in Kiernan's eyes and Phoebe read the message, *who better than the Devil understood wicked pleasure?*

She caught sight of the duke standing in the group Kiernan had left, and the thin lipped expression on his face. "My lord," she said to Kiernan, "I believe your father plans to take you over his knee."

Kiernan laughed, but didn't look at him. That, Phoebe was certain, was purposeful.

"He's quite capable." Kiernan's attention shifted to her uncle. "Lord Albery."

"My lord," her uncle said.

Kiernan grinned. "Kiernan will do." He took a step to Phoebe's aunt. "Lady Albery, you grow more lovely each time we meet."

She demurred, but Phoebe didn't miss the fleeting, but distinct, sultry look in her eyes. So her aunt wasn't above a flirtation with her soon-to-be nephew.

"Lord Ashlund." She curtsied.

Kiernan gave her a roughish look. "Lords and curtsies will soon grow tiresome among us." He winked at her. "We'll leave that in the public world."

Lady Albery gave a graceful nod. "As you wish, Kiernan."

He smiled broadly. "Excellent."

"May I present Lady Albery's son," Phoebe's uncle said, "Ty Humphrey, Baron Arlington."

Kiernan's gaze shifted onto Ty, and Ty gave a slight bow. "My lord."

"Arlington," Kiernan said with a civility that Phoebe noticed didn't hold the warmth he'd extended to her aunt and uncle.

The orchestra began playing a waltz and he faced her. "I believe this first dance belongs to me, Miss Wallington." His gaze shifted to her aunt. "But if you would do me the honor, Lady Albery, I will claim a dance with you later in the evening?"

"Of course." She slipped her hand into the crook of Lord Albery's arm.

Kiernan extended his arm to Phoebe. She accepted and he led her to the dance floor. He pulled her closer than was acceptable and she kept her gaze level with his chest as he stepped into the music in perfect time. Her heart stuttered when his muscled legs pressed against her thighs with each subtle direction to the music. A tremor in her stomach weakened her knees and she knew an instant of fear that she would stumble.

"You look lovely," he said.

"Thank you, my lord."

"No, that's not right," he said.

Phoebe snapped her head up to meet his gaze.

"*Lovely* is for your aunt." His blue eyes bore into her. "You are beautiful."

Damn him, he truly was the Devil—and knew it. "If you keep looking at me like that, your father will take you over his knee," she said.

He grimaced. "You're right. He's liable to hire a chaperone as I suggested."

"Chaperone?" Phoebe saw her efforts at spying going up in smoke. "By heavens, Ashlund, what have you done?"

He grinned. "I like it when you say my name like that."

She rolled her eyes. "Good Lord."

His arm tightened around her waist and he maneuvered into a turn. Her breasts pressed against his chest and she recalled the duchess'

155

suggestion that she *try out the goods*. A picture flashed of her bare breasts pressed against his naked chest and her nipples hardened to stony points. The room spun. Phoebe buried her face his chest and held on for dear life. His hold tightened—if that was possible—and she detected the bulge pressing into her hip.

"Damnation, Phoebe, you've done me in."

"What?" she began, but found herself whirled away from the other dancers and being hurried through the open balcony doors. Cool air washed over her and snapped her mind to attention. "We're on the balcony," she said.

He halted at the railing that faced the gardens. Phoebe glanced back toward the ballroom. People standing near the door yanked their eyes away from her direct gaze.

"What have you done?" she demanded.

Elbows on the railing, Kiernan leaned forward, staring out into the gardens. "Unless you want that chaperone, I suggest you don't hug me like that again—in public."

"What?" She recalled his thick erection pressed against her. "Oh."

His head shifted in her direction. "Oh?"

"When you made the turn, it made me a bit dizzy."

He studied her. "Did it now?"

"You have a healthy ego, Ashlund."

"I still like the way you say my name."

She shot him a reproving look. Her head had cleared and she was feeling more herself, more the way she needed to feel in order to deal with this man. A man, she suddenly remembered, who was using every underhanded piece of weaponry in his arsenal.

"I assume you saw the article in the *Satirist*?" she asked.

He nodded. "I did, and I'm sorry. I know you'd hoped to avoid a scandal."

"I should have been able to avoid a scandal."

"That is seldom the way such matters work," he said.

"Especially when the prospective groom is involved."

His brow furrowed. "You think I informed the *Satirist* of our escapade?"

"I think it's a very convenient happenstance for you."

"Not especially."

"No?" she said. "A scandal practically ensures I must marry you."

"Practically?" he said.

"Ah ha!" she exclaimed. "You did do it."

"No. I didn't."

"Why should I believe you?"

He straightened. "Because I've never lied to you."

Was about Alan Hay and his band? Had Kiernan truly never lied to her?

"I didn't give the story to the paper," he said with finality.

"I didn't give you leave to read my mind, sir." He hadn't exactly, but he was closer than she liked. "Why should I believe you?"

A corner of his mouth twitched. "I don't need a scandal. You're going to marry me anyway."

She threw her hands in the air. "You're impossible."

"So I've been told. He straightened from the wall. "I suppose we should rejoin the party." He extended his elbow and she laid her hand in the crook of his arm. "I like that as well," he said.

And Phoebe was startled to realize that she liked it too.

The music ended and Phoebe thanked Lord Phillips for the dance as she noted that Kiernan and his father were stepping from the ballroom into a hallway. With the party in full swing and the men gone, now was her chance to look around. Lord Phillips offered his arm and she allowed him to escort her off the dance floor.

"It's intolerably hot," she said. "Don't you think?"

"Indeed, I do," he replied. "Would you like some refreshment?"

She smiled. "Sir, you're a mind reader."

He gave a slight bow, then started through the crowd toward the buffet table located on the other side of the massive room. She started for the same hallway Kiernan had taken and didn't breathe until she entered the corridor. She hurried to the end, then took a sharp right. As expected, a set of rear stairs was located up ahead. She sent up a prayer that she not encounter any servants. Thankfully, the ballroom was located on the second floor, and she reached the third level of the four-story mansion without being seen. If her calculations were correct, the family private quarters would be on this level.

As hoped, the floor was deserted. Likely, the servants were helping with the party below. Orchestra music filtered up from the ballroom. Otherwise, all was silent. The first door opened into a small bedroom that looked unused. The second door opened upon what had to be the lady's bedroom. A low fire burned in the hearth and cast enough light that Phoebe was able to cross to the adjoining door she hoped led to the master's chambers. She'd calculated right. A fire also burned in this room and she surveyed the room. A small secretary sat near the window to the right of the hearth. She hurried to the desk, and a quick look revealed only blank writing paper and pen.

Another door was located on the far wall and Phoebe tried the door. It opened upon a modest study. Here is where the duke might keep personal documents. Apprehension twisted her stomach. What if father and son were in league? Would a duke betray his Queen? In the five years

157

that Phoebe had been spying for England, she'd never once doubted her conviction. Her assignments had posed no real threat to her, had caused no personal conflict. It was bound to happen eventually, but she would have paid a ransom for the time to have been anytime but now.

Phoebe shrugged off the thought and hurried to the desk. She opened the two drawers located on the right side of the desk, but found only writing paper and newspapers. She faced the walnut cabinet that sat against the wall behind the desk and began rifling through the drawers only to find accountings, personal letters and the like. She sat in the desk chair and scanned the dates on the letters and stopped at a letter from the magistrate in Glasgow dated two days after her arrival at Brahan Seer.

> *To His Grace the Duke of Ashlund*
> *Your Grace,*
>
>> *There is no doubt in my mind that the fire that demolished the two cottages was, as you suspected, started with lamp oil. Our investigation in the area where your men chased the arsonists turned up a small swath of common MacGregor plaide. This evidence, coupled with the fact that someone broke into the desk in your library – while nothing of value anywhere in the castle was taken – is enough for me to pursue the matter.*

Phoebe stared at the words someone *broke into your desk.* The magistrate believed the fire might be connected to someone searching the duke's desk? Why would anyone set a fire just to search the desk? Why not simply steal into the castle in the dead of night? Phoebe recalled Kiernan's familiarity with the occupants of the cottage down to the very details of knowing the personal items they had lost, and the duke's knowledge of the families who had lost their homes. Father and son knew their tenants well. A stranger who entered the castle would be noticed. Kiernan said the MacGregors weren't involved in any fighting. Had he been telling the truth? Who would kill just to search someone's private belongings…and what did the duke and marquess have that was worth killing for? Phoebe read on.

>> *However, there are two other incidents that give me pause. Four days after the fire, we found a man murdered near the Glaistig Uain. This is strange enough – as you know, murders aren't common in this area. What compounds this mystery is that witnesses at the inn identified the man as having been there that day. He was seen with several other men, two of whom are the men your son killed during his attempted kidnapping.*

Phoebe paused. What two men had Kiernan shot? Had the magistrate returned to the scene of the crime and – understanding struck. The two men the magistrate spoke of weren't men Kiernan had killed, but were Bob and the other man she had shot. The second man hadn't lived? She closed her eyes and took a deep breath. The two men were criminals, but she had killed them, nonetheless. And, she realized with shock, Kiernan had taken responsibility for their deaths. Damn him, damn him to hell. He was going to twist her heart inside out before she was done with this business.

She returned her attention to the letter.

> *From all indications, the man we found dead was in the company of two men when he was shot, but we have no idea who those men were. I have yet to identify the dead man or the two men Kiernan killed, but it's clear they were all party to your son's attempted kidnapping. I can't say if they have any connection with the fire, but we have your description of the one man sighted near the village the night of the fire. If I find anything further, I will contact you immediately. Of course, if you think of anything more, or if anything else happens that you believe connects to this case, please contact me immediately.*
> John Glen, Chief Magistrate, Glasgow

Phoebe didn't like the coincidence of the dead men and the arson any better than did the magistrate. The two had to be connected. A horrifying thought struck. Kiernan had accused Adam of being the arsonist. Had he told his father of his suspicions? If the Duke of Ashlund made accusations against Adam—a sound outside in the hallway caught her attention. The distinct murmur of men's voice filtered to her.

Phoebe jumped to her feet and shoved the letters back into the drawer. She hesitated. Where were the men headed? The study had a hallway door. She raced for the adjoining door. Whoever it was, if they entered one of these rooms, she could step into the empty room and close the connecting door before they entered. The voices came closer and she realized they had paused outside the study.

Phoebe eased the adjoining door open a crack as the study door opened and her uncle's voice sounded loud and clear, "You're too generous, Your Grace."

She peered through the slit at her uncle, the duke, and his son.

"He's a fine animal," the duke replied. "You're making a good investment." He motioned to the couch near the fireplace. "Kiernan, would you fetch us a drink?" The duke looked at her uncle. "Do you like scotch?"

"I do, Your Grace. Thank you."

"Marcus will do," the duke said, "Or MacGregor, if you prefer."

Her uncle looked startled, but said, "Of course, Marcus."

They sat on the couch and a moment later Kiernan handed them drinks then sat on the wing backed chair opposite them. "How is Phoebe adjusting to the idea of marriage?" he asked.

"It will take some time," he replied.

Kiernan laughed. "So I gather."

Her uncle surprised her by saying, "You have done the right thing, Lord Ashlund, and I am grateful."

Kiernan's expression sobered. "I couldn't have done otherwise."

"But you could have," her uncle said. "Many men in your position would have."

Kiernan cast his father a sideways glance, "True."

"My solicitor will have the contract drawn up. The dowry — "

"I promised Phoebe her inheritance is hers," Kiernan cut in. "Please see to it that the contract is clear in this matter."

Her uncle gave a nod. "You are generous."

As for a dowry," Kiernan began — Phoebe's heart thudded — "I will have to give that some thought."

"Kiernan," the duke said.

"You can't take all the fun out of this, Father."

"Careful, lad, I can."

"Maybe," he replied, humor in his voice. "But I don't need her money. I am the groom, however, and I do deserve something."

His father mirrored her thoughts when he replied, "I have no doubts the lady will give you exactly what you deserve," then added, "Please bring me the newspaper from the desk in my study."

Phoebe clapped a hand over her mouth, barely stifling a gasp as Kiernan rose. She whirled and raced across the room. At the door, she yanked it open and stepped outside, carefully clicking it shut behind her. She started for the servants' stairs, but a woman's laughter in the stairway stopped her. By heavens, someone was coming up the stairs.

Phoebe pivoted and ran down the hallway to the main stairs before realizing her mistake. Anyone who might be in the foyer below would see her descend the staircase. She continued past the stairs to the room one door down from the duke's and slipped inside. A small fired burned in the hearth and Phoebe immediately realized her horrible mistake. She had entered Kiernan MacGregor's room.

Fifteen minutes later, Phoebe cracked the door to see one of the maids busying herself with a flower arrangement on a table a little way down the hallway. The girl disappeared into the room beside the table and Phoebe glimpsed the edge of a bed in the room. The second maid entered the room. For the next few minutes, Phoebe waited for the girls to leave or close the door, but they moved from within the room to the hallways so that she dared not step from her hiding place. Thankfully, she hadn't heard the men leave the duke's study, which meant Kiernan and her uncle hadn't yet missed her.

A door opened and she heard the duke's voice. Her uncle answered, but his words were cut off when the door closed. Alarm jumpstarted Phoebe's pulse. That had to be Kiernan who left the meeting. Once he returned to the ballroom, he would quickly discover her absence. She forced a slow breath and watched for him. The pad of boots on carpet approached the stairs opposite his bedroom. She waited see him descend the stairs, but he didn't come into view. An instant later, Phoebe realized he was headed for his bedroom.

She took a faltering step back from the door and turned, wildly searching for a hiding place. The armoire was too small. Damn him for not sharing the vanity of so many men of his position who kept more clothes than they could possibly wear in a lifetime. There was no changing closet in this room. The balcony might offer a hiding place — the footsteps were near. Too late. Phoebe lunged for the bed.

When the door opened and the marquess stopped dead, his eyes on her, Phoebe didn't break the connection. His gaze slid down her face to her breasts, which were bared beyond even the sensibilities of the demimonde. She had yanked one gown strap off her shoulder and the comb from her hair, then flung herself onto the mattress. Phoebe lay, one hand thrown over her head, her hair in disarray across the quilt. She couldn't stop the slow release of the breath she held or the slow intake of breath to refill her lungs. In the light of the low fire, his gaze sharpened the instant before he closed the door softly behind him and clicked the lock into place. She stifled a gasp, but was sure he couldn't miss the rise and fall of her breasts caused by the thud of her heart against her chest.

Kiernan leaned his shoulders against the door, crossed his arms over his chest, and lifted a lazy brow. "I'm wondering how you got past the girls out there."

"*That* is what you have to say at a moment like this?"

"Forgive me, my dear, but you've been so concerned about your reputation that I'm a little surprised you would take such a chance."

"No worries, my lord, when I sneaked into your room they weren't on this floor."

"Indeed?"

The bemused note in his voice was unexpected. Phoebe started to push into a sitting position. "If you are worried — "

"I'm not the least bit worried," he cut in, and she stilled.

She was sure he wasn't, damn him. Phoebe relaxed back onto the bed, her arm draped across her midsection. His eyes flicked onto the action, then came back to her face.

"Is something wrong, my lord?" she asked. "Are you upset I'm here? You did tell me to try out the goods." *By heavens, those had been the duchess' words, not his.*

"That is certainly one way of putting it," he replied.

Kiernan pushed off the door and her heart beat faster as he drew closer. He reached the bed, stopped, and stared down at her. Heat rose to her cheeks and she fought the urge to squirm under his scrutiny. Thankfully—or perhaps not so thankfully—he lowered himself to sit on the mattress beside her. Phoebe had expected something more direct, like yanking up her skirts, unbuttoning his pants, then lying on top of her and—she released a shaky breath.

"Are you all right, my dear?"

"Fine, my lord. You?"

"Better than I can remember."

She wanted to throttle him.

"I like this dress."

"The duchess' choice," Phoebe replied.

A corner of his mouth twitched. He lifted a thick lock of her hair and rubbed the tress between his fingers, then dropped it and slipped a warm finger beneath the strap still on her shoulder. Phoebe flinched and his eyes shifted onto her face. She lay still as a mouse and thought perhaps he was going to call a halt to the seduction—heaven help her, she had no idea where that would leave her. Instead, he slid the strap down her shoulder so that both breasts were exposed nearly to her nipples. She couldn't say where this left her, either.

He trailed the finger down her shoulder past her collar bone and over the rise of one breast. She shivered. His finger moved closer to the edge of her bodice. He dipped down into the valley between her breasts and up the other. Warmth centered in her stomach and worked its way downward in a radiating wave. His finger slid inside her bodice and the wave peaked when he caressed a nipple. The juncture between her legs tightened and a dizzying current brought with it an unfamiliar energy.

What was wrong with her? This was dangerous territory and was most certainly not what she'd had in mind when she'd jumped on his bed. What had she had in mind? To seduce him—or pretend to seduce him—not the other way around. But how did she go about seducing him? The thought was cut off when he kissed her. As she remembered, his mouth was soft and warm, but now there was an insistence that caused her limbs to go weak. His tongue flicked at her lips and she opened without hesitation. He plunged inside, soft, sweet, and so warm that Phoebe wondered how such a large man could be so gentle.

Think, she commanded her failing wits. If she wasn't careful, he would have an inescapable reason to force her to marry him. A memory flashed of happening upon Heddy and one of her paramours in an erotic embrace while closeted away in a private room at a party. Phoebe twirled her tongue around Kiernan's while reaching with one hand to cup his groin. He stilled and heat raced through her at the unexpected feel of the long, hard length beneath her fingers. She hadn't looked, hadn't realized that he was fully erect. Fully erect? That part of him seemed ready to break free of his trousers. How was that possible in the few minutes since he'd sat down?

He broke the kiss and lifted his face a bare inch from hers. Her throat went dry, but there was no turning back now. She massaged him.

"*Phoebe.*"

The rasp in his voice startled her, but she immediately understood the advantage and gently raked her nails along his rigid length.

"By God, Phoebe, if you keep that up—"

She raked her nails harder, and he covered her hand with his, flattening her palm over him. The steel rod pulsed. Yes, she had the advantage. This, according to Heddy, would bring a man to quick climax—and without any resistance on his part.

His gaze shifted from her face and he grasped both straps and eased them down to uncover her breasts. Cool air washed over her flesh, tightening her nipples. He drew a sharp breath and bent toward her. In the haze of confusion she was aware of the tickle of his hair on her cheek, then the flick of his tongue against—by heavens—her nipple. His hand still covered hers over the hard part of him, urging her to knead him. She complied and couldn't resist the desire to attempt to wrap her fingers around his shaft.

He shoved her hand aside and embarrassment washed over her. He had detected her inexperience. But Phoebe realized he was unfastening his trousers and, when he grasped her hand and brought it back to him, her fingers closed around his bare flesh. For an instant, she wondered if she would faint, but he sucked her nipple into his mouth and the pleasure caused her fingers to convulse around his rod. He groaned and she squeezed tighter.

He released her nipple and pressed his lips to her ear. "Hold me tight, love, as tight as you want. Then move like this."

To her shock, he guided her hand up and down in a slow pistoning motion. Down until his flesh pulled so tight she feared she would hurt him, then up until his penis nearly slipped from her grasp.

"Tighter, Phoebe," he urged.

"I-I don't want to hurt you, my lord."

He gave a husky chuckle that made her feel warm all over.

"You can't hurt me," he said. "In fact, you may abuse me all you like."

She squeezed tighter and continued the up and down motion. He slowly thrust into her hand as his teeth closed over her ear lobe. An unexpected picture rose of him thrusting inside her. She heard a whimper,

163

then realized the sound emanated from her. His hand cupped the juncture between her legs.

"*Sir.*"

"Turnabout is fair play, Phoebe. I would be no gentleman if I let you pleasure me while I did not return the favor. Now you keep on as you are and we'll both benefit, I promise."

Panic flooded her. Heddy had said men went insane when a woman touched them in this manner. Kiernan gently massaged her mound. Faster, she realized, she had to stroke him faster. That would bring him to a frenzy, and once he'd reached his pleasure they would be finished. She increased her speed on his erection.

"Slow down," he ordered.

Moisture on the tip of his shaft slicked her fingers. He ceased his attentions on her sex and she breathed a sigh of relief only to find he'd yanked her skirt to her thigh.

"Doesn't this please you?" she asked, and squeezed his erection on the up motion.

"It pleases me *too* much," he growled.

Then how was he able to think of touching her?

He slipped a hand beneath her skirt, and his warm fingers on the sensitive flesh of her inner thigh caused her to jump. The feather light tickle across the curls covering her sex startled her and her rhythm faltered. Good Lord, she had to take back the advantage. She grabbed him with her other hand, covering his member from tip to root.

"You vixen," he murmured.

In the next instant he had her skirt up around her waist.

"My lord," she cried.

"Hush," he commanded. "The maids have the hearing of gods."

He pushed her legs apart and shock immobilized her when his head descended and his mouth closed over the most intimate part of her where her drawers were open at the crotch. She squirmed in surprise, then drew a sharp breath at the pleasure that rippled through her. He wasn't—he couldn't be—he was. He was sucking and, dear God in heaven, she couldn't think. Pleasure shot through her. The sucking stopped, then his tongue thrust inside her.

"Dear Lord!"

"Quiet," he warned, then, "Keep your hold tight on me. That will bring you even greater pleasure."

She jammed the fingers of one hand into his hair, while the other hand gripped his erection. She yanked on his hair and he grunted, then began sucking again.

"My lord," she pleaded.

"Soon, love," he said against her flesh, all the while making her wild. The knowledge that his mouth was pressed intimately against her flesh warred with the notion that this was not supposed to happen.

Need coursed through her and Phoebe bucked in surprise. The friction of her movement against his mouth sent a compelling wave of longing through her and she shoved his face deeper between her legs. He laughed. She recalled somewhere in the distant part of her brain that she was supposed to be driving him insane with need, and she managed to squeeze him.

"Don't stop," he urged, and again began sucking.

Phoebe feared she would lose her mind. Somehow, the thick, hot male part of him she held incited her lust. Then his finger slipped inside her. Strange sensations radiated within her channel. He thrust quickly and her body seized in a spasm of blinding pleasure. His hand encircled hers with an iron grip that squeezed his rod. He groaned and sucked her harder. Another spasm rocked her and she bucked.

"Damnation," he cursed.

The room blurred around her.

"Phoebe," he rasped, and she realized he had shoved her hand aside. Kiernan gripped his shaft and pumped his seed onto the blanket beside her. He unexpectedly grabbed the edge of the blanket and made a quick swipe of his penis. "I should have hired the damn chaperone," he muttered.

"What?" she said.

"I imagine he wanted to get back to Phoebe." Her uncle's voice came from the hallway.

Phoebe bolted upright.

"If you're looking for His Lordship," Brenda said, "I saw him go into his chambers earlier, Your Grace."

Phoebe drew a sharp breath.

"If you wanted my father and your uncle to call a minister to marry us this instant, you've done it," Kiernan whispered. "We may need that special license after all — if your uncle *and* my father don't murder me."

He yanked her skirt down.

"I believe I'll return to the party," Lord Albery said.

"I'll be down directly," Kiernan's father replied.

"Get down on the other side of the bed," Kiernan ordered Phoebe.

"He's bound to notice your..." She glanced meaningfully at his groin.

"No." he yanked his trousers up over his nearly flaccid cock. "You saw to that."

Her cheeks reddened, and he was torn between laughter and wanting to paddle her bottom. She had sneaked into his room and let him do to her what even some mistresses wouldn't allow, then blushed at the fact that she had gotten him off with a bang that nearly brought him to his knees.

165

He wasn't certain what his future wife was doing snooping in his bedchambers, but he was reasonably certain seduction hadn't been on the agenda. His plan had been just as foolhardy. He intended to give her a good scare. But the devil had gotten into her and she'd managed to make him forget good sense, as well as his promise to his father. Well, not quite, but his father was sure to see no distinction between bedding a lady true and proper and fucking her with his tongue.

"The other side of the bed," Kiernan ordered, and hurried to the door.

With a careful turn, he unlocked the door and hoped like hell his father hadn't heard the tiny click. He whirled. Phoebe was out of view and, in four long strides, Kiernan reached the secretary on the left wall.

He landed in the desk chair and yanked papers from the drawer in the instant before the door opened. He waited an instant as if breaking from deep concentration, then looked at his father.

"What are you doing?" he asked.

"This letter from Harris has weighed on my mind."

"Harris informed me that the cottages will be rebuilt by month's end. He can manage the project. You have other matters to deal with."

Kiernan wondered how Phoebe liked being referred to as 'other matters.' How much of his conversation with his father and her uncle had she overheard before ducking into his room? He was relatively certain that's where she'd been, then got trapped when the maids arrived on this floor. His father stepped into the room and closed the door behind him. Kiernan silently cursed. His father would pick now to discuss something private. Kiernan rose, hoping to forestall him saying something neither of them wanted overheard. He was going to have to tell Phoebe the truth about his involvement with Clachair, but he hoped to hear from the man first.

"Send the maids to the kitchen on some errand," his father said.

Kiernan stilled. This was a strange order. "As you wish, Father."

"And, Kiernan."

"Yes?"

"Please inform Miss Wallington that I see no reason for a year's engagement. I am certain her uncle will agree."

Kiernan canted his head in acknowledgement and his father left— leaving the door wide open. Kiernan started forward, then his gaze caught on Phoebe's comb on the bed.

Chapter Sixteen

Phoebe leaned back in the chair at her secretary and opened the note from Kiernan, his second missive in as many days.

> *Phoebe,*
>
> *I left word to have this small wedding gift forwarded to you if it arrived while I was away. There will be many more gifts forthcoming — Elise looks for every excuse to give gifts. She tells me she plans to spend time with you while my father and I are away — again, I apologize, but our business in Suffolk simply can't wait. I hope this book gives you something to do until my return.*
>
> *Kiernan*

She reread the line: *I hope this book gives you something to do until my return.* In other words, *if you're busy reading, you'll stay out of trouble.* Confound the man's arrogance. He'd seen her in a bookstore and decided he could manipulate her with a book. Phoebe pulled the large package from the desk and unwrapped the paper to reveal three leather-bound books inside a leather-trimmed box. She drew a sharp breath at sight of the author and title: *Frankenstein, Mary Shelley.* Carefully, she pulled volume one from the box and turned to the title page.

> *London*
> *Printed for Lackington, Hughes, Harding, Mavor, & Jones Finsbury Square*
> *1818*

She brushed her fingers over the date, 1818. An early edition. She'd underestimated Kiernan MacGregor. He knew exactly what he was doing — and could all-too-easily succeed in distracting her. If that distraction didn't work, he'd arranged for Elise to spend time with her while he was gone. This explained the duchess' appearance on her doorstep yesterday, less than an hour after Phoebe sent word that she would leave for Scotland the next day. She hadn't been surprised when the duchess protested in favor of waiting for the men to return. Phoebe's assurance that she would go alone brought a knowing smile to Elise's face, and she said, *"Actually, it's a fine idea. After all, they will likely catch up with us on the road."*

Phoebe gently inserted the book back into the box. She hoped the men would be gone long enough for her and the duchess to reach Scotland...and for Phoebe to catch her breath. Two days had passed since the *interlude* with Kiernan and she couldn't seem to regain her equilibrium. It seems the duchess had been correct. God help her, Kiernan MacGregor was, indeed, an experienced lover. A tender lover, damn his soul, and Phoebe had only tasted of his talents. She shivered as she had a hundred times since that night, the feel of his rigid staff between her fingers still so real...the memory of his tongue inside her—Molly appeared in the open doorway of Phoebe's bedchamber.

"The duchess' coach has arrived, Miss."

"Thank you, Molly. This trunk is ready. Please inform Gaylon."

"Are you all right?" the maid asked.

She smiled. "Distracted. I'm fine."

Molly left and Phoebe gathered her reticule, the two books she had purchased, and her cloak, then made her way to the parlor where the duchess and her aunt waited.

Elise smiled. "I hope I'm not too early."

"Not at all. Gaylon should have my trunks loaded right away." She sat on the sofa beside her aunt.

"Phoebe," Lady Albery said, "are you sure you won't change your mind and wait until Lord Ashlund returns?"

"We've discussed this, Aunt. My uncle has afforded four men as escort in addition to Calders. Plus, we have the duchess' entourage. We're quite safe."

"You really should take Molly with you," Lady Albery continued.

"No thank you. As I said, I'm not accustomed to traveling with a maid, so I won't miss her."

"Don't worry," the duchess said, "I have Sue. She can deal very nicely with the both of us."

Lady Albery tsked, but Phoebe only nodded and wondered how much time she'd have in Scotland before her nemesis caught up with her.

Three quarters of an hour later, they drove through the gate, leaving her aunt waving a woeful handkerchief.

"Are you and your aunt close?" Elise asked.

"No," Phoebe replied. "Though, the way she has acted these last few days, one would think she was losing a daughter."

"Yes, one would." Elise smiled. "So, we're off. I can't tell you how pleased I am to have you visit Ashlund. We're going to have a wonderful time."

"Where exactly is Ashlund?"

"Two hours north of Edinburgh."

"Not in the Highlands then?" Phoebe asked.

Elise shook her head. "No. It's another two hour ride before you enter the southernmost part of the Highlands. Tell me, did you like Brahan Seer?"

"I did. The castle is beautiful and Loch Katrine is spectacular."

"Yes," Elise smiled, "it is magnificent. Marcus and I spend a great deal of time there. Though, with the education of the twins, we don't stay as long as we used to." She sighed. "I would prefer they received their education there, but my husband insists they receive a formal education in Edinburgh."

"Is that where Lord Ashlund studied?" Phoebe asked.

"No, he studied at Oxford, which is why Ethan is to study at the university in Edinburgh."

"Ethan?"

"Our son. Our daughter is Jacqueline."

"I see, and what does Lord Ashlund having studied in Oxford have to do with your son studying in Edinburgh?"

A twinkle entered Elise's eyes. "Marcus feels one son educated by the English is enough. I know what you're thinking," she went on. "He has an American wife and his future daughter-in-law is English."

"Ma'am, I would never say such a thing," Phoebe demurred.

"It's not all English he dislikes," the duchess said with a laugh in her voice, "only the ones who attempt to give MacGregor land to their English kinsmen. Of course, the Scottish crown has been known to do the same."

"It's a wonder the MacGregors aren't homeless, one and all," Phoebe said.

"Many are," Elise replied.

"Your Grace, forgive me, I forgot—"

"It isn't your history, Phoebe. We have many good books on Highland history in Ashlund. If you are interested, I'm sure Kiernan will take you to visit many of the places where historical events took place." She grimaced. "Beware, though, it's likely to turn into a long journey. You'll soon learn that every road in the Highlands is famous for some battle or another."

Phoebe glanced at Elise, whose tired face said three days in a carriage and now horseback had taken its toll.

"Perhaps we should stop at the next inn?" Phoebe said.

169

"Oh no," Elise replied. "It is just past five o'clock. The horses have been in their traces for a mere two hours. Do you mind riding at night? It'll be dark soon."

"Not at all." The guards who rode with them could withstand the chill, but the duchess had her cloak wrapped tightly about her. "Though, the night is cold."

"Would you prefer the carriage?"

Phoebe shook her head. "No, ma'am. To be honest, only pouring rain or snow can compel me to ride inside a carriage when I have a good mount. I was thinking of you."

Elise smiled. "I'm of the same mind. If we are to reach Ashlund by the end of the week, we must stay on course." She sighed. "It's good to be in Scotland again. I made arrangements for accommodations with cousins. They are only two hours away."

"How is it you were able to arrange lodging at so late a date?"

Elise gave her a reproachful look and Phoebe knew she was, again, being reprimanded for being so formal. *Time will solve your dilemma, Phoebe,* she had said the day they'd left London. *You'll soon grow tired of the formality in your own family.*

"I sent word the night you informed me you wanted to leave," Elise said.

"You're sure they won't mind?"

"Quite sure."

"If you—by heavens." Phoebe drew a sharp breath at sight of an overturned coach that came into view around the bend. The vehicle lay on its side, wheels spinning. "Calders," she called, but he yelled, "Whoa!" and pulled back on the carriage reins.

There was a shriek from their coach and Phoebe realized Sue had been take unawares by the sudden stop. Donald, who rode ahead of them, along with Niall, Elise's private guard, kicked their horses into a gallop. Phoebe dug her heels into her mount and followed. The men arrived at the fallen carriage and vaulted from their saddles. An instant later Phoebe arrived at the overturned coach.

"Dear God," she exclaimed at sight of the wheeler's hind feet pinned by the carriage tongue.

His front hooves were curled up and his belly pressed to the road. His head was turned back as the driver worked to loose the animal, talking softly as another man straddled his neck trying to prevent his struggles from inflicting further damage. Phoebe noted the horses badly skinned hind legs. If he lived, there would be swelling and serious bruises.

Phoebe leapt from her saddle as Elise arrived with the coach close behind. Calders halted a safe distance behind the downed vehicle, tossed the reins to the livery, then jumped to the ground.

"Is the wheeler all right?" Phoebe called to the man who stood some feet away, calming the second horse.

The man nodded.

"Where are the other—" She spotted two horses standing side by side just within over of the thickening forest.

"We've got to get the harness off and lift the tongue," cried the man who worked to loose the fallen horse.

Donald and Niall rushed to the front of the carriage and Phoebe followed.

"Ye havena' got a knife, man?" Niall demanded. Without waiting for an answer, he whipped a dagger from his boot, bent, and, in one swift slice, cut the harness. He then swung around and straddled the tongue, facing the horse. Squatting, he took a deep breath and gripped the wood. With a great heave, he rose slowly, lifting the tongue. The carriage creaked and a moan came from the compartment.

"For God's sake, man," Niall said in a strained whisper, "get the beast out."

The man on the horse's neck jumped off and the other man urged the horse up. The horse gave a low whinny and struggled to his feet. The driver drew him away from the carriage. Slowly, Niall lowered the tongue. The instant it touched the ground, Calders jumped onto the side of the coach. Niall leapt over the tongue and bound up beside him so fast, Phoebe blinked.

"A beast of a man," she murmured.

"Precisely the reason my husband insists he accompany me everywhere I go." Elise stepped forward and, placing her palms on the coach, craned her neck in order to see inside the compartment.

Niall glanced over her shoulder. "Your Grace." He ceased yanking on the carriage door and jumped lightly to the ground. Phoebe's mouth fell open and she stepped back when he lifted the duchess bodily from the ground and set her back away from the carriage.

"Dinna' come any closer," he admonished as if talking to a child.

"Niall," Elise threw her cloak over her shoulders, "out of my way."

"Nay, Your Grace," he replied. "His Grace wouldna' allow you near the carriage and neither can I."

A loud creak drew Phoebe's attention back to the carriage. Donald stood atop the vehicle, where and he and Calders managed to wrench the door open. Donald lowered himself inside the coach.

"The lass first," he called up. Calders squatted, lifted the woman from the doorway, then motioned for Niall to take her.

"Dinna' move, Your Grace," Niall ordered, and returned to the carriage.

Calders gently lowered the woman into his arms, and Phoebe and Elise hurried alongside as Niall strode several paces from the carriage. He laid the woman in the wet grass and Elise went to her knees beside her, pressed an ear at her chest, then looked up at Phoebe.

"A strong heartbeat. Quick, there's a bottle of water in the carriage, and smelling salts in my reticule."

Phoebe started to turn, but Sue shouted from the carriage door, "I'll get it."

An instant later, Sue returned with the salts and water. Niall and Calders approached, the gentleman who had been inside the carriage slouched between them, an arm slung over each of their shoulders. They lowered him to the ground next to the woman. He remained upright and pressed his palm against his forehead.

"My wife," the man whispered.

"She'll live," Elise said, and took the smelling salts Sue held out and opened them beneath the woman's nose. The woman turned her head aside, but Elise kept the salts beneath her nose.

"Douglas," the woman moaned, again turning her head away from the smelling salts.

Elise brought the bottle even closer to her nose. The woman's eyes opened and she tried to sit up. "No, no," Elise said, holding her down. "Phoebe, wet a handkerchief."

Phoebe retrieved a handkerchief from her pocket, wet it with the water Sue had brought, then handed it to Elise.

"What happened?" the woman demanded, then said in a frantic voice, "My husband."

"It's all right, Andrea," Douglas said, "I'm here."

She gave a small cry and reached for him.

The short, stout man gave her a crooked smile. "Quite all right, my dear." He squeezed her hand.

Elise began wiping Andrea's forehead.

"Where is Gerald?" Andrea asked.

Douglas glanced at the men who inspected the horse that had been pinned. "He is well, my dear. It looks as though he was able to save the horse." Douglas looked up at Niall, who stood over the group. "Is there any sign of the other two horses?"

"They're not far." Niall pointed to the trees to the right of the carriage. "I saw them in the forest."

"Round them up," Elise said.

Niall nodded to Donald, who took off in the direction of the horses.

"What happened?" Phoebe asked.

"We hit a hole earlier in the day," Douglas replied. "When we stopped at the inn just down the road, they were supposed to have checked the wheels. The driver was sure he felt some unsteadiness in the rear, right wheel."

"You're lucky it was a front wheel that came off," Phoebe said.

172

"Indeed," he agreed. "Though, if those fools at the inn had done their job properly we wouldn't have needed luck. Damn it—pardon me ladies." He inclined his head in apology, then cleared his throat and went on. "We were moving along at a nice trot when I heard a shriek from one of the horses. The next thing, the coach lurched and we went over."

"We had better see to the repair of that wheel," Phoebe said, then stopped and looked at Elise. "Provided, that is all right with you, Your Grace."

"Your Grace!" Douglas burst out. He began struggling to his feet.

"Please," Elise said, "don't move until our men can assist you."

"Come on, man," Niall said to Calders. "Let's see to the wheel." The two strode toward the carriage as Andrea sat up.

"Oh dear," she said. "Your Grace, you must forgive us, we had no idea."

Elise patted Andrea's arm. "You've done nothing that requires my forgiveness." She cast a sidelong glance at Phoebe, then leaned close and murmured, "Perhaps this will teach you to call me by name."

Phoebe's eyes widened in surprise, but she managed to stifle the mirth.

"Lord Douglas Ingersol at your service, Your Grace," Douglas said and again attempted to gain his feet.

Donald returned and Elise nodded to him.

"Help Lord Ingersol to his feet, please." She looked at Douglas. "Let's get you two into our carriage. It's nearly dark. We have no idea how long the repairs will take and there's no need for us to sit on the wet ground."

A few minutes later, Lord and Lady Ingersol, along with Elise, were tucked safely into the carriage. Phoebe went to the fallen carriage to see how the repairs fared.

"It doesn't look as though we'll be able to make repairs on the wheel here," Calders informed her.

"The night is clear and the moon full," Phoebe said. "There isn't enough light?"

"The wheel is cracked. It'll have to be repaired, or perhaps even replaced."

She nodded. "I'll tell the duchess." Phoebe hurried to the carriage. She opened the door and surveyed the occupants. "Niall and Calders inform me the wheel is cracked. The repairs can't be done here."

Elise looked at Lord Ingersol. "It seems we must leave your carriage here. We'll have the wheel repaired and send Niall back with your men to bring it onward. The Orwell Inn is forty-five minutes ahead. We will stop there for the night."

"Your Grace," Lady Ingersol said, "we can't impose upon you."

"Our men can deal with the repairs," Lord Ingersol said. "You needn't bother yourself any further."

"Nonsense," Elise said, "we'll make sure the carriage is brought safely to the inn this evening." She addressed Phoebe. "Do you know how much longer we'll be?"

"Not long, I think. The horses are rounded up and Niall is loading the wheel. It looks as if your wheeler isn't seriously injured."

Lord Ingersol looked relieved. "A good horse," he said. "I would have hated losing him."

"I'll have your trunks loaded onto our carriage and check on how much longer we'll be," Phoebe said.

"If they can hurry?" Elise said, and Phoebe nodded, then turned away and started for the other carriage where the men were already retrieving the trunks.

The company rode at a trot, Phoebe on horseback with the men. She regretted the little time they would lose by stopping at the inn, but after the time spent rescuing Lord and Lady Ingersol there was no question of pressing on. Perhaps they might leave early enough in the morning to recover some of the lost time. Phoebe jarred from her thoughts when she realized that Niall had pulled his pistol from his waistband, even as she registered a rustle of leaves somewhere beyond the road. She wheeled around in unison with Niall to face the approaching rider.

"Halt," growled Niall, his weapon aimed at the rider as he broke from the forest.

A cry went up from Calders, who had clearly spotted the newcomer, and Donald rounded the carriage.

The duchess' carriage door swung open. "Phoebe," Elise's called. "Niall, what's happening?"

"By heavens." Phoebe stared at the newcomer as he cleared the forest and moonlight illuminated his face. "What is he doing here?"

Chapter Seventeen

"Don't shoot," Phoebe cried. "I know this man."

Niall didn't move a muscle. "Come forward ye bloody fool," he said. "I'm not inclined to heed the lady until I see your weapon on the ground."

Phoebe groaned. This is what an Englishman got for stepping onto Scottish soil. "Adam," she called, "what in God's name are you doing here?"

Adam reached into his coat.

"Careful," Niall warned, and Adam opened his coat, revealing the pistol stuffed into his waistcoat. He lifted the weapon with forefinger and thumb and tossed it to the ground.

Calders came to a halt next to Niall. "What's he doing here?"

"You've no other pistol?" demanded Niall.

"No," Adam replied.

Phoebe whipped her head around at hearing someone alight from the carriage and saw it was the duchess. Lord Ingersol stepped from the carriage behind her, leaving his wife and Sue crowded in the doorway peering out.

"What's going on here?" Ingersoll asked as if he were in charge. "Do you know this man?"

Phoebe ignored him and turned back to the duchess' men. "Niall, put away your weapon. I've known this man since the schoolroom. Satisfy yourself that you've taught him not to sneak up on a carriage traveling at night. And you, Adam, thank God for a full moon or I might have shot you myself. Why are you skulking about in the forest?"

"I didn't care for this bend in the road," he replied. "If I encounter a highwayman, I prefer being the one to catch him off guard."

"It didn't occur to you that if you were to catch me off guard I might shoot you?"

"You didn't."

Phoebe rolled her eyes. "What are you doing here?"

Elise approached. "Is that Mr. Branbury?"

"It is," Phoebe replied, and started toward him.

He dismounted and came forward, meeting her halfway. "Phoebe," he said, and she heard the tender note in his voice and realized his intent.

"Oh, Adam, you're only causing yourself pain by coming here."

"Phoebe," he began again, then looked at the crowd gathered. "Over here," he motioned toward his horse, "I'd like a private moment."

"Quite inappropriate," Ingersol muttered.

"Phoebe," Elise called. "Perhaps Mr. Branbury would care to join us at the inn?"

"Forgive the intrusion, Your Grace," Adam gave a gallant bow.

"Indeed," Elise said, surprising Phoebe with her icy tone. "Lord Ashlund won't appreciate his future wife being waylaid on the road."

"Phoebe and I are close friends," he replied. "I would die to protect her honor."

Elise raised a brow. "You damage her honor by insisting upon privacy."

Even in the muted light of the moon, Phoebe saw his face redden.

"Here here, now," Lord Ingersol came forward, "if the young lady is engaged to another man, what right have you to be bothering her?"

Adam stiffened and looked pleadingly at Elise. "It is of the utmost importance that I speak with Phoebe. I will keep her but a moment."

"Phoebe," Elise began, but Phoebe stopped her.

"Your Grace, Adam is an old friend. I owe him, at the very least, a moment of my time. We will only be a few feet away. Rest assured, Mr. Branbury's intentions are honorable." She turned and started toward the trees. "Don't dally, Adam," she said in a whisper. "One of them is bound to protest in earnest at any second."

Adam hastened to follow her.

When they reached the edge of the tress, Phoebe whirled. "What in God's name is wrong with you?"

"Phoebe—"

"No," she said, "don't bother explaining, it's quite clear why you're here, not only to me, but to every person standing over there."

"I had no idea there would be such an entourage. Phoebe." He took her hand in his.

"Please, Adam, don't do this." She tried to pull free, but he held tight and took a step deeper into the trees.

He stopped within the shadows and blurted, "We could reach Gretna Green in a few hours."

"Adam—" she started, but the despair in his voice halted the intended retort. "Adam," she said more softly, and squeezed his hand, "you worry me. I've never seen you like this."

"Desperation drives a man."

A strange pang went through her. "I have never misled you."

"There was a time…"

"Once, yes, but we were young. How often have I explained it was infatuation?"

"You deemed it infatuation after reading your father's letter," he retorted.

Phoebe stiffened. Adam and Alistair were the only two people who knew about the letter. She regretted both.

"I care for you. Adam, but you go too far." She added in frustration, "For God's sake, why force me to hurt you? I have always been honest with you."

He dropped her hand as if he held hot coals. "Honest with me? You're not honest with yourself. How am I to believe you are capable of being honest with me?"

"You have the most abominable way of making me wish I had shot you."

"How does your future husband feel about your quest, Phoebe?" Adam demanded, and she was startled to realize how much he knew about her. Worse, how obvious she'd been in regards to her feelings about her father.

"I have had enough." She whirled, but he caught her arm.

"Oh, no you don't. Answer me."

An instant of silence passed.

"I'll be damned," he breathed. "You haven't told him."

She jerked her arm free and turned to go.

"That's unfair, don't you think?" he snapped. "Doesn't the poor fellow have the right to know your heart belongs to another man?"

Phoebe whirled. "How dare you?"

"Phoebe," Adam said, his voice suddenly soft, "I know what your father means to you. Fool that I am, I would share you with him. Can your new love say that?"

"Why are you doing this?" she asked. "I can change nothing."

"You know why. I love—"

The deafening roar of a shot rang out and Adam staggered backward a pace.

"Adam?"

Phoebe stood frozen for an instant, confused, then, lunged toward him. She grabbed his outstretched hand. He gripped her fingers, then his hold slackened and he slumped against her. His knees buckled and Phoebe caught him, his weight dragging her down with him. They landed together, her on her knees, him cradled in her arms.

Adam grasped her hand. "Phoebe." The word was a mere whisper.

Something warm spread across her abdomen and she touched the sticky substance seeping from his chest.

He grabbed her shoulder, dragging her face closer to his. "I'm sorry."

"No, no, quiet," she said through tears.

"I—" Adam coughed hard "—love—"

He went limp.

"Adam." She felt for a heartbeat, her hand wet with blood, but found no pulse thrumming against his neck. "Dear God. Adam. No!"

An unexpected sound penetrated her mind. The pounding of boots on ground? Phoebe looked up, barely able to focus on the two men who skidded to a halt beside her. She hugged Adam, ignoring the iron grip on her arm. She shook the hand off, then glanced sharply up. The drawn pistol the man held registered in her brain.

"Why?" she cried, and lunged for his weapon.

"Phoebe!" Kiernan jerked the pistol aside, sending the shot into the darkness. "Mather!" he shouted as Phoebe wrestled for the gun.

"I'm all right, sir," he called. "You missed me by at least an inch."

Phoebe's grip slipped and Kiernan's chest clenched at the realization that the slick warmth on her hands was blood. He wrenched the pistol free of her grasp, then stuffed it into his waistband and went down on his knees beside her.

"*Phoebe*." He gripped her shoulders. "Are you hurt—did he hurt you? Who is he?"

"Miss!" a man called from the edge of the trees.

"Phoebe." Kiernan felt her face, her neck and down her bodice, but found no wound or blood soaked fabric. His mind raced. Had the man she still hugged been shot? "What happened?" Kiernan demanded.

The noisy pounding of feet on the ground was followed by Elise calling, "Phoebe," as she hurried into view.

"Back, Duchess," Niall shouted, and shoved past her, then stopped. "Laird?"

Phoebe looked at his stepmother. "Elise, I—he—"

With one hand, Kiernan crushed Phoebe as close as he could, given that she kept a tenacious hold on the man. With the other hand, he felt for a pulse on the man's neck. Nothing. Two other men appeared beside Niall.

"Phoebe," Kiernan said, but she shook her head violently. He grabbed her to lift her, but she struck out at him.

"No," she cried, but he yanked her up. The man slid from her lap. "Adam." Phoebe clutched at him as Kiernan lifted her into his arms.

He hugged her, pressing her face into the crook of his neck. Hot and wet, her tears bathed his skin. "Bring him," Kiernan ordered Mather.

Mather hoisted Adam over his shoulder.

"Duchess," Niall said, and she led the way past the onlookers out onto the road.

Kiernan headed for their coach.

A woman standing near the carriage shrank back as he passed. "She shot him," she gasped an instant later when Mather appeared carrying the dead man.

Calders ran ahead and opened the carriage door for Kiernan.

"Goodness," Sue exclaimed, and scooted away from Kiernan. "What—"

"Get out," he ordered.

The girl's eyes widened and her gaze flicked to the blood that stained his shirt and Phoebe's bodice. She scrambled from the carriage and Kiernan stepped into the compartment. Elise followed, slamming the door behind her.

"What the bloody hell is going on?" he demanded, settling back and enfolding Phoebe closer.

Elise shook her head. "I'm not sure. Phoebe was speaking with Mr. Branbury. Suddenly, there was a shot and," she looked anxiously at Phoebe, whose crying had softened, "and the next thing we knew, we saw you with her. What happened?"

"I'm as confused as you. I was following the carriage with the intention of catching up not long after you left the inn, but I found tracks that led off the road. I became concerned it was highwaymen. This Branbury—Adam—what was he doing here?"

Phoebe gripped the lapels of Kiernan's coat. "Why? Why?" she demanded.

"Shh, love." Kiernan stroked her hair. He looked at Elise. "What the hell was she doing with him?"

"We tried to stop her. It was clear he had come to talk her out of marrying you."

"And you didn't stop her?" he snarled, then, "Bloody hell. Forgive me, Elise."

"Never mind," she said. "I met Mr. Branbury at Shyerton Hall. He didn't seem violent. Did he try to force her to go with him?"

Phoebe abruptly sat up and tried to shove from Kiernan's lap.

"No." He held her tight.

"Release me," she hissed, and batted at his chest with a vehemence that startled him.

Kiernan hesitated, then complied. She flung herself to the seat across from him, beside Elise.

"Why—" A sob broke past her lips.

"Phoebe." He leaned forward.

"Don't." She scooted to the corner away from him.

Kiernan exchanged a confused look with Elise.

"You didn't shoot him?" Phoebe asked, her voice little more than a whisper.

"Damnation, of course not. Why would I?"

"Perhaps you thought the situation was something it wasn't?"

"Such as?"

"If you thought he was a lover."

"If you wanted him, I wouldn't have stopped you," Kiernan replied. "You assured me you'd known him since childhood, but weren't interested in him."

"You didn't know who he was. You once told me I could come as go as I please, so long as I had *no secret assignation.*"

Kiernan pulled the pistol from his waistband and extended it toward her, butt first. "You heard the single shot. There was no time for a reload."

Phoebe's mouth twisted. "That is not the only pistol you own."

He stuffed the gun back into his waistband. "Do you honestly think I shot him?"

"Kiernan," Elise said in a calm voice.

He looked at her, then returned his gaze to Phoebe. "I assumed you shot him in self-defense."

Phoebe lifted her chin. "Adam would never hurt me."

Kiernan raised a brow. "This is the same Adam you said tried to kidnap you the night I kidnapped you?"

"He didn't send those men."

"How can you be so sure?"

Phoebe turned her head aside.

"Miss Wallington," he snapped. Her eyes jerked to meet his and his heart wrenched at the pain he read on her face. He reached into his coat pocket and produced a handkerchief. "Here, take this."

She glanced at his hand, took the handkerchief, then blew her nose. "Adam's response when I mentioned that night proved he knew nothing." She wiped her eyes. "I have never known him to lie. In fact, I thought it was him only because I could think of no one else, but kidnapping isn't in his nature. He was—" she hiccupped a small sob and Kiernan felt his heart constrict "—he was as you saw him tonight." Tears streamed down her face. "He came here, faced the wrath of a duchess, to beg me once again to marry him." She lifted her chin. "I wasn't *in* love with him, but I did love him."

"Listen to me." Kiernan scooted to the side and slid forward so that his legs were on each side of hers. "I didn't shoot him. Listen," he emphasized, when she shook her head and looked away, "I did not shoot him." He paused, then said softly, "If you shot him, I know it was self-defense." Her eyes widened, but he went on. "You needn't worry about telling me the truth."

"You bastard." She raised her hand and Kiernan caught her arm mid-swing.

He held her gaze. "All right, then, who shot him?"

She looked as if he had slapped her. "I—" Her brow knit in confusion.

Kiernan released her hand and looked at Elise. "Who are the strangers?"

"Their carriage—"

"Yes," he interrupted impatiently, "I saw that. Do you know who they are?"

"Lord and Lady Ingersol," she replied.

"Are you acquainted with them?"

"No. But it couldn't have been them. They were with me when the shot was fired."

"What about the men in their party?" Kiernan asked.

Startlement washed over Elise's features. "We were all outside. I didn't want to return to the carriage until Phoebe returned. I saw them step into the trees, but never dreamed—Oh, Kiernan," tears sprang to her eyes, "I'm so sorry."

"Please, Elise," he said, "keep your wits about you."

"Yes." She nodded and swiped at her tears with the back of her hand. "Of course."

He looked again at Phoebe. "You're sure—"

"I did not shoot him," she snapped. "I'm not even carrying a weapon."

That was true—or, at least, he hadn't seen a weapon. He had to search the area.

Phoebe burst into tears again. "Where is he? Dear God, we left him out there."

"We didn't leave him out there. Mather brought him." Her eyes widened, and he said, "I will see to him. Elise." He looked meaningfully at her, and she nodded.

Elise wrapped an arm around Phoebe and pulled her close. "Come, Phoebe," she soothed as Kiernan opened the door. "That's it, yes. Cry all you like." And he clicked the door closed behind him.

Despite Phoebe's objections, he held her. She fought it, fought him. Not outwardly, for he made it clear her efforts were useless, but from within. She fought to shrink from the arm resting reassuringly on her hip, fought to ignore the rise and fall of the chest he pressed her face against. He had taken off his greatcoat and wrapped it around her. Her cheek lay against the soft linen of his shirt and her senses swirled with the smell of him. The scent of Sandalwood she had noticed that first night he appeared in her carriage. Despite the stink of Adam's blood on his shirt, Kiernan smelled as though he had just bathed. His scent comforted—but she despised the comfort—oh, how she despised it. How much comfort was Adam—she sobbed and Kiernan's arms tightened around her.

"Shh, love," he whispered so softly she knew neither Elise nor Sue could have heard even in the close confines of the carriage. "We're nearly there." He smoothed her hair and Phoebe melted into a river of dreams.

It seemed she had slept a lifetime, yet she felt as if her eyes had only just closed. Phoebe was aware of arms lifting her. She looked up, her sight catching the angular jut of a man's jaw. She reached to touch a lock of raven hair that curled where neck met shoulder, but stopped when the roof of the carriage gave way to a clear night sky. She blinked up into the light of a full moon and nestled into the crook of Kiernan's neck when cool air rushed across her face.

So quiet here. Phoebe opened her eyes. She lay on a bed in a room she didn't recognize. Still, something in the flicker of light cast by the fire in the hearth sent a ripple of security through her. She gazed in wonder at the sea green canopy that draped the bed before again closing her eyes.

Voices, soft, murmured nearby. Had she slept? Her head turned toward the sound as though it was a mechanical object controlled by something other than her will. Phoebe opened her eyes and saw only the blur of objects. A figure moved toward her and sat on the bed beside her. She tilted to the side toward the weight on the mattress. She focused on the figure, trying to understand the sense of familiarity she felt.

"Uncle?" Phoebe said and reached up to touch his face.

"Shh," he replied. "Sleep." A tiny strand of hair was brushed back from her face. "It won't be long now," he said. "Sleep while you can."

And she did.

"Phoebe."

Her name came to her as though an echo from a distant canyon.

"Phoebe."

Large hands grasped her shoulders. She tensed, then relaxed upon understanding the gentleness in the touch. She felt a little shake to her body.

"Phoebe, wake up. It's time."

Time? She tried to recall a forgotten appointment.

"Wake up." The voice grew more insistent.

Phoebe opened her eyes and blinked into the face above her.

"This isn't what I had planned," he was saying. "Not what you had planned, I know. But so much more than your reputation is at stake now."

"Reputation," she repeated groggily.

"Yes."

"Ashlund." She slowly wrapped her fingers around the wrist gripping her shoulder. *Flesh and blood.* Indeed, he was with her in this unfamiliar place.

"Yes," he said. "Can you get up?"

"Must I?"

He broke into a brief smile and she realized his brow had been furrowed in a fierce frown.

"You must. Though, I promise you a good bed once we are—"

"What time is it?" she interrupted.

"Five-thirty."

Phoebe glanced at the curtained window and detected no sunlight. She frowned. "I slept an entire day away?"

"You haven't, sweetheart. It is five-thirty in the morning."

"Morning?" She sat up, forcing him back as he released her. The room spun around her. She tried to focus on him. "What are you doing in my chambers at this ungodly hour? Is this my bedchamber?" she added more to herself than him, glancing down to find she was dressed in nothing but a shift. "Rather improper, you being here."

Kiernan took her hand in his. "Propriety is of little consequence at this point."

"I beg your pardon." Her stomach gave a lurch to match the dizziness in her head. "My agreeing to come to Scotland gives you no rights to my bed."

A tender smile touched his mouth. "I know. The necessity of what lays ahead is what forces me to overstep the boundaries of gentlemanly behavior. I pray you'll forgive me. We have a trip ahead of us, but it's what awaits us there I have come to explain." He gave her an odd look, then said, "Is the idea of marriage to me really so appalling?"

"Marriage? Why the devil are we discussing marriage at five—" Badgering her in the dawn hours was going too far. She kicked. He grasped her shoulders and forced her back against the pillows.

"Phoebe," he said, his voice firm, his expression now burning with a fervor that startled her. "Do you remember what happened last night?"

"I—dear God." She stilled. "Is Adam really dead?"

"Yes."

She stared at him, her breathing heavy. "*You.*"

He shook his head. "We have been over this. I had a single pistol."

"But you could have—"

"When have you known me to carry more than a single weapon?"

That stopped her. She recalled that first night when he had waylaid her. "*Never thought I'd need more than one shot,*" he had said. And he hadn't even shot those men...had he?

She focused on him. "Who?" Her voice caught. "Why?"

"I don't know. I didn't know the man, remember?"

She flushed. "I never dreamed he would —" Tears threatened again.

"I know." Kiernan squeezed her shoulder, then released her. "Up." He pulled her into a sitting position. "As hard as it may be to believe, we have a larger problem at the moment."

He stood and Phoebe swung her feet over the edge of the bed. She pulled the blanket around her shoulders. "What could possibly be worse?"

"Lord and Lady Ingersol."

"What of them?" she croaked, keeping her eyes on the floor in an effort to slow the dizziness.

He regarded her for a moment, "You remember nothing of the evening?"

She jerked her head up. "Lord Ashlund. I shall remember it for the rest of my life."

"Afterwards," he insisted. "Do you remember what happened after I arrived?"

Phoebe thought for a moment. "You took me to the carriage. The duchess was there. You had a pistol."

"The one that fired when you grabbed it."

"Yes."

Kiernan sat down beside her. "Lord and Lady Ingersol believe you killed Branbury."

"What?" she exclaimed. "That's ridiculous."

"Forgive me, my dear, but it is not a farfetched notion."

"I would never harm him."

"Consider how it looks."

Phoebe opened her mouth to argue, but muttered instead, "By heavens."

He smiled. "Never fear, I will remedy the situation."

"I don't see — oh no." She shook her finger at him. "No you don't."

"*Phoebe.*"

She jumped to her feet only to have the room spin in a violent circle about her. In the next instant, Kiernan's arms encircled her.

"Easy, sweetheart," he said, holding her steady against him.

Phoebe nearly fell into his solid warmth and she didn't resist when her held he tighter. The strong thump of his heart forced the rise and fall of his chest against her cheek. Eyes closed, she breathed deep of his familiar scent. Memory rushed forward of the carriage ride last night and —

"The highwayman." She yanked her head back and looked up at him.

He stroked her hair. "What?"

"You told the duchess that you were following someone who you feared might be a highwayman intent upon waylaying us. What did you find? Oh, my lord, this man could be the killer."

"He very well could be. Unfortunately, I didn't find him."

"What?" she cried. "We must find him. We must try."

"I agree, which is why I have someone searching for him."

"You do?"

"I do."

She buried her face in his chest. "Lord Ashlund, thank you."

He gave a laugh. "Lord Ashlund? Why so formal, Phoebe. In a few hours we'll be married."

"What?" Then she recalled the reason for his visit. Phoebe shoved at his chest. "Let me go!"

He grasped her shoulders. "Stop it. Don't you understand? Once you're my wife, they can't touch you."

Her mind whirled. "Wh-what?"

"As my wife, they cannot touch you. I won't chance a constable knocking on my door. Not just yet, anyway. So you see why we must leave for Brahan Seer immediately. The arrangements have been made for a small service when we arrive."

"My lord!"

Afterwards, it will be my word against theirs," he cut in. "They saw nothing."

"Neither did you."

"Technically, not quite true."

"Technically, you did not," she nearly shouted.

"I reached you before anyone else, and I searched the area. I found no weapon. You couldn't have thrown the gun far had you shot him."

"Good of you to clear my name."

"I would have been a fool not to investigate."

Phoebe pushed away from him. "Indeed."

His brow wrinkled.

She couldn't believe it. Her cynicism had wounded him.

"Had you told me you shot him, Phoebe, it would have made no difference."

"Yet you looked for a weapon."

"I did," he replied. "It will be much easier to swear that I didn't find a weapon when I truly didn't. Not to mention, I had no intention of leaving any evidence behind to be found later. Have you considered the possibility it wasn't Branbury the killer meant to shoot?"

"By heavens." She sat down on the bed again and looked up at him. "Who would want to kill me? Adam said if he were to meet a highwayman, he wanted to be the one to surprise him. Perhaps there really was a highwayman—"

"A common highwayman who hid in the trees and killed a man he didn't know? To what end?"

Someone who had meant to kill her, not Adam? Phoebe felt the room begin to spiral again and she lay back on the bed.

185

Chapter Eighteen

Brahan Seer lay half a day's ride ahead of them. That was half a day too long, as far as Kiernan was concerned.

"She hasn't uttered more than a word in response to my efforts at conversation," Elise told him as they walked the grounds of the Glaistig Uain.

"Not surprising," he replied. She'd said even less to him. "You sent word to Father?"

"Yes, though it's likely he is already on his way to us and won't receive the message." She lapsed into silence for a moment, then said, "He will be deeply upset if he misses your wedding, Kiernan."

"I won't wait. God only knows what trouble Lord Ingersol and his wife have already set into motion. Who was this Branbury, Elise?"

She sighed. "I only met him once. But in answer to the question I know you're thinking, she gave no indication of having any tenderness for him."

"You were obviously wrong on that score," he said between tight lips.

"No," she replied patiently. "They were clearly well acquainted, but she didn't act the part of a woman in love. In fact, she seemed very displeased with him."

Kiernan kept his eyes straight ahead. "Lovers quarrel?"

"No, it wasn't that sort of thing at all."

"I'll have to trust your judgment in the matter, but her upset seems to go beyond that of a friend dying."

Elise slipped a hand into the crook of his arm and tugged him to a halt. "Kiernan."

Kiernan met her gaze.

"He died in her arms."

Kiernan covered her hand with his and gave it a squeeze before starting forward again. "Why was he there?"

"He was in love with her."

"Yes, that was obvious even to me, but waylaying her on the road was a highly irregular way to go about pursuing her. Damnation, first someone tries to abduct her—" He caught the surprised look on Elise's face. "Father didn't tell you?"

"No," she replied.

"Well, the night Phoebe and I met—"

"Would this be the night you abducted her?"

He gave her a dry look. "Indeed, madam."

"Ahh." She faced forward and they started walking again.

"There was someone else attempting the same thing," he said.

"Good Lord, you aren't serious?"

"Very serious."

"Why wasn't I informed?"

The harsh note in her voice surprised him. "It didn't occur to me. I suppose, I assumed Father told you."

Her eyes narrowed. "Had I known that, I would have been more forceful in trying to stop Phoebe from making this trip. Don't think I'm not aware that you blame me for not stopping her."

"Blame you?" Did he blame her? "Elise, she was determined."

"Was her uncle aware that someone else attempted to kidnap her?"

Kiernan halted. "I-at the time, Phoebe was sure she knew Branbury was the kidnapper, so I didn't feel—" He broke off.

"Didn't feel what?" Elise demanded.

"Damnation, Elise."

She lifted a brow. "I know exactly what your father and you would have done if I kept that sort of secret."

He knew she was recalling a time when she had kept just such a secret and had nearly got her brother *and* him killed. That had been a terrible time for them all, and he had often wondered if she'd fully forgiven herself for the deception—and his father for nearly killing her brother. Would Phoebe forgive him for setting her life on this new course? Did she blame him for her friend's murder? Could she accept him despite being forced into marriage?

"I was wrong," he said.

Elise's lips pursed, but she began walking again and said, "Who was this kidnapper?"

"I believed it was Branbury, but Phoebe swears it wasn't him. Given that he was willing to chase her clear to Scotland, I'm not so sure. By the way, until this mystery is solved, Phoebe isn't to go anywhere without a guard."

"Ahh, that explains why Donald is always nearby," Elise said. "You may use Niall, also, if you like."

He shook his head. "No. It's best if you both have someone near at all times. I would prefer to think it was Branbury who had tried to adduct her that night," Kiernan went on with his previous thought. "A midnight run for Gretna Green would be harmless enough,"

"Yes. If it wasn't him, the kidnapper is still out there."

"Just as Branbury's killer is still out there."

"You're certain it was deliberate murder?" she asked. "It is possible a highwayman shot him."

"Possible, but unlikely," he replied. "Which means I have to discover whether or not Branbury was the intended victim."

Elise gasped. "Why would anyone want to kill Phoebe?"

"That is what I intend to find out."

Kiernan opened the door to the women's salon at Brahan Seer.

Phoebe didn't turn from where she sat staring at the fire, but said, "Are you ready, Lord Ashlund?"

He closed the door and crossed to the couch. "No need to rush." He sat down beside her and she looked at him. Her brow furrowed as her gaze shifted downward and he realized she was surprised to see him in a kilt. A hint of amusement shone in her eyes, then vanished.

"What did the constable have to say about Adam's murder?" she asked.

"I sent word to the magistrate from Glasgow. He's someone we trust and the closest magistrate. I haven't heard back from him yet, but rest assured, he'll conduct a thorough investigation."

"I can't hide forever."

"We aren't hiding, Phoebe, but we must prepare for whatever that fool Ingersoll has in mind."

"Adam was a good man," she said. "I owe it to him to face his family."

"It's not your fault he was shot."

Her brow rose. "It was you who suggested he wasn't the intended victim."

"That doesn't make it your fault."

Something flickered across her face. A sense of knowledge, he realized.

"He was there to beg me to marry him—to run off to Gretna Green that very moment, in fact."

"I see. Why didn't you accept?"

"I...I wasn't in love with him."

"Are you sure?" He glimpsed the moisture in her eyes before she ducked her head. "Phoebe," he began, but she pushed to her feet.

He stood and reached for her. She turned away, but he grasped her arm and turned her toward him.

"Let me go," she said through a sob. "He is gone. You needn't worry that he is any threat to—"

Kiernan pulled her close. "Hush," he said. "You misunderstand."

"I understand well enough."

The tears in her voice wrenched at his heart. "No, sweetheart, you don't." He pressed her closer and leaned his chin on her head.

She sagged against him. "He's dead, for-for what?"

"I wish I knew."

"You can bloody well believe—" she hiccupped "—I'll find out." She sobbed softly into his coat. "Don't think you can stop me." She hiccupped again. "Or that our marriage will stop me."

Kiernan placed a finger beneath her chin and tilted her face up. "I wouldn't dream of stopping you."

She stared, eyes wide, cheeks stained with tears. Desire swept through him. *Steady,* he warned himself. *Now isn't the time*—He froze when she reached up and wrapped a hand around his neck. She drew his face to hers. Her lips touched his. She's distraught, he reminded himself. She will regret her actions, but when she arched her breasts against his chest, his resolve failed. He devoured her mouth. Her small whimper sent blood pounding through his veins and his cock throbbed with staggering need. He became aware that her fingers had tangled in the hair at the nape of his neck. His erection pulsed. Warm, insistent, her lips parted, and he swept his tongue inside. Her tongue flicked against his and he sucked her into his mouth.

She gave a small gasp and melted against him. Kiernan cupped her buttocks and undulated her mound against his erection. By God, her touch set him on fire. They were to be married in minutes, their wedding night was only hours away. Could he wait? He had only to lift his kilt and he would be inside her in seconds. Would she let him? She broke the kiss and he was sure she'd come to her senses, but she slid her mouth along his jaw and down his neck. When she breathed deep he thought he would lose his mind. Kiernan thrust gently against her. Pleasure radiated through his cock and he groaned.

Kiernan gripped her buttocks and lifted her from the floor, took one step and eased her onto the couch. He came down on her, kissing her hard as he yanked up her skirt and slipped his hand between her legs. His finger met her slick heat. She was so wet. Kiernan buried his face in her hair and slid a finger inside her. So tight.

"Phoebe," he whispered.

She stiffened.

His head spun.

"My God," she cried, and he jerked his head up.

189

His mind snapped into focus on her wide-eyed expression of shock.
"No." She shook her head.
"Sweetheart—"
"Not this, not now."
He yanked his finger from inside her.
"No," she cried more softly, this time.
He cursed and rose, pulling her to her feet.
"It's wrong," she said through tears.
Kiernan held her close. "I know," he soothed. "It's my fault, all my fault." And it was.

Phoebe's gaze fell from the afternoon sun shining through the stained glass window of the chapel to the sprig of white heather Kiernan had pinned to the bodice of the light green dress that served as her wedding gown. From the corner of her eye, she caught sight of her hand resting on his, and the thick gold band he had placed on her ring finger.

The reverend's "You may kiss the bride," registered faintly in her mind. Yet, she understood quite clearly the meaning when Kiernan's tender grip on her hands loosened and his finger curved under her chin. Her gaze flitted past the lock of golden hair that had come loose from its binding and across the strange sight of his kilted figure as he tipped her face up toward his.

"Lady Ashlund," he said in a quiet voice, and brushed a kiss across her lips.

Her mind flooded with the memory of their earlier interlude and Phoebe experienced the same flush she had when Kiernan lowered himself onto her. Her mind clouded as it had in that moment, then shame followed, just as it had then. But the slick heat between her legs didn't fade. He slipped an arm around her and turned to face the small crowd who sat in the little chapel. Kiernan's hold on her waist tightened and he halted, staring at his father, who stood at the end of the aisle. Kiernan started forward again, and Phoebe allowed him to lead her down the aisle.

"Father." Kiernan stopped before the duke and extended his hand, but his father grasped his shoulders and pulled him into an embrace.

The duke released him, then turned smiling to Phoebe. He winked. "A bit sooner than you had anticipated, lass, but a fine thing, nonetheless."

"Your Grace." She started to curtsy.

He caught her hand, stopping her. "Father will do." He kissed her cheek. "Now, let me look at you." He took a step back. "A fine thing, indeed." He drew her close and hugged her. "Don't fret," he said into her ear. "All will be well."

To her great surprise, relief rushed through her. The duke released her, and Phoebe turned to see Elise standing behind her. The duke stepped past Phoebe.

"Marcus." Elise fell into his arms.

Just as a bride might fall into her groom's embrace, Phoebe couldn't help noticing, and a sudden urge to cry swept over her. She ducked her head with the intention of turning away, but the strong arm that slid around her waist startled her. She recognized Kiernan's touch. He held her steady as the duchess withdrew from her husband's embrace. Phoebe caught sight of her misty eyes and was sure she, too, would give into the tears that hung perilously close to the surface. When Elise embraced her, she remained silent, but gave Phoebe a squeeze, then returned to stand beside her husband.

Phoebe recognized the fiery redhead who next approached. Earlier, Elise had introduced Phoebe earlier to Sophie, the duke's cousin, and her husband, Justin. "How wonderful that you have managed to settle this rascal down," Sophie said with a lilt of Scottish brogue. She glanced affectionately at Kiernan, then looking back at Phoebe, added, "I'm pleased to meet you, Lady Ashlund."

Justin stepped up and said, "*Mille failte dhuit le d'bhreid, Fad do re gun robh thu slan. Moran laithean dhuit is sith, Le d'mhaitheas is le d'ni bhi fas.*"

Phoebe frowned, and Kiernan's warm breath washed over her ear when he bent and whispered, "A thousand welcomes to you with your marriage kerchief. May you be healthy all your days, may you be blessed with long life and peace. May you grow old with goodness and with riches."

She looked at Justin, though her mind was on the cool metal of the ring on the finger of the hand Kiernan held. Phoebe smiled. "Thank you, my lord."

Justin kissed her cheek, then shook hands with Kiernan. "My congratulations," he said, and moved on.

Mather stepped up. "Lady Ashlund." He bowed.

"Mather," Phoebe said with an unexpected rush of affection. She took his hand and gave it a squeeze. "I'm so glad you're here."

"Thank you, ma'am," he replied, his face flush. He extricated his hand from hers and moved on.

Phoebe recognized the captain of Brahan Seer as he stepped up.

"*Meal do naigheachd!*" he said.

She gave him a bemused look.

"Congratulations to ye, Lady Ashlund," he said with a smile, and went on.

The last guest stopped before them "Ye have a fine lad, there," Winnie said. "I saw his father birthed, and have known Kiernan from nigh the day he was born." Her eyes grew moist. "Fine lad." She placed a hand on Phoebe's shoulder and squeezed before brushing past her.

Kiernan angled his head toward Phoebe and said through the corner of his mouth, "Are you sure you're up for the celebration?"

191

"You can't disappoint your tenants," Phoebe replied.

"I'm sorry, Phoebe, but they insisted on a celebration."

"Don't trouble yourself, Lord Ashlund," she said. "It's only fitting they should offer their best wishes."

"You need stay only a few minutes, then you can excuse yourself. No one will think much of your retiring early for the evening."

The small celebration, Phoebe noted, as they rounded the bend that led from the chapel to the castle, spilled from the great hall into the courtyard. She faltered, then decided it was far better to face a crowd of strangers, than any single anxious face. All were indeed strangers, aside from those few who had attended the ceremony, yet they greeted her as though she was no stranger, and certainly not English.

The guests hadn't waited for the bride and groom to join them before beginning the merriment. Though the food on the long table had remained untouched, scotch, wine, and other spirits had been indulged in without hesitation. A shout went up as Phoebe and Kiernan passed through the doorway. Kiernan's arm jerked from her waist as he was pulled from her side by a rowdy group of men. He received hearty slaps on the back and comments in Gaelic, which no one translated. The men began dragging Kiernan away. He glanced helplessly over his shoulder. She raised a questioning brow, but he shrugged and turned his attention to his comrades.

"Come along, Phoebe," a woman said behind her.

Phoebe turned to see Elise step up beside her.

"Chances are, you won't see Kiernan the rest of the evening. The women usually gather near the hearth and leave the rest of the room to the men." She smiled. "Much safer that way."

Phoebe looked at the men milling about, laughing loudly, slapping one another on the back, and generally ignoring the more civilized niceties. "Yes," Phoebe agreed. "I see your point."

Elise took Phoebe's hand and led Phoebe through the crowd. "The women you are about to meet are rather unique. Teachers, healers, even one political activist. Each a leader in her own right."

"Educated women, out here?" Phoebe asked.

"In their own way," Elise said, and pushed through a wall of men.

"Och, m'lady," one man said, jumping out of her way.

She nodded, moving on. "Only two actually read, however."

A serving girl carrying a tray rattling with mugs and glasses of containing a variety of drinks stopped just ahead of them. Phoebe snatched one of the glasses as she passed the girl. Phoebe lifted the glass and was taking a large swig just as Elise brought them to a halt near the hearth.

"Ladies," Elise said, "may I present the bride, Phoebe MacGregor, Marchioness of Ashlund."

Phoebe sputtered and wheezed as the scotch blazed a scorching path down her wind pipe. She wiped her mouth with the back of her hand as she swung her gaze onto the women. Through bleary eyes she saw their attentions' were firmly fixed on her. She stared back.

"Rather odd the first time you hear it, isn't it?" Elise asked, and the women broke into gales of laughter.

The faces of the women before Phoebe blurred. She sighed and took another gulp of scotch.

"Phoebe," Elise said gently, "perhaps you would like to retire for the evening?"

Phoebe surveyed the crowded room. "What time is it?" she asked even as the clock on the mantle chimed. She grimaced. "By heavens, must they make such racket?"

"It's nine o'clock," Elise replied. "Would you like to eat a little something before bed? You haven't had a thing all evening."

"Forgive me, Your Grace," Phoebe said, "but I have, indeed, had something." She finished off the contents of her glass. Phoebe didn't miss the look the duchess exchanged with one of the women. "Don't trouble yourself, ma'am," Phoebe said, "I'm quite capable of holding my liquor. Much to my misfortune," she added under her breath.

"Still," Elise persisted, "let's have something to eat."

"Thank you, but no."

"Bed then?" Elise said.

Phoebe thought for a moment. "Yes, I think that would be a fine idea. Where am I to sleep?"

"Come along, I'll show you."

There was a moment Phoebe thought she would be ill. The long corridor they traveled seemed to be a maze. She didn't recall such twists and turns in her previous stay at Brahan Seer. At last, they stepped into a brightly lit corridor much wider than the one they had been in and she took a deep breath.

"Are you all right?" Elise asked.

Phoebe nodded. Elise gave her an unsure look, but continued down the hallway. She stopped in front of the fourth door, opened it, and stepped back, indicating Phoebe should enter ahead of her. Phoebe stepped inside. A fire burned in the hearth on the far right wall. Four candles burned in the candelabra that sat on a table against the wall in front of her. A canopied bed sat to the left, and on the silk cover lay scattered the petals of various flowers. The nightgown laid out with obvious care on the foot of the bed, however, is what snagged her attention.

"A bridal chamber," she muttered.

Elise whisked past her without a word, yet, Phoebe knew the duchess understood she had forgotten the reason for tonight's revelries.

"Shall I have a bath drawn for you?"

"Good God, no." Phoebe gasped. "Oh, forgive me, Your Grace, I didn't—"

"No bath, it is, then." Elise turned down the bed. "We're in the south wing, in case you wondered." She stopped and looked at Phoebe. "Do you plan on standing in the doorway all night?"

Phoebe looked about her as if suddenly realizing where she was. "No, ma'am, of course not." She stepped into the room, despite a sudden desire to turn and run. "The, er, south wing, you say?" she said, taking each step as if it were her first.

"Yes." Elise fluffed the pillows rather vigorously. "On the third floor."

"Ahh," Phoebe said.

Once no more fluffing of the bedcovers and pillows was humanly possible, Elise straightened. "Let me help you out of that dress." She started toward her.

"If you don't mind, Your Grace, I prefer to do it myself."

Elise stopped. "I can have someone sent up."

Phoebe shook her head. "Really, I prefer to be alone for a little while."

"It's customary for someone to sit with the bride, you know."

"I know. I appreciate your concern, but really, I am best left to myself now."

Elise nodded. "If Kiernan remains below, I'll check on you a little later."

Phoebe grabbed her arm as she passed. "I beg you, Elise, don't hurry him."

Elise patted the hand that gripped her. "Perhaps a little sleep will do you good."

"Indeed."

Elise went to the door, but paused in the doorway. "If you need anything…"

"I promise to call for you."

Elise closed the door behind her with a soft click.

Phoebe turned to the sideboard beneath the window, centering her attention on the decanter there. "I believe I have all I need."

Kiernan opened the door to the bridal chamber. Phoebe wasn't sleeping as she should have been, given the wee hours of the morning. Though, upon first glance, one might have thought she slept, he knew she only lounged. It wasn't the fact she was still fully dressed that gave away her state, or that only the blonde lock that had come free earlier was the only hair out of place, but more the way she sat on the bed, head back against the pillows propped up behind her. A crystal tumbler sat listed slightly in her lap, yet, her grip on the glass clearly held the object in check. Brandy, by the look of things. Kiernan smiled, the decanter, only a third full, sat on the table beside the bed, near enough to reach without inconveniencing the drinker from her leisure.

"Where are your merry wishers?" Phoebe asked, a slight slur in the word 'wishers.'

Kiernan stepped inside and closed the door. "Thank you for reminding me." He bolted the door. "The moment they realize my absence, they'll be upon us."

Phoebe lifted her head from the pillow and finished her drink with a quick flourish of her hand and a backward jerk of her head. She laid her head back again and, eyes closed, groped with her right hand for the decanter. Finding it, she brought it onto her lap and poured a fair amount of liquid into the tumbler. When trying to place the decanter back on the table, however, she missed, and was forced to open her eyes to keep from dropping it on the floor.

Kiernan crossed to the sideboard and got a glass, then went to the bed and sat down beside her. As he poured a drink, Phoebe opened one eye.

"If you finish that off, Lord Ashlund, I will ask that you fetch another decanter."

He placed the nearly empty decanter back on the night stand. "What are we drinking to?"

"You won't like it."

"Don't tell me you are wishing for my demise already."

Her eyes shot open. "Fool," she muttered. "Adam." The single word was clear, but her hand shook slightly as she downed another swig of her drink.

"Ah, yes." Kiernan raised his glass. "To Adam." He saluted and finished his drink in one swallow.

Phoebe lay back, once again, as though dozing.

Kiernan glanced at the decanter, then at her glass. "You've been up here for some time," he commented.

"This is where the bride is supposed to be."

Kiernan sat his glass on the table. "His death isn't your fault, Phoebe."

Her eyes opened and she regarded him. "You don't know that."

"You didn't shoot him."

"Ohh," she said, jerking her hand. Brandy sloshed over the rim of her glass onto her hand. "Now, see what you've done." Phoebe transferred her glass to the other hand, then sucked the brandy from her fingers.

"We have more brandy," he said. "You needn't worry about a few spilt drops."

"I'll worry about anything I please," she retorted.

"So I see."

Phoebe halted the sucking and regarded him. "You think I'm foolish for caring about—about—" She stopped, her eyes widening.

"Adam," Kiernan prodded gently.

Tears abruptly filled her eyes.

"Phoebe." Kiernan scooted closer to her.

"Oh, go away," she blubbered.

She shoved at him, tipping over the glass on her lap and spilling brandy on her dress. He rose and Phoebe swung her legs over the edge of the bed. She attempted to brush the liquid from her dress while he hurried to the armoire and returned with several handkerchiefs. He tried dabbing at the liquid but she pushed his hand aside.

"It's too late for that." Phoebe stood. She swayed, and Kiernan gripped her elbow to steady her. She shook him off. "I'm all right." But in two steps, she fell straight to her backside.

He pulled her to her feet, then scooped her into his arms. "If you're going to drink, my dear, I suggest you stay in bed."

"Oh, you'd like that." She hiccupped. "Wouldn't you?"

Kiernan laid her on the bed, then sat beside her and rolled her onto her side. He began unbuttoning the row of buttons that went down the back of the dress.

"What are you doing?" she demanded.

"Getting you ready for bed. I'm surprised Elise didn't help you."

"Told her not to," Phoebe replied in the voice of a petulant child. "And I don't want your help either."

"You're going to have a devil of a headache in the morning. Sleeping in this tight gown won't help your mood."

"My mood is fine."

"Indeed." Kiernan finished the last button and turned her onto her back. He brought her to a sitting position and began pulling the long sleeves from off her arms.

"I ought to shoot you for this," she mumbled, then more tears appeared. "I told Adam he made me wish I had shot him. Oh, but men are abom-abommmmniible."

Kiernan halted in tugging off the second sleeve and looked at her. "Why didn't you simply marry him, Phoebe?"

"Abomb-abomnbe—"she frowned ferociously as if it were his fault she couldn't speak. "Abob-abib—Oh! Horrid! That's what you all are."

He pulled the sleeve off, then, standing, stripped the dress from her. She shivered in the chemise. Kiernan tossed the dress onto a nearby chair, then gently pushed her back onto the mattress and sat beside her. He ignored her breasts, straining against her chemise, the nipples dark beneath the fabric, and reached behind her. Kiernan brought her to a sitting position, hugging her to his chest as he attempted to free the covers she sat on.

"I'm not in the mood for this." She jammed her forced between her breasts pressed and his chest.

He continued to struggle the blanket beneath. "I would suggest, then, keeping your hands to yourself."

She gave a halfhearted swipe to his chin. "Self-defense," she mumbled into his neck.

"God help me." He slipped a hand beneath her buttocks and lifted her enough to free the covers.

Phoebe batted at his arm. "I'm not interested in your attentions tonight."

"My dear," he said, laying her back onto crisp linen sheets, "as much as I might like to, I am not in the habit of taking advantage of women who are deep in their cups, even if the woman is my wife."

Phoebe's eyes popped open. "Wife," she said as her hand went to her mouth and she belched.

"Phoebe," Kiernan said sharply.

"Oh dear," she said through another belch.

Kiernan whirled and, spying the object he was searching for sitting near the nightstand, scooped it up and faced Phoebe.

"By heavens," she cried, "not the chamber pot again."

He dropped to his knees, hoisted her into a sitting position and shoved the pot under her nose.

Phoebe shook her head. "Out of the way, Ashlund."

Kiernan started to argue, but she scooted to the edge of the bed and shoved to her feet. She dropped to her knees and it was clear her stomach would not be put off any longer. Kiernan once again shoved the chamber pot in front of her. She grasped its edges and vomited.

Laughter abruptly echoed in the hallway outside the door.

"Damnation," Kiernan cursed as the laughter grew louder. The entire male population of Brahan Seer had decided to congregate outside their room.

Phoebe retched again.

A loud pounding sounded at the door. "Bhalgaire!" said John, a man from the village. "Ye canna' escape us." Shouts of agreement went up and more pounding followed. "You may be anxious to see the lassie, but you won't get off so easily."

"Too late, lads," Kiernan called.

More laughter. "It's never too late," another voice answered in between Phoebe's gasps. "Now open the door. We won't look." At this, raucous guffaws abounded and were mingled with more bawdy comments.

Phoebe leaned over, her head nearly touching the chamber pot. Kiernan placed a hand on her head to steady her. She pushed him away, but ceased such efforts in favor of once again gripping the chamber pot and heaving into it. The noise outside the room abruptly stopped.

"What in God's name are you doing to her?" came the calm voice of his childhood friend David.

"Go on, now, lads," Kiernan urged. "You've done enough damage for one night."

There was a pause, then, David said, "Sounds to us as if it is you who have done the damage. What's wrong?"

Kiernan looked down at Phoebe who, though breathing heavily, had ceased retching. "Nothing," he called.

"There are fifteen of us, at least. We can easily break the door."

Kiernan sighed. "Will you be all right, Phoebe?"

She shot him a sidelong glance that could only mean she might be all right, but his future good health was uncertain. He rose and went to the door. He unbolted the door, then quickly stepped outside.

Kiernan caught sight of his father at the back of the crowd before saying, "Enough, lads, she's simply celebrated a little too vigorously."

The men's eyes widened and somewhere in the middle of the group someone said, "You don't mean she—"

"Drunk as a skunk?" put in another.

Kiernan didn't miss the twitch at the corner of his father's mouth and was certain the duke was thinking that this was merely the first of many ways in which Phoebe would repay Kiernan for waylaying her coach.

"Never saw a woman who could hold her liquor," said David.

"Don't be too sure about that," Kiernan said. "From what I saw, she drank quite a bit before retiring, and the decanter of brandy in the bedchamber was nearly empty when I arrived."

John frowned. "Not natural for a woman to drink so much."

"Well," Kiernan said, clearing his throat, "Phoebe is a rather unusual woman. Now, if you will excuse me."

For a moment it seemed the men might proceed with the wedding night tradition of forcing their way into the bridal chambers but his father said, "Come along, lads. There's plenty more scotch downstairs for us."

One by one, they turned away. Kiernan backed into the room, keeping a wary eye on them until he had the door closed and bolted again. He turned back to Phoebe. She had crawled back into bed and lay curled up on her side, this time, sleeping quite soundly.

Chapter Nineteen

A heavy weight over Phoebe's shoulder pinned her to the bed in the darkness. The mass of heat that molded to the curve of her back pressed closer. She stirred and the weight on her shoulder slipped beneath her arm and wrapped itself around her waist. Vague images of people laughing, food, drink, and a dark face, floated through her mind. She concentrated, trying to comprehend their meaning when the unmistakable hard length of a man pressing against her buttocks registered in her brain. The warmth around her waist crept upward and closed with a gentle caress around a breast.

Phoebe gave a small cry of surprise.

"Shh, sweetheart," came a soft male voice in her ear. "It's me."

He kissed her ear and warmth rippled through her. He rocked gently against her and her body gave an answering throb that so startled her, it was a moment before she realized his hand was sliding downward. Phoebe wriggled in his grasp. His hand cupped the feminine part of her through her chemise.

He sighed and began inching up the fabric. The material brushed lightly over the stiff curls of her woman's mound. She was aware the instant the linen exposed her, for his fingers caressed her. He probed, parting the folds with a careful touch until, at last, he slipped a finger inside her wet channel.

Phoebe gripped the sheets as he moved his finger in and out. She was only beginning to adjusting to the sensation when she felt a flick to the sensitive nub that now throbbed with every tiny thrust me made.

"By heavens," she whispered. "This is something new."

He chuckled in her ear. "But the beginning of many firsts, my dear."

Her mind swirled with vague possibilities, all ending with the same exquisite pressure she now experienced. He stopped abruptly, and Phoebe felt as though she teetered on a precipice she longed to jump into. He rolled her onto her back and came down on top of her. His weight pressed her into the bed. The memory of Brandon crushing her beneath him in much the same way flashed before her, but was banished immediately by a rough kiss to her mouth.

Kiernan released her mouth and nipped at her ear. "Only you and I in the wedding bed," he whispered.

Phoebe gasped. Had she said Brandon's name aloud?

Kiernan's mouth, hard and insistent, slid down her throat, while he moved his shaft in easy motion against her. He grasped her chemise and tried to tug it down her shoulders, but the linen fit snuggly over her breasts. His hands explored her chest, and his fingers gripped the top of the chemise. Even as she felt his muscles tighten she realized his intent.

Phoebe gasped as he rent the cloth. His mouth closed over a hardened nipple. She sunk her fingers into his hair. The heavy locks slid like satin through her fingers just as she knew they would. Thick and soft like—her breath caught, he must have lifted the cloth of his nightdress, for the velvety hard length of his shaft brushed against her thigh, then probed the nestle of curls. He found quick entrance between her damp folds. A thrill shot through her body, followed by the physical pleasure of his rubbing.

"Don't wait any longer," she whispered, and she felt his body tighten in the instant before he surged forward—Phoebe bolted upright, a deep wheezing breath bringing her full awake and blinking into the sunlit room.

She blinked harder, her breath coming in heavy spurts, and looked at the empty space beside her on the bed. She raised a hand, unable to endure any longer the shaft of sunlight that dove in a relentless stream through the window and directly across her line of sight. Turning her head aside, she groped at her bodice to find the chemise she had worn under her dress was in one piece. She hazarded a glance at the foot of the bed and saw that the nightgown that had been laid out for the wedding night lay crumpled in a corner of the bed.

What had happened last night? The arrival at Brahan Seer, the wedding, the reception, her memory faltered—Kiernan, he had come to the bridal chamber, they drank brandy together. Phoebe scrambled back so that the sunlight no longer fell over her, and she looked about the room. There, on the chair, lay her dress, no doubt a mess that would need ironing, but still intact.

She had desired no groom, the memory of Adam's death still too recent, the horror of his blood on her hands, too fresh to want the touch of a man. Yet, she had managed, nonetheless, to give herself over far more gladly than was seemly, and no groom had been needed! Heat flooded her cheeks. The memory of Kiernan's grasp tightening as he gave her the kiss that made them man and wife came to mind. No! She had not wanted him.

200

Yet, again, came the recollection of his tall frame, blue eyes stark against swarthy skin, and black hair that had gone uncut. The muscled flesh of his legs visible between his kilt and boots. Phoebe balled a hand into a fist and hit the pillow on the side of the bed as hard as she could.

"Oh, Adam," she cried, "I am no friend. To the bitter end, I am no friend."

She threw herself on the pillow and cried.

It was ten o'clock before Phoebe made an appearance downstairs. She had considered staying in bed—the pounding in her head caused by the overindulgence of brandy last night enough to keep her buried beneath the covers—but she realized waiting would only make facing her husband and his family all the more difficult. To her relief, none of the MacGregors she wished to avoid were in the great hall.

"Marcus has gone to the village," Winnie told her as she directed her in a chair at the kitchen table. "Anabele," Winnie called to one of the maids, "fetch a cup of tea for Lady Ashlund."

Phoebe placed a hand over the housekeeper's, "You're an angel, Winnie, and, please, Phoebe will do."

The housekeeper grinned. "Aye," she said and seated herself at the table. "Elise is about somewhere in the keep."

Phoebe nodded.

Winnie hesitated. "Your husband, well," she gave Phoebe a sheepish look, "he isn't here."

A rush of relief flooded Phoebe, then she wondered where he was "Where is he?"

"Up north is all I know. He doesn't confide in me."

Neither does he confide in his wife, Phoebe thought. Then her heart sank. So here she was, married to a man who was quite possibly a traitor. Was this how her mother had felt?

Phoebe had noticed the interested looks she'd gotten from the women as she sat with Winnie, but the girl who just left had stared unabashedly.

"Have I done something?" Phoebe asked Winnie.

The housekeeper laughed. "They're curious."

She should have known. "Curious as to how the marquess kidnapped me?"

"Aye. His antics surprised even Marcus this time. Kiernan is an unusual man."

Phoebe had to agree.

"He's the most English of the MacGregors, which makes him too proper at times."

"Too proper?" A tremor rippled through her stomach at recollection of the night Kiernan had caught her in his bedchambers. He'd been anything but proper.

"Aye," Winnie said. "But he loves a good joke and just can't help getting himself into trouble." She grinned. "You're proof of that."

Phoebe had to admit to being more than a little curious. "Am I the worst trouble he's gotten into?"

"I would say so, but he doesn't seem to mind one bit." Phoebe's cheeks warmed and Winnie laughed again. "I imagine you gave him a dose of his own medicine."

If that were true, she wouldn't be in the Highlands married to him.

"But ye needn't worry," Winnie went on. "I'm sure he will settle down now that he's married."

Settle down? Wasn't that what he expected of her? He said she would have the freedom to do as she pleased, but he also wanted children. Kiernan's sons would be magnificent. The face of a dark haired, blue-eyed boy arose in her mind.

"And he's a Highlander through and through," Winnie said. "He understands his duty."

"Duty?" Phoebe repeated.

"Aye, he learned firsthand as a young boy when they watched Marcus' cousin hang for attempted murder."

The vision evaporated. "The duke has a cousin who was hanged for murder?" Phoebe blurted.

Winnie nodded. "The son of his laird raped a girl in the village and David demanded he be brought before the magistrate. The earl denied his son was guilty, so David tried forcing him to go. Of course, the earl then called in the magistrate and accused David of trying to kill the viscount. Marcus was ready to lead a revolt, but his father forbade it. There was enough blood being shed by the feud between us and the Campbells. Cameron knew the king wasn't in the mood for another MacGregor war."

"If he was innocent, surely something could have been done," Phoebe said.

"He may not have been innocent by their standards."

Phoebe recalled Kiernan's words the day they rode into Brahan Seer. *"This is untamed country, far outside the reach of traditional law. The nineteenth century won't ride to our rescue any quicker than the Queen's men will."*

Had England failed her Scottish subjects in this case?

"Either way," Winnie said, "by the time Cameron got wind of it, David was all but hung. Marcus took Kiernan with him and they said goodbye to David."

Phoebe started. "The duke forced his son to watch?"

"Kiernan was young, but you can rest assured he won't forget the price MacGregors pay."

202

"No," Phoebe murmured. "He won't forget."

What better reason to commit treason than knowing that one's country won't defend you? Wasn't that what had happened to her father? He had given his life in service of his country, and had been betrayed by the very people who appointed him protector. Phoebe was startled by the unexpected memory of the duke's words when Kiernan came to the library the day she had told him of her father. *"Your future wife was just telling me of her father's involvement with Arthur Thistlewood. You wouldn't remember, you were a boy then, but Thistlewood was found guilty of high treason and hanged in 1820."*

Was it so strange that he remembered Arthur Thistlewood with such clarity after all these years? Perhaps not. The days after the Cato Street Conspiracy, the populace had demanded Arthur Thistlewood and his cohorts' heads—and had gotten them. The duke had shown surprise when Kiernan commented that Phoebe knew something of assassinations—that, she thought, should have given the duke pause, but he hadn't missed a beat, damn him. Neither had Kiernan, she realized. She'd forgotten, but when Kiernan asked what her father had to do with Arthur Thistlewood, and she answered that he was one of the men accused of taking part in the assassination attempt, recognition had flickered in his eyes.

Had he made the connection between Phoebe Wallington and Mason Wallington? If so, why not say something? But the answer was too obvious. Her heart beat faster. Kiernan recognized the name. Just as the duke did, she realized with a start. When Phoebe told him her name, he'd been surprised. He'd passed his surprise off as having known a murderer with the name Wallington, but that had been a lie. *Both* father and son knew who her father was.

"Forgive me, Winnie," Phoebe said, "but would you mind terribly if I excused myself? I'm rather tired."

"I'm not surprised," she clucked. "Go on up to your room and I'll have Anabele bring some lunch."

"Cold chicken and perhaps some bread would be nice, or anything of that sort." Anything that would withstand a long ride.

The housekeeper smiled. "She'll be up directly."

Phoebe went first to the library. As hoped, she quickly located a map of the Highlands. She shoved the map under her arm and checked the corridor. Seeing it was empty, she hurried to the room she'd shared with Kiernan last night. She had only just arrived when a knock sounded at the door.

Phoebe put the map into the armoire, then called, "Come in." The door opened and Anabele entered carrying a tray of food. "Good morning, Anabele. Set the tray there, please."

The girl deposited the tray on the secretary.

"Thank you," Phoebe said.

The girl turned to leave, but halted and said, "What's this?"

Phoebe turned as she scooped up something off the floor.

Anabele turned, a sheath of folded paper in hand. "It has your name on it, my lady." The maid hurried to Phoebe and gave her the note.

"Thank you," Phoebe said, and she left.

Phoebe unfolded the note and caught sight of Kiernan's signature at the bottom.

Phoebe,

> *Forgive me for leaving the day after our wedding. Unfortunately, I have business that can't wait. I will return in two or three days. I promise to make this up to you.*

Your husband,
Kiernan

Phoebe stared at the words *your husband* and cursed the flutter in her stomach. In five years as a spy, she hadn't gotten into one speck of trouble. Inside of a fortnight of meeting Kiernan MacGregor, she'd become entangled with traitors and murderers, and was married to a man who was likely the ringleader. A sudden desire to cry rushed to the surface. She swiped at the moisture in the corner of one eye. Kiernan was off taking care of his business. She intended to do the same.

Phoebe refolded the note, crossed to the door and quietly bolted the door, then retrieved the map from the armoire and sat back down at the desk. The map had no index. She began searching for the Dornoth Firth, the port John Stafford had referenced in his journal, the port Alistair preferred when he left Scotland for France.

She moved her gaze along the southeastern coast and reached for a biscuit. "Firth of Clyde," she repeated. Loch after loch passed beneath her gaze, and she grew frustrated as her eye traveled up the full length of the east coast and along the north. Then she found it. "Dornoth Firth!" she exclaimed. And there was Tain, south of the channel.

Phoebe searched far to the south. She groped for the tea cup and, finding it, lifted it to her lips. She followed the clan names down the map; Menzies, Campbell, Macnab, *MacGregor*. She took another sip of tea and calculated the ride to be two days. Longer than she'd hoped, which gave her concern over traveling the mountainous terrain alone. She would have to hire an escort for at least part of the way, and a quick look told her Perth was a large enough city to procure a reputable escort. If she left her escort in Inverness, the trip from there to Tain was only a few hours.

She glanced at the clock on the desk. Eleven thirty. Late in the day to begin such a journey, but should she wait, her new relatives would likely descend upon her. She lifted the lid that covered the plate on her tray.

Cold chicken, just as she'd requested. Perfect for a long trip and, as expected, enough for three meals. Phoebe couldn't help a smile. Winnie was a good soul.

Within twenty minutes, Phoebe had retrieved the tower percussion pistol she'd hidden in her trunk, and had bundled the remaining food, then hid each in the pockets of her dress. After another quick study of the map, she completed her ensemble with a voluminous cloak. Phoebe took a deep breath and opened the door. Through the winding corridors of Brahan Seer, she headed for the seldom traveled front entrance. There, she slipped out and strolled across the courtyard, praying none of her new relatives would appear.

As she had done the last time she'd been at Brahan Seer, Phoebe walked down the hill, but skirted the fringes of the village. Winnie said the duke was in the village, and Phoebe held her breath until she reached the stables and found them unattended. She located blanket, saddle and tack, and within fifteen minutes, had saddled a gelding. Phoebe stopped even as she lifted a booted foot into the stirrup. Her husband was gone, he wouldn't miss her, but the duke and duchess were sure to sound the alarm upon discovering her absence.

Phoebe looked down the length of the stables. Opposite the stalls was a door, slightly ajar. She hurried to the tack room and slowly pushed the door open. As hoped, the stable master's office. Inside she found a quill. Notes, bills and miscellaneous papers were stacked in two neat piles on the left side of the desk. Phoebe rifled through the papers until she found one that was blank on the bottom half. She creased the paper, placed the crease on the edge of the desk, and neatly tore the empty half from the rest of the sheet.

She sat at the desk's chair and scribbled a note.

Elise,

> *Forgive my leaving like this, but I know you and the duke will not agree to let me go. I believe you will understand that I can't let Adam's killer go unpunished. I am returning to London to deal with the matter myself. I believe that the longer I wait, the harder it will be to catch the murderer.*
>
> *My marriage to Lord Ashlund will give me immunity against any allegations, so please rest easy in my safety. I will send word as soon as I arrive to Shyerton Hall.*

Yours,
Phoebe

She folded the note and wrote the duchess' name on the outside then leaned it against the ink well and quit the modest office.

That special sense that John Stafford wrote of, that sense that *every investigator must have to survive*, had roared to life in Phoebe, and she knew that the trail to her father—to her husband—were somehow connected. Thanks to John Stafford, she also knew that trail began with Lord Alistair Redgrave in Tain, Scotland.

"How does your future husband feel about your quest?" Adam had asked the night he was murdered.

Phoebe planned to find the answer to that question.

Phoebe caught sight of the tiny Achilty Inn up ahead. A shopkeeper in Orrin had recommended the inn as the last one until Tain. She had left behind in Inverness the two men she'd hired on the recommendation of the minister at St. Paul's church in Perth. This, she had reasoned, was a safer course of action than taking a recommendation from the local magistrate, who was far more likely to be just the person the duke would contact if he was on her trail. Tain was but three or four hours away. An easy ride, but her horse was fagged and it was nearly ten at night.

Obtaining lodgings proved easy. Highlanders, Phoebe reflected, were a friendly lot. She recalled the night Kiernan had been shot, and the English innkeeper's wife when they sought lodging. Phoebe received no such shabby treatment from the Scottish innkeeper's wife, who now bustled her up to a room.

"Ye look fair starved," the woman said, glancing over her shoulder at Phoebe as she opened the door to a room.

Phoebe followed her into the modest room.

"Och," the woman said. "That John. He made the fire, but didn't have sense enough to close the window." She went to the open window and tugged it closed. She turned her attention to the bed. "What brings you all the way out here?" she asked as she drew back the blankets.

"Forgive me, madam," Phoebe replied, "I know it's highly irregular for a woman to travel alone."

The woman looked at Phoebe, not a trace of apprehension or recrimination on her face, and smiled.

Phoebe managed a blush. "You see," she stammered and looked down at the floor, "I am newly married—"

"Well, now," the woman interjected as she lifted a pillow and began fluffing it.

Phoebe looked up at her. "And, well, you see, my husband went away on business. He had not expected to be gone long, but it's been a month now, and…well, I miss him terribly."

"Aye," the woman clucked, "and rightly so."

"So, I decided, if Muhammad won't come to the mountain, I'd bring the mountain to Muhammad."

The woman paused in fluffing the pillow, a confused look on her face.

"If he can't come to me," Phoebe offered gently, "I'll go to him."

The woman's face brightened. "A fine wife," she said, then frowned. "But do you no' think it's a bit dangerous traveling on your own like this?"

"Oh, well, I didn't start out on my own," Phoebe said, stripping off her gloves. "I had a servant with me. You'll laugh." She tossed her gloves on the chair that sat before the crackling fire. "The foolishness of men."

The woman's eyes brightened.

Phoebe giggled. "You see, he fell from his horse and broke his leg."

"No!" the woman exclaimed, her eyes widening.

Phoebe nodded vigorously. "And my husband is forever worrying I'll hurt myself." She laughed again. "Can you imagine? It was I who had to save him."

The woman laughed. "Aye, lass, that's often the way it is. They think it's them who saves us, but who is it that saves them from themselves?" She snorted, adding, "The weaker sex," and both women laughed.

"Well," Phoebe went on, "it was no more dangerous for me to continue on, than it was to turn back."

The woman's expression turned more serious. "Surely, you could have gotten another escort, though?"

Phoebe affected a look of abashment. "Do you think I should have? Oh dear." She sat on the chair, crushing her gloves. "Jared is sure to be angry with me."

"Now, now," the woman said, and waddled to Phoebe's side. "You did what ye thought was best. And, you're all right, aren't you?"

"Oh, indeed, I am. Quite well."

The woman patted Phoebe's arm. "No harm done, then. But," she said with a serious look, "you never know who you might meet traveling in these parts." She gave a succinct nod. "We'll find you someone to go the rest of the way with you."

"Can you spare someone?"

"Well, perhaps we can send John." She looked thoughtful. "I'll ask my husband."

"Your husband owns the inn?" Phoebe asked, as if in awe.

The woman smiled. "He does."

"Oh, but I didn't know. Pray, forgive me."

A pleased look passed over the woman's face. "Och. There's nothing to forgive."

"What is your name, madam?" Phoebe asked.

"Mrs. MacKenzie. Now," she said, "you get—"

There was a knock at the door. Phoebe and the innkeeper's wife both looked toward the door, which stood ajar.

"Sally," Mrs. MacKenzie cried, when a young woman carrying a tray pushed open the door.

"Over here." Mrs. MacKenzie pointed to the small table beside Phoebe's chair.

The girl brought the tray to the table.

"You're too kind." Phoebe stood.

"Never mind," Mrs. MacKenzie said. "You must eat. Now, Sally, fetch a little warm water for—" she looked to Phoebe.

"Mrs. MacGregor," Phoebe replied.

As hoped, Mrs. MacKenzie beamed. "Mrs. MacGregor." Sally hurried from the room and Mrs. MacKenzie looked at Phoebe. "If you need anything, my room is at the end of the hall."

"Again," Phoebe took Mrs. MacKenzie's hand in hers, "you're too kind."

The housekeeper blushed and patted Phoebe's hand. "Get some rest, lass. We'll have a nice breakfast in the morning and get you settled on your way."

A shame, Phoebe thought, to have to miss such an enjoyable meal.

Five hours rest had revived Phoebe and her horse. She buckled the billets on the animal's saddle when a prickling sense of familiarity caused her to pause in the dim light of the stall. She grasped the stirrup and laid it quietly against the horse's belly, then crept to the stall door. She peeked out into the darkness, searching one side of the stable, then the other. She discerned no movement and ducked back into the stall, pausing to listen. All remained quiet.

Skulking about in the night made one suspicious. Unfortunately, she had learned long ago that she was the suspicious sort. She turned back to the horse. The fact that the inn stood within sight of the stables didn't help. A guilty conscious, she thought, remembering the kind Mrs. MacKenzie. Again, she wondered if leaving in the middle of the night wouldn't be more memorable, than allowing the good housekeeper to send an escort from whom she would be forced to escape. Phoebe started toward the lamp that hung on the inside wall of the stable, but whirled abruptly. That had definitely been a sound. She placed a hand on the gelding's nose and edged past him to the door. She looked out but, again, not so much as a piece of straw stirred. She stepped out and groped along the stalls to the stable doors.

The door was still ajar as she's left it when she entered and Phoebe leaned forward to peer around the edge. She froze. Outside in the pre-dawn shadows, at the very end of the stables, stood a man. His profile faced her, and he was deep in quiet conversation with someone who remained out of view on the other side of the stables.

The sense of familiarity she had experienced earlier returned. The man's features were indiscernible and his build wasn't out of the ordinary. He lifted his arm and placed a palm against the edge of the barn, leaning into the building. Phoebe's pulse jumped. It couldn't be. Her mind flashed back to the day when Alan Hay had arrived at the Green Lady Inn, and that night when Robbie held her at gunpoint in the barn. This time, the outline of a short hanger hunting sword protruding from his waistband was unmistakable.

The Highland map she had consulted before leaving Brahan Seer came to mind. By heavens, she had paid the districts no mind when she consulted the map, caring only for the location of Tain. Her brain hadn't registered the fact that the Sutherland district lay just above Tain.

Robbie's hand dropped away from the building. He stepped forward and she lost sight of him behind the stable. She waited to the count of three, then pushed the door open another few inches and stole from the stable. She crept to the edge of the building. There came the soft nicker of a horse. She halted at discerning the faint murmur of voices, then hurried to the far end the building. Phoebe peeked around the corner. Robbie stood, hand on the saddle pummel, ready to mount his horse. The other man, while talking in a whisper she couldn't distinguish, was obviously agitated.

Robbie shook his head and mounted. The man grabbed Robbie's arm. Robbie pulled back on the reins and the horse whirled, forcing the man back. Robbie didn't look back, but continued alongside the stables. The man took a step in Robbie's direction. Phoebe drew back and hurried back toward the stable door. She slipped inside and watched. The man appeared from around the stable an instant later and quickly passed from view. Phoebe peeked around the corner of the door and saw he was headed toward the inn.

"You never know who you might meet traveling in these parts," Mrs. MacKenzie had said.

What better person to see criminals on their way than a kindly old innkeeper's wife? Phoebe wondered. She hurried to her horse. She had been convinced she would find some connection between her father and Kiernan MacGregor, but hadn't been able to figure out what that connection might be. Seeing Robbie Hay here was too fantastical to be coincidence. There was no doubt that he would lead her to her husband. Lord Ashlund was, indeed, aiding criminals.

Her heart jumped. What if the recognition she'd glimpsed in Kiernan's eyes when she'd talked about her father was more than mere recognition of his name? What if it was also the knowledge that his future father-in-law was a man who would see him hanged for treason given the chance? She'd often wondered how her father had occupied himself all these years. Despite the deceit by the men who had made him an outlaw, he loved his country. He had remained in contact with Alistair. Could that mean he had somehow continued to serve his country? Her excitement took a dive. If true, could that account for Kiernan's unwavering

209

determination to marry her? What better way to control her father than by controlling her?

Phoebe wasn't surprised when Robbie headed north. She was surprised, however, when instead of heading east toward Tain, he continued north of the channel, then veered east into Dornoth Firth.

The elevation grew steeper and when she crested a large hill, she stopped. Below the densely forested hillside lay the coast and the sprawling port city of Dornoch. She searched the hill for Robbie and caught sight of him picking his way down the mountain. She followed.

The city was large enough that Phoebe hoped Robbie wouldn't recognize her among the bustle of the crowded street. He rode at such a slow pace that she realized he was less likely to notice a woman strolling the boardwalk, than a woman on horseback. She stopped in front of a shop, dismounted, and tied the reins to the post outside the shop, then sauntered down the street in Robbie's wake.

He continued through town without stopping. When the crowd thinned, she began to fear that Dornoch wasn't his destination. The sun had begun its descent and she would lose him if she was forced to retrieve her horse. She breathed a sigh of relief when he stopped on the edge of town in front of a three-story house with an overhead sign that read *Madam Duvall's Boarding House.* Robbie dismounted and went inside.

Two men approached her on the walkway. Phoebe paused and gazed through the window of a general store. She studied a pot that was displayed, while waiting for the men to pass. As they neared the boarding house, a window on the second floor opened and a woman stuck her head out. A woman, Phoebe noted, who could not be mistaken for anything other than the prostitute she was.

"*Cheri,*" the woman called in a thick French accent.

The two men paused at the door and looked up.

"Adele," one man replied and threw her a kiss.

The woman disappeared back into the house and the man in the lead opened the door to the brothel and entered with the other close behind. Phoebe turned, looked both ways, then crossed the street and headed back into town.

Chapter Twenty

At the sound of a sharp knock, Kiernan swung his gaze from Madam Duvall to the drawing room door. The door opened and her butler entered.

"Someone to see the Lord Ashlund," he announced in formal tones.

Kiernan looked at Madam Duvall, who sat on the settee beside his chair. "Was I to see someone else today?"

"No monsieur," she replied. "Only Robbie and, as you know, he arrived over an hour ago."

Kiernan turned his attention to the butler. "He didn't say who he was?"

"Said you would know him, sir."

Kiernan rose and removed a pistol from a nearby desk. "Show him in, Phillip. Letty, meet our guest at the door, if you please." Kiernan strode to the door and leaned against the wall to the left.

A moment later, a familiar figure entered the room.

"What the devil?" Kiernan exclaimed.

The Earl of Stoneleigh whirled to face him. Regan eyed the gun Kiernan pointed at him, then ran his gaze down the length of Kiernan's kilt.

"Never seen you looking so…"

Kiernan lowered in the weapon. "What are you doing here?"

"I could ask you the same thing," Regan replied.

"No, you can't."

Regan turned his attention to Letty, though he addressed Kiernan, "You're being rather rude, you know. Madam." Regan lifted her hand to his lips.

"Sir," she replied with a tilt of her head.

"Letty," Kiernan said, "do you mind? I need a word with our visitor."

Kiernan waited until Letty closed the door behind her, then said, "What are you doing here, Stoneleigh?"

"Stoneleigh?" Regan grimaced. "I have annoyed you." He threw himself down onto the sofa. "It's been a long trip. Aren't you going to offer me something a drink?"

"Will it get anything out of you?"

"You know how relaxed I get after a drink."

"Begin the tale," Kiernan said, "and I might not have you drawn and quartered."

Regan lifted a brow. "Don't think I've ever seen you so testy before."

Kiernan went to the sideboard. He set the pistol on the cabinet, then lifted the stopper off the decanter of port. "I wasn't expecting guests."

"Then you're due for another shock."

Kiernan paused in pouring the drinks to look at Regan. "What does that mean?"

"Your wife is here. I assume," he added, "given that you're staying in a brothel, you didn't bring her with you."

"Phoebe? Here?" Kiernan shook his head and finished pouring the drinks. "Impossible. She's back at Brahan Seer, and she would have no idea I'm here—speaking of which, how did you know I was here?"

"Your horse."

"The Andalusian?" Kiernan picked up the two drinks and crossed to Regan. "So, you happened to be in Dornoch and spotted my horse?" He handed a drink to Regan, then sat down in his chair.

"Right."

"Not many Englishmen happen to be in Dornoch, Scotland, Regan."

"I had no idea you were here."

"Then why are you here?"

Regan sipped the port. "It's been far too long since I've had good port." He met Kiernan's gaze. "It was, indeed, Phoebe I saw."

"She has no way of knowing I'm here. Not to mention, my father would never let her go." The memory of how both he and his father had 'let her go' the last time they had been at Brahan Seer came to mind.

"She wore no bonnet," Regan said. "Never does, as you know. There is no mistaking that golden hair." He took another sip of port.

"Why hasn't she already stormed Madame Duvall's?"

The earl laughed. "How many wives expect to find their husbands at a brothel two days after their wedding?"

Kiernan narrowed his eyes. "You know a great deal too much about my life these days."

He rose, crossed to the secretary and scribbled a note to his cousin to discreetly search for a newcomer, a woman with golden hair and...how did he describe her figure? He decided against the extra description. If Phoebe was in Dornoch, Androu would pick her out of the crowd without any trouble. If she was here, he would congratulate her on her excellent tracking skills—then paddle her pretty bottom. He had a great deal more to learn about his wife than he thought. Kiernan paused while signing the note. What if he wasn't the reason she was here? He cast Regan a glance, then went to the door and called for Phillip. The butler appeared a moment later and Kiernan gave him the note.

"Please have this delivered to Androu immediately." Phillip gave a small bow and started to turn, but Kiernan said, "Oh, and Phillip, please inform Mather we will meet at our friend's place. We've had too many unexpected visitors today for my liking. You will find him at Rhoda's. He may stay there until our appointed meeting time. He's likely to murder me in my sleep if I ask him to leave her before necessary."

Phillip bowed and left the room.

Kiernan closed the door, then returned to his seat and said to the earl, "Start at the beginning."

Regan took another drink, then said, "I know my turning up here is odd—odd enough, I suppose, that I do owe you an explanation. Though, after I've told you my story, I hope you'll see your way to show me the same consideration. I find it just as strange finding you here. First, I must ask you keep this information to yourself, and don't interfere."

"Has this anything to do with me?"

"No."

"Then, I can't see a problem. I don't make a habit of interfering, you know."

Regan cleared his throat and Kiernan scowled.

"You'll never let me live down my matchmaking debacle, will you?" Kiernan asked.

"Neither will Phoebe," Regan laughed. "Though it didn't turn out all that terrible for you."

No, he had to agree, it hadn't turned out badly at all.

"Now, as to my being here," Regan said. "I'm on the trail of a criminal."

Kiernan paused with his glass halfway to his lips. "What criminal would that be?"

Regan grinned. "Hard to believe, isn't it? Who would have thought of me as a doer of justice, righter of wrongs?"

Kiernan took the forestalled sip. "Not I."

"Well, you would be right. The long and short of it is, I've been commissioned by the government to keep an eye on Lord Ronald Harrington."

"What are you talking about?"

"Harrington is being investigated on matters of national security."

"National security?" Kiernan blurted, then cursed the government official who had commissioned Stoneleigh in hopes he would stumble

213

upon the secret other *real* British spies had failed to find. When Kiernan discovered the idiot's identity, he would whip him for throwing Regan in his path. "Lord Harrington has an unimpeachable reputation," Kiernan said. "Not to mention, you're no spy."

"No, I'm not. But it came to the notice of a certain someone in the government that I'm an acquaintance of his and," he shrugged, "well, he asked me to help out."

"And out of the goodness of your heart you agreed?"

"It's something of an adventure."

"I've never known you to apply yourself to anything for longer than a month."

"Not so. I did graduate Cambridge with honors."

"Only because your father threatened to enlist you in the military."

"Can you imagine?" Regan looked aghast. "Not even a commission."

"What's behind this, Regan? I don't believe you would follow a suspected spy all the way out here for the Crown."

"No. I wouldn't." Regan leaned forward. "I have a particular interest in Harrington, or, rather, a friend of his. I'm of the mind that Harrington is involved."

"Involved in what, the treason he's suspected of?"

"Well, as to that," he laughed, "I can't say. No, this involves my father."

"Your father? How is the marquess involved in this?"

Regan shook his head. "No, not Stoneleigh, my real father."

"Your real father? Regan, you've gone mad."

"I know, it's a devil of a mess. About two years ago, I discovered some letters written to my mother from a Lord Henry Ballmore. Quite personal, love letters, in fact. Seems she was to marry Ballmore, and she was pregnant at the time."

"Bloody hell," Kiernan whispered.

"Quite right," Regan agreed. "Of course, I confronted her and found out that Ballmore was my real father. They were, as I said, to be married, but Ballmore was killed outside a theatre in York before the marriage took place. She met Stoneleigh, who, despite her condition, wished to marry her."

"I'm sorry, Regan," Kiernan said.

"Never mind about that. I never knew the man, though, it was a shock, and I was furious with Mother for keeping it from me."

"I don't know that she had a great deal of choice."

"No, I suppose not. And Stoneleigh has been good to me. Still, I couldn't help being curious about Ballmore, so I did some investigating and discovered he had a little actress on the side."

"Common enough," Kiernan commented.

"True, but he wasn't the only one. Lord Niles Mallory was in love with the girl as well. Sarah—" Regan snapped his fingers lightly "—some obscure woman, no one we would have heard of—Hazelton, yes, that's it. Anyway, Ballmore and Mallory were both chasing after her."

"Mallory, isn't he the fellow who made all that racket about the labor laws in the House of Lords a few years ago?" *The same man who, so many years ago, accused Phoebe's father, Mason Wallington, of being a traitor to the Crown?*

"That's him," Regan said. "What do you think of this? I found that Mallory was in York when my father was there."

Kiernan studied him. "What are you saying?'

"I read the reports. Ballmore's death was no ordinary mugging. He was beaten."

"Muggers often beat their victims."

Regan shook his head. "This sort of beating was fueled by rage, the kind of beating one gets in a brawl."

"Those records would have to be over thirty years old. How did you manage to glean so much detailed information? Don't you think perhaps you're reading into this what you wish to find?"

"I knew you would think so. But God help me, it's true. I spoke with the young officer—he's not so young now. He was, by his own word, 'the embodiment of all an officer of the law should be.' He went to great lengths to document and investigate all crimes under his jurisdiction."

"If he suspected foul play of a different nature, why didn't he investigate?'

"He did, only he didn't connect Mallory, and hit a dead end."

"How did you connect Mallory?"

"It wasn't well known that Mallory was in love with Sarah. When Ballmore was killed, Sarah kept quiet about Mallory. He set her up with a stipend. But, she died a few years ago and, of course, the money stopped. She has a daughter, Harriet, who threatened to bring Mallory's involvement in Sarah's life to the attention of the authorities, but something happened to scare her into silence."

"Mallory threatened her?"

"I don't think it was Mallory. I think it was Harrington."

"Harrington? Why would he concern himself with Mallory?"

Regan shrugged. "Damned if I know, but I would bet a month's allowance he did."

But Kiernan was suddenly certain he knew why. Here was the answer to how Harrington had coerced Mallory into falsely denouncing Wallington.

"But you have no real evidence the two are connected," Kiernan said.

"No." Regan sat forward, his expression a combination of excitement and sober speculation. "But it's obvious Mallory despises Harrington, and the hate goes deep. Harrington passes it off as Mallory being angry the labor bill didn't pass. Harrington opposed him on it. Yet, you find the two men in one another's company a great deal."

"And you have found yourself in their company of late? Just as you were the other night at the Halsey ball," Kiernan said.

"I was acquainting myself with Mallory, which, of course, had me in Harrington's company. Hence the reason I was recruited."

"How is it this mess has brought you here?"

"Harrington is here."

"Harrington? What is he is doing here?" Kiernan demanded, but knew the answer—and didn't like it.

"I have no idea," Regan said. "I'm not even sure what prompted me to follow him."

Kiernan cursed again. "Stoneleigh, I might have you whipped after all."

The Andalusian. There was no mistaking the horse. Phoebe had seen the creature while at Brahan Seer. It was unlikely there was another like it in all of Scotland. The animal belonged to the Marquess of Ashlund. Her husband. She nodded to the stable master, who was saying, "The hotel is just a little ways down the main street."

"Yes," she replied. "I rode past it."

The man smiled. "Aye, then, ye know where you're going."

"Indeed," Phoebe said, and smiled despite the fact her heart was breaking. She knew exactly where she was going.

Her dear husband was holed up in a brothel. Phoebe had worried that asking the stable master where she could find the owner of the Adulusian would raise suspicion, so she had begun her search where Robbie's trail had ended: at Madam Duvall's. It was dark, but she leisurely strolled along the boardwalk and kept her hood over her hair, both unnecessary precautions. As she neared the brothel, a man turned, stared, then hurried into Madam Duvall's. Phoebe realized that the Marquess of Ashlund was at the brothel. She also knew that Kiernan was being apprised of the fact that his wife was in town. In another moment, he would also know she stood across the street from his hiding place.

With a sigh, Phoebe drew back the hood of her cloak and crossed the street to the house. She started to knock, but changed her mind and opened the door, then stepped inside.

A hulking monster of a man stood a few feet from the door and turned. "Beg your pardon, Miss," he said in a heavy Scottish accent. "But you must be in the wrong place."

Oh how she wished that were true. "I'm here to see my husband."

Annoyance flashed in his eyes. "We don't allow ladies at Madam Duvall's."

Of that she was sure.

He took a step toward her and Phoebe pulled the pistol from her pocket. He halted.

"Micah," called a woman as she stepped out from a room to the right.

"Madam Duvall, I presume?" Phoebe asked without taking her eyes from the bodyguard.

"There's no need for the weapon, madam," she replied.

"That remains to be seen," Phoebe said. "Please inform Lord Ashlund that his wife is here."

"Wife? I wasn't aware His Lordship had married."

Her heart lurched. He hadn't told anyone he was married. Her reaction was stupid, she knew, but she wasn't going to deny the hurt.

"Where is he?" Phoebe demanded of Madam Duvall.

Uncertainty flickered across her face, but she nodded toward the hallway. "Upstairs. Come with me." She started down the hallway.

Phoebe gave the bodyguard a wide birth, then pocketed the gun and followed Madam Duvall down the corridor, up two flights of stairs, and down another corridor. Madam Duvall stopped before a set of double doors, gave a perfunctory knock, and entered.

"Lord Ashlund—"

"Yes, Letty," Kiernan interrupted. He sat across the lavishly furnished bedchamber at a secretary, his back turned. He confirmed Phoebe's suspicions when he said, "Show my wife in." He continued writing as Phoebe entered, and Madam Duvall left, closing the doors behind her. He laid down his pen and rolled his chair around to face her. He wore a kilt, as he had for their wedding. She couldn't halt the flick of her gaze to his muscled calves. The man could drive a woman wild. He *had* driven her wild.

"You never cease to amaze me." He leaned back in his chair and crossed his arms over his chest. "Where does my father think you are?"

"On my way to London to see Adam's family."

Kiernan nodded. "And how did you find me?"

"The Andalusian."

"That horse is likely to get me killed." Kiernan rose and strode to her. Once at her side, he caught her hand and raised it to his lips. "Things aren't what they appear, my dear."

Ah, Phoebe reflected with a stab of sadness, if only they were as simple as they appeared. "I suppose it's my fault you've sought solace in a brothel," she said. He gave her a questioning look, and she added, "I wasn't a proper bride on our wedding night."

Amusement flickered in his eyes. "I will have to remember your love of brandy, but I doubt you believe the fact we didn't consummate our marriage is why I'm here."

"What else am I to assume?"

"What indeed?" he murmured.

Kiernan reached up and she stilled when he undid the clasp on her cloak. His warm fingers brushed her collarbone and gooseflesh raced down her arms. He swung the cloak from around her shoulders and tossed it onto a nearby chair. Then, with a firm hand on her elbow, he directed her to the couch that faced the fireplace. She sat down and he lowered himself onto the cushion beside her.

"I should have told you the truth," he began, "well...before now, at any rate."

"What truth would that be, my lord?"

"You recall the Highlanders who have been displaced from their homes these past years? You may not be aware of it, but many are wanted criminals."

Phoebe lifted one shoulder in a shrug. "When one plans the assassination of noblewomen..."

A corner of his mouth lifted. "I felt sure you hadn't forgotten."

"It is difficult to forget when one is threatened at gun point."

"Desperate people do desperate things," he replied. "But, if you recall, it was you who pointed out that Robbie's pistol wasn't loaded, and *you* stopped me from beating him to death."

"I remember," she said—and she also remembered a line from her father's letter. *You cannot comprehend the fine line between reason and desperation when all choices have been eliminated.*

"Desperation does not excuse murder," she told her husband.

"Surely, you understand how those in power might manipulate others' desperation for their own means?" Kiernan asked.

It is shocking to learn that one's leaders are willing to sacrifice their countrymen for money and power came another startling salvo from her father's letter.

Then it seemed Kiernan had read her mind when he asked, "How does a man take back that which was stolen from him by his betters?"

"He-there are channels one goes through." She clamped down on the strange sense of indecision that muddled her brain. "Protocol. *Not* murder."

Kiernan gave a gentle smile that caused her chest to tighten.

"Ahh," he said. "And the men who have been trampled upon should trust those in power, those who robbed them, cast them from their homes like animals—and worse—to follow this *protocol*?"

218

The words were barely out of his mouth when her mind flooded with *those few rich and powerful men who rule supreme in our society have stolen our rights.*

Anger shot through her. "You condone murder under any circumstances?"

"I should ignore the innocent who are murdered by their masters, yet bring to justice those men who strike back at their murderous overlords?" he said, but might as well have repeated her father's words, *Ironically, had I known then what I know now, I would be guilty of their accusations.*

The tears she'd held in check since discovering Kiernan was in Dornoch burned the corners of her eyes. It was as if he had read her father's letter. But that letter lay in the bottom of a drawer in England.

"How can you understand?" she demanded. "You've never faced hunger, cold, the prospect of no home."

"Perhaps not," he agreed. "But Ashlunds are also MacGregors, and MacGregors live under threat. You will remember Zachariah and his men."

Phoebe drew a sharp breath. She had taken Zachariah for a man who double-crossed an employer, who had masterminded the kidnapping of a wealthy marquess. But Kiernan inferred that the employer wanted Kiernan MacGregor the man, not the British nobleman.

Phoebe lifted her chin. "Kiernan MacGregor may face many dangers, but what chance is there the Marquess of Ashlund will ever stand accused of treason?"

Kiernan didn't break from her stare. "After today, very great. You see, I am confessing to you my part in aiding criminals escape the fate their government would impose upon them."

"You are in league with them," she cried.

"In league with them for what, a plot to kill a woman hundreds of miles away?"

Phoebe glared at him. "The duchess would not be so blasé about the plotting of her murder."

He gave a short laugh. "She would like nothing better than to send those men to the gallows for something that never happened."

"You're twisting the truth. Their plot to murder *anyone* is a crime."

"Can you so easily judge and condemn a man who has had even the most basic rights denied him?" Kiernan asked.

Would it shock you to hear that I relish the day I shall destroy my accusers? They have taken all I hold dear: you, our darling Phoebe and, lastly, "my freedom," she said out loud. Surprise flickered in Kiernan's eyes, and she added, "I am not their judge. The law must deal with them."

"You mean the law dispensed by people like the duchess, or perhaps those gracious men in the House of Lords? Say, Lord Ronald Harrington, who makes the very laws that protect them?"

219

"Lord Harrington?"

You cannot know how my accusers make even the most abhorrent criminal look like one of God's angels. I sorely underestimated the depth of their deceit.

Her head swam. Surely her father hadn't meant—

"You think I'm wrong to slip the hangman's noose from around the necks of accused criminals?" Kiernan asked.

Just as I did yours, she knew he was thinking, and could no longer hold back the tears.

"Damnation, Phoebe." He pulled her close. "I'm not as bad as all that, I promise," he said. "I've been a terrible suitor and a worse husband. Finding me here is inexcusable, and my confession in such surroundings..."

His confession? He had confessed to aiding criminals. Criminals he believed were victims...just as his kinsmen David had been? Winnie was right, Kiernan hadn't forgotten.

"I shouldn't have left you only a day after our marriage," he said.

She became aware of the heat of his fingers around her waist. Phoebe shook her head in an effort to clear the haze in her mind.

"And, while I forgive you, you are correct," he said. "We didn't consummate our marriage."

He shifted and the moist warmth of his lips touched her throat. His mouth moved in what seemed infinitesimal increments along her neck. Shivers raced along her flesh. His mouth slid onto her ear.

"This is, perhaps, not the most fitting place," he whispered, his breath skimming across her skin, "but you have me at a disadvantage. Your touch drives me wild."

She vaguely remembered trying to drive him wild, stroking his engorged member—that she remembered too well—but he'd gotten the better of her.

"Technically," he went on, his deep voice moving over her like silk as he ran his tongue along the edge of her ear, "this isn't our wedding night. Therefore, it's not as if I'm a complete cad. Can you forgive me for, yet, one more transgression?" His mouth glided across her cheek. "I promise to be a better husband afterwards." He covered her mouth with his and dragged her against him.

Her breasts, crushed against his chest, ached. She exhaled, her breath mingling with his. A soft moan emanate from her throat. He slid a hand up her back and ran his fingers along her neck just below the hairline.

Phoebe shivered.

He pulled her to her feet. Her legs felt like rubber.

"Steady, sweetheart."

He turned her until her back faced him and pushed aside her hair. With one arm around her waist, he held her close while kissing her neck. She was vaguely aware of him unbuttoning her dress, but the sensation of his mouth on the sensitive skin of her neck muddled her brain. A moment later, he pushed the dress from her shoulders and it slipped to the floor. He grasped her chemise and began pulling it over her head.

"My lord," she cried, but he had the garment off her and a chill raced across her flesh.

He turned her and her skin heated when his gaze dropped to her naked breasts.

"Sir," she began, but he cut her off with a kiss, then lifted her into his arms and crossed to the bed. He laid her on the mattress and she knew she should push him away, leave, run as far away from him as she could. But when he lowered himself onto her, a dizzying current spun the room. Then he kissed her and she was sure she was drowning. He trailed kisses along her cheek and down her throat to her shoulder.

"Sweetheart," he said, and Phoebe felt herself floating between the real and unreal.

He filled her senses.

Kiernan shoved off of the bed and in seconds had his boots off. He rose, loosened his belt, then unwrapped his kilt. Phoebe's heart jumped in the instant before the plaide dropped to the floor and she couldn't tear her gaze from his shaft. He was just as he'd been that night in his chambers: thick, rigid, and—heaven help her—in definite proportion to his size. He began unbuttoning his shirt.

Her heart beat faster. What in God's name was she doing? She hadn't come here to seduce her husband. She had come looking for her father. Kiernan braced one knee on the bed, then bent and kissed her. Phoebe started to shove him away, but her palms connected with the hard flesh of his chest. Her eyes flew open and the sight of her fingers splayed against the dark expanse of muscle caused her to knead the unyielding flesh. He drew back a fraction and she tore her gaze from the mesmerizing sight to see that his blue eyes had darkened to a hard glitter.

He shucked his shirt, then came down on top of her. Her breath hitched and she clutched his shoulders. The softer contours of her body submitted to his hard planes, and his engorged member lay thick and heavy on her belly. Her nipples rose to marbled points against his chest and the juncture between her legs tightened in response. She couldn't halt the reaction and a throb thrummed from the most intimate part of her.

Kieran covered her mouth with his as he shifted, then began a slow glide of his shaft through her curls and along her belly. Phoebe sucked in a breath and he slipped his tongue inside her mouth. He gave another slow thrust of his shaft, this time caressing the tip of the throbbing point between her legs. Phoebe startled at the pleasure that radiated through her. Feather light, one hand skimmed along her arm, over her shoulder, then covered her breast. Kneading the breast, he broke the kiss and slid his mouth along her cheek, down her neck to the other breast. An instant later, he sucked a nipple into his mouth.

She was slowly going insane.

He reached between their bodies and Phoebe gasped when his warm finger stroked her heated sex. He flicked his tongue on her nipple as his finger teased, stroked, urged her to want more…to want him. She gripped his shoulders in an effort to halt the whirl of sensations, but the feel of steel beneath her fingers compelled her to pull him closer instead.

The stroking ceased and she realized he was fitting his shaft to the entrance of her channel. Her stomach did a somersault. This was as far as she and Brandon had gotten—though the journey had been nothing like this. She hadn't lost her mind with Brandon. The tip of Kiernan's penis eased into her. Phoebe tensed.

"Easy, love," he whispered. "We have all night."

She flushed. He had guessed the truth? But how?

He inched deeper. She held her breath as his girth stretched her. This was strange. He reached between them and began stroking her again, this time with more fervor. She clamped her legs around his hips.

"That's it," he coaxed, and massaged her faster.

Her mind confused the sensation with his deeper penetration. He had stopped, hadn't he? Need rose on a tide and she remembered this same feeling from the night he'd given her pleasure. God forgive her, she wanted that now. He began flicking her sensitive nub. She lifted her hips and in the next instant he shoved into her hilt deep. A split second of tearing pain, then he lay on her unmoving.

She waited, suddenly lucid and uncertain. Did a wife tell her husband to get himself off her when he had just taken her virginity?

His chest rose then fell with a deep breath…and he kissed her. Warmth began a slow spread through her. He grasped her hands, raised them over her head and threaded his fingers with hers. Then he began moving inside her. This was nothing like a moment ago. He slid effortlessly in and out of her slick channel. Her heart rate kicked up. His hips rocked against her with each slow stroke of his rod along her walls. Phoebe laced her fingers more tightly with his. He thrust faster, harder. She drew a shaky breath. Pleasure tickled at the edges of consciousness. She clamped her legs around his hips and startled at the sensations that radiated through her. Tentatively, she lifted her hips to meet his surge. The tip of his penis seemed to crash into the back of her wall.

He groaned and crushed her deeper into the mattress with a fierce thrust. A mixture of pleasure and pain shot through her. His hips slammed into her with each powerful plunge deeper. Kiernan abruptly shifted and sucked a nipple into his mouth. Blinding pleasure surged through Phoebe. She squeezed her eyes shut. A bright white light blurred her vision behind her eyelids. Her muscles tightened around Kiernan in climax. A hoarse groan rumbled through his chest and he ground himself against her. He released her fingers and slid his arms around her, squeezing so that she could scarce catch her breath. But the discomfort was flooded by the ripples of aftershock that radiated through her body. He pounded into her, then gave a final thrust that seemed to reach clear to her core.

"Phoebe."

The hoarse whisper sent a strange ripple of emotion through her as the pleasure subsided on smaller then smaller waves. He thrust again, slowly. Phoebe wrapped her arms around his shoulders in the last seconds as he moved inside her then finally relaxed.

They lay unmoving for a long moment, their bodies slicked with sweat, then Kiernan slid from her. Cool air washed over her heated flesh. He pulled the blanket up over them, then tugged her backside against him. Phoebe blinked at the stars that winked in the night sky through the window, then closed her eyes.

Chapter Twenty-One

*P*hoebe awoke chilled. She glanced around the darkened room, her eyes unfocused. She shivered and tugged the bedcovers up over her shoulders—then remembered. By heavens, she had let her husband bed her in a brothel. Worse, she'd liked it.

A faint noise sounded. She shifted her gaze to the left where a sliver of light shone beneath a door she thought opened to a closet. Did the door connect to another room? She threw back the covers and grimaced when cool air rolled across her naked body. Phoebe pulled a blanket from the bed, wrapped it around her, and crept to the door. She placed her ear against the wood but heard nothing, so lowered herself onto her knees and looked under the door. Another door was visible fifteen feet away. A closet connected another room, she realized, and the opposite door was open.

Phoebe stood and slowly turned the knob. The door clicked open, and she waited for any sounds of alert, but silence followed. Carefully, she inched opened the door and the murmur of Kiernan's voice reached her. She strained to make out his words, but his voice was pitched too low. She tiptoed across the floor to the door and peeked through the crack. Her view included an armoire beside a window. She eased closer to the door and cocked her ear as close to the opening as possible.

Kiernan quieted, another voice murmured something, then Kiernan said, "What better way to catch a traitor?"

"We should go," the man said.

Kiernan sighed. "I had more pleasant plans for the morning, but if we hurry, I may make it back before my wife wakes. Give me a moment."

Phoebe's pulse jumped. Footsteps approached the door. She sprinted for the opposite door and reached it in two leaps, carefully shut it, and ran the last few paces to the bed. She threw the blanket over her as she turned toward the wall. A moment later, the door softly clicked and the soft pad of feet neared, then stopped. Phoebe forced even breathing as if asleep, and he left. She waited another moment, then sprang from the bed and dressed.

Moonlight shone through fast moving clouds, illuminating the two men's tracks in the moist ground. Not that Phoebe had to track them. In the distance, they walked down the main street, their great coats fanned out around them like bat wings. She hugged her cloak tighter, keeping a hand pressed against the pistol in her pocket, and hurried through the shadows cast by the shops that lined the deserted street.

The men took a right turn down a narrow lane. She rushed to the edge of the building and peeked around the corner. When they were far enough ahead, she hugged the wall and followed. They wound their way through the streets for another fifteen minutes as the tang of salt air intensified.

They walked another ten minutes and she grew concerned. Sunrise was but an hour away. Minutes later, the distinct caw of the sea's scavenger birds broke the nightly silence.

Kiernan and his companion slowed and Phoebe halted at the nearest cottage and pressed close to the building. The men angled toward a house and she watched as they reached the door and knocked. The door opened and dim light splashed out into the darkness. They stepped inside and the door closed.

When Phoebe reached the cottage, she made a quick inspection that revealed no open windows. She glanced up at the sky and prayed she didn't have long to wait.

Light fingered across the dark sky in gray streaks. Another quarter of an hour and the sun would peak over the horizon. A door clicked open and Phoebe crept from the side of the cottage to the rear. A low murmur of voices was followed by the light crunch of boots on the rocky terrain. Their footsteps began to fade and she hurried to the edge of the cottage and peered around the corner. Four figures silhouetted by the gray dawn passed along the lane.

Minutes later, the sun's rim edged up the sky. Shops had replaced cottages, and sailors and merchants milled about the street. Phoebe kept the hood of her cloak around her face while walking on the opposite side of the street a safe distance behind the men. The man who had accompanied Kiernan from Madam Duvall's was with him, along with Mather, but the third man was a stranger.

The street veered to the right and Phoebe slowed as she rounded the corner. A bay jutted inland and several ships stood docked in the water. The men rounded a shop and disappeared from view. She slowed in front of the shop and gazed in the window at the nautical almanacs and supplies displayed in the window. Two men appeared from around the building and she waited until they passed before continuing to the building edge. At the end of that lane, past several buildings, a single ship bobbed at the dock. The lane was empty except for Kiernan and two of companions—Mather was gone—and they stood near the gangplank.

The stranger to Kiernan's right clapped him on the back as a sailor appeared on deck and called to them from the ship. The stranger raised a hand in salute, turning so that she glimpsed his profile. The sailor waved back then disappeared below. Phoebe stared at the man, whose back was once again facing her. There was something—

"Are ye lost, lass?" a deep voice rumbled.

Phoebe turned toward the speaker. A large Highlander stood beside her, a revolver shoved into one side of his belt, and pistol in the other.

"Oh, no." She smiled. "I am just wondering who that man is. He looks familiar. Do you know him?" She motioned toward the stranger.

The Highlander glanced at them. "Which one? I know them all."

"Who are they?"

"A lady doesn't ask about strange men," he said.

"A lady can ask about her husband's associates," she replied.

He gave her a curious look, then said, "The one standing to your husband's left is David MacKenzie."

She scowled. "How do you know which man is my husband?"

He raised a brow. "I know David's wife. The other," he motioned to the man with his back to them, "is fifty-seven years old."

"Men his age marry," she said. "What is his name?"

"Clachair."

"Clachair?" She jerked her gaze onto him and, as if finally realizing she was there, Kiernan looked in her direction.

Clachair turned, and Phoebe stared into eyes identical to those belonging to the man in the portrait that hung over the salon fireplace in her uncle's London home: her father's eyes. Recognition registered on his face, and her surroundings swam around her in a swirl of black. Iron fingers closed around her arm. Phoebe snapped from the faint and nearly tripped when the man pulled her toward Kiernan and Clachair, who were now walking in her direction. Her legs felt like jelly and she suddenly didn't want to talk to either of them—ever. A strange sense of panic welled up and she yanked in an effort to free herself from the man.

"*Sir.*" She yanked harder.

A shot rang out, whizzing past them from the street behind them. The man shoved her to the ground and yanked the revolver from his belt. She started to scramble up.

"Androu!" Kiernan shouted. "Get her out of here."

Phoebe twisted in an effort to look in Kiernan's direction, but Androu swept her into a bear hug and in three long steps, reached the gag between the nearest building, and dropped her onto her feet. She pulled the pistol from her cloak.

Androu glanced back. "By the Saints, are ye daft, woman?" He knocked the weapon from her hand with a heavy-handed swipe.

She cried out as the pistol sailed into the lane. "You fool! Hand over your revolver."

His brows snapped down in a frown. "I'm not of a mind to be shot by a woman."

Another gun report sounded. A woman screamed.

Androu's head whipped around and he peered past the building toward the ship. "Run, MacGregor," he shouted, and fired.

Phoebe hugged the opposite building and peered out toward the ship. She caught sight of Kiernan an instant before he lunged into their alley. Another shot blasted, this time, from the direction of the ship, and Androu fired back.

Kiernan seized Phoebe's shoulders. "Are you all right?"

She nodded.

"What in God's name are you doing here? Never mind. In the future, I'll entertain guests someplace other than a room next to our bedchamber."

"Kiernan." Phoebe gasped his lapel. "That man—Clachair—is my father."

Kiernan's expression softened. "I know. I meant to tell you, but," he flashed a lopsided grin, "you distracted me. That's why I'm here. I had to tell your father I'd married you."

Tears threatened again. "What?"

"Stay back!" Androu shouted, then, "There the bloody bastards are!" He fired again.

Kiernan gave her a hard shake. "Do not move, Lady Ashlund, or I swear by God Almighty, I'll spank your bare arse in the town square." He released her and pulled the revolver from his waistband as he sidled up to the building's edge and peered into the lane. "Your handiwork?" he said to Androu.

"Aye, got him through the heart."

"Damn good shot. No sign of the others. How many did you count?"

"Two, maybe three. They made MacDougal's place, nearest the ship."

"Clachair," Kiernan shouted, "Stay down."

"Has Clach—my father—no weapon?" Phoebe demanded.

"No."

"Why not?"

Kiernan's attention remained on the street. "He's a man of peace, Phoebe."

A tremor shook her. "I always knew he was a peaceful man. No such man could be a traitor."

Kiernan's gaze shifted onto her. "I believe we discussed this last night."

She felt her eyes widen and he lifted a brow in confirmation of her thoughts: her father was the Clachair wanted by the Crown because, like Kiernan, he was aiding criminals. He was, indeed, a traitor.

Her jaw tightened, then she whirled on Androu. "Give me your spare pistol."

He cast a shocked look at Kiernan.

"Do as she says," Kiernan instructed.

Androu looked dubious, but pulled the pistol from his waistband and extended it butt first.

She looked at the pistol. "Had you not knocked my Blanch pistol from my grasp, I would not have to make do with this archaic piece of machinery."

Androu looked offended. "'Tis a respectable Scottish pistol."

"Flintlock," Phoebe muttered. "Care to trade the Pepperbox for this pistol?"

His eyes narrowed, then he swung his gaze onto Kiernan. "I'll go find the bastards for you."

Kiernan shook his head. "I must ask that you do something far more important."

Understanding struck like lightning and Phoebe began backing up.

"Stay where you are, Phoebe, or that spanking will be forthcoming," Kiernan said without taking his eyes off of Androu, and she halted when he added, "She's my wife, Androu."

Something in the way he said 'my wife' sent a tremor through her stomach.

"Aye," Androu replied, and Kiernan faced her.

"He's my father," she pleaded.

Kiernan stepped forward and grasped her shoulders. "And he's my friend, for many years."

"Years?" she repeated.

"Yes, love, years. Now trust me." He flashed the all-too-familiar grin, and added, "After all, you're my wife—spy and all." He cut off her gasp with a hard kiss, then shoved her into Androu's arms. "Whatever you do, Androu, don't let her out of your sight. She's a very clever woman. Sit on her, if necessary."

"MacGregor," she shouted, but Androu hefted her up like a sack of potatoes and raced down the tiny alley.

Kiernan glanced back at her, then looked both ways down the lane and disappeared, headed toward the ship.

"Release me," Phoebe ordered, and jammed the pistol into Androu's side. "Or I'll shoot."

He halted at the edge of the building. "No you won't. Unless you wish to explain to your husband that you shot his cousin's husband."

Phoebe ceased pacing and whirled when the door of the general store creaked open. The crowd that had gathered in the shop fell silent. Phoebe looked past them, past Androu, who sat in the front of the shop, gaze steady on the door, to see another villager enter the store. Androu didn't look back at her, but rose, and moved to the window. He leaned against the wall and stared outside.

Phoebe joined him. "Why haven't they returned? It's been over an hour."

He straightened from the wall. "Perhaps we'll find out now."

Phoebe looked out the window and recognized the man approaching as one of the men Androu had sent to help Kiernan.

"Don't leave this spot," Androu ordered, and headed for the door.

Phoebe watched through the window as the man stepped up on to the boardwalk and began talking with Androu. The man waved his arms in heated conversation and Androu glanced back in her direction. The man grew still as Androu spoke. The man spoke again, and Androu cast a quick glance in her direction. A moment later, the man turned and hurried down the street, and Androu entered the shop.

"The bast—er, criminal has taken to the forest and MacGregor has gone for him," he said. "Murphy is gathering more men for the hunt."

Phoebe cast an anxious glance at the darkening clouds.

"Your husband will be all right, lass."

"Damn him," she muttered. "And damn my father. Damn them both."

"Your father?"

Phoebe shifted her gaze to him. "How many men have joined the search?"

"Enough," he replied. "MacGregor wants me to take you back to, er..."

"Madam Duvall's?" Phoebe snorted. "Try that, sir, and I'll shoot off your bollocks."

Androu sighed. "Your husband was afraid you'd say something like that. Christine," he called over his shoulder, "cut me several strips of material, lass."

Aside from the drum of rain pelting the house, all had remained quiet since Phoebe returned to Madam Duvall's two hours ago. Arm draped across the back of the couch, both feet tucked beneath her skirts on the couch, she stared out the drawing room window into a private garden. The front door opened in the foyer and Phoebe checked a start of terror at the murmur of voices. Kiernan appeared first in the doorway. His raven

229

lay hair matted against his forehead and neck, and his coat dripped water on the carpet, but it was the harsh look in his eyes that frightened Phoebe.

Lord Stoneleigh stepped into the room next.

"Lord Stonel—" His name died on her lips when he cleared the doorway and another figured entered the light of the room, his body half visible behind the large frame of her husband.

Kiernan stepped aside, allowing Mason Wallington to enter the room. Phoebe remained as still as a statue, arm slung over the top of the couch, not a lock of golden hair askew from where the tresses were piled high atop her head. For an instant, Kiernan feared the shock might cause her to swoon, then she blinked, breaking the spell.

"Hello, sir," she said.

"Sir?" Mason repeated.

He crossed the room and pulled her up and into a hug. Regan seated himself in a chair to Kiernan's right, and a long silence passed until Mason at last held Phoebe at arm's length and stared into her eyes.

"Sir?" he repeated.

She shrugged. "Now that you're here, I find I'm not sure what to do with you."

He laughed and hugged her again, then released her and urged her back onto the couch, sitting beside her.

"What happened?" she asked, looking from him to Kiernan.

"We caught five of the men, but one escaped, perhaps two," Kiernan replied. "We have a dozen men on their trail. We'll find them."

Her gaze shifted onto Mason. "My guess is they were sent by Lord Harrington."

"You know who he is?" he asked.

"Yes."

He glanced at Kiernan, then Regan.

Phoebe frowned then turned toward Kiernan. "What—Oh. You think I'm connected with Lord Harrington, that I led him here."

"Phoebe—" Mason began, but she cut him off.

"There's no need to apologize. You may not be far from the truth."

He placed a hand over hers. "Being associated with Alistair Redgrave does not mean you are associated with Lord Harrington."

"But how—" she began, then understanding shone in her eyes. "Of course. Lord Redgrave has known all along where you were and apprised you of my...activities."

"I'm sorry, Phoebe. There was no other way. I wasn't willing to risk your life by telling you the truth."

She looked at Kiernan. "And you, sir, you weren't willing to risk your wife knowing too much about you?"

"I have been honest about my intentions, Phoebe. I didn't know you were a spy until yesterday—which—" he laughed, "—doesn't speak highly of my deductive abilities."

"How did you know that Redgrave knew of my whereabouts?" Mason asked her.

"I didn't, until recently. Do you remember John Stafford?"

Mason looked surprised. "Of course. He headed the operation to capture the Cato Street conspirators."

"He died recently," she said.

Mason's eyes clouded. "He was a good man. But what has he to do with you?"

"He sent me a journal of his private investigation into the allegations against you. He believed you were innocent."

"Well, damn it all." Mason laughed. "Redgrave told me of the investigation. I should have known John would keep a thorough account. I suppose I also should have known my daughter would follow that trail."

"You were my final quarry," she said, "but I was headed for Tain."

"Ahh," Mason said, "Galbraith, Redgrave's trail."

"Yes."

"How did you end up in Dornoch?" Kiernan asked.

Phoebe lifted a brow. "Robbie."

"Robbie?"

"The Achilty Inn?" she said.

Kiernan groaned. "You have a knack for being at just the right place, my dear." And he had to admit, he liked that.

"It's in the blood," Mason said.

"Quite right," Kiernan said, and winked at Phoebe. "I'll have to remember that in the future."

"And I will have to remember that my husband is a schemer."

"Phoebe—" he began, but she cut her gaze onto Mason.

"Was my abduction your doing? Why concoct such a ridiculous scheme?"

"That," he said, "was pure chance."

Phoebe snorted. "I don't believe you."

"Your kidnapping is exactly what it seems," Kiernan said. "And is all my fault," he added when she narrowed her eyes.

"It's too fantastical," she said.

"I did tell you that when I saw you that night, I intended to secure an introduction. If you hadn't been in that carriage, it would have only been a matter of time before I found you...and fell in love with you."

Her lips parted in surprise and a blush reddened her cheeks. Kiernan was suddenly certain he would never tire of that reaction.

"Have you lost your mind?" she demanded.

"I lost my mind the night I waylaid your coach."

The blush deepened and she cast an embarrassed glance at her father. There came a sharp rap on the door and it opened.

"Forgive me," Madam Duvall said, "but you have another guest." She stepped aside and Kiernan straightened from the wall when the one man he didn't want to see stepped into the room.

Phoebe shoved to her feet.

Lord Ronald Harrington stopped three paces inside the room, his gaze locked on her father. "Tell your daughter and Lord Ashlund to relax. I wouldn't get a round off without receiving a bullet for my trouble." He gave a gracious nod to Phoebe. "Miss Wallington is quite a good shot."

"That's Lady Ashlund," Kiernan said.

Lord Harrington appeared surprised. "My congratulations."

Phoebe tensed, then felt her father's warm fingers grasp hers. Her heart pounded. What was Lord Harrington doing here? Alistair's words as written in John Stafford's journal raced to the forefront of her mind, "*The criminals you deal with are nothing like Harrington. He has power and connections that are unimpeachable.*" What was Lord Harrington's part in her father being accused? Her father gently pulled her back onto the couch. And Lord Harrington's gaze shifted to him.

"You are looking well, Wallington."

"You look as if you've eaten and drunk too much," he replied.

"The price of sitting at my desk so much. I wouldn't have thought of looking for you in Scotland," he said. "Clachair was rumored to be in France. Clachair: bricklayer, stonemason." He raised a brow. "The name was simply too obvious."

Phoebe jerked her gaze onto her father. Clachair: Mason. She hadn't made the connection.

He smiled softly, as if reading her mind, and said, "It took my daughter to find me."

Pain stabbed through her. She'd told Lord Redgrave her suspicions about Kiernan being in contact with Clachair, and the information had reached Lord Harrington. She squeezed her father's hand and he squeezed back.

"Actually, she isn't responsible for my being here," Lord Harrington said. "You have Lord Ashlund to thank for us finding you. Mason, your association with him is just a fortunate happenstance." He looked at Kiernan. "Really, my dear boy, aiding criminals?" He made a tsking sound. "When wanted criminals began to disappear, we knew someone was helping them leave the country. We placed several individuals among the ranks of the rebel rousers who were complaining about the government's financial endeavors in Scotland."

"Wilson," her father murmured.

Lord Harrington lifted his brows. "He was one of our agents. I gather his disappearance was your doing?"

"Yes, only we didn't kill him, but shipped him to a penal colony in Australia."

"Poor devil," Harrington muttered.

"Poor devil, indeed," her father said. "He was a maniacal killer. What do you want, Ronald?"

Phoebe's stomach knotted. What did he want? She opened her mouth to ask—demand—answers, but her father said, "You were a fool to come here. You must know it's not safe for you here."

Harrington gave him an indulgent look. "Surely, you don't think I was foolish enough to come here without informing someone?"

"That is exactly what I think," her father replied. "It's likely the only person you informed was Mallory, and, should you not return, he would gladly consign you to the devil."

Lord Harrington laughed. "Mallory is a good fellow, but certainly not the man to trust in such matters."

Who might Harrington have trusted? Phoebe looked at Lord Stoneleigh. What was the earl doing here?

"It is not I our dear Lord Harrington speaks of," Lord Stoneleigh said, clearly noticing her glance. "I am but a spectator."

Lord Harrington snorted. "I am aware of the connection between Stoneleigh and Ashlund. I had no intention of entrusting my fate to him. Besides, it isn't Lord Stoneleigh wants."

"Perhaps not," the earl agreed.

Phoebe could no longer stand the suspense. "What's going on?" she demanded.

"Later, my dear," Kiernan said quietly.

Before she could reply, Lord Harrington said to her father, "You stand accused of treason. It pains me, but the evidence against you is too great to ignore."

"Evidence you created," she cut in.

His eyes shifted onto her. "Beware, Lady Ashlund, you don't want to be found guilty of treason, as well."

"There is a great deal of evidence that says my father isn't guilty, sir. But his innocence isn't the question. The question is: why are you here?"

"He's here to kill me," her father said.

"His attempt to assassinate you at the dock failed. I am asking why he is here, in this room."

"Lord Harrington has come to guarantee his safe retreat," Lord Stoneleigh said.

"No one will accost you," her father said. "None of our men, that is. I cannot vouch for others."

Harrington inclined his head. "That is all I ask."

Phoebe glanced around the room in shock. "You can't just let him go."

Her father regarded her. "What would you have me do, kill him in cold blood?"

"I-I don't know, but to simply release him. What about the penal colony in Australia?"

"A man of his stature would attract far too much attention," Kiernan said.

"By heavens," she murmured.

"Exactly," her father replied."

"It's time you retired, Mason," Lord Harrington said.

Her father smiled, and Phoebe glimpsed a hint of the young man whose portrait hung over the mantle in her uncle's home. "I have no intention of allowing you to manipulate more men into the gallows."

"You and I both know Thistlewood was mad."

"The ends do not justify the means."

Lord Harrington straightened. "I am in the Queen's service. It is my duty to seek out and destroy all dissidents."

"My God." Her father shook his head. "You're as mad as Thistlewood was. Go home. You've done enough damage—" he glanced at her "—for a lifetime." He looked back at Harrington. "Don't come back. I won't be here, but others will be. And, Ronald, should you give me reason, I will return to England and kill you."

"You?" He gave a derisive laugh. "I wager you still don't own a pistol."

Her father stared, an answering glitter in his eyes. A thrill shot through Phoebe.

"If I hear so much as a whisper from you against my daughter, I will kill you," he said.

"Not to worry." Kiernan interjected. "I own a very respectable arsenal of pistols and I don't suffer the same aversion to violence that Mason does. Now, there's ship bound for England. I can get you aboard."

Harrington's jaw visibly tightened.

"Excellent," Her father stood and started toward the two men.

Phoebe jumped to her feet. "Don't think for a moment you're leaving me behind." She followed her father to the door.

Kiernan grasped her arm. "My dear—"

"Unless you intend on tying me up, I am going," she said.

"The idea does hold some appeal," he replied.

"I assure you, sir, it does not."

Kiernan sighed, and she disengaged her arm, then cast an inquiring look at her father. He smiled in amusement, then inclined his head in acquiescence.

"You won't accompany us, Regan?" Kiernan asked.

The earl stretched his legs and shook his head. "If you don't mind, I think I'll stay here and better acquaint myself with this establishment."

They headed out the door into the hallway where the bodyguard opened the front door for them. Phoebe started forward, but Kiernan grasped her arm.

"If you don't mind," he said, "Lord Harrington will go first."

"Then I will follow," her father said.

"Far be it from me to disagree with my father-in-law," Kiernan replied, keeping a grip on her arm.

"Ronald." Her father waved him forward.

"You have become suspicious in your old age," Lord Harrington commented, and stepped from the house onto the walkway. He tugged his coat closed and began buttoning it against the chill afternoon air.

Her father paused for a fraction of a second, then started out the door. Kiernan took a step forward.

A shot rang out.

Chapter Twenty-Two

"*F*ather!"

Phoebe's shout blared in Kiernan's ears. He shoved her back through the door, then threw a backhanded punch at Harrington as a second shot blasted. Harrington slammed into the building and Kiernan lunged for Mason in the instant he hit the walkway. Kiernan jammed his arms beneath his shoulders and hauled him back through the door and out of view of the open door.

Phoebe fell to her knees beside him. "He's been shot," she cried.

Feet raced across the overhead floorboards. Kiernan glanced at the open door. Harrington was gone. He didn't like that any better than if Harrington stood there with a gun to finish off the job.

Kiernan stripped off his coat and shoved it in front of Phoebe. "Staunch the blood."

She looked at him, eyes dazed.

"You've done it before," he shouted. "For me. Snap to, Phoebe."

She grabbed the coat and he yanked the revolver from his waistband and flattened himself against the wall near the door. Cautiously, he peered around the doorjamb. Harrington was nowhere in sight.

"God damn bastard," he cursed.

"MacGregor," Mason said in a harsh whisper.

"Father," Phoebe cried in unison with the snap of Kiernan's head in their direction.

"Shh," Mason said. His eyes shifted to Kiernan. "Get her to safety."

"I'm not leaving you," she said through tears.

Letty appeared on the stair landing with Regan two steps behind, a revolver in his hand. "*Mon dieu*," she breathed in unison with Regan's "Good God."

Regan pushed past her and she followed. She stopped beside Mason, as Regan sidled up to the door opposite Kiernan.

"What happened?"

Before Kiernan could answer, the pounding of boots on the wooden walkway pulled his attention back to the street. Douglas and Androu were racing along the walkway on the opposite side of the street.

"Stay back," Kiernan shouted. "The shooter is still out there."

"No, he's not," a man called from between one of the buildings across the street.

Kiernan aimed his pistol in the direction of the man's voice.

"Don't shoot, for Christ's sake," Regan said. "He's one of us."

Alistair Redgrave emerged from the alley, hands raised, but Kiernan didn't miss the revolver protruding from his waistband.

"What the hell are you doing here, Redgrave?" Kiernan demanded.

"Alistair?" Phoebe called.

"Stopping you from getting your head shot off," Redgrave called back. "Your shooter is back there." He motioned toward the alley behind him. "Dead."

"Androu, Douglas, go have a look," Kiernan ordered. "And start a search for Harrington."

The men took off at a run.

"Redgrave," Kiernan said, "if I don't like your explanation, I'll kill you." He glanced at Regan. "I'll deal with you as well. You didn't tell me the entire story behind why you're here."

"Blame Her Majesty," Regan said. "I was sworn to secrecy."

"The devil with your secrets. Redgrave," he called, "get in here and help with your friend." Kiernan shoved the pistol into his pocket. "Come along, Regan, we'll need you as well." He hurried to Mason. "Letty, a room with fresh linens and a doctor, if you please."

She nodded and called "Margaret," as she hurried through the drawing room door.

Redgrave appeared in the doorway and reached them an instant later. He knelt beside Mason.

"You're sure you got the man?" Kiernan demanded.

"A bullet through the heart."

"Any sign of Harrington?" Kiernan asked.

Phoebe gasped. He followed the direction of her stare and saw Harrington in the doorway with a gun. Kiernan grabbed for his pistol as the deafening roar of a shot rang out in the room. Harrington's eyes widened in shock, then he toppled backwards. Kiernan shifted his gaze to Letty, who stood in the drawing room doorway, a revolver pointed at Harrington. A small curl of smoke lifted from the barrel of her gun.

"I saw him pass by the window," she said. "He was skulking. That is never a good sign."

"No," Kiernan agreed, it isn't." He looked at Regan. "She beat you to the shot."

"I put the damn revolver in my belt."

"Never underestimate a woman. Let's get Mason to a bed. Where are we taking him, Letty?"

She lowered the weapon. "Third floor, second door on the right."

"Third floor?" Kiernan grunted as they lifted Mason. He didn't like the looks of the man. His eyes were closed and his chest didn't rise and fall with its usual vigor. "You plan to make us work, madam."

"The third floor is safer than the second floor," Letty replied, unruffled. "And that bed is unused."

"Yes, well," he cast a glance at Phoebe, who stood beside him, eyes fixed on her father, face wet with tears, "*unused* is exactly what we need."

The doctor had done all he could. Her father's life now lay in God's hands. To have come so far, to be so close, only to have him taken from her was too cruel. The candle beside his bed cast the only light in the darkened room and Phoebe felt her mind sliding into sleep. She jerked herself awake. She couldn't sleep. She couldn't leave her father's side. She had to be here, ward off death until her father was strong enough to fight that dark angel himself. He hadn't stirred since he'd closed his eyes before Kiernan and Alistair carried him upstairs. As long as he kept breathing, his strength would increase and, once he was rested enough, he would wake up.

But he didn't wake that night, and when Kiernan returned to the room as dawn once inched across the sky, Phoebe shook her head before he said what she knew he was going to say.

"I won't leave," she insisted. "If you carry me out and tie me up, I'll wrench free even if I leave my skin behind."

Kiernan lifted her from the chair and she struck out at him with her fists. He hugged her tight, then sat in the chair and settled her on his lap. She collapsed into his solid warmth and cried.

Phoebe sat across the carriage from her husband and studied him. Eyes closed, he leaned to the side, shoulder wedged against the corner. The worry lines around his eyes were softened, but she feared he didn't sleep. He had slept little in the last two weeks, perhaps even less than she. They both kept watch by her father's side while he lay in bed, his soul trapped between this world and the next. Kiernan had hovered over her as if it had been she who lay on death's door. There had been nights she prayed God would take her instead of her father. Phoebe took a slow, deep breath.

He had spared them both.

She looked out the window. The sun hung just above the trees in the west. Soft orange veiled the evening sky. Was the sky as beautiful in America? Phoebe smiled gently. She would ask her father. Despite Lord

Harrington's death, they all agreed her father was no longer safe in Scotland. Only after Alistair discovered who Harrington had confided in, could she travel to America to visit her father where he was on his way to stay with the duchess' brother.

Alistair. Gratitude welled up in her in the too-familiar desire to cry. His intervention had saved her father's life, and probably Kiernan's as well. She still couldn't believe that Lord Stoneleigh had been informing Alistair all along of Lord Harrington's comings and goings, and that it was Alistair who had instructed Lord Stoneleigh to follow him to Scotland. Kiernan had been furious that Regan hadn't told him that Redgrave was there, and that they suspected the real attempt on her father's life was yet to come.

"It was obvious that the assassination attempt at the docks was badly done." Alistair had laughed. *"Harrington would have made a very bad spy."*

Thank God for that small favor.

She shifted her attention back to Kiernan. He had placed himself in harm's way when he dragged her father into Madam Duvall's—he had put himself in harm's way half a dozen times since meeting her. And yet, he had said he loved her. There, without hesitation, in front of everyone at Madam Duvall's. He hadn't said it since, but she'd recalled the words a thousand times, and still had no idea what to think.

Phoebe lowered her gaze to where his shirt lay open at the neck. He wore no cravat. His arms lay crossed over his broad chest, his coat, unbuttoned, hung at his sides, and his legs were stretched out diagonally across the carriage floor. She glanced out the window. They were at least an hour and a half from her uncle's estate in Carlisle. Plenty of time... Would Mather and the two men the duke had insisted accompany them guess what was going on inside the carriage?

She carefully pulled the window curtain closed, then set aside the blanket Kiernan had draped over her legs when they left the inn after lunch. Phoebe placed one foot on the left of his legs, and the other on the right, then pulled up her skirts and grasped his shoulders as she straddled him.

Kiernan's eye shot open and he seized her shoulders, eyes momentarily unfocused in the dim lamplight. Phoebe lowered her gaze to his chest and began unbuttoning the top button on his shirt. She unbuttoned the next button and the next, until his chest lay bare. She removed the Highland belt pistol from his waistband and set the weapon on the opposite cushion, then flattened her palms on his chest and pushed aside the shirt. Then she kissed a nipple. The rise and fall of his chest grew heavier. She took the nipple into her mouth. His quick intake of breath brought an answering pulse from the place between her legs.

Kiernan's fingers tightened on her shoulders. She sucked harder. He drew her body closer. She moved to the other nipple and administered the same treatment. He shifted, brushing her head with his chin as he straightened. His shaft pressed enthusiastically beneath her buttocks. She slid her tongue up his chest to his neck, found his ear, and nibbled on the lobe. Kiernan pressed her down, grinding her against his arousal. The carriage hit a bump in the road, forcing her weight down on him with a sudden jolt, and he grunted. Moving her hands downward, Phoebe skimmed his chest until she found the first button on his trousers.

Her knuckles brushed the tip of his shaft as she pushed the button through its hole and she snapped her head up, meeting his gaze. The blaze in his eyes brought on a heady dizziness. By heavens, he liked what she was doing. With trembling fingers, she pushed the next button through its hole. Another, and the top of the trousers opened, revealing the upper half of his erection.

In quick succession, she unbuttoned the remaining three buttons. Her mouth went dry at sight of his engorged rod resting on his belly. She slowly wrapped her fingers around him. The carriage rocked slightly, and Kiernan arched his hips, sliding his shaft between her fingers. He pulled her against him. The carriage shifted and she accidentally gave him a hard squeeze. He groaned.

"Careful, my dear," he whispered hoarsely in her ear, "or you may bring too quick an end to this."

Phoebe released him and shifted on her knees until her cleft hovered over his erection. The gentle rocking of the carriage teased their joining as Phoebe lowered herself onto him. Kiernan slid his hands beneath her skirts, up her thighs to her waist. She kissed him slowly and he let her. His fingers flexed against her waist. She broke the kiss, then braced her hands on his shoulders as she slid up, then down again. Up, then down again, and again until Kiernan's hold on her turned fierce.

He quickened their rhythm. Bringing her down hard, he filled her to the hilt. Ripples of pleasure radiated deep within her. When he lifted and brought her down on him again, he arched his hips, meeting the stroke in midair. Phoebe trembled. He gave another hard thrust, gripping her bottom and grinding them together. He groaned, his head thrown back. Phoebe kissed him where neck met shoulder and nipped at his flesh. Kiernan hugged her close and she slid her arms around his neck.

He moved in her, circling slowly, the base of his shaft rubbing with firm insistence against her swollen sex. Phoebe gasped at the unexpected jolt of pleasure. He abruptly turned and lowered her onto her back and loomed over her, thrusting hard.

He kissed her, then whispered in her ear, "Together this time." He reached between them and massaged her sex.

Need coursed through her. He massaged faster. Climax ripped through her. Her breath caught, then pleasure shot through her on another, more intense wave. Kiernan ripped his hand away from her sex and, braced on one elbow, gripped her shoulder with the other hand and plunged deep inside her. She arched her hips, meeting his powerful thrust, and he groaned with his own release.

An unexpected shout came from Mather. Kiernan's head snapped in the direction of the door. A pounding on the top of the carriage followed and he yanked his shaft from inside her as they came to a thunderous halt. Phoebe felt herself slipping from the seat, but Kiernan caught her and shoved her back against the cushion. She sat up and he had his trousers buttoned in the next second. He grabbed the revolver from the opposite seat as a shot rang out, followed by a heavy thud up top.

"Don't do it!" shouted a man.

"Stand down, lads!" Mather yelled, and all went silent.

The carriage door flung open and Phoebe stared at a man and the Wilkinson double barrel over-and-under pistol he pointed at Kiernan.

"Well, well," he said through a kerchief that covered the lower half of his face, "what have we got here?" He glanced at Kiernan's open shirt.

Kiernan began buttoning his shirt. "Did you kill any of my men?"

"Never mind them," the man said. "I'm more interested in what you've been helping yourself to in this carriage."

"Are you willing to murder five people for a bit of sport?" Kiernan demanded.

"Never heard the fancy call fucking his wife a bit o' sport.'"

"She would be nothing more to you. What do you want?"

The man's eyes narrowed and her heart jumped. He intended to pull the trigger. Vaguely, she registered the other two masked highwaymen on horseback behind him, their weapons trained on the men up top. Then she kicked the man's arm. His arm flew upwards and the gun fired as Kiernan lunged for him. They hit the ground hard and Phoebe seized the revolver Kiernan had dropped.

The coach rocked, and the largest of the highwaymen shouted, "Don't move!"

Kiernan jumped to his feet, dragging the man with him. The man's scarf had twisted loose, revealing a square, whiskered jaw. The smaller of the mounted men leveled his gun on them. Phoebe leaned through the doorway and fired at him. His horse screamed as its rider jerked and slid from the saddle. Kiernan plowed a heavy blow into his opponent's jaw. The man stumbled backwards and tripped. He hit the ground near his fallen pistol. Kiernan lunged forward as the man snatched up the gun, and swung it onto Kiernan.

Phoebe cried out. A shot blasted and her vision blurred in the second before her mind registered Kiernan's opponent limp on the ground, blood spreading in a dark stain across his dirty shirt. She cut her gaze onto Mather, who gripped a revolver pointed at the dead man. Another shot blasted and she jumped.

"Nobody move," the remaining brigand shouted. "Or I'll shoot the lady."

The man pointed a dual barrel pistol at her. The long barrel ensured deadly accuracy. She would be dead before she hit the ground.

"You've got one shot," Kiernan snarled. "Get out while you still can."

The sudden beat of horse's hooves sounded through the trees.

"Drop your weapons!" a voice shouted.

"What the—" The brigand's curse cut short when a man burst from the trees.

Phoebe blinked, uncertain that the newcomer was really her cousin Ty Humphrey. The highwayman backed his horse and fired his revolver. Kiernan lunged for her. Ty came to a skidding halt as Kiernan's arms closed around her. Phoebe glimpsed the Blunderbuss pistol Ty aimed at the retreating highwayman in the instant before she landed on the ground, Kiernan on top of her.

Chapter Twenty-Three

*A*ccording to John Glen, the magistrate in Glasgow, there was no mistaking the bullet wounds that had killed Adam. He'd been shot with a Dragon, a pistol-sized Blunderbuss favored by pirates in the previous century; a weapon which was still loved by those who wanted to ensure they didn't miss their target while inflicting the maximum amount damage to their victims. Not a common weapon in this modern age, but Phoebe knew one man who owned a Blunderbuss.

She slipped into her uncle's townhouse through the kitchen door. As expected, all was quiet. The housekeeper and cook napped through midday in order to fortify themselves for the evening hours when Lady Albery made her greatest demands. Phoebe's uncle was still in Carlisle, and she prayed Ty was anywhere but home. If she encountered him, she was liable to put a bullet through him.

She hurried through the kitchen and up the main stairs, where she had less chance of encountering servants. Her aunt was adamant that only upstairs maids were allowed on the main staircases, and then only to polish the wood. On the third floor, Phoebe made her way to Ty's room. She knocked and, when no answer came, she slipped inside. She began her search with the desk on the left wall and halted when she discovered a letter from the Duke of Ashlund.

> *To Charles Wallington, Viscount Albery*
> *Sir,*
> *I write in regards to the marriage of my son, Kiernan MacGregor, Marquess of Ashlund, to your niece, Phoebe Wallington. This announcement will come as a surprise, but be advised there are circumstances surrounding this engagement we must discuss privately. The formal announcement has been dispatched to the post and will appear in print, at the earliest, the day you receive this letter, at the latest, the next.*

I will be in London within the week and shall call upon you immediately.
Signed,
Marcus McGregor, Duke of Ashlund

The letter the duke sent to her uncle? What was Ty doing with it?

She refolded the note and slipped it into her pocket, then finished looking through the drawer. Next, she searched the armoire without success. The nightstand followed and her heart jumped into her throat when she opened the drawer and stared down at the Blunderbuss. This was the weapon he'd carried two nights ago when the highwaymen ambushed them. Phoebe hadn't forgotten the look on the first highwayman's face, and his intent to shoot Kiernan. Highwaymen were almost unheard of in their modern times, and murder without provocation by a highwayman didn't make sense. A great many things didn't make sense. Like why Ty killed Adam.

Tears rushed to the surface and Phoebe was forced to sit on the bed in order to slow the turn of her stomach that threatened to bring up her breakfast. She had to maintain control, had find something, anything, that gave her a clue as to why Ty had killed Adam. It made no sense. She started to close the drawer, then decided to take the pistol. Phoebe hid the Blunderbuss in her pocket with the letter, but was forced to maintain a grip on the heavy weapon. She left the room, carefully closed the door, then hurried down the hall toward the library.

"You're sure no one will come up here?" a muffled male voice asked.

Phoebe's attention jumped to her aunt's closed door up ahead.

"Yes," Lady Albery replied. "Mrs. Jenkins and Cook are napping, and I left strict orders not to be disturbed for the afternoon. The maids won't dare venture upstairs until I call for them."

"But you called for me," the man said.

"You know I can't go a day without you," she replied in a sultry voice.

Phoebe stifled a gasp. Her aunt had a lover?

"You like that?"

"Yes," she gasped with a breathless moan. "Don't be gentle, Clive, fuck me hard."

Phoebe's stomach roiled.

"Happy to oblige," he said in a gritty voice.

Something in his voice gave her pause and she slowed. What was it?

Lady Albery cried out.

Phoebe stumbled, then caught herself. Dear God, she had to get away from there. She raced past her aunt's room, but couldn't drown out the sounds of the man's grunts and her aunt's moan. Phoebe reached the stairs and nearly tripped over her skirts on the first step. She yanked up her skirts and raced down the stairs. She reached the ground floor and left by the front door.

Once on the main street, she hailed a passing cab and collapsed onto the seat. "Oh, uncle," she sobbed, and couldn't halt the flood of tears.

When Phoebe arrived at the duke and duchess' home where she and Kiernan were staying were staying, she'd composed herself enough so that the servants wouldn't be able to detect her anxiety. She needed time to think, to figure out what Ty was doing with the note from the duke, and how she was going to tell her uncle about his wife. Tears threatened again, but Phoebe forced them back as she nodded to the butler.

"I'll be in my room, Hinks. I'm not to be disturbed."

He gave an austere cant of his head and she took the stairs at a leisurely pace. When she reached her room, Phoebe sat on the bed and burst into tears again. She wasn't wholly surprised her aunt was unfaithful, but her uncle would be. How was she going to tell him? The door to the antechamber connecting her room to Kiernan's opened and he stood in the doorway. Phoebe drew a sharp breath.

"What's wrong?" He strode to the bed.

"N-nothing."

"Give me any trouble, Phoebe, and I'll turn you over my knee."

She blinked, then ire shot through her. "You've threatened that many a time, my lord. I don't believe you."

Kiernan stood quietly for a moment. "It sounds as if you would like a spanking."

"What I would like is to be left alone."

"What's wrong?" His attention dropped to the pocket with the Blunderbuss.

His brow furrowed, but she realized his intent too late. Kiernan seized her arm, yanked her to her feet, and pulled the pistol from the pocket. The note fluttered to the floor.

"What's this?" He shoved the pistol close to her face.

Something in his tone gave her pause, and she realized he'd read the magistrate's report on Adam's death. He thought the weapon was hers…that she'd killed Adam.

Kiernan released her and snatched up the letter. She stood frozen as he read it.

His gaze shifted to her face. "What are you doing with my father's letter? Damnation, Phoebe, I know this isn't your weapon. What have you done?"

She considered telling him to go to the devil, but realized she couldn't sacrifice Adam's justice—and her uncle's life—for her own anger. "It belongs to my cousin Ty. As you have clearly guessed, I read John Glen's report on Adam's bullet wounds. I recalled that Ty was carrying a Blunderbuss when he happened upon us on the road."

"And the letter?" Kiernan demanded.

"That, too, I found in Ty's room."

Kiernan's mouth thinned. "Ty's room? You were snooping in Arlington's room? You are not to go back there. No more playing spy."

"*Playing* spy? I am a spy."

"Not anymore."

"I warned you, sir, that marriage would not change me. I'll come and go as I please, continue on as I always have."

He gave her a critical look. "I see. So it is you whose life won't change, while you brought me to task for believing I wouldn't change with marriage."

"I never asked you to change, and I made it perfectly clear I wouldn't."

He stepped close, towering over her. "A wife who wishes to attend parties is one thing. A fiancée who is spying and doesn't tell her future husband is quite another."

"I never planned on marrying you," she replied.

He nodded. "So I gather."

"If you are dissatisfied with the union, have the marriage annulled."

Kiernan scowled. "I have no intention of letting you go."

"Why? I have been nothing but trouble for you."

He snorted. "No truer words have been spoken, but that doesn't mean I don't love you."

Her mouth parted in surprise.

He lifted a brow. "What have you to say to that, madam?"

Phoebe narrowed her eyes. "I think that you are once again trying to charm me."

A speculative glint appeared in his eyes. "I haven't *charmed* you in two days."

Her cheeks flushed hot with the memory of how *she* had charmed him in their carriage.

"I am going to keep a closer watch on you, wife. There will no sleeping in the lady's chamber tonight. I want you in my bed."

She stared. "You're insane."

"Be that as it may, I warn you, when I return home, should I find you in this bed instead of mine, I will remove you to my bed and tie you there. As you know, I'm quite capable of carrying out *that* threat. Though you haven't learned where that can lead." He turned and started for the anteroom.

"By heavens," she exclaimed. "I have no intention of sitting idly by while you—"

He whirled. "What?"

"Where are you going?" she demanded.

"I have a meeting." He lifted the note and shook it. "I suspect you now know who is responsible for the story in the *Satirist*."

With that he whirled and left.

Phoebe stared. She hadn't told him about Clive.

Phoebe started awake when the clock in the library chimed. The book she'd been reading thunked as it struck the carpet and the second chime told her she'd slept for an hour. The fire had died to coal red embers and her blanket hung half off the couch where she lay. She considered putting another log on the fire, but pulled the blanket over her shoulders instead. Either Kiernan hadn't returned home, or he hadn't yet found her. The mansion was a labyrinth of rooms. He might have looked for her and given up. No, she decided. He hadn't exaggerated when he said he was a relentless hunter. He would search every nook and cranny of the mansion—then make her pay for the effort.

She wasn't strictly disobeying him—the idea she had to obey rankled beyond reason—after all, she hadn't gone to sleep in *her* bed. She had decided to tell him that she'd waited up in order to tell him about Clive...and that she remembered what it was that caught her attention when she'd heard his voice. Her aunt's lover was the highwayman who escaped.

The door opened with a quiet click. Phoebe froze, Kiernan's words rolling around in her head "...*you will pay the piper. That is me, madam, in case you think otherwise.*"

By heavens, she was actually trembling. Phoebe inched her head up until she could peek over the top of the couch. Her heart jumped into her throat. The man sitting at the duke's desk wasn't Kiernan.

"He was last seen at the Davenport soirée?" Kiernan asked of Mather as they descended the steps of his club.

"That was the report an hour ago, sir."

"So he is ensuring that witnesses can testify to his whereabouts. Good. And you're sure he knows I was contacted by someone anxious to sell me information about a man who hired him to kill me while in Scotland?"

"Mr. Sykes is known for not keeping a secret. I feel certain he has told Baron Arlington's valet the story."

They reached Kiernan's coach. "Here is where we part ways, Mather."

"I must protest once again, sir. I feel certain your father wouldn't approve of this plan."

Kiernan swung open the carriage door. "No, he wouldn't. In you go."

"I really should go with you."

"We've discussed this," Kiernan said. "I'm an easier target alone. Besides, I have half a dozen officers from the Metropolitan Police on the case."

"A bullet or a knife can find its mark before they police reach you."

"One way or another, Arlington intends to kill me. Then he will force Phoebe to marry him. I can't allow either."

"Your father is sure to send me packing once he learns I not only didn't stop you, but I aided you," he grumbled.

"We won't tell him." Mather still hesitated, and Kiernan laid a hand on his back. "Go on, my friend."

He sighed, but stepped into the carriage. Kiernan closed the door and started down the sidewalk. Ten minutes later, he turned into the nearest gaming hell.

An hour and several whiskies later, Kiernan left the club five hundred pounds poorer than when he entered. The big man sitting in the corner quietly drinking had cast him enough covert glances that Kiernan knew him to be his would-be killer. Kiernan couldn't help a grimace. Phoebe's cousin wasn't taking any chances. He'd hired a man a head taller than Kiernan.

Kiernan began an unsteady walk down the sidewalk. The pad of footsteps followed a moment later, and he was impressed that the big man could tread so lightly. This brigand might be a more practiced killer than Arlington's previous employees. A hansom cab passed. Kiernan flicked the passenger a glance and rubbed his chin as if scratching an itch. The man didn't twitch a muscle, but Kiernan knew he'd seen the signal. Kiernan made a sudden left into one of the appointed alleys. As expected, the footsteps quickened.

Up ahead, yellow lamplight spilled across the cobblestone from around a sharp turn. His assailant would want to catch him before he reached the light. The footsteps grew louder and Kiernan yanked free the pistol stuffed into his waistband, and turned. The man stopped ten feet away. Kiernan glimpsed a glint of metal an instant before the man drew back his hand, knife poised to throw.

Another man stepped into view behind Kiernan's assailant in the instant before Kiernan fired. The killer jerked to the left and hit the wall. Kiernan's mind registered the knife flying through the air toward him and he dove to the right. A shadow fell across his path and another shot blasted. The ping of metal striking metal whizzed an inch past his ear. He hit the ground and rolled. Boots pounded on cobblestone as he shoved to his feet. Two Metropolitan Police officers were yanking the man to his feet. Kiernan turned as two more officers rushed around the bend where Mather stood, his revolver pointed heavenward.

Kiernan scanned the cobblestones and spied the knife a few feet away. He took two steps, scooped up the weapon, and strode to Mather. Kiernan held the knife to the light. A small chip was visible in the hilt.

He looked at Mather. "You always were a good shot."

"A necessity, sir," he replied, and Kiernan knew he meant, *you really are a pain in the arse.*

Phoebe ducked her head down behind the couch. Her heart thundered. What was Ty doing here? What should she do? She had no weapon, hadn't thought she needed one. If she remained quiet, he might not discover her. Once he left the room, she could alert someone to his presence.

She willed her heart to stop its panicked rhythm and worked to slow her breathing. Ty would be rifling through the duke's desk for one reason only: he believed the duke knew something—no, not the duke, she realized. Kiernan. But what? Her confrontation with Kiernan a few hours ago slammed into her memory. He had taken the Blunderbuss and his father's letter. Surely those items weren't what Ty was looking for. They weren't incriminating enough for him to risk sneaking into the duke's home, and he couldn't know that she had taken them.

Her cousin had been acting strange of late. She'd seen no dark mood from him as she usually did when he gambled. He'd been more responsible, even concerned for her marriage, her inheritance. *"Ashlund is filthy rich,"* Ty had said. *"How could he possibly need your paltry fifteen thousand pound yearly income?"*

The memory made her realize that Ty never courted any of the ladies who could bring to him the modest inheritance a baron might expect. Surely, he must want a woman who could bring something to the marriage. Perhaps even a fifteen thousand pound yearly income? Her stomach clenched. It was too coincidental that her aunt's lover Clive was the highwayman who escaped, and Ty had miraculously arrived in time to save them from the brigand. Dear God, they had to be in league together. But that didn't explain why he'd killed Adam.

A shadow fell across her, and Ty came into view standing behind the couch. She gave a cry.

He placed his palms on the top of the couch and leaned forward. "Enjoying spying on me, Cousin?"

Her mind jumped to a dozen different answers before she recalled they were in the duke's home and they both knew he had no reason to be there.

Phoebe shoved off the couch as Ty grabbed for her. She thudded onto the carpet, then seized the bottom of the couch and heaved with all her might. He slammed onto the carpet, the couch on top of him. Phoebe sprang to her feet and lunged past him for the door, but iron fingers seized her ankle. She crashed to the carpet, kicking. The heel of her free foot landed a blow to his jaw before he grabbed the foot. She screamed. Ty was on her in an instant. His hand clamped over her mouth, pinning her to the floor. The pistol in his waistband dug into her hip.

"Where is it?" he hissed.

She shook her head to say she didn't understand.

"Don't toy with me, Phoebe. I want that letter."

She grabbed the wrist of the hand over her mouth.

"Stop it or I'll kill you right here," he snarled.

She stilled.

"Now, I'm going to remove my hand," he said. "Scream and I'll knock you from here to hell and back. Understand?"

She nodded.

Tentatively, his hold loosened. Phoebe made no move to scream and he lifted his hand from her mouth.

"You fool," she said. "My husband will return any moment and when he does—"

"The letter," he hissed.

Her heart pounded. Ty showed no fear that Kiernan might arrive. Terror twisted through her. She recalled the highwayman who, without provocation, intended to shoot Kiernan. Her chest constricted. Ty had sent them—paid them—to kill her husband. And she didn't have to wonder why. If Kiernan died, she would be a very rich woman. Her fifteen thousand pound yearly income would, then indeed, be paltry. But that didn't explain Adam.

"Why?" she demanded.

His face contorted in fury. "He intended to force to go to Gretna Green with him."

Phoebe closed her eyes. Ty had known exactly who the *why* referred to. She opened her eyes. "You miscalculated."

"I won't make that mistake again."

She started to tell him there wouldn't be a next time, but he cut her off.

"Where's the letter Phoebe? Tell me or I kill you, then your husband."

Panic ripped through her. She forced all thought from her mind— except one. "What letter?"

"The letter your husband received from the man in Scotland."

She had no idea what he was talking about, but said, "Kiernan keeps all personal papers in his bedchambers."

Ty shoved to his feet, dragging her with him. He drew the pistol from his waistband. "One peep and I'll blow your brains out."

She nodded.

"Which floor?" he demanded.

"Third floor, west wing."

"Any servants about?"

She shook her head. "The duke and duchess don't allow them to work into the night."

"How magnanimous of them," he said, and prodded her toward the door.

The turn of the doorknob stopped them short.

250

Ty cursed. Phoebe rammed her elbow into his ribs and wrenched free of his grip as she dove right. He swung his pistol toward her and she rolled. A shot resounded and she jumped before realizing that Ty hadn't fired. Her vision snapped into focus onto Kiernan, who strode across the room, still gripping the pistol he'd fired.

Ty scrambled to his feet. Blood stained the left side of his shirt over his ribs. Mather appeared in the doorway, a revolver in hand, but Kiernan reached Ty. Kiernan threw aside his gun and drove a heavy blow into Ty's belly. Ty dropped to his knees. Kiernan seized his lapel and lifted. Her cousin rammed his head into Kiernan's gut and drove him backwards until they crashed into a chair.

Phoebe jumped to her feet. "Mather! Do something."

Mather looked at her, brow raised.

Kiernan rammed an elbow into Ty's shoulder. Phoebe spied Ty's pistol lying on the floor near her foot and she snatched up the weapon. The two men were on their feet again. She pointed the weapon at Ty as Mather reached her side.

"No, Lady Ashlund." He eased the weapon downward. "You might hit His Lordship and I've worked far too hard this evening to keep him from getting shot."

The duke appeared in the doorway, a revolver in hand, as Kiernan's fist slammed Ty's jaw. The blow lifted her cousin off his feet and slammed him into the coffee table. Wood splintered and he went limp.

"What in bloody hell is going on?" the duke demanded.

Phoebe glimpsed Elise in the hallway. He glanced back at her, then looked back at Kiernan.

"We have Mr. Branbury's killer," Kiernan said in a dark voice that sent a shiver down her back. "I'll explain all — " he glanced at Phoebe, eyes dark with fury " — tomorrow."

In three paces, he was at her side and grabbed her arm. "What the hell happened?"

"I fell asleep in the library when Ty — "

"The library?" he cut in.

Ty groaned.

Kiernan looked at Mather. "Mather, if you please. I believe Richard has a cell reserved for the baron."

"With pleasure, sir."

Mather strode to where Ty stirred, then seized him by the collar and dragged him to his feet. Ty swayed but stood on his own when Mather released him.

"Can't have that," Mather said, and threw a hard uppercut to Ty's jaw. Ty crumpled to the floor, then Mather hauled him over his shoulder and started for the door. "Your Grace," he said as he passed the duke. "Ma'am," he nodded to the duchess, and disappeared down the hall.

251

Kiernan's grip on Phoebe's arm tightened. "Lady Ashlund, I warned you what would happen if I returned home to find you anywhere but in my bed."

She flushed. "Sir, I—"

He dragged her to the couch near the window and dropped onto the cushion, hauling her over his lap, and yanking her nightgown up over her buttocks. She gasped.

"Kiernan," Elise began.

"Lass," the duke cut in, and Phoebe snapped her head in their direction. The duke gave his wife a warning shake of his head.

Embarrassed warmth spread up Phoebe's cheeks. She couldn't believe it. The duke was going to stand by while his son spanked her bare bottom!

Kiernan's hold on her waist tightened. She twisted in an effort to break free, but his arm pinned her more tightly to his lap. A slap sounded before the stinging registered in her mind. Before she could yelp, his broad palm again connected with the sensitive skin of her buttocks.

"Release me!" She thrashed.

He smacked her again.

"MacGregor," she shouted. "I will put a bullet through your—" Another slap followed, harder this time. "That hurts!"

Kiernan gave yet another stinging swat, then shoved to his feet, dragging her with him. She jerked her head up, eyes narrowed in fury.

He lifted a brow. "I believe you know what is to follow."

Confusion gave way to understanding. "You had best never untie me, for I will brain you in your sleep."

He gave a nod. "I am pleased that your plans include me. Come along."

She dug in her heels, but he hugged her to his side and forced her to match step with him. "Father," he said as they neared the door. He smiled at the duchess, who stared wide-eyed. "Elise."

Once through the doorway, Kiernan lifted Phoebe so that her feet left the carpet. She gave him a hard kick, but he didn't slow, and instead took the stairs two at a time. They reached his room and he strode to the bed. Kiernan dropped her feet onto the floor only to grab the waist of her nightgown.

Phoebe realized his intent. "I beg—"

Fabric covered her mouth and blocked her vision. She brought her arms down in an attempt to thwart him, but heard a rip and relented. Kiernan yanked the nightgown from over her head, then pushed her onto the mattress. He snatched a handkerchief from his pocket and swung a leg over her hips. His weight pinned her to the mattress and Phoebe found herself facing the thick bulge in his trousers.

Kiernan finished tying Phoebe's hands to the bedpost, then straightened to survey his handiwork. Her arms were stretched back over her head, causing her breasts to jut forward in daring invitation. The base of his engorged cock pressed her flat belly with a need that bordered on pain. For a horrifying instant, when he'd seen her in Arlington's grip, Kiernan thought he'd lost her and he'd gone out of his mind. Yet even her here, safe, he still teetered on the edge of losing his mind.

He braced his palms on each side of her and brought his face close to hers.

"Beware, my lord," she said in a soft voice.

His cock jumped.

Kiernan shoved to his feet and slid his gaze over the curve of her breasts and down her belly. When his gaze reached the blonde curls that disappeared into the juncture between her legs his erection beat against the constraints of his trousers as if it had a mind of its own. When it came to Phoebe that wasn't far from the truth.

He brought his eyes back to her face to find her staring with…boredom? Damnation, the little hellcat was challenging him. That's what she'd been doing when she chose the library instead of his bed. Kiernan shucked his coat then yanked loose the knot on his cravat. With slow deliberation, he slid the cloth from his neck, tossed it aside then unfastened the buttons on his shirt. When he shoved the fabric off his shoulders, her gaze dropped to his chest.

Kiernan let the shirt fall, then unfastened his trousers. He kept his attention on her face, but her eyes remained fixed on his fingers as he freed the last button and shoved the trousers down and over his hips. Her mouth parted and, when she swallowed, his erection pulsed. She gave a small gasp and it was all he could do to keep from mounting and fucking her like a wild bull. Kiernan forced his breathing to slow and lowered himself onto her.

Her full curves melted beneath him. His heart raced and he covered a breast with his palm. The nipple pressed into his hand and he watched her face as he kneaded the warm flesh. She wiggled beneath him and for an instant he thought he would spend himself on her belly.

"I think some movement is required, sir."

Kiernan stilled. "What's that you say?"

"You are awfully…large."

Was she talking about his body or his cock?

Kiernan urged her legs apart and settled his hips between her thighs. "We'll start with an heir," he said.

Gently, he reminded himself as he fitted the tip of his penis to the opening of her channel. God, but he wanted to drive into her until she screamed his name.

"Once he's safe in the nursery," he went on, "a daughter will follow." Her slick folds allowed easy entrance and her gasp when he inched inside caused his scrotum to contract. "After that," he kissed her cheek, "we'll get you fat with my third child." He slid a wet kiss from her cheek to her ear, and drove hilt deep in one hard thrust.

She drew a sharp breath.

Kiernan lifted onto his elbows and looked at her. "What have you to say now, wife?"

She stared up at him. "I say that puts me exactly where I predicted: at your beck and call."

He shook his head. "No, love. That puts me at *your* beck and call."

Kiernan reached up and yanked free the handkerchief that bound her hands.

Her eyes narrowed. "What sort of knot was that? A highwayman's hitch, I wager."

He lifted a brow. "Only a highwayman would use a highwayman's hitch?"

She nodded and Kiernan moved inside her in slow, easy strokes.

"By heavens," she said in a breathless voice that wound through him like a siren's song. "I suppose that'll do."

"Will it?" he asked.

She nodded and wound her arms around his neck.

"Do you think you might one day love me?" he asked.

Her breasts rose and fell with the quickening of her breath. "That depends."

"Depends on what?" Kiernan drew a nipple into his mouth.

She sighed. "Whether or not you can keep my ennui at bay."

Kiernan snapped his head up. "Ennui, you say?"

She nodded and he felt that same sense of helplessness he'd felt that moment he'd entered her coach. There was only one answer. He stroked faster in her channel. Pleasure mounted.

"Do you like that, love?" he asked.

"Yes," she whispered with an arch of her hips that met his thrust.

"Then I am certain I can keep your boredom at bay—and so much more."

Her gaze locked with his. "All right, then," she whispered. "I love you."

That was all Kiernan needed to hear.

# # #

Afterward

For those who might think that I allowed my imagination to run rampant with government conspiracies, mass assassinations, and revolutions, I refer you to the book *Enemies of the State: The Cato Street Conspiracy* by M. J. Trow, which was a major source for the history I used in *My Highland Lord*. Years ago, when I wrote the first draft of this book, there was very little information available on The Cato Street Conspiracy. Now, however, there are a few good books like Mr. Trow's *Enemies of the State*, and they prove once again that fact is far stranger than fiction. Of course, I only touched upon the intricate web woven by the British government in an effort to maintain the status quo during The Cato Street Conspiracy, and the lengths to which so-called radicals were willing to go in order to achieve their revolutions. I took a few liberties and added a character or two in order to tell Phoebe and Kiernan's story, but the history is solid. I hope you found it as interesting as I did.

From the author:

I admit that I like leaving a story with the hero and heroine in bed. This is romance, after all, and what better way to face the future than in each other's arms? If you enjoyed reading about Kiernan and Phoebe's journey of love, perhaps you would also like to learn just how Kiernan's father, the duke, came to fall in love with an American woman. For your pleasure, I have included sample chapters of My Highland Love.

Enjoy, and remember, *"Where there is love, there is life."* Mahatma Ghandi.

Tarah

My Highland Love

How does a woman tell her betrothed she murdered her first husband?

Elise Kingston is a wanted woman. Nothing, not even Highlander Marcus MacGregor, will stop her from returning home to ensure that the man responsible for her daughter's death hangs.

Until she must choose between his life and her revenge.

Chapter One

America
Winter 1825

"*The Lord giveth and the Lord taketh away.*" Or so her eulogy would begin.

The heavy gold wedding band clinked loudly in the silence as he grasped the crystal tumbler sitting on the desk before him. He raised the glass in salutation and whispered into the darkness, "To the dead, may they rot in their watery graves." He finished the whiskey in one swallow.

And what of that which had been hers? He smiled. The law would see that her wealth remained where it should — with him. A finality settled about the room.

Soon, life would begin.

* * * *

Solway Firth, Scottish-English border

Elise jumped at the sound of approaching footsteps and sloshed tea from the cup at her lips. The ship's stateroom door opened and her grip tightened around the delicate cup handle. Her husband ducked to miss the

257

top of the doorway as he entered. He stopped, his gaze fixing on the medical journal that lay open on the secretary beside her. A corner of his mouth curved upward with a derisive twist and his eyes met hers.

With deliberate disinterest, Elise slipped the paper she'd been making notes on between the pages of the journal and took the forestalled sip of afternoon tea. She grimaced. The tea had grown cold in the two hours it had sat untouched. She placed the cup on the saucer, then turned a page in the book. As Robert clicked the door shut behind him, the ship's stern lifted with another wave. She gripped the desk when the stern dropped into the swell's trough. Thunder, the first on the month-long voyage, rumbled. She released the desk. This storm had grown into more than a mere squall.

Robert stepped to her side. "What are you doing?"

"Nothi—" He snatched the paper from the book. "Robert!" She would have leapt to her feet, but her legs were shakier than her hands.

He scanned the paper, then looked at her. "You refuse to let the matter lie."

"You don't care that the doctors couldn't identify what killed your daughter?"

"She is dead. What difference can it possibly make?"

Her pulse jumped. *None for you. Because you murdered her.*

He tossed the paper aside. "This has gone far enough."

Elise lifted her gaze to his face. She once thought those blue eyes so sensual. "I couldn't agree more."

"Indeed?"

The ship heaved.

"I will give you a divorce," she said.

"Divorce?" A hard gleam entered his eyes. "I mean to be a widower."

She caught sight of the bulge in his waistband. Her pulse quickened. Why hadn't she noticed the pistol when he entered?

Elise shook her head. "You can't possibly hope to succeed. Steven will—"

"Your illustrious brother is in the bowels of the ship, overseeing the handling of the two crewmen accused of theft."

Her blood chilled. When her father was alive, he made sure the men employed by Landen Shipping were of good reputation. Much had changed since his death.

"One of the men is wanted for murder," Robert said.

"Murder?" she blurted. "Why would a stranger murder me?"

Robert lifted a lock of her dark hair. "Not a stranger. A spurned lover." He dropped the hair, then gripped the arms of her chair and leaned forward. "Once the board members of Landen Shipping identify your body as Elisabeth Kingston, the stipulation in your father's will shall be satisfied and your stock is mine."

The roar of blood pounded through her ears. If he killed her now, he would never pay for murdering their daughter. And she intended that he pay.

Elise lunged for the letter opener lying in one of the secretary compartments. The ship pitched as her fingers clamped onto the makeshift weapon. As Robert yanked her to her feet, she swung the letter opener. Bone-deep pain raced up her arm when the hard mass of his forearm blocked her blow. The letter opener clattered to the wooden floor.

She glimpsed his rage-contorted features before he whipped her around and crushed her to his chest, pinning her arms to her sides with one powerful arm. He dragged her two paces and snatched up the woolen scarf lying on the bed. In one swift movement, he wound it around her neck.

Robert released her waist, grabbed the scarf's dangling end, and yanked it tight around her neck. Elise clawed at the scarf. Her nails dug into the soft skin of her neck. Her legs buckled and he jerked her against him. His knees jabbed into her back and jolts of pain shot up both sides of her spine. She gulped for air.

His breath was thick in her ear as he whispered, "Did you really think we would let you control fifty-one percent of Landen Shipping?" He gave a vicious yank on the scarf.

No! her mind screamed in tandem with another thunder roll. Too late, she understood the lengths to which he would go to gain control of her inheritance.

The scarf tightened. Her sight dimmed. Cold. She was so cold.

Amelia, my daughter, I come to you — the scarf went slack. Elise dropped to her knees, wheezing in convulsive gasps of air. Despite the racking coughs which shook her, she forced her head up. A blurry form stood in the doorway. *Steven.*

The scarf dropped to her shoulders and she yanked it from her neck. Robert stepped in front of her and reached into his coat. *The pistol.* He had murdered her daughter — he would not take Steven from her. Elise lunged forward and bit into his calf with the ferocity of a lioness.

Robert roared. The ship bucked. Locked like beast and prey, they tumbled forward and slammed against the desk chair. The chair broke with the force of their weight. The secretary lamp crashed to the floor. Whale oil spilled across the wooden floor; a river of fire raced atop the thin layer toward the bed.

Steven yanked her up and shoved her toward the door. Robert scrambled to his feet as Steven whirled and rammed his fist into Robert's jaw. Her husband fell against the doorjamb, nearly colliding with her. Elise jumped back with a cry. Robert charged Steven and caught him around the shoulders, driving him back onto the bed.

The ship bucked. Elise staggered across the cabin, hit her hip against the secretary, and fell. The medical journal thudded to the floor between her and the thick ribbon of fire. Her heart skipped a beat when Robert slammed his fist into Steven's jaw.

She reached for the open book and glimpsed the picture of the belladonna, the deadly nightshade plant. Fury swept through her anew. She snatched up the book, searing the edge of her palm on the fire as she pushed to her feet. Elise leapt forward, book held high, and swung at Robert with all her strength. *May this belladonna kill you as your powdered belladonna killed our daughter.* The crack of book against skull penetrated the ringing in her ears. Robert fell limp atop Steven.

The discarded scarf suddenly blazed. Elise whirled. Smoke choked her as fire burned the bed coverings only inches from Robert's hand. Steven grabbed her wrist and dragged her toward the door. He scooped up the pistol as they crossed the threshold and they stumbled down the corridor to the ladder leading up to the deck.

"Go!" he yelled, and lifted her onto the first tread.

Elise frantically pulled herself up the steep ladder to the door and shoved it upward. Rain pelted her like tiny needles. She ducked her head down as she scrambled onto the deck. An instant later, Steven joined her. He whirled toward the poop deck where Captain Morrison and his first mate yelled at the crewmen who clung to the masts while furiously pulling up the remaining sails and lashing them to the spars.

Steven pulled her toward the poop deck's ladder. "Stay here!" he yelled above the howling wind, and forced her fingers around the side of the ladder.

The ship heaved to starboard as he hurried up the ladder and Elise hugged the riser. A wave broke over the railing and slammed her against the wood. She sputtered, tasting the tang of salt as she gasped for air.

A garbled shout from the captain brought her attention upward. He stared at two men scuttling down the mizzen mast. They landed, leapt over the railing onto the main deck and disappeared through the door leading to the deck below. They had gone to extinguish the fire. If they didn't succeed, the ship would go down.

Elise squinted through the rain at Steven. He leaned in close to the captain. The lamp, burning in the binnacle, illuminated the guarded glance the captain sent her way. A shock jolted her. Robert had lied to the captain about her—perhaps had even implicated Steven in her so-called insanity. The captain's expression darkened. He faced his first mate.

The ship's bow plunged headlong into a wave with a force that threw Elise to the deck and sent her sliding across the slippery surface. Steven shouted her name as she slammed into the ship's gunwale. Pain shot through her shoulder. He rushed down the ladder, the captain on his heels. Another wave hammered the ship. Steven staggered to her side and pulled her to her feet. The ship lurched. Elise clutched at her brother as they fell to the deck. Pain radiated through her arm and up her shoulder. The door to below deck swung open. Elise froze.

Robert.

He pointed a pistol at her. Her heart leapt into her throat. Steven sprang to his feet in front of her.

"No!" she screamed.

She spotted the pistol lying inches away and realized it had fallen from Steven's waistband. She snatched up the weapon, rolled to face Robert, and fired. The report of the pistol sounded in unison with another shot.

A wave cleared the railing. Steven disappeared in the wash of seawater. Elise grasped the cold wood railing and pulled herself to her feet. She blinked stinging saltwater from her eyes and took a startled step backwards at seeing her husband laying across the threshold. Steven lay several feet to her right. She drew a sharp breath. A dark patch stained his vest below his heart. *Dear God, where had the bullet lodged?*

She started toward Steven. The ship listed hard to port. She fought the backward momentum and managed two steps before another wave crested. The deck lurched and she was airborne. She braced for impact against the deck. Howling wind matched her scream as she flew past the railing and plummeted into darkness—then collided with rock-hard water.

Cold clamped onto her. Rain beat into the sea with quick, heavy blows of a thousand tiny hammers. She kicked. Thick, icy ribbons of water propelled her upward. She blinked. Murky shapes glided past. This was Amelia's grave. Elise surfaced, her first gasp taking in rainwater. She coughed and flailed. A heavy sheet of water towered, then slapped her against the ocean's surface. The wave leveled and she shook hair from her eyes. Thirty feet away, the *Amelia* bounced on the waves like a toy. Her brother had named the ship. But Amelia was gone. Steven, only twenty-two, was also gone.

A figure appeared at the ship's railing. The lamp high atop the poop deck burned despite the pouring rain. Elise gasped. Could he be— "Steven!" she yelled, kicking hard in an effort to leap above another towering wave. Her skirts tangled her legs, but she kicked harder, waving both arms. The man only hacked at the bow rope of the longboat with a sword. "Steven!" she shouted.

The bow of the longboat dropped, swinging wildly as the man staggered the few steps to the rope holding the stern. A wave crashed over Elise and she surfaced to see the longboat adrift and the figure looking out over the railing. Her heart sank. The light silhouetted the man—and the captain's hat he wore. Tears choked her. It had been the captain and not Steven.

Elise pulled her skirts around her waist and knotted them, then began swimming toward the boat. Another wave grabbed the *Amelia*, tossing her farther away. The captain's hat lifted with the wind and sailed into the sea. She took a quick breath and dove headlong into the wave that threatened to throw her back the way she'd come. She came up, twisting frantically in the water until she located the ship. She swam toward the longboat, her gaze steady on the *Amelia*. Then the lamp dimmed… and winked out.

Chapter Two

*E*ngland lay far behind him, though not far enough. Never far enough. Marcus breathed deep of the crisp spring air. The scents of pine and heather filled his nostrils. Highland air. None sweeter existed. His horse nickered as if in agreement, and Marcus brushed a hand along the chestnut's shoulder.

"It is good to be home," Erin spoke beside him.

Grunts of agreement went up from the six other men riding in the company, and Marcus answered, "Aye," despite the regret of leaving his son in the hands of the Sassenach.

He surveyed the wooded land before him — MacGregor land. Bought with Ashlund gold, held by MacGregor might, and rich with the blood of his ancestors.

"If King George has his way," Erin said, "your father will follow the Duchess of Sutherland's example and lease this land to the English."

Marcus jerked his attention onto the young man. Erin's broad grin reached from ear to ear, nearly touching the edges of his thick mane of dark hair. The lad read him too easily.

"These roads are riddled with enough thieves," Marcus said with a mock scowl. His horse shifted, muscles bunching with the effort of cresting the hill they ascended. "My father is no more likely to give an inch to the English than I am to give up the treasure I have tucked away in these hills."

"What?" Erin turned to his comrades. "I told you he hid Ashlund gold without telling us." Marcus bit back a laugh when the lad looked at him and added, "Lord Phillip still complains highwaymen stole his daughter's dowry while on the way to Edinburgh." He gave Marcus a comical look that said *you know nothing of that, do you?*

"Lord Allerton broke the engagement after highwaymen stole the dowry," put in another of the men. "Said Lord Phillip meant to cheat him."

"Lord Allerton is likely the thief," Marcus said. "The gold was the better part of the bargain."

"Lord Phillip's daughter is an attractive sort," Erin mused. "Much like bread pudding. Sturdy, with just the right jiggle."

A round of guffaws went up and one aging warrior cuffed Erin across the back of his neck. They gained the hill and Marcus's laughter died at sight of the figure hurrying across the open field below. He gave an abrupt signal for silence. The men obeyed and only the chirping of spring birds filled the air.

"Tavis," Elise snapped, finally within hearing range of the boy and his sister, "this time you've gone too far and have endangered your sister by leaving the castle."

His attention remained fixed on the thickening woods at the bottom of the hill and her frustration gave way to concern. They were only minutes from the village—a bare half an hour from the keep and safely on MacGregor land—but the boy had intended to go farther—much farther. He had just turned fourteen, old enough to carry out the resolve to find the men who had murdered his father, and too young to understand the danger.

Bonnie tugged on her cloak and Elise looked down at her. The little girl grinned and pointed to the wildflowers surrounding them. Elise smiled, then shoved back the hood of her cloak. Bonnie squatted to pick the flowers. Elise's heart wrenched. If only their father still lived. He would teach Tavis a lesson. Of course, if Shamus still lived, Tavis wouldn't be hunting for murderers.

Those men were guilty of killing an innocent, yet no effort had been made to bring them to justice. The disquiet that always hovered close to the surface caused a nervous tremor to ripple through her stomach. While Shamus's murderers would likely never go before a judge, if Price found her, his version of justice would be in the form of a noose around her neck for the crime of defending herself against a man who had tried to kill her—twice.

Any doubts about her stepfather's part in Amelia's death had been dispelled a month after arriving at Brahan Seer when she read a recent edition of the London *Sunday Times* brought by relatives for Michael MacGregor. She found no mention of the *Amelia's* sinking. Instead, a ten thousand pound reward for information leading to the whereabouts of her *body* was printed in the announcements section.

Reward? Bounty is what it was.

The advertisement gave the appearance that Price was living up to his obligations as President of Landen Shipping. But she knew he intended she reach Boston dead — and reach Boston she would, for without her body, he would have to wait five years before taking control of her fifty-one percent of Landen Shipping. She intended to slip the noose over his head first.

Elise caught sight of her trembling fingers, and her stomach heaved with the memory of Amelia's body sliding noiselessly from the ship into the ocean. She choked back despair. If she had suspected that Robert had been poisoning her daughter even a few months earlier —

"Flowers!"

Elise jerked at Bonnie's squeal. The girl stood with a handful of flowers extended toward her. Elise brushed her fingers across the white petals of the stitchwort and the lavender butterwort. She was a fool to involve herself with the people here, but when Shamus was murdered she been unable to remain withdrawn.

"Riders," Tavis said.

Elise tensed. "Where?"

"There." Tavis pointed into the trees.

She leaned forward and traced the line of his arm with her gaze. A horse's rump slipped out of sight into the denser forest. Goose bumps raced across her arms.

Elise straightened and yanked Bonnie into her arms "It will be dark soon — " Tavis faced her and she stopped short when his gaze focused on something behind her.

Elise looked over her shoulder. Half a dozen riders emerged from the forest across the meadow. She started. Good Lord, what had possessed her to leave Brahan Seer without a pistol? She was as big a fool as Tavis and without the excuse of youth. She slid Bonnie to the ground as the warriors approached. They halted fifteen feet away. Elise edged Bonnie behind her when one of the men urged his horse closer. Her pulse jumped. Was it possible to become accustomed to the size of these Highland men?

She flushed at the spectacle of his open shirt but couldn't stop her gaze from sliding along the velvety dark hair that trailed downward and tapered off behind a white lawn shirt negligently tucked into his kilt. The large sword strapped to his hip broke the fascination.

How many had perished at the point of that weapon?

The hard muscles of his chest and arms gave evidence — many.

The man directed a clipped sentence in Gaelic to Tavis. The boy started past her, but she caught his arm. The men wore the red and green *plaide* of her benefactors the MacGregors, but were strangers.

"What do you want?" She cursed the curt demand that had bypassed good sense in favor of a willing tongue.

Except for a flicker of surprise across the man's face, he sat unmoving.

Elise winced inwardly, remembering her American accent, but said in a clear voice, "I asked what you want."

265

Leather groaned when he leaned forward on his saddle. He shifted the reins to the hand resting in casual indolence on his leg and replied in English, "I asked the boy why he is unarmed outside the castle with two females."

Caught off guard by the deep vibrancy of his soft burr, her heart skipped a beat. "We don't need weapons on MacGregor land." She kept her tone unhurried.

"The MacGregor's reach extends as far as the solitude of this glen?" he asked.

"We are only fifteen minutes from the village," she said. "But his reach is well beyond this place."

"He is great, indeed," the warrior said.

"You know him?"

"I do."

She lifted Bonnie. "Then you know he would wreak vengeance on any who dared harm his own."

"Aye," the man answered. "The MacGregor would hunt them down like dogs. Only," he paused, "how would he know who to hunt?"

She gave him a disgusted look. "I tracked these children. You think he cannot track you?"

"A fine point," he agreed.

"Good." She took a step forward. "Now, we will be getting home."

"Aye, you should be getting home." He urged his horse to intercept. Elise set Bonnie down, shoving her in Tavis's direction. "And," the man went on, "we will take you." The warriors closed in around them. "The lad will ride with Erin. Give the little one to Kyle, and you," his eyes came back hard on Elise, "will ride with me."

The heat in his gaze sent a flush through her, but her ire piqued. "We do not accept favors from strangers."

His gaze unexpectedly deepened.

She stilled. *What the devil? Was that amusement on his face?*

"We are not strangers," he said. There was no mistaking the laughter in his eyes now. "Are we, Tavis?" His gaze shifted to the boy.

"Nay," he replied with a shy smile. "No' strangers at all, laird."

"You know this man?" Elise asked.

"He is the laird's son."

"Marcus!" Bonnie cried, peeking from behind Elise's skirts.

Elise looked at him. Marcus? *This* was the son Cameron had spoken of with such affection these past months? It suddenly seemed comical that she had doubted Cameron's stories of his son's exploits on the battlefield. She had believed the aging chief's stories were exaggerations, but the giant of a man before her was clearly capable of every feat with which his father had credited him.

Prodded by the revelation, she discerned the resemblance between father and son. Though grey sprinkled Cameron's hair, the two shared the same unruly, dark hair, the same build... and... "You have his eyes," she said.

He chuckled.

Heat flooded her cheeks. She pulled Bonnie into her arms. "You might have said who you were." She gave him an assessing look. "Only that wouldn't have been half as much fun. Who will take the child?"

His gaze fixed on the hand she had wrapped around Bonnie and the small burn scar that remained as a testament of her folly. His attention broke when a voice from behind her said in a thick brogue, "'Tis me ye be looking for, lass." She turned to a weathered warrior who urged his mount forward.

Elise handed Bonnie up to him. Stepping back, she bumped into the large body of a horse. Before she could move, an arm encircled her from behind, pulling her upward across hard thighs. A tremor shot through her. She hadn't been this close to a man's body since—since those first months of her seven-year marriage.

Panic seized her in a quick, hard rush. The trees blurred as her mind plunged backward in time to the touch of the man who had promised till death do them part. Her husband's gentle hand on their wedding night splintered into his violent grip the night he'd tried to murder her—the movement of thighs beneath her buttocks broke the trance as Marcus MacGregor spurred his horse into motion. His arms tightened around her and she held her breath, praying he couldn't hear her thudding heart.

The ambling movement of the bulky horse lifted her from Marcus's lap. She clutched at his shirt. Her knuckles brushed his bare chest and she jerked back as if singed by hot coals. Her body lifted again with the horse's next step and she instinctively threw her arms around Marcus's forearm. His hold tightened as rich laughter rumbled through his chest.

"Do not worry, lass. Upon pain of death, I swear, you will not slip from my arms until your feet touch down at Brahan Seer."

Elise grimaced, then straightened in an effort to shift from the sword hilt digging into her back.

"What's wrong?" He leaned her back in his arms and gazed down at her.

She stared. Robert had never looked so—she sat upright. "I've simply never ridden a horse in this manner."

"There are many ways to ride a horse, lass," he said softly.

Elise snapped her gaze to his face, then jerked back when her lips nearly brushed his. She felt herself slip and clutched at his free arm even as the arm around her crushed her closer. Her breasts pressed against his chest where his shirt lay open. Heat penetrated her bodice, hardening her nipples. A surprising warmth sparked between her legs. She caught sight of his smile an instant before she dropped her gaze.

267

Their ascent steepened. Marcus closed the circle of his arms around the woman's waist. She leaned into him. It was a shame she wore a cloak. Without it, her bare arms would lay against his chest. He hardened. *Bloody hell*. Shift even a hair's breadth and the challenge he'd seen in her gaze an hour ago would resurface, accompanied by a slap across his face.

She had betrayed no fear when he came upon her—other than her open assessment of his weapon. Odd his sword should be what frightened her. She must have known if he meant mischief, he needed no weapon save his body. An erotic picture arose of her straddling him, breasts arched so he could suckle each until she begged him to lift her onto his erection.

He forced back the vision and focused on her determination to defend the children with her life... or perhaps, her body. He smiled, then gritted his teeth when he further hardened at the memory of her leaning over Tavis's shoulders as she scanned the forest for the riders he'd sent. Hands braced on her knees, her posture revealed the curve of a firm derriere.

When she turned at their approach, the wind had blown her brown hair about her shoulders, bringing his attention to the sensual curve of modest breasts visible just above the edge of her bodice. He envisioned hips tapering into long legs and wondered what those legs would feel like wrapped tightly around his waist while he thrust deep inside her.

Her accent had caught him off guard. What was an American woman doing on MacGregor land, and how had she come to know Tavis and Bonnie well enough to track them through the woods? Hot fury shot through him. The little fool. Had the wrong man come upon her, she might well have ended up like Katie.

The majestic heights of Brahan Seer's west tower abruptly loomed in the distance. Marcus's steed unexpectedly faltered, then steadied. The woman tensed and Marcus's body pulsed. He closed his eyes, breathed deep of her hair, then looked again at the tower. For the first time in his life, he regretted the sight. His ride with her cradled in his arms would soon end.

Higher they climbed, until Brahan Seer's walls became visible. The gates were open. At their approach, his captain Daniel hailed from the battlements. Marcus nodded as they rode through the entry. Inside the courtyard, he halted and Daniel appeared at his side.

"Elise," he addressed the woman, surprise apparent on his features. He glanced at the children, his gaze lingering on Bonnie. His mouth tightened. "Mayhap Marcus can take a hand with you, Tavis. Get along, and take your sister. Your mother will be worried."

Marcus handed Elise down to him. Before Marcus's feet touched the ground, she had started toward the castle. He dismounted and clasped

Daniel's hand while watching from the corner of his eye the sway of her cloak about her hips as she answered a welcoming smile from two of his men headed toward the stables.

"What were they doing out alone?" Marcus demanded of Daniel.

"I've ordered the boy not to go wandering the woods," he replied.

"And Bonnie?"

"This is the first. I imagine she chased after her brother."

Elise turned the corner around the castle and Marcus cut his gaze onto her the instant before she disappeared. Lust shot to the surface and tightened his shaft, but he turned back to Daniel. "Why is Shamus letting his children run wild — never mind. I'll speak to him. You look well."

Daniel hesitated, then said, "Chloe is with child."

Marcus smiled in genuine pleasure. "Congratulations, man."

Daniel smiled, then took the reins as Marcus turned toward the castle.

Through the busy courtyard, he answered greetings, but his thoughts remained on the image of Elise as she vanished from sight. She had a forthright, strong quality. Yet — he bent his head to breathe her lingering scent from his clothes — the lavender bouquet in her hair was decidedly feminine. It would be some time before he forgot the feel of her buttocks across his thighs. But then, perhaps he wouldn't have to. Marcus entered the great hall to find his father sitting alone in his chair at the head of the table.

Cameron brightened. "So, ye decided to come home?"

Relaxing warmth rippled through Marcus.

"Tired of wandering the land?" Cameron made a wide sweeping gesture.

"You knew I was on my way, but, aye." He stopped at the chair to his father's right and lowered himself onto the seat. "I am pleased to be home."

"How is my grandson? I see you did not bring him with you."

Marcus sighed. "Nay, Father. You knew I wouldn't."

Cameron snorted. "We would not want to offend the mighty Sassenach."

"Father," Marcus said in a low tone.

Cameron shook his head. "The clan never asked you to concede to the English, you know. *I* never asked for it. Did you ever wonder if the sacrifice is worth your son?"

"Aye," Marcus murmured. He'd wondered. Politics had ruled the MacGregor clan for centuries and that wasn't easily changed. He paused. "Have I been gone too long, or is something different about the great hall?"

"You have the right of it, lad." Eyes that mirrored his own looked back at him. "More than you can imagine."

Marcus looked about the room. "I can't quite place it. What's happened?"

Cameron took a long, exaggerated draught of ale.

269

"*Cameron.*"

"Enough of your looks, lad. They do not work with me." He chuckled. "I taught them to you. Remember? It is no mystery, really. Look around. When did you last see the tapestries so bright, the floors so clean?" He motioned toward the wall that ran the length of the room, framed by stairs on either end. "When have you seen the weapons so polished?"

Marcus scanned the nearly two hundred gleaming weapons mounted across the wall. He rose and walked the wall's length, perusing the weapons. Each one glistened, some nearly as bright as newly forged steel. He glanced at the floor. The stone looked as if it had just been laid.

He looked at his father. "What happened?"

"The women came one day—or rather, one month—and swept out the cobwebs, cleaned the floors, the tapestries, weapons."

Marcus rose and crossed the room to the kitchen door where the women worked. The housekeeper sat at the kitchen table. Ancient blue eyes, still shining with the bloom of youth, smiled back at him. Winnie had been present at his birth. Marcus knew she loved him like the son she'd never had. He, in turn, regarded her with as much affection as he had his own mother.

She turned her attention to the raw chicken she carved. "So, you've returned at last."

"Aye, milady."

A corner of her mouth twitched with amusement.

"I am looking forward to the company of some fine lasses tonight," he said. "'Tis a long and lonely trip I've had. Perhaps next time I shall take you with me." He gave her a roguish wink before striding back to his seat in the hall.

Marcus lowered himself into the chair he had occupied earlier. "Must have taken an army just to shine the weapons alone. Not to mention the walls and floors."

"It did. You will see the same throughout the castle. Not a room went untouched."

"Whatever possessed them to do it?"

"It was the hand of a sweet lass," Cameron replied.

"Which one? Not Winnie—"

"Nay. The lass Shannon and Josh found washed ashore on the coast. They brought her when they returned from the south."

"Washed ashore?"

"An American woman. Her ship perished in a fire."

"American?"

Cameron scowled. "Are you deaf? Shannon is the one who discovered her at Solway Firth."

"What in God's name was she doing there?"

Cameron gave his chin a speculative scratch. "Damned if I know.

270

They were headed for London."

"London? Sailing through Solway Firth requires sailing around the north of Ireland. That would add a week or more to the journey."

His father's mouth twisted into a wry grin. "You know the English, probably got lost."

"I thought you said she was American."

"English, American, 'tis all the same." Cameron's expression sobered. "But dinna' mistake me, she is a fine lass. She came to us just after you left for Ashlund four months ago. You should have seen her when they brought her here. Proud little thing."

"Proud, indeed," Marcus repeated.

"'Tis what I said." Cameron eyed him. "Are you sure something isn't ailing you?"

Marcus shook his head.

"At first, she didn't say much," Cameron went on. "But I could see a storm brewed in her head. Then one day, she informed me Brahan Seer was in dire need of something." He sighed deeply. "She was more right than she knew."

Marcus understood his father's meaning. His mother's death five years ago had affected Cameron dramatically. Only last year had his father finally sought female comfort. The gaping hole created by her absence left them both thirsting for a firm, feminine hand.

"It's a miracle she survived the fire," Cameron said. "'Course, if you knew her, you would not be surprised."

"I believe I do," Marcus remarked.

"What? You only just arrived."

"I picked up passengers on the way home — Tavis, little Bonnie, and an American woman." Marcus related the tale. "I recognized her accent," he ended. "Got accustomed to it while on campaign in America."

Cameron smiled. "Elise is forever chasing after those children."

"Why?"

His father's expression darkened. "Shamus was murdered."

Marcus straightened. "Murdered?"

"Aye."

"By God, how — Lauren, what of her?"

Sadness softened the hard lines around his father's mouth. "She is fine, in body, but... her mind has no' been the same since Shamus died. We tried consoling her, but she will have none of it."

A tingling sensation crept up Marcus's back. "What happened?"

"We found him just over the border in Montal Cove with his skull bashed in."

"Any idea who did it?"

"Aye," Cameron said. "Campbells."

Marcus surged to his feet. He strode to the wall, where hung the

271

claymore belonging to his ancestor Ryan MacGregor, the man who saved their clan from annihilation. Marcus ran a finger along the blade, the cold, hard steel heating his blood as nothing else could. Except... *Campbells.*

Had two centuries of bloodshed not been enough?

Fifty years ago, King George finally proclaimed the MacGregors no longer outlaws and restored their Highland name. General John Murray, Marcus's great uncle, was named clan chief. Only recently, the MacGregors were given a place of honor in the escort, which carried the "Honors of Scotland" before the sovereign. Marcus had been there, marching alongside his clansmen.

Too many dark years had passed under this cloud. Would the hunted feeling Ryan MacGregor experienced ever fade from the clan? Perhaps it would have been better if Helena hadn't saved Ryan that fateful day so long ago. But Ryan had lived, and his clan thrived, not by the sword, but by the timeless power of gold. Aye, the Ashlund name Helena gave Ryan saved them. Yet, Ryan MacGregor's soul demanded recompense.

How could Ryan rest while his people still perished?

Marcus removed his hand from the sword and faced his father. "It's time the MacGregors brought down the Campbell dogs."

Feminine laughter spilled from the kitchen into the great hall during the evening meal. Marcus sighed with contentment. Light from sconces flickered like a great, filmy curtain across the room. Two serving girls carrying trays of food stepped from the kitchen, and the men, who blocked the doorway, parted. The sense of contentment came as an almost unconscious realization. He had missed sharing the evening meal with his clansmen. Marcus leaned forward, arms crossed in front of him on the table, and returned his attention to the conversation with Cameron and Daniel.

"We will be ready at first light, laird," Daniel said.

"The Campbells will not be expecting trouble," Cameron put in.

"If word has reached them that I've returned, they may be," Marcus said.

Cameron grunted. "Lot of good it will do."

The feminine voice Marcus had been waiting for filtered out from within the kitchen. "Easy now, Andrea," Elise said.

The conversation between his father and Daniel faded as Marcus watched for her amongst the men who crowded between the door and table. The thought of seeing her beautiful body heated his blood. Elise stepped from the kitchen, balancing a plate of salmon. She passed the table's end where he sat and carefully picked her way through the men until reaching the middle of the table. She set the oval platter between the chicken and mutton.

"Beth, place the carrots to the left. Andrea—" She took the plate of potatoes from the girl, then set it to the right and turned toward the kitchen.

"Elise," one of the young warriors called, "come, talk with us, lass."

Her mouth quirked. "If I play with you, who will finish dinner?"

The man's hearty chuckle gave evidence she hadn't fooled him, and he approached with friends in tow.

Cameron stood. "Elise," he called over the men's heads, "come here."

She turned. When her gaze met Cameron's, warmth filled her eyes. She dried her hands on her apron and headed in his direction.

"Go on, lads," Cameron said to the men who teased her. "You have better things to do than dally with the lassies."

When she came within arm's reach, he gripped her shoulders. "Meet my son. He's returned today." He turned her.

Her gaze met Marcus's. Her smile faltered but quickly transformed into polite civility. "We've met."

"Oh?" Cameron replied, all innocence.

"Yes. He came by when Tavis, Bonnie, and I were on our way home this afternoon."

"Ahh," Cameron said, then turned and gave the man beside him an energetic greeting.

Elise looked again at Marcus and motioned toward the kitchen. "I have work to do."

"Aye," he said. The memory of her breasts pressed against his chest caused him to harden.

She backed up a few steps, then turned and ran headlong into the man behind her. He reached to steady her. A flush colored her cheeks and Marcus bit back a laugh when she dodged the warrior. Marcus leaned forward, catching one last look at her backside before she disappeared through the kitchen door.

Author Bio

Award winning author Tarah Scott cut her teeth on authors such as Georgette Heyer, Zane Grey, and Amanda Quick. Her favorite book is a Tale of Two Cities, with Gone With the Wind as a close second. She writes modern classical romance, and paranormal and romantic suspense. Tarah grew up in Texas and currently resides in Westchester County, New York with her daughter.

Also by Tarah Scott:
My Highland Love
Highland Lords Series
Lord Keeper
A Knight of Passion
The Pendulum: Legacy of the Celtic Brooch
When a Rose Blooms
Labyrinth
An Improper Wife
Hawk and the Cougar
Double Bang!
Born Into Fire

Award Winning Titles:
Lord Keeper
Golden Rose Best Historical of 2011
First place in the 2004 RWA CoLoNY Happy Endings contest
Third place in the Greater Seattle Chapter RWA's 2003
Emerald City

My Highland Lord
Indie Romance Convention Readers Choice Award 2013

COMING SOON
How to Tame a Highland Earl
Death Comes for a Knight

As T.C. Archer
Chain Reaction: Phenom League
Full Throttle
Sasha's Calling
Trouble at the Hotel Baba Ghanoush
For His Eyes Only
Winter in Paradise

COMING SOON
In the Company of Kate
Behind Enemy Lines: Phenom League
Yeoman's Curse